*To Carol —
Best wishes &
surf's up!*

A Novel

Gordon Gumpertz

Durban House

Copyright © 2008, Gordon Gumpertz

All rights reserved. No part of this book may be used or reproduced in any manner whatsoever without the written permission of the Publisher.

Printed in the United States of America.

For information address:
Durban House Publishing Company, Inc.
7502 Greenville Avenue, Suite 500
Dallas, Texas 75231

Library of Congress Cataloging-in-Publication Data

Gumpertz, Gordon

Tsunami / Gordon Gumpertz

Library of Congress Control Number: 2006923983

p. cm.

ISBN: 978-1-930754-80-5

First Edition

10 9 8 7 6 5 4 3 2 1

Visit our Web site at

http://www.durbanhouse.com

Dedicated to my beautiful wife, Jenny, whose encouragement, idea sharing, and critical eye contributed greatly to the writing of *Tsunami*.

prologue

The container ship *Moro Prince*, bound from Manila to Los Angeles, had enjoyed three days of smooth sailing. The last piece of rough weather had been a heavy tropical storm between Guam and Wake Island, kicking up twenty- to thirty-foot seas. Now the ocean was calm, with a three-foot swell and a gentle trailing breeze. The temperature was comfortable, the sky cloudless, the humidity low.

Able Seaman Fidelio Magsaysay had been standing bow watch for the past hour. With the weather clear and the sea empty, he found it hard to concentrate. He scanned his quadrant out to the horizon as slowly and carefully as he could manage, then fixed on something close by to rest his eyes before starting the process again.

After one of his sweeps, Fidelio thought he saw something out there. Dead ahead. Just coming up over the horizon. He raised his binoculars, studied a moment, then lowered them to his chest. He pressed the talk button on his handset and waited till a voice replied, "Bridge."

"Funny-looking cloud bank dead ahead. Low lying."

Fidelio's report came through on the speaker. The captain and the chief mate raised their binoculars almost in unison. "What do you make of it?" asked the captain.

"I don't know," the mate said. "Nothing like that's been reported in this area. Strange cloud. Little bit dirty looking. Probably a local weather system."

"Yeah, probably, but then, you know…" The captain paused. "I saw something like this once before. Java Sea, October of 2010. A week later a whole fucking island disappeared."

"What was it, like a volcano? You think this…?"

"Looks like we can skirt it, whatever the hell it is." He turned to the helmsman. "Change course to zero five zero. We'll run north of it, then correct our heading as we go around the damn thing."

The captain wondered whether this was something that should be reported. To play it safe, he said, "Mr. Mate, fix our position."

The mate pressed a key on the GPS panel. He announced the longitude and latitude and pointed to the spot on the chart. "That puts us here. One thousand three hundred eleven nautical miles west southwest of San Pedro."

"Okay," said the captain. "Make a log entry that we've come across a strange cloud formation. Then make a radio report to NOAA in San Francisco."

Able Seaman Magsaysay first felt the course change in his feet, and realized the bow was swinging slowly to port. Two hours later the *Moro Prince* had the cloud on its starboard beam. The color of the water had changed from blue to milky green. The air was warmer. He took off his denim work shirt, then his T-shirt. He was naked to the waist but couldn't stop sweating. The humidity almost smothered him. Once in a while the breeze shifted and an odd smell came wafting in from the direction of the cloud. A smell that was not of the sea. A smell of molten heat that came from some other part of the earth.

one

The Science Institute of the Pacific, more commonly known as SciPac, spread out over thirty acres in the foothills of the Sierra Madre range northeast of Los Angeles. The glass-clad, low-rise buildings made it look more like a research facility than a college campus, but it housed one of the world's leading universities in the geophysical sciences.

In a small office in the seismology department, Dr. Leilani Sanches's pulse picked up a beat as she studied the satellite image on her computer screen. She stretched her small figure across the desk to fine-tune the satellite resolution. A dense, whitish-gray cloud rose from the sea directly over the Shark Fin undersea mountain range in the mid-Pacific. She clicked it up to maximum enlargement. "It's broken the surface for the first time," she said to her lab assistant, Gus Belmondo.

Gus adjusted his round glasses, propped a hand on Lani's desk, and stared at the monitor. "Wow! The water's actually boiling where the plume comes out. That's one hell of a lot of heat!"

She brushed wisps of silky black hair away from her ears. A few strands had tumbled free of the casual twist and jeweled dolphin clip above the nape of her neck. She stretched again to retune the satellite, the tail of her white boat-neck T-shirt pulling up over her stone-washed jeans, revealing an inch of coffee-and-cream island skin. Her gold-brown eyes stayed riveted on the growing ash plume. "Is this data going into the model? Automatic feed's working?"

"Like a charm," said Gus, green eyes smiling behind his glasses. "Data's being fed into the model as it comes in. I hate to ask, but is it time to worry?"

"Let's take a look." Lani clicked the mouse and replaced the satellite view with a full-color, real-time simulation of Seamount Gilman, the undersea volcano. The equipment hummed while she and Gus studied the computer-generated model of the volcano, the ocean around it, and the ground beneath. Everything seemed to be playing out as her hypothesis had predicted. The worst could happen.

New seams were opening up about two kilometers below the mountain as they watched. Scorching hot magma poured into the mountain from the new seams, the red color spreading and deepening. Carbon dioxide, sulfur dioxide, and the other gasses from deep within the earth, displayed in shades of green, grew denser and packed into every corner of the mountain. Earthquakes showed up as bright blue starbursts, rippling out in concentric circles as the shock waves traveled.

Gus leaned his tall frame down for another look. "This baby's rockin' and rollin'."

Lani craned forward in her chair and refocused her eyes on the screen. Her words were tinged with awe. "More than one magma chamber must be feeding the volcano."

She studied the magma volume for another few moments, then zoomed to a closeup of one side of the mountain. "Is that a bulge?"

Gus leaned in again, closer. A dome-shaped protrusion was beginning to swell on the east flank. "If that baby ruptures..."

There was a knock on Lani's open door. Dr. Margaret Bradshaw, her boss, stood in the doorway. A blue-eyed blonde, she was immaculately dressed in a black suit, black hose, and black shoes, her short hair brushed and sprayed. She was an inch or two under six feet, statuesque. "Just got your message about the ash plume."

Gus picked up Lani's quick eye shift and head jerk. He left the room. Lani switched back to the satellite view of the volcano.

Margaret placed herself behind Lani's chair and watched as the cloud on the screen continued expanding. "No cause for alarm. This will release some of the pressure and calm things down."

Lani shook her head. *Damn*, she thought. *Here we go again.* "The pressure's still building. I think I've got a good feel for what's going on out there."

Margaret's reply had an edge. "I know you consider this your very own volcano, but other scientists with much more experience are studying it too. They don't seem nearly as concerned."

Lani didn't respond. Maybe she did consider this her very own volcano, but with good reason. She'd been assigned to the Murray Fracture Zone project two years before. The Murray, a fault line running west along the seafloor for nearly three thousand miles from Southern California to a point north of the Hawaiian Islands, was thought to have gone permanently inactive twenty thousand years before, right after the creation of the Shark Fin undersea range. It was a surprise when new low-level seismic activity was detected near the Murray's midpoint. The experts thought it most likely came from the torque of accelerated plate movement. That scientific opinion prevailed for several years until Lani published her paper. She was the first to associate the low-level quakes with magma transport, the initial step in the fueling of a volcano.

Lani tapped her keyboard. The satellite photo of the volcanic plume disappeared, replaced by a map of the ocean floor fifteen hundred statute miles off the California coast. She pointed to the Shark Fin range, midpoint on the Murray. "These high peaks are all ancient volcanoes. But it's this one here, Seamount Gilman, that's decided to come back to life. And it's big, a real monster."

Margaret sniffed. "This is not the Indian Ocean. The nearest subduction zone is two thousand miles away. If your volcano does stay alive, it'll probably be more like an undersea Kilauea. Active but not dangerous."

Lani flicked a silky strand away from her ear. She told herself not to lose sight of the big picture—the ominous events unfolding under the sea. "I wish that were the case… just island-building. But this one is behaving more like a Krakatau or Saint Helens."

Margaret smoothed a wrinkle out of her black suit jacket. "I hardly think it's that dire."

"Then how do you account for the swarms of quakes? The crust fracturing over a wide area? The widening seams? The heavy intrusion of magma? The magma's superheating the water leaking into the mountain. It's building up a really big head of steam and gas."

Margaret clearly didn't want to understand. "Must be a hot spot under that mountain. Probably an old one. Hot spots don't just crop up out of nowhere. And they don't produce violent volcanoes."

"Kilauea's a hot spot volcano, and it had a huge blowout in 1790. Killed eighty people. But this is more than that. The magma's too heavy, and with all the quake activity, it looks like the Murray's building up to a major slippage."

"Look, Lani, fracture zones are not subduction zones. No plate convergence, no subduction, no dangerous volcanoes."

"That's the accepted theory. This is the exception to the rule."

Margaret adjusted a gold filigree bracelet. "I know you were a star at Princeton when you came to SciPac for your PhD. But you're inexperienced and you're not a trained oceanographer or volcanologist. You simply don't have the background that gives me a high degree of confidence in this theory of yours."

Lani stroked another key. Densely packed mathematical formulae filled the screen. "My model says there's at least a fifty percent probability of a major blowout."

"I've seen your model and your math before." Margaret inspected her polished nails.

"Then why don't you understand?" Lani kept her voice deliberately soft.

"Oh, I think I understand quite well when someone's going off half-cocked."

Lani stifled her growing urge to strike back. It was more important to convince Margaret that the pressure building up inside the volcano was even stronger than Mount Saint Helens just before it blew. Lani switched back to the color simulation and zoomed in on the pubescent bulge in the mountain's flank. "Don't you see, if the bulge expands, all it'll take is one strong quake to rupture it and set off a major explosion."

Margaret gave Lani an impatient look. "You're asking me to buy into this Rube Goldberg idea of yours, and I just can't. You're saying *if* Seamount Gilman is indeed a stratovolcano…"

"Which I'm sure it is…"

"…and *if* it explodes with the force of a Krakatau, and *if* the earth's crust under the volcano disintegrates from the shock, and *if*, as a result, the entire mountain collapses inward down into an empty magma chamber, then the combination of events will displace enough water and release enough energy to produce a giant tsunami."

Margaret's patronizing tone and the cocked eyebrow rankled Lani, but her reply was straightforward, her words strong and clear. "Yes. Fifty-fifty chance."

Margaret looked at her watch. "Look, Lani, I'm late for a meeting."

Frustration forced Lani's words out in a high-pressure stream. "I've talked to the tsunami warning centers in Honolulu and Palmer, Alaska. They're worried about this thing, too. They're not discounting my theory out of hand. I'm sending them my calculations."

Margaret gave her a stony look. "Who else have you contacted?"

"The Hawaii Volcano Observatory and the Cascades Observatory. They also want to see my numbers."

Margaret folded her arms. "Let's get this straight. Nothing goes out to anyone without my approval. I don't want any rumors coming out of my seismology department about a giant tsunami getting ready to hit the California coast."

Lani felt like Seamount Gilman… ready to explode. "It could happen. And it's standard practice to share data with other—"

Margaret's color intensified under her makeup. "If your ideas get out, everyone'll panic and it'll make SciPac look ridiculous. So keep a lid on it until I tell you otherwise. And don't even think about trying to go over my head." She slammed the door as she left.

Gus came back in, eyes owlish behind his thick lenses. "I don't think she understands."

Lani smacked her hand down on her desk. "She's more interested in her hairdo than the safety of five million people!" How could someone with Margaret's credentials be so dense? Was she so stuck in traditional thinking it blinded her to new ideas? Or was it just professional jealousy? Whatever the reason, it was obvious she was going to keep belittling Lani's work and keep pressuring her to give in.

Lani tightened her gut muscles. Come what may, she would not back down.

"What are you going to do?" said Gus.

Lani frowned, gold sparks in her angry brown eyes. "I don't know. But I have to do something."

Lani had never been in this part of Arcadia before, near the old race track. She drove slowly in the fading twilight, looking for

Carleton Cohen's home. Cohen was Dean of the School of Earth Sciences, and Margaret's boss. The houses looked big and comfortable, on wide lots with an abundance of shrubbery in front. Probably built in the 1960s. She spotted the number and pulled her aging red Corolla up to the curb. She started to get out, then got back in and closed the door. Cohen probably wouldn't even want to listen. She was disturbing him at home. She'd be asking him to go against one of his own department heads. Her chances really weren't very good. And if he reported her, her career was over.

She drew in a deep breath, then let it out slowly through puckered lips. She'd been raised to obey the rules and respect authority. Maybe she was being too impulsive. Maybe she should think it over. But obeying the rules in this case could result in enormous loss of life. Should she protect herself by going along? Or get the truth out whatever the cost? The lives of five million people might be on the line.

She rang the bell and waited. A man in a red plaid flannel shirt, chino pants, and running shoes opened the door. He was in his late sixties, and everything about him seemed round: round face, round belly, round pale blue eyes behind rimless glasses, and circular fringe of gray hair. "Yes?"

Lani heard his shortness of breath and hoped he was well enough to see her. She swallowed hard. "I don't know if you remember me, Dr. Cohen, but I'm in seismology. We met a couple—"

Cohen's round face broke into a smile. "Oh, sure, I remember you. Leilani Sanches, right? You're working on the volcano. Come in."

As Lani stepped inside, she noticed a woman standing to one side of the door. Cohen introduced her as his wife.

Cohen stretched his arm toward the far end of the hall and said to Lani, "Let's go into my office."

His wife put a hand on his arm. "Not too late, dear. You have to save your strength."

He nodded and led Lani into a large room that had been made into a comfortable study.

Cohen said, "This used to be our family room. When the kids left, we converted it to a home office." He pointed to a leather armchair. "Sit down and tell me what's on your mind."

"Your wife looked concerned. I feel like I'm intruding."

Cohen chuckled. "She likes to fuss. It's nothing. No big deal. So, tell me…"

"You're sure?"

"Yes, it's okay. I'm sure. Go ahead."

"My computer model says the volcano's on the verge of exploding. If it does, it could set off a major tsunami."

Cohen's eyes widened. "How major?"

Lani met his questioning gaze. "The model projects a series of hundred-foot waves. Maybe two hundred."

Cohen stared. "Really? Here? In California?"

"The coastline from Oceanside to Santa Barbara would take the brunt. San Diego not quite as bad."

"That means L.A. would be right in the middle. You've explained all this to Dr. Bradshaw?"

Lani nodded. "Margaret doesn't agree with my model or my theory. She told me there's nothing to worry about and to sit on it."

Cohen leaned back in his desk chair. "I'd feel better if the problem came to me through Margaret. Have you made your case as strongly as you can?"

Lani sighed. "Several times."

"If she has all the facts, why does she want you to sit on it?"

Lani shifted forward in her chair. "She thinks it's a shield volcano, just pumping out a little harmless basalt lava."

"Makes sense, given its location."

Lani's face took on more color. "But it's not acting like one. It has all the earmarks of a stratovolcano… or a rhyolite."

Cohen chuckled. "Rhyolite? We haven't had one of those

since the Marsden explosion." The Marsden Depression was a huge undersea caldera north of the Mendocino Fracture Zone, fifty kilometers across and five kilometers deep.

Lani spoke excitedly, leaning forward in the leather chair. "Based on the rate and direction of tectonic plate drift, the blowout that gave us the Marsden two million years ago would be exactly where Seamount Gilman is today."

Cohen studied Lani with questioning eyes. "But that would mean a massive hot spot. I don't think there's one still around that's big enough to do the kind of damage you're talking about."

She pressed ahead. "What if the volcano's being fed from two sources? A humongous hot spot plus subduction."

"That's a big *if*."

"Dr. Cohen, that part of the Murray is acting weird. The quake activity along the fault line just won't quit. Like one side of the fault is trying to slide under the other."

Cohen's brow wrinkled. "That usually only happens where tectonic plates come together, but if there's a weakness on one side of the fault—unlikely but not impossible."

Lani, face flushed, said, "I think the fault slippage and quakes are opening up fissures to the heavier, hotter magma. When that material hits the lighter hot-spot magma—"

Cohen hesitated. "A lethal mix. I guess it's possible." His mouth twisted as if he were tasting something sour. "I can see how important this is to you, but I think you ought to give Margaret one more try. It'd be much better if this comes through channels."

Lani stood up. "I know I'm risking my job and my future in seismology by going over Margaret's head, but I'm convinced my model's right. I think it's urgent to put out a tsunami warning for the entire shoreline between San Diego and Santa Barbara."

Cohen studied Lani for several seconds. "I'm willing to listen, but you better have some damn strong arguments. If you can't convince me…"

"I know, you'll have to tell Margaret and that'll be it for me. But that's fair. If I didn't think I could prove my point, I wouldn't be here."

The door opened and Cohen's wife came in with a glass of water and a small dish full of pills. "Time for dessert," she said, and left the dish on the table next to him.

Cohen made a face. "Yum, yum. My favorites." He swallowed the pills with one gulp. "I can't give you more than an hour. She's right. I have to get my rest." He pointed to his computer. "Okay, let's get started."

Lani went to his desk. "After I access my model, I'll bring up the graphic simulation to show you conditions on the site, then go to the mathematical formulae the simulation is based on."

The one hour extended to two. Cohen went through Lani's math a second time, then clicked back to the simulation. It would take an enormous blast to break the earth's crust and cause the inward collapse of the mountain into the emptied magma chamber beneath it, but if those conditions did come together, then Lani's scenario was possible. Cohen turned to look directly at her. "Your model says fifty percent probability. I don't know if I'd go that far, but I'd say there's a fair chance."

"If it does happen the way the model predicts, do you think there'd be enough ocean displacement to kick off a tsunami?"

Cohen didn't answer immediately. He swung back to the monitor for a moment, drummed his fingers, then nodded. "Yes. A big one."

Flooded with relief, Lani had the impulse to hug him. Instead, tears brimmed and spilled down her cheeks.

Cohen turned off the computer and handed Lani a tissue. "I'll talk to Margaret when I get back to my office. I'll tell her your project needs a second look." He smiled. "But now I'd better be a good boy and get some rest."

"May I ask one more favor? I've been on the Internet with Ocean Research Labs in La Jolla. They're sending one of their research ships out to the volcano and invited me to go with them. I didn't even ask Margaret, because I knew she wouldn't approve it."

Cohen asked, "Who invited you, and what will you do out there?"

"Richard Costello's the ORL project manager. He said I could go down in their submersible and take a firsthand look at the mountain. It'll help me validate the model."

"I know Costello," said Cohen, nodding approval. "He's tops in marine geology. When does the ship leave?"

"Six tomorrow morning. The *Carlsbad*."

Cohen put out a hand as if to restrain her eagerness. "Lani, your model raises enough urgent questions to be taken seriously, but the way we're going about it sure as hell breaks the rules, and it'll really bend Margaret all out of shape. But I'll call her at home and tell her I've okayed your trip, and the three of us should sit down together and hash this thing out. I'll try to square things with her as much as I can."

Lani wrote on a pad on Cohen's desk. "Here's Dr. Costello's cell phone number. He's probably on board by now."

"Okay. I'll call and tell him you're authorized to make the trip."

"As an official representative of SciPac?" Lani urged.

Cohen smiled. "Of course. Why don't you wait? I'll make both calls now."

The call to Costello was short, and the one to Margaret long. Cohen finally ended it by saying, "Yes, I know how out of order the whole thing is, but I happen to agree with her math and her model's projections. All I'm suggesting is the three of us sit down and go over this together after she gets back and I'm back in my office. Are we agreed? Good."

Lani whispered, "I don't know how to thank you." Emotion threatened to swamp her again.

"Just keep doing good work."

She squeezed his hand and left.

~ ~

The 297-foot research vessel *Carlsbad* reached the volcano on the morning of the fourth day at sea. Lani was the first to spot the plume. She'd gotten up before dawn, borrowed the captain's powerful long-range binoculars, and planted herself on the wing of the bridge. A few minutes before 9:00, she picked up a faint smudge on the horizon and yelled, "There it is! Just a little off to the left."

The captain reclaimed his binoculars. "Right you are. Volcano smoke one point off the port bow. But it's over the horizon, still a good piece away. We'll correct course and be there in two to three hours."

At 11:20 Lani stood on the main deck near the bow, watching the crew of the *Carlsbad* put out sea anchors a half mile from the volcano. The water had been changing color, from dark blue to milky green, for the past half hour. A whitish-gray column of steam, smoke, and ash rose out of a boiling sea and churned upward for two miles or more. The overwhelming smell of sulfur and chlorine, mixed with intense heat and 98 percent humidity, made breathing hard and painful.

Richard Costello, the project manager from Ocean Research Laboratories, suddenly appeared beside her, two surgical masks dangling from one hand. Lani thought he looked like the scarecrow in *The Wizard of Oz*. Tall, skinny as a stick, all arms and legs. He was in his late thirties, thinning brown hair pulled back in a ponytail, with eyes the aquamarine of reef water, now bloodshot from the bad air.

He handed her one of the masks. "Captain says we're pulling back another mile. Too much toxic sulfur dioxide and CO2 in the air."

She coughed. "Not enough oxygen for sure."

"Let's go below and take a look at the instruments. Air's better down there."

"I'll be down in a few minutes. I want to look at the plume a little while longer."

He slipped on his mask and pointed to hers. "Then put that on," he said, his voice muffled. "It'll filter out the larger particulates. When you come down, expect scary instrument readings. Swarms of quakes along the fault line and under the mountain. Not too deep, either. And we're picking up a harmonic tremor for the first time."

She put on her mask and adjusted the strings. "The tremor usually comes a few days ahead of a blowout."

"Yes, but how many?"

"I need to go down in the sub and check out the mountain while there's still time."

Costello studied the whitecaps. "Not today. Seas are too rough for launching. Probably first thing tomorrow. By the way, you'll have a guest aboard."

"You?"

"No, I'll be controlling the operation from the ship. The Coast Guard is sending someone."

Lani blew a derisive puff of air through the mask. "That's all I need. Some clunky sailor looking over my shoulder."

"He's supposed to assess the degree of danger and report back."

Even with the mask, the toxic air had her breathing heavily. "Can't he stay on the ship and do that?"

They watched the crew pull in the sea anchors, inverted canvas cones on long lines that acted like drags to keep the ship from drifting. Costello said, "Admiral Carson wants a first-hand report. I told him his man could make the dive with you."

The ship got underway again, its bow turning slowly away from the volcano. Lani said, "How did the Coast Guard get involved? My boss at SciPac doesn't want anybody to know anything about this."

"Balls!" said Costello. "You can't keep this a secret. Our computer model at Ocean Research shows a much lower chance of a tsunami than yours, but we all know the seamount is unstable and dangerous. I thought the Coast Guard should know too, so I called the head guy."

Lani nodded. "I'm glad you sounded the alarm. If having the sailor aboard is the price I pay, then so be it. But he can't interfere."

"Right," said Costello. "Just a passive observer. That's the deal."

The ship came to a gradual stop at its new position, and the crew paid out the sea anchors again. Lani said, "Air's better," and pulled off her mask.

"Still stinks, but you can breathe now." Costello pulled his mask down below his chin.

Lani closed her eyes and listened. "What's that popping sound?"

"That'll be your clunky sailor. He's coming special delivery in a long-range helicopter."

She scanned the sky. "I see it."

Costello trained binoculars in the direction Lani pointed. "U.S. Coast Guard. That's the one."

~ ~

A voice in his headset awakened Dave Steel. "We have the volcano cloud dead ahead, and we're locked onto the ship's locater signal. Should be there in a few minutes."

The rhythmic thumping of the rotors and the whine of the jet engines had put him to sleep almost as soon as the long-range chopper cleared the coastline four hours ago. He unbuckled from his rear seat and craned forward between the pilot and copilot to get a better look. "Secure your seatbelt," said the pilot. "I see the ship."

They hovered about two hundred feet above the *Carlsbad*, the landing pad on the ship's fantail rising, falling, tilting at crazy angles. Dave said, "Looks like we've got a ten- to twelve-foot swell down there."

"Not a problem," said the pilot. "It'll just take a few minutes to perch the bird on the deck."

They inched down to a gentle landing, and the pilot began refueling for his return to base. Dave took off his helmet and followed an escort to the main salon, which the crew and research staff used as a conference room, dining hall, and recreation room.

A small woman in T-shirt and jeans and a tall, thin man waited for him. A crewman in denim work shirt and black watch cap filled three mugs with hot coffee.

The tall man said, "You must be Commander Steel. I'm Richard Costello, and this is Lani Sanches."

The six-foot, sandy-haired Coast Guardsman shook hands. "I'm Dave." His lopsided smile crinkled the skin around his alert blue eyes. He had a prominent nose peeling from too much sun and ears to match. "I'm here to observe and write a report on the situation for Admiral Carson."

"Call me anything but Dick," said Costello. "I'll answer to Richard, Rich, Ricky, or almost anything else." He turned to Lani. "We borrowed Dr. Sanches from SciPac. She'll be in charge when you go down in the submersible."

"Lani," she said, shaking hands.

Her hand rested in Dave's for a moment and her eyes met his. Her smile faded. She turned away and picked up her coffee.

Dave studied her with interest. There was a hint of Asia in the cheekbones and facial planes, and her dark brown eyes were large and full of curiosity. A well-formed, smallish nose. Lips on the full side. And even though the T-shirt and faded jeans weren't high fashion, she'd probably look great in whatever she wore.

He thought he'd seen "welcome aboard" in her smile for a moment, followed by a quick cold shoulder. Maybe she thought he was butting in where he didn't belong, and resented his presence. He'd try not to make waves, but his first duty was to gather accurate facts and write a report for Admiral Carson.

"Cream or sugar?" Lani looked at him for a few moments, tray in hand.

"No thanks. I take it black." He tried to think of something more to say, but she turned away, set the tray down, and started chatting with Costello.

Dave's eyes lingered on her straight back, the nape of her neck, and the rhinestone dolphin hair clip. She seemed friendly enough, up to a point, and quite reserved beyond that. But she was probably smart as hell, and she radiated energy and resolve, so the working relationship should be okay.

Costello said, "The sea's a little rough for launching the submersible today, so we'll go at daybreak. After you're settled and have a bite of lunch, we'll talk about what you'll be looking for when you go down tomorrow. I'll bring you up-to-date on the readings we've been getting on our instruments since we've been on station."

The mess steward cleared the lunch dishes, and they settled down with fresh coffee. Costello told Dave the volcano had been extremely active and he wasn't sure how much longer they'd be able to stay on station. "We've been getting swarms of small quakes, most under 2.5 but with a few in the 3-to-4-point five range."

"Would you believe 117 separate quakes over the past twenty-four hours?" Lani asked.

Dave paused to do the math. "One every twelve minutes?"

Richard nodded. "On average, but they come in clusters, most occurring two to three miles under the fault line, a few directly under the volcano."

Lani brushed a strand of hair from her forehead. "The ones right under the volcano are worrisome."

Richard tapped the handle of his white coffee mug. "The cloudiness in the water comes from the high concentrations of CO_2, sulfuric acid, and nitric acid."

Lani said, "When we go down tomorrow, I'll be looking for fissures and major cracking along the side of the mountain. Bulging or other signs of weakness. See if there's lava flow as well as ash, and whether it's coming out of the top or a hole in the side."

"The closer you get to the mountain, the murkier it gets," said Richard, "and the warmer. The air conditioning in the sub won't hold up if the hull gets too warm, so keep an eye on your temperature gauge. If the air in the sub reaches a hundred Fahrenheit, you're to head for the surface. Anything over that starts to cook the controls."

two

The morning dawned cloudless, but ash from the volcano filled the sky and filtered the sun's rays. The sea had calmed to a three- to-four-foot swell.

The submersible was in the water, snugged against the side of the ship and ready for boarding. It looked like a twenty-foot watermelon with a flat front and a conning tower hatch on top. It was painted bright orange with a small blue and white NOAA emblem on the side, and had a small manipulator crane tucked behind the conning tower. The two large, round view ports in front, eight smaller ports, and two powerful spotlights mounted like ears in front of the conning tower gave it a big-eyed creature-from-outer-space look.

"Sure you want to come?" Lani asked Dave. She'd removed her jeweled clip and fed her long silky hair through the back of her baseball cap, securing the ponytail with a blue terry band. "You can wait for me on deck, you know."

He shook his head. "Better see for myself. Have to write an accurate report for the admiral. Besides, they already stuck these sensors all over my body."

Lani smiled. "They'll get itchy. It won't be that comfortable."

"No problem."

She watched him for a few moments. He seemed to be settled in well, and she liked the way he was adapting. "Have you had any scientific training?"

"Majored in geology at Colorado State before the Coast Guard Academy."

"Okay," she said. "Just remember, you're not in charge of anything when we're in the sub. Nels is our skipper and he's in charge of the boat. I'm the boss when it comes to the research. I say what we observe and what we measure and how and when we do things when we're down there. Understood?"

"Got it," Dave said. "I'm along for the ride."

Lani settled next to Dr. Nels Lindstrom, the sub operator. Dave squeezed into a small pull-down seat directly behind them. The infrared light revealed a crowded cockpit resembling an advanced jetliner. A black steering wheel and propulsion control handle rode against the operator's knees. Mounted around and above the two large view ports were panels of gauges, dials, indicator lights, an array of switches in different colors, a video screen, a sonar screen, and a communications board.

"Cozy," Dave said.

Lani said, "Cramped is a better word." She couldn't see much when they first submerged. The water started out green with foamy bubbles, then grew clearer but gradually darker as they went down.

They'd been down about ten minutes when Richard Costello's voice came over the speaker. "Question for Dave. Do you suffer from claustrophobia? Your blood pressure and heart rate are slightly elevated, plus we're getting an occasional panic spike."

"Guilty, but it's under control."

Lani glared at Dave, her voice an angry undertone. "Why didn't you tell me? I don't want *anything* to interfere with this dive. It's too important."

"I'm okay," said Dave. "I even get this way on my own ship when I go into cramped spaces below, but it never interferes with duty. No problem."

She saw beads of sweat on Dave's forehead. She fervently hoped he wouldn't let her down. "We have sedatives in the medical kit."

He shook his head. "I do relaxation exercises."

She lightly touched his arm. "I don't know why you came, if it's so hard for you."

"Duty," he said. "Pure and simple."

Lani turned to look at her instruments. "Water's getting warmer," she said to Nels.

"We're two hundred meters down and directly above the base of the volcano," Nels said. "Temperature's already up to twenty-seven degrees Celsius."

"About eighty Fahrenheit," she interpreted for Dave.

"No need to translate. Coast Guard's all Celsius and metric now."

"How deep on this first dive?" Nels asked.

"To the base of the mountain," said Lani.

Nels paused a moment. "All in one bite? Hull pressure and water temperature will be extreme down there. And the deeper we go, the closer to the side of the volcano we get."

"I want to get to the bottom ASAP and slowly circle the volcano on our way up. We'll pull out if it gets too hot."

"We're down three hundred meters now," Nels said, "level with the top of the mountain, about eight hundred meters away from the side."

Dave said, "So we have an active volcanic peak that rises fourteen thousand feet above the ocean floor with another thousand feet of water on top of it, is that the picture?"

Nels and Lani nodded.

Halfway down, at twenty-five hundred meters, Nels pointed to the temperature readout. "Thirty-five degrees."

"Ninety-five Fahrenheit," said Dave.

"Shall we check with Project Control, see what Richard thinks?"

asked Nels.

"No," said Lani. "Richard's looking at the same data we have. If he's worried, he'll let us know. Let's keep going down till we hit forty."

"I'm not sure what'll happen," Nels said. "This sub has never been in water over twenty-five Celsius." A few minutes later, he said, "We're about to hit the wall. Temperature's thirty-eight, which is Richard's limit—a hundred Fahrenheit. The boat's sluggish. I say it's too dangerous to go deeper without an okay from Project Control."

Lani said, "If the ash and gas are coming out a side vent at about this depth, we're probably approaching the hottest point. We might be able to break past it down into colder water."

Nels shook his head. "What if it's ruptured near the base? I'm responsible for the safety of the boat. I'd rather check with Richard."

Costello's voice came over the intercom. "My readout panel tells me you're at a decision point. Go or no-go, right?"

Lani switched to Talk on Costello's channel. "I think we have a good chance of breaking past this level into cooler water. Satellite soundings show possibility of venting at this depth."

"Nels, how are the controls?"

"Sloppy. We're almost 100 degrees Fahrenheit inside, and our gauges are showing sea water temperature on the hull over 150. If it gets any hotter, I won't be able to steer and we might lose power."

"What if we pull back away from the volcano and then continue our dive?" asked Lani.

There was a momentary delay before Richard answered. "Might work. Nels, head away from the seamount another kilometer. If it's cool enough there, go ahead and submerge to the bottom. Then work your way back slowly toward the base of the volcano. If it gets too hot at any point, you have the authority to abort the mission and return to the ship."

Lani said, "I still want to circle the mountain on the way up.

When we hit that layer of hot water at twenty-five hundred meters maybe we can sail up through it to cooler water and continue circling."

"That's up to Nels," Costello said. "The skipper has the final word on go or no-go."

The water and inside air temperature cooled markedly as they pulled away from the mountain. "We're going down," said Nels.

It took over an hour to work along the bottom, back to the base of the volcano. Their powerful searchlights illuminated a strange gray world of undulating rocky seafloor, an occasional tentacled plant, or an eel-like creature peering from a shadowed cave or hole. Condensation began coating the view ports.

Nels switched on the defrost circuit. "You're right, Lani. It's cooler. The major venting has to be further up, like you said."

They slowly circled the volcano on their way back to the surface. Lani kept up a running commentary, monitored and recorded on the *Carlsbad*, noting the jumble of huge black volcanic boulders carpeting the deeply creased, dark gray slopes of the cone-shaped mountain.

Richard Costello interrupted her. "Did you say you're seeing some bulging?"

"Starting at the four-thousand-meter level. East flank of the mountain. Significant bulge developing. Probably a thousand meters across. Protrudes at the center about a hundred meters. Looks like a big blister."

"We're heating up," said Nels. "Depth is three thousand meters."

Richard said, "My gauges show the air in the vehicle is getting hotter, along with the water outside."

Nels said, "We're all running in sweat. Internal systems are cranking at max, but not designed to handle these extreme conditions."

"Must smell great down there."

"If you like the aroma of old gym socks. Also the hull has

been under severe pressure longer than it should. Lots of creaking and groaning. Starting to risk a seam failure."

Lani's words tumbled out. "I can see the bottom of the rift. We're coming up just below a massive split in the side of the volcano. Fire, steam, smoke, ash pouring out. What a show!"

"Earthquakes are picking up in frequency and intensity." Richard's voice contained a note of urgency. "The bulging, the side venting, and this new earthquake data, plus the condition of the boat… it's too dangerous down there. Head for the surface. Now!"

"Just a few more minutes, Richard? I need to get closer to the bottom of the fissure."

"We're exceeding our heat limits again," said Nels. "Having trouble steering."

"Five more minutes?" pleaded Lani.

"What do you think, Nels? Can you give her a couple more minutes?"

"Two minutes max, then we're bailing out. Where do you want to go, Lani?"

"As close to the side of the mountain as you can, just below the fissure."

"I'll try. But the stuff pouring out the side is creating a hot updraft. Could drag us in closer than we want."

They felt a gentle bump.

"What was that?" said Dave.

"Damn!" Nels said. "Current sucked us up against the mountain. Hold on."

The propulsion revved up and the boat vibrated like a jack hammer as Nels tried to get free of the volcano's grip. "We're stuck," he said. "Must be snagged on something."

"I've got a good view of the fissure, and I'm getting some great shots," said Lani.

"That won't help us get off the side of this volcano."

"Getting real hot," said Dave.

Nels said, "The longer we stay in this current, the hotter the hull'll get and the hotter it'll get inside."

Lani's excitement at being so close to the volcano finally gave way to concern about their situation. "Can you get the outside videocam focused on the problem?"

"Coming up on the monitor now. We're wedged between two outcroppings. Jammed in there pretty tight."

"The lower outcropping looks a little loose," said Dave. "Instead of trying to back out, how about going forward and down."

"Worth a try," said Nels, "but another shot or two of full power will just about use up our battery pack."

Lani said, "If we don't break away within the next two or three minutes, it won't matter anyway. We'll slowly cook to death. Let's do it."

Nels nodded. "Here goes. We'll put pressure on that bottom rock and see if we can break out." He pushed forward on the power control and the steering wheel. The sound of the motor built to a high whine, then almost a screech as he applied full power. The infrared light flickered and dimmed.

Nothing happened. Lani leaned against Nels and reached back to touch Dave's arm. "Come on," she commanded. "Let's rock this thing front to back—like we're on a swing. Weight forward when I say *front*, and backward when I say *back*." She started chanting, and the three of them pushed back and leaned forward in unison. After a few tries, the little sub rocked forward a bit and Nels gave the boat his last shot of full power.

There was a grinding sound. The lower outcropping gave way and the sub shifted free.

Back aboard the *Carlsbad*, an angry Richard Costello sat with elbows on the wardroom table, leaning forward and shaking his head so that his ponytail wagged slowly back and forth. "When I gave you the extra two minutes, I didn't say you could go in that close. Your scientific curiosity very nearly cost three lives and a multimillion-dollar submarine. And my career."

"I thought my first-hand observations would contribute," said Lani.

"Sure." Richard eyed her. "We know a lot more about the condition of the volcano than we did before. Reinforcing our decision to get the hell out of here. I've told the captain to bring the sub aboard and get underway for La Jolla. The radio room is setting up a rendezvous point with a Coast Guard chopper, and we'll have both of you off the ship this afternoon."

Lani's eyebrows went up. "You're sending me back in the helicopter?"

Richard nodded.

She took off her cap and shook her hair loose, refastening it with the clip. "Sorry you're angry with me."

"Don't get me wrong," he said. "You're a first-rate scientist and you gave us some important data. But there's a line you don't cross, even for the sake of science."

"How about for the sake of the five million people who live along the Southern California coast? Do you want another Indian Ocean disaster?"

Richard studied Lani for a moment. "The circumstances are totally different, and your tsunami theory is still only a theory. No doubt in my mind the mountain's going to blow. Just a matter of when. But whether the concussion will be strong enough to blast a hole in the crust and cause an inward collapse of the mountain is still open to question."

"My math says it will. The main magma chamber's two kilometers directly under the volcano and it's huge. If the blast breaks through, there's your ready-made caldera."

"We're studying your math back at Ocean Research, and we're doing our own simulations. At this point, we're not ready to agree or disagree."

Dave said, "Can you both drop this professional crap and

give me some solid information for my report to Admiral Carson? What are the chances of a two-hundred-foot tsunami?"

"Better than fifty-fifty," said Lani. She looked at Richard.

He hesitated. "Under Lani's optimum conditions, the blast could be big enough to set off your killer tsunami."

She said, "There's nothing between here and the coast to slow a wave down once it gets started."

Richard added quickly, "I'm not sure the chances of it happening are anywhere near fifty-fifty. I'd be more inclined to put it in the range of ten percent. And I don't know how destructive it'd be. The height of the wave would depend on the force of the blast and the size of the collapse, if any. Could be big, could be puny."

"So the possibilities are these," Dave said. "Number one, nothing happens. The volcano subsides and is never heard from again. Two, the volcano blows but the mountain stays intact. Tsunami, if any, not serious. And three, the whole shot. Big blast. Big hole. Big collapse. Big wave."

"Fair summation," said Lani. "A tsunami travels five to six hundred miles an hour in deep water. It'd hit the coast of Southern California just under three hours after the event."

"Ships at sea are safe because the wave stays on the ocean floor, right?"

"Hardly noticeable on the surface. Just a ripple." Lani thrust her hand up and over. "Rises as the bottom shallows and builds to its full height as it comes ashore."

"How far inland would a wave that big go?"

"In low-lying areas, probably a mile to a mile and a half. Maybe two," said Costello.

Dave looked at Lani. "That figure of five million you threw out a while back. Is that how many people live within two miles of the ocean between San Diego and Santa Barbara?"

"My best estimate."

"Zero chance of moving that many people to safety in two or

three hours," Dave said. "They'd have to be evacuated before the warning system picks up the wave."

"Amen," said Lani. "I think the evacuation order should be given right now."

Richard looked at her. "Better be careful with that one. I think you should let someone higher up the ladder make that decision."

Lani stared at the table.

Costello said, "And I hate to give you more bad news after all you've been through today."

She looked up. "What?"

"Dean Carleton Cohen died following bypass surgery. I just got an e-mail. Everything seemed to be okay, but he was hit by a stroke and they couldn't save him. Really sorry."

Lani felt suddenly empty. Cohen was such a nice man. He was also the one person at SciPac who believed in her theory and could help her.

"And I got a phone call from Margaret Bradshaw," said Costello. "She wanted to know who gave the okay for you to come on this trip. I said Dean Cohen approved it, and she said that was news to her."

Lani's golden-tan skin turned pale. "She's lying. I was there when he called her."

"Bottom line, Lani, she says she doesn't know anything about it, and orders you back immediately."

Lani kneaded her brow. "This has to be the worst day of my life. First I come close to wrecking the sub. Now Dean Cohen's gone, and there's no one at SciPac to back me up."

"He did call me. I'll back you up on that one," said Richard.

"Yes, but if Margaret says Dean Cohen might have called you but didn't call her, then I'm still in the soup."

A crewman stuck his head in the door. "Dr. Costello, the captain says the chopper will pick up the passengers in about twenty minutes, so please have them ready."

On the way back, Lani and Dave occupied the two rear seats. Both wore blue flight suits and helmets fitted with earphones and boom mikes. After an hour of silence, Dave leaned over and pointed to the intercom button. "I'm sorry everything went wrong for you today."

She gave him a weak smile.

Her face framed by the helmet was really quite pretty, he thought. The sadness in her eyes gave her a softer look. He said, "I don't have the background to understand the higher-order math behind your model, but judging by the way that mountain was acting, I'd say you probably know what you're talking about. I'll do what I can with Admiral Carson."

"Thanks, but I'm afraid that won't help me at SciPac. They'll say I went over my department chair's head and either demote me or get rid of me altogether."

"Don't be so pessimistic. Things'll work out okay. Just let me know what I can do to help."

She looked at him for a long time. "You really mean it, don't you?"

"Whatever's in my power." He smiled and gave her a thumbs-up. "Think positive."

She usually tuned out when she heard *positive thinking,* but this blue-eyed Coast Guardsman seemed so sincere. There was something solid and steady about him that made her feel a little more hopeful.

~~

Back in the lab for the first time since her trip to the volcano, Lani turned on her monitor, poured a cup of coffee, and was reading an e-mail. She was to be in Margaret's office at 9:00 to explain her unauthorized visit to the dean and her unauthorized trip on the *Carlsbad*. The phone rang as she stared at the screen.

"Dr. Sanches? This is Porter Sinclair, Science Editor of the *Los Angeles Times*. Can I talk to you for a minute?"

"Sorry, Mr. Sinclair. You'll have to talk to my department head, Dr. Bradshaw. Or the public information office. They handle all press contact."

"It's about the volcano that's been erupting out in the Pacific. I just talked to Dr. Bradshaw and she gave me some information on it, but I understand you're the manager on the project and thought you could fill in some details."

"I'd like to help out, but you'll have to go with the information Dr. Bradshaw gave you."

Silence spun down the line. "Well, let me tell you what she said. Then you can decide whether you want to add anything."

Lani didn't respond, and he continued. "She says it's a volcano that's been dormant for a long time, and now has suddenly come to life. It's venting a lot of steam and ash, but'll eventually peter out and go dormant again. Is that the way you see it?"

"I'll discuss it with Dr. Bradshaw and someone will get back to you if there are any changes." Lani hung up and fixed her eyes on the computer screen. She tried to hold her irritation down so she could think things through. She picked up a pen to jot down a list of points to discuss with Margaret. The pen made a popping sound when she threw it back down on the pad.

Lani headed into Margaret Bradshaw's office at 9:00, knowing she was in for a bad time but determined to get in the first shot. "Did you tell Porter Sinclair this is a tame volcano? That it'll just peter out and go dormant? How could you say that when you know it's on the verge of a blowout?"

Margaret's reply held an icy edge. "I think we have some other issues to cover first."

"No, let's go ahead and talk about the volcano," said a man off to her left.

Lani glanced in surprise at the figure sitting in the corner with his legs crossed.

"Lani, this is the president of the university," said Margaret. "Dr. Sylvester Purvis."

"We met at a reception for new staff at the faculty club," said Purvis.

"If I'd known you were here, I wouldn't have—"

"Maybe it's just as well. Dr. Bradshaw and I were just discussing press coverage of the volcano. And the importance of caution."

Lani took in the scene quickly. She looked at Purvis's face and then Margaret's. Plainly, the subject had been something other than press coverage.

"We have to be sure of our ground," said Margaret. "It wouldn't be unusual for a volcano to go quiet after some initial activity."

"But I was there. Close enough to touch it. The mountain's ready to blow."

Margaret took a navy blue suit jacket off a hanger behind the door and put it on. "That leads us to the main reason we're here. Can you explain to Dr. Purvis and me why you went over my head to Dean Cohen, and why you went with Ocean Research to the volcano without permission?"

Lani didn't know whether to look at Margaret or the university president, so she glanced back and forth, from one to the other, as if watching a tennis match. "I went to Dean Cohen because my model says there's a fifty-fifty chance Southern California will be hit by a killer tsunami, and I was ordered to forget it. I went to the volcano because Dean Cohen called Ocean Research Labs and okayed the trip. He also called Margaret and got her agreement."

Margaret's voice was sharp. "I received no such call."

Lani focused on Margaret. "I was there when he called you and heard him talking to you."

"Who did he talk to at ORL?" asked Purvis.

"The project manager, Richard Costello."

Purvis cleared his throat. "Lani, even if Dean Cohen did make one or both of those calls, you still violated university policy when you saw him without Margaret's approval."

"I'm convinced the lives of five million people are at stake."

"I'm sure you are," said Purvis, "but your model's only a model. No one can be sure the volcano will erupt, or exactly what would happen if it did. I think you showed very poor judgment."

Lani had expected a showdown with Margaret, but wasn't prepared for broadsides from the university president too. She said, with some desperation in her voice, "But if you'd been in that sub with me and seen how dangerous that mountain is..."

"Margaret's filled me in on your theory," said Purvis. "A giant caldera explosion starts a major seismic sea wave." He smiled at Lani. His eyes lingered on her face. "And while I think you might be jumping to conclusions, your science on this one shows a bold approach. And you're a passionate advocate for your own ideas."

Purvis's overtones made Lani uncomfortable. She saw Margaret's face flush. The hard stare and tight mouth signaled more than displeasure. What kind of snake pit had she stepped into?

"But we can't afford to make a mistake," continued Purvis. "The university depends on the goodwill of both the public and private sectors for our funding. And giving your theory to the press before we've had a chance to have it reviewed by other scientists just wouldn't be a good idea."

"I'd welcome a scientific debate, but the problem is time. We might have thirty days. Or maybe only thirty minutes."

"But it's been releasing steam and ash," said Margaret. "Surely that's reducing the pressure."

"That's from a rift in the side. It's releasing some pressure, but not enough. The crater on top is sealed. The magma's extremely rich in silica. Very heavy. Tends to self-seal and keep the steam and gas inside. Big bulge on one side of the mountain. Pressure's building."

"So you think it could turn out to be an underwater Saint Helens or Krakatau," said Purvis.

Lani nodded. "Has all the earmarks."

Purvis began tapping his fingertips together. "I'll talk to the new dean of earth sciences about setting up a panel of experts. We'll get the top people in seismology, oceanography, and volcanology. Are you willing to have your work reviewed by that kind of panel?"

"I'd welcome it."

"If the experts agree there's a crisis, then I think we'd want to go to the authorities. If not, we can let it ride. Will you go along with that?"

"How soon can you get these experts together?"

"They're all busy people, but we'll set it up as fast as we can."

"I hope that's soon enough."

"The main thing is we have to work together," said Purvis. "I know you feel strongly about this, but it wouldn't serve any purpose to go off on your own. If you made any kind of public statement without the full backing of the institute, it'd make us all look bad and…"

"People might panic," said Margaret.

Purvis continued. "If it led to evacuating the coastal zone, you can imagine the hysteria. Local economies would suffer. The business community and public officials who support us would be extremely upset. So I need your promise you'll be a team player. That you won't say anything publicly about this without clearance."

Lani studied the ceiling for a moment, then looked at Purvis and nodded. "Okay, I promise. My own opinion is there's not enough time to get that panel together, but I'll be a team player and keep my mouth shut."

"Good," said Purvis. "I'll take Margaret's complaint about your breaking university rules under advisement. It's a separate issue. In the meantime, you can stay in your present position at the lab, and we'll keep working together on press information." He dismissed her with a nod.

Lani had been back in her office for only a few minutes when Margaret Bradshaw called. "Dr. Purvis wants a memo from you laying out your position in detail."

"How soon does he need it?"

"Get it to me no later than two. I'll walk it over to him."

"You want the whole picture? Gas analysis and pressure measurements, seismic activity, fracturing and diking, magma analysis and transport volume, fault line stress numbers, where the rift is, where the bulge is and what it looks like? In other words, all the reasons why I think the volcano will explode, why it'll collapse, how much ocean that'll displace, and how big a wave it'll make?"

"As complete as possible," said Margaret. "He wants you to present your case as strongly as you can."

Lani's computer clock said she had less than five hours to put something together. "Should be able to have a two- or three-page summary of the situation by then. Will that do?"

"Perfect." She hung up.

Margaret was out when Lani came by with the finished memo. Margaret's secretary was leaving for lunch and asked her to put it on Margaret's desk. Lani laid the report on her boss's desk and went on to a meeting of the project staff.

Rear Admiral Yarnell Carson wore two stars and two hats: as head of Twentieth Coast Guard District, stretching from Point Loma near the Mexican border to Morro Bay in Central California; and head of Pacific Command, which took in the West Coast, Alaska, and Hawaii.

Carson was an inch taller than Dave Steel and wider across the shoulders. Everything about him was crisp, from the clean, square lines of his jaw and nose to the neatly pressed, light blue short-sleeved shirt that set off his dark brown eyes and ebony skin. He put down the report and looked at Dave. "You say maybe it will, maybe it won't. What the hell am I supposed to do with that?"

"The experts don't agree, sir. My own sense is that Seamount

Gilman is in a very dangerous state, ready to blow apart any moment. But maybe that's because I was inside a little sardine can of a sub that got stuck against the side of that volcano. I studied some geology at Colorado State, but I'm no expert on this kind of stuff."

The admiral shifted in his chair and picked up a brass letter opener, which caught the light as he rotated it slowly in his strong hands. "Okay, so what's the disagreement?"

"Dr. Sanches thinks there's a fifty percent chance of the whole thing happening. The volcano exploding with enough force to blow a hole in the earth's crust under the volcano, and the mountain collapsing inward into the hole. All in a matter of minutes. *Bam bam.* Sudden release of enough energy to make a two-hundred-foot tsunami.

"The ORL guy, Dr. Costello, also thinks the volcano will explode, but only puts the possibility of a major tsunami at ten percent. Says too many things would have to come together to produce that result."

"Even ten percent is high, as far as I'm concerned," said Carson. "Do we have a set of inundation maps for this area?"

"I'll check it out. If not, I'll call the Corps of Engineers and local emergency people and see what they have."

"Try NOAA, too. But any tsunami inundation map that's ever been drawn up probably wouldn't factor in a two-hundred footer." Carson rested the letter knife on his desk and fell silent.

Dave's glance wandered to an empty corner near the filing cabinet. "Where's the bat?"

Carson laughed, the sound somewhere between amusement and exasperation. "Cynthia said it got in her way when she filed, so I moved it over there." He jerked his thumb toward a corner by the window. "Did I ever tell you about the bat?"

Dave didn't want to deprive the admiral the pleasure of retelling his favorite story. "I know you played double-A ball."

"Yeah, I was a good catcher. Had a strong arm and runners

were afraid to steal on me, but I could never get my batting average above two-fifty. The manager said my chances of making it to the majors, even triple-A, weren't that good."

"Is that when you opted for the Coast Guard?"

"I had one more game to play before I left for the academy. My last game with the team. My last at-bat. We were behind four to two. Bases loaded."

The admiral rose, gripped an imaginary bat, and leaned into home plate. "The pitcher tried to sneak a fastball past me and I hit the mother right on the button." He ripped the air, rotating hips and shoulders, arms finishing high. "Got it all. Grand slam. Won the game. They never even found the ball. Kept my lucky bat with me ever since. Every ship, every shore duty station. Wherever the bat's gone, good things have happened."

Yeoman Cynthia Gates's voice came over the intercom. "Sir, an e-mail just came in from somebody at SciPac. Dr. Sylvester Purvis."

Carson sat and clicked on the SciPac message. "Purvis says he's setting up a panel of scientific experts to review the volcano data. He'll advise if the panel says the situation is critical."

"The situation looked pretty damn critical to me when I was down there."

"We can't do anything official till we're asked, or receive orders from upstairs. I'll alert the commandant's office in Washington that we may have to act fast. In the meantime, I want you to track down those inundation maps and put together an evacuation plan."

"For the whole coast?"

Admiral Carson nodded. "Santa Barbara to San Diego. A plan to move everybody back at least two miles."

"How soon?"

"I want it on my desk one week from today. Oh-eight-hundred."

"I'll need help," Dave said. "We'll have to contact dozens of other agencies and local jurisdictions. I better have some people who are good at logistics."

"I'm setting up an incident command with you as operations chief. That puts you in charge of tsunami readiness for the entire coast from Santa Barbara south. You'll have first call on personnel and equipment."

"I'll need a heelo, and I'd like to have Baldy Spangler as my pilot."

The admiral nodded. "Just issue the order. By the way, that gun smuggling problem is building up to a crisis. We're meeting with the FBI to set up a joint task force. You'll be our point man."

"Anything new?"

Carson shook his head. "They're killing a lot of people. Two o'clock tomorrow in my office."

"Aye aye, sir."

Carson watched Dave go out the door. It was more fun when he was that rank and that age and in the thick of the action. When Violet was alive, and the kids were little. Violet had been gone five years, the kids had their own lives, and now he had a much bigger family: the twelve hundred men and women in his command. And the safety of the ports, coastline, and coastal waters from San Diego to Alaska to Hawaii that all rested on his shoulders.

He'd been told he was on the short list being considered for next vice-commandant of the Coast Guard. If he was passed over, he might take early retirement. But maybe not. His desk chronometer said the time was 1800, and fatigue etched his jawline. He picked up a scale model of the *Adak*, his first cutter, his first Persian Gulf patrol. How many years ago?

Yeoman Gates's voice came through on the intercom. "Sir, the commander of Alaska District is on the line. Says it's urgent." Carson heaved a sigh and reached for the phone. When he spoke, his voice was strong.

three

Harley Wamp liked to get out early to the construction site. He'd gotten up a little after 5:00 when he heard the plop of the morning paper on his front steps. Normally he'd read the paper for a few minutes while having a cup of coffee, then shave, shower, and head for Serenidad. But this day was starting out with a different twist. He'd just seen the headline in the *L.A. Times*: *200-FT TSUNAMI MAY SMASH SO CAL COAST.*

Dyspeptic was the best way to describe Wamp's personality. His stomach was constantly full of gas, he was suspicious of the motives of others, and his outlook on life was elemental: to get anything done, you did what you had to do. He was under six feet, but on the burly side, with hard eyes and big fists. He'd been butting heads with builders, contractors, and suppliers for more years than he cared to remember, and in his early days was known to have personally beaten up a few of them for trying to cheat on a contract.

He'd started as a construction supervisor with Southern Coast Land twenty-five years before. The owners liked his tough, no-nonsense way of getting things done. After a number of promotions, he'd been invited to join their board of directors. The company went public, the original owners died, and Wamp found himself in charge. He'd worked his way up the ladder to become president of Southern Coast Land, the second-largest residential developer in the United States, and winners in a bidding war for the ten thousand choice seaside acres once known as Camp Pendleton. His big hands had softened with office work, but his eyes remained hard.

The new city of Serenidad was a make-or-break proposition for Harley Wamp and Southern Coast Land. They'd elected to cut out the independent builders and do it themselves, functioning as both developer and builder. Wamp had run the numbers. By letting suppliers bid the whole job, and accepting materials in trainload lots, they'd be able to build in an extra twenty percent profit on each house. They'd stretched their credit lines to the limit and taken in an investment partner in order to make the winning bid and finance the enormous construction costs of a whole new city on the coast, stretching from San Clemente to Oceanside. There was no room for error. Everything had to work on schedule and on budget down to the last nail if they were to pull this thing out.

So far so good. It had been a tough grind, but they'd gotten through the governmental clearance and permitting stages, and were deep into the project. It didn't hurt that Southern Coast Land was a major contributor to the reelection campaigns of every elected official involved at the state and county levels.

The development was to be built out in six phases. All six were in some form of construction, from site grading to final paint. In the first phase, known as Ocean Aire Estates, model homes had been completed and houses were in the final stages of construction. Down payments received based on lot locations and architects' renderings poured in. The last time he checked, they'd taken in over fifty million dollars. If everything kept going according to plan, they'd clear a fortune. On the other hand, they owed billions to the banks. If the plan became destabilized in any major way, total disaster was a stark probability.

Wamp read the headline again. His hand started to shake and

he felt like he was about to have the mother of all gas attacks. As he read the story, his fear turned to anger. He threw the paper against the wall, called his secretary, and told her to call a board meeting for 8:00. When she reminded him that it was 5:00 in the morning, he told her, "Get 'em outta bed if you have to. Just get their asses in there by eight."

Wamp was on the construction site by first light. He inspected the grading that had been done the day before, then drove back to phase two where two hundred houses were in framing. He parked and went into one. His practiced eye told him everything was in code, the materials and workmanship good enough for their purposes. The location and look of the place would get them the price they wanted. Buyers didn't really seem to care about the quality of the lumber or hardware, or whether a door frame was perfectly true.

His next stop was the construction shack, where he had a standing 6:00 a.m. meeting with the general contractor. He chewed out the general for letting the electrical sub get behind schedule, and told him the framing bills were coming in too high and he wouldn't pay a nickel more than the estimate.

He got to Southern Coast Land's corporate offices near the John Wayne Airport just in time for the meeting. He walked to the head of the conference table but didn't sit down. He bunched up the front page of the *Times* in his fist. "You guys seen this pile of shit?"

He rode right over the nods and yesses. "If we don't do something about it and do it damn quick, this could start a goddamn panic and kill our sales dead. Who's gonna wanna buy a million-dollar house near the ocean if they think the damn thing's gonna be washed away by a tidal wave? And if our sales stop, our income stream stops and we're fucking upside down."

"Is there anything to this at all?" asked one of the board members.

"Did you read the whole thing?" Wamp glared. "It's only the

theory of some bubblehead out there at SciPac named Leilani, for Chrissake. The *Times* interviewed some top authorities on this stuff. They all say the odds of all that happening are very, very long. They say even if there is a volcano out there and even if it does explode, the chances of it being big enough to start a tidal wave that'll clobber our coast here are next to nil.

"So the job of this board is to make sure our buyers don't panic, and keep right on putting down those down payments. Period. That's all that counts. How do we do that? We do that by making hamburger out of Dr. Leilani Sanches. Make her look like a jerk. Some wacko who wants to get her name in the paper so bad she's willing to do anything. As you people know, we've always given big to SciPac. Just got through endowing a chair of something or other. Sylvester Purvis owes me one…"

One of the board members asked, "Can we get him to put out a retraction?"

"You bet your ass," said Wamp. "I'm telling Purvis to issue a statement saying Leilani's science is all wrong and there's nothing to worry about. And we'll get a bunch of leading scientists to come out saying the same thing."

"Can we count on that?"

"They can be bought like anybody else. With the kinda money we're offering, no problem. The governor and the mayors of all the beach cities are gonna release statements saying everything's okay. And we're gonna get that smear campaign cranked into high gear. When we get through with her, Leilani Sanches is gonna wish she was back on the beach doing the hula hula."

Wamp waited for somebody to say something. When everyone remained silent, he said, "Okay, I'll call Sylvester Purvis. You guys get busy and make up a list of scientists who'll be willing to see things our way. Make sure they know it's a two-thousand-dollar-a-day consulting assignment. We'll have the lobbyists go to work on the politicians. And we'll get our PR firm to start the smear campaign on Miss Leilani. Get people laughing at her, like she's the biggest crackpot to come down the pike. Jokes on the late night shows, stuff like that. That oughta be enough to get her ass fired."

~~

George Hacker hated being short. Now that he was putting on weight, he hated it even more. He knew his five-foot-four-inch frame wasn't designed to carry 185 pounds. He couldn't zip his pants all the way up anymore. His tight collars made his small gray eyes bulge like a toad's. Reluctantly, he'd had his tailor come in and measure him for a completely new wardrobe.

Hacker's feelings about his looks were offset to a large degree by his knowledge that he was the most powerful man in Asian shipping. He knew there were questions about the tactics he'd used to take over the Blue Star Line fifteen years before, but he gave them little thought, knowing they were raised by people who went through life following sets of rules made for suckers. People who didn't understand that in the dog-eat-dog world of international business, you had to take what you wanted by any means at your disposal.

Before China took over Hong Kong, he had seriously considered moving his large fleet to Singapore or Manila. That was before his lengthy talks with Chinese government officials and his generous contributions to the recreation fund of the People's Liberation Army. Now he was convinced that conditions in Hong Kong would remain at least as favorable as they had been under the British.

Hacker's office had a panoramic view of the docks in the Tai Po district. He walked to the window and looked down with satisfaction. Eleven Blue Star container ships were being loaded with Chinese goods destined for the U.S. and Europe. Four of his tankers pumped Middle Eastern crude to the refineries in Kowloon. Another fifty-one Blue Star tankers and forty-two container ships were in ports around the world or on the high seas. All making money. He smiled. Not bad for an orphaned kid who'd started his career running cocaine for the longshoremen when the banana boats came into New York Harbor from Central America.

He cast a reconfirming glance at the line of photos on his office walls. He'd posed with just about every world leader. The British Prime Minister, the Brazilian Trade Minister, the American President, kings, sheiks, and mullahs. No big deal that he'd paid to have the shots taken from a low angle to make himself look taller. The intercom buzzed. The British-accented voice of Dixon Mallory, his executive vice president, came over the speaker. "I have those numbers."

Hacker grunted. "Bring 'em in. They better be good." The only thing George Hacker and Dixon Mallory had in common was their zest for making money by whatever means it took to make it. Actually, Hacker didn't like Mallory very much. Too much of a snob. Oxford. All the right clubs and the right friends. The right looks. Aside from business, they didn't have much to talk about. But Mallory was useful. Smart, not bogged down by some preacher's ideas of right and wrong, and he was able to open doors that even George Hacker, the powerful head of Blue Star Shipping, couldn't open on his own.

Mallory, six-one and slender, with cool hazel eyes, wore his impeccably tailored linen suit with casual ease. He got right to the point. "I've talked to the factory. I told them we'd take more production but they'd have to lower their price. After a good deal of agonized screaming, the owner came down from five to four dollars a unit, including the first loaded clip. Extra loaded clips are reduced to a dollar from a dollar and a half. He can add a shift and give us another sixty thousand units a month."

"You're too easy," said Hacker. "I woulda kicked him in the ass and got another half buck."

Dixon Mallory examined a manicured nail. "If we're going to roll this product out across the U.S., we have to have a dependable production source. Besides, every time we increase the order, I'll tell him he has to bring the price down. We'll get our extra half-dollar, and more."

"What about the distributor in the States?"

"That was a little more difficult," said Mallory. "I explained that we're raising his price ten dollars on the guns and two dollars on the clips. And he has to take another sixty thousand guns a month, plus an additional hundred and eighty thousand clips."

"What'd he say?"

The hazel eyes lightened and his mouth pulled up in a half smile. "I believe his first words were 'No way, José.' Said he'd have to start charging forty instead of twenty-five and demand would dry up. I told him the product's in such high demand, it isn't that price sensitive. Then he admitted the specialty gun's a hot item and people will pay. He says he's expanding east with his distribution network and could take care of the extra volume."

"I'm not sure I want that asshole expanding his territory," said Hacker. "Tell him he has to sell the extra volume on the Coast, and he better get his ass in gear. Anyhow, we're getting some good publicity. The *L.A. Times* calls our product the scourge of the city. Number one killer of young males and cops."

"The timing is excellent. It should increase product demand considerably."

"You sound like a fucking professor," said Hacker. "Have you run the numbers?"

Mallory smiled, urbane, just this side of patronizing. "You have a way with words, George. Factoring in the lower acquisition cost plus the increase per unit on both the guns and the clips, our margin more than doubles. Then with the extra production…"

Hacker had already figured it in his head but he asked the question anyhow. "How much extra you figure we'll clear a month?"

Mallory bent over the calculator on Hacker's desk and quickly ran a column of numbers. "Around six million per month more than before. An extra seventy-two million a year. It should make the bottom line look pretty good."

"Bottom line already looks good. This'll make it look better." His eyes found the new photo on the wall, the Chinese premier. Another short guy with balls.

~ ~

Dave walked back into Admiral Carson's office, where two people from the FBI push-pinned a large map of the United States onto the wall. The admiral nodded him toward a chair.

FBI Agent Jiro Yamaguchi, a muscular five-foot ten with close-cropped black hair, circled the West Coast with his pointer. "This is where they're coming in, L.A. taking the brunt. Sixty-five to seventy percent. The rest spread out over San Francisco, San Diego, Portland, Seattle. For the moment, the problem is pretty well confined to the inner cities on the coast, but starting to spread east. Denver police found them on three suspects last week."

"We've got to stop the flow," said the other FBI man, Assistant Director Albert Lewis. "Otherwise there'll be a lot more dead cops." He pulled a small black gun out of his pocket and placed it on Admiral Carson's desk. "Here's one of the little bastards. Deadliest street weapon we've ever come across."

Jiro Yamaguchi took a loaded clip out of his pocket and held it up, his black eyes looking intently from Dave to the admiral. "Clip's only four inches long. Holds sixty rounds of high-velocity hollow point in a double row of thirty. The gun's fully automatic. Fires the whole clip in five seconds. Rips a person apart." He slid the clip into the gun butt, thumbed on the safety, and put it back on the admiral's desk.

"That's why they're called Rippers," said Lewis.

Carson reached across his desk and picked up the weapon. He held it at eye level for a moment, then gripped the butt and put his finger along the trigger guard. "Hmmmm. Light, thin, about a third the size of a big frame pistol." He handed the gun to Dave.

Dave let the pistol rest in the palm of his hand. "If these things are killing a lot of Americans, any possibility it's a terrorist attack?"

Admiral Carson shook his head. "No, the Secretary of Homeland Security told the Coast Guard Commandant somebody's in this for the money. And they're making a lot of it."

Dave felt the compact pistol warm in his hand. It was obscene and deadly. "I've seen these on the news, but it's the first time I've handled one. Feels like a plastic toy."

"That's the horrible side of this thing," Jiro said. "Kids go right from the plastic gun in the toy chest to this killing machine. Even fits a small hand."

Carson took the gun from Dave, released the clip, removed a bullet, and held it between his thumb and forefinger. "Smaller than a twenty-two."

"Right," said Jiro. "Two millimeter. Smallest caliber pistol we've seen, and by far the most lethal. You can carry one in a pants pocket with no imprint. Mostly plastic, so metal detectors don't pick them up."

"There's a little outline of a dog on the grip," said Admiral Carson.

"Yeah, they're also called Dogs," said Jiro. "Stand on a street corner anyplace in South Central or the east side and ask for a Dog or a Ripper. You'll have one in five minutes, and it'll only cost you twenty-five bucks. Plus five bucks apiece for the loaded clips."

"Some factory someplace in Asia turns these out by the thousands every day," Director Lewis said. "They're being smuggled in somehow, and sold so cheap almost any school kid can get one on his weekly allowance."

"It's not only gangbangers getting killed by these things," said Jiro. He held the gun out between thumb and forefinger. "Dozens of kids in grade school and middle school have died by Rippers. This is the way kids settle arguments nowadays. They pull these out and start shooting."

"When cops try to intervene, their flak jackets don't protect them," said Lewis. "The shooter points at the face and empties sixty shots in two seconds. Not much left of the cop's head. We've got to find out how these things are coming in and cut off the flow."

Dave pointed to the map on the wall. "You seem pretty sure they're coming in by sea."

Jiro stepped away from the map. "We've eliminated air because of the high cost of air freight. To sell these on the street as cheaply as they do, the guns have to be manufactured cheap and shipped in bulk at low cost. That means by sea."

Dave said, "They can't be running contraband into deserted coves at midnight, like the old-time rum runners. We track every inbound ship by radar. If there's any deviation from a normal port of call, we check them out by air or sea patrol, then board and inspect if anything's not right. My guess is the guns come in hidden in the middle of normal cargo."

Carson said to Lewis, "Looks like Washington has appointed us a committee of two to solve this problem."

Lewis said, "That appears to be the situation. A joint FBI-Coast Guard operation to put an end to this gun smuggling. Jiro's our lead agent on the case."

The admiral said, "I'm assigning Commander Steel to work with Jiro. Dave graduated number one in his class at New London, and the Coast Guard sent him to Columbia for his master's in criminology. Thought we'd give him a chance to use the training and get some of the taxpayers' money back."

Jiro shook Dave's hand with an eager smile. "When can we get together? I'm anxious to push ahead on this."

"I'm leaving for sea duty. Checking out a Russian trawler fleet that's dipping inside the two-hundred-mile line. Back in about two weeks. We can start then."

"Let your XO take the trawler patrol," said Carson. "Why not start tomorrow?"

"Your place or mine?" asked Jiro.

"I'll come over to the bureau," Dave said.

Aboard the Coast Guard cutter *Farallon*, Dave laid out the interdiction plan he'd drawn up after his meeting with Jiro Yamaguchi. His group executive officer, Lieutenant Commander Justin Riley, and the ship's skipper, Lieutenant Elaine DuBois, looked and listened. The cutter rocked gently, its bumpers quietly thump-thumping against the jetty as the bow wave of an outbound tanker washed against its sides.

"We don't know how they're coming in," said Dave, "but the FBI has ruled out air, so it has to be by ship. The Rippers come in small boxes. A case of forty-eight would be about the size of a case of canned corn. A whole shipment could easily be hidden behind a false wall in a shipping container."

Riley, small and wiry, with a black crewcut and slate-blue eyes, asked, "Once the guns get here, how do they get them ashore?"

"We're really flying blind." Dave waited while the boatswains mate's PA announcement ordered sweepers fore and aft. "Don't know how the guns are shipped, or how they're brought ashore. The only things we're sure of is they're manufactured in Asia, and killing a lot of our kids and quite a few cops."

DuBois wore winter blues tailored to fit her five-foot ten-inch, slim-waisted figure. Her shag-cut hair matched her oak-brown eyes. "Any orders on how to proceed?"

Dave said, "It's likely the guns get here in shipping containers disguised as something else. Tennis shoes, canned beer, you name it… guns packed in the same boxes and loaded in the middle of the container. Customs would probably check a dozen boxes out of the front of the container and then pass it through."

Riley said, "They're already spot-checking containers for terrorist stuff like bombs and poison gas."

"They've got their hands full." Dave moved a radar maintenance manual off the chart table. "This is our show, and we'll have to take a completely different approach."

DuBois said, "Such as?"

"Intercept cargo ships coming from Asian ports. I'm especially interested in Blue Star. Their home port is in the source area, and they bring in a big chunk of Asian cargo."

"We can't board foreign-flagged vessels without cause."

Beyond the bridge's windscreen, a tug glided by, tethered to the stern of a Japanese container ship. "If they're clean, I agree," Dave said. "But a safety violation or anything suspicious is just cause. Let's board as many as we can."

Riley smiled. "Strap on the gun belt and board at sea?"

"Sure, when it's something obvious," said Dave. "If it's marginal, escort them into port and let Marine Safety do a fine-tooth job."

"You're really trying to rattle their cage."

"If we put on enough pressure, maybe we can flush something out."

"So," said DuBois, "if we can't count enough life boats, or there are too many people on deck, or it looks like there's a fire hazard or health hazard, or if the ship's listing or riding too low in the water, we board or escort, depending on the situation."

"Exactly," said Dave. "When we inspect, we keep an eye out for false bulkheads, containers that have been modified, compartments where things can be hidden."

Riley said, "Blue Star ships are newer, and kept in pretty good condition."

Dave switched on the electronic chart table. "Probably can't board, but when their annuals come up let's make the most of it. Beef up our inspection teams. Stretch out the process. Poke in every corner. That's the best I can do at the moment."

They huddled over the glowing display of the coastal waters. "Let's position the group's cutters to intercept the maximum number of container ships coming into San Pedro, Long Beach, San Diego."

"How far out do we pick them up?"

Dave said, "We'll have air group give us positions and course headings, then meet them at the twelve-mile line."

The Officer of the Deck's voice crackled on the intercom. "Admiral on board, sir."

"At ease," said a voice from the door of the bridge. Steel, DuBois, and Riley snapped salutes as they turned and greeted Admiral Carson.

Dave took him through the steps they'd been discussing. "So as of now, our top priority switches from illegal aliens to gun running."

The admiral nodded and was quiet for a moment. "That's correct, but we can't let up on illegal alien smuggling, either. Like that old rust bucket we stopped last week. The one with the hundred and fifty illegals jammed in the forward hold. Sorry we had to send them back. Don't blame these people for wanting to come here and try to find a better life, but our job is to uphold the law of the land, not pass judgment." The chart table glow highlighted his firm jaw.

The three subordinates had heard Carson's opinions before, but they respected him as a capable leader and gave him their full attention.

The admiral said, "It's too bad we have to put up these walls against immigration. All four of us standing on this deck today are here because our ancestors were immigrants. In my case they didn't come of their own free will. They were chained in the hold of a slaver. But Riley's people probably came looking for a better life."

"Yep, in steerage. Escaping the potato famine."

Admiral Carson looked at Dave. "You look like yours came over on the Mayflower."

"Steerage too," said Dave. "From Poland back in the late eighteen-hundreds. The name was Stielokowicz or something like that. The immigration inspector shortened it to Steel."

Carson looked at Lieutenant DuBois.

"I'm a Cajun from New Orleans," she said. "My ancestors were chased out of France and emigrated to Nova Scotia. The British chased them out of Nova Scotia and they wound up in the bayous of Louisiana."

The admiral nodded, a satisfied smile on his face. "Okay, enough pontificating. Let's get down to business. Dave, bring me up-to-date on your meetings with the FBI about this gun problem."

"We're taking a close look at Blue Star Lines. According to the shipping schedules, Blue Star puts more container ships into Pacific Coast ports than any other line."

Carson grunted. "Blue Star's out of Hong Kong, right?"

"Yes, and that's near the manufacturing source. Also, Jiro said two tips just came in from their contacts in Hong Kong. One was to check for false bottoms in the Blue Star containers. He's filling me in on the other one later, after he talks to Hong Kong again."

"How are you following up?"

"Jiro and I are going over to Pacific Container Terminal this evening, undercover as longshoremen. We've got union cards, assigned to work a Blue Star ship that starts unloading tonight. He's driving a rig that stacks containers, and I'm on a gang offloading containers onto trailers."

"Doesn't sound like you'll have time to do much inspecting."

Dave shook his head. "We'll check the containers while we're handling them… look for telltale signs, like rivets in the wrong place. You never know, something might pop up."

Carson said, "I'd like to talk to Commander Steel for a minute."

DuBois and Riley saluted and left.

"Glad to see you dealing with the smuggling problem, but this tsunami thing has me worried too. Are you giving enough time to the evac plan?"

Dave turned off the electronic chart table. "It's kind of a juggling act, but things are coming together. The report'll be ready on time."

The admiral nodded. "The Russian trawler fleet?"

"I've briefed Riley. He's using this as his flagship. They'll be getting underway in a couple of hours. He'll keep in touch on a secure circuit and advise if they run into unexpected problems."

"And you're to keep me posted on everything. Are we clear on that?"

Dave hesitated, then said quietly, "Yes, sir. Understood."

Carson's eyes softened. "If you have any questions, now's the time to get them out."

"Nothing important," said Dave. "Just wondering what to do with my spare time. I have midnight to six open."

What could have been a blast of hot anger turned into a belly laugh. "We can always use another bartender at the club. Available for the late shift?"

Dave grinned. "Yes, sir. I mix an excellent martini and a more-than-passable rum punch."

Dave kept his weight down to a trim one-sixty on a six-foot frame by skipping desserts and eating salads. He ran five kilometers most mornings before breakfast. He tried to get in a half-dozen sets of tennis on weekends, and he worked out on the nautilus machines at the gym two nights a week. He thought he was in pretty good shape, but the repetitive motion of handling container after container, hour after hour, had his arms and shoulders aching.

Three massive hammerhead cranes worked alongside the *China Star* unloading hundreds of semi-truck-size cargo containers. The crane operator clamped onto the top corners of the container with a spreader and lowered each one down to a chassis, a special truck trailer. Dave removed twist locks from the bottom corners of each container as it came down, and helped the crane operator seat the container on the chassis. There was no letup. No sooner would they get one container set, than another came down out of the sky.

It was 3:00 in the morning and Dave had been at it for more than five hours. Despite his physical effort, he was doing his best to check every container he handled, scanning the sides for an extra line of screws or rivets that might mark the location of a false bottom. So far, he'd found nothing suspicious.

Jiro Yamaguchi had put in a few summers working as a heavy equipment operator before becoming an FBI agent. Tonight he'd been assigned the job of moving containers coming directly onto the floor of the dock from the other end of the ship. He drove a top handler, a machine about the size of a large forklift, that stacked the containers in rows for later pickup. As he lifted each container, he checked for telltale signs, but to that point had found nothing out of the ordinary. Once in a while, on his way to pick up his next container, he circled past Dave, who gave him almost imperceptible shoulder shrugs or head shakes.

During the 2:00 a.m. lunch break, Jiro, in frustration, had casually asked a couple of the longshoremen if they'd noticed anything different about the Blue Star containers over the past few months. Both shook their heads.

It was just after 4:00 in the morning, two hours to go before the end of the shift. Dave had seated the latest container on a chassis. He glanced toward the bow of the ship, looking for Jiro.

As he watched, the forward crane deposited a new container on the dock and Jiro moved his machine into position to lift it. The spreader released the container and began rising straight up to grab another one. After traveling a few feet, the heavy claw seemed to stick in midair directly over Jiro's head. In trying to free it, the operator jerked one side up and sent a ton of cast-iron spreader swinging out in a fifty-foot arc. Just as Jiro moved in to clamp onto the container, the spreader came flying back like a wrecking ball and smashed into the side of Jiro's machine, demolishing it and sending Jiro slamming to the ground.

All the longshoremen ran to the scene. A stunned and bruised

Jiro sat near the wreckage, still clutching the detached steering wheel. Dave squatted down and put a hand on his friend's arm.

Jiro ran his fingers through his close-cropped black hair, trying to shake away the fog. He screwed up his face. "What hit me? Felt like an A-bomb blew me right out of my seat with this damn wheel in my hands."

The shift foreman told Dave to drive Jiro to the emergency room to get him checked for broken bones. "You and your buddy'll both get paid for the full shift. But don't come back tomorrow. You're bad luck."

In the car, Jiro said he was pretty beat up, but nothing was broken. They opted for breakfast instead of the emergency room.

Dave saw the lights of a coffee shop taking shape in the thin, predawn fog. He pulled into the parking lot and read the sign. "Black Cat. It fits."

Tendrils of steam from two cups of hot coffee intertwined and then disappeared through the holes in the dingy acoustical tiles. "Accident or attempted homicide?" asked Dave.

"I got antsy earlier and asked a couple of dumb questions." Jiro peeled the paper bottom off a warm blueberry muffin. "I think this was their answer. I'm lucky I survived."

"Somebody doesn't want us snooping around."

Jiro washed down a large bite of muffin with a gulp of coffee. "It could mean we've stumbled into some drug deal. Or we're on the right track and Blue Star is involved in gun smuggling."

"Come on," said Dave, "I'll drive you to your car, and then I've got to get back to base to wrap up the evacuation plan."

"I saw the headlines in the paper. You really think there'll be a tsunami?"

Dave put his coffee down. "I have a duffel next to my front door, packed and ready to go."

"Glad I don't live near the beach," said Jiro. "Back to the gun smuggling. Did you notice the size of that container holding yard?"

Dave nodded. "Acres. Must be ten thousand loaded containers in there."

"That may be where they transfer the merchandise."

"If that's the other Hong Kong tip, I hope it's better than the first one."

Jiro speared the last muffin crumb and licked it off the end of his fork. "That *is* the other Hong Kong tip."

"You think it's reliable?"

Jiro shrugged. "Any lead's worth pursuing. The transfer's supposed to take place around two tomorrow morning. We might catch them in the act if we're there first. Are you willing?"

"You're not suggesting anything illegal, are you?"

Jiro tilted a hand back and forth. "Not sure about illegal but, for sure, dangerous as hell."

Dave grinned. "Why didn't you say so?"

~~

At just past midnight Dave and Jiro pulled up in front of the vast holding yard where hundreds of Blue Star containers were salted in among thousands of others.

Jiro showed his FBI shield to the lone security guard. "The director's office called."

The guard stood under a light outside his prefabricated hut, running a ballpoint down his clipboard. "How do you spell that?"

Jiro spelled *Yamaguchi*.

"Yeah. Here it is. How long will you guys be in there?"

"Couple hours maybe," said Jiro. "Why?"

"Have to lock you in. Can't leave the gate open that long." He nodded to the cell phone on Jiro's belt. "Call when you're finished." He gave them a number.

The center of the yard was well lighted by clusters of lights on high poles, but the brightness gradually faded into shadow at the far edges. The aisles between the containers appeared almost totally black.

"First thing to do is locate the Blue Star section," said Jiro.

"Flashlights okay?"

"Only for the next half hour." Jiro zipped up his navy blue FBI windbreaker against the chilly wind blowing in from the ocean. "I want to start our stakeout no later than one. After that, no lights, no noise."

"What happens if we catch them in the act?"

"Depends on how many there are." Jiro glanced at Dave's gun belt.

Dave nodded. "Beretta nine-millimeter, standard issue. I don't wear it very often anymore, but tonight might be a good time for it."

Jiro patted the holster under his windbreaker. "Glock 23. If there're too many of them, I'll call for backup."

At the first intersection, Jiro said, "Let's work down parallel aisles and stay within yelling distance. If you find a Blue Star container, flick your light over to my aisle and yell or something."

They started at the far end of the yard. Dave launched down a dark canyon of forty-foot shipping containers stacked three high. He shone his light on the sides, looking for the familiar Blue Star. He met up with Jiro at the end of the first aisle, shook his head, and did a U-turn down the next aisle, continuing the search.

After a half dozen long aisles, Dave looked at his watch. Jiro's half hour was almost up and they still hadn't found the Blue Star section. The yard was too big for a quick search, so he'd just have to keep looking till Jiro said to stop. Maybe they'd get lucky.

Dave walked two more aisles without results. He began to think they'd picked the wrong part of the yard when he spotted his first Blue Star. Then another and another. He checked his watch again. Three minutes to spare. They could pick a spot and settle down for the stakeout. He spotted Jiro's light in the next aisle and yelled, "Got 'em!"

The beam from Jiro's flashlight suddenly wobbled. At the same moment, Dave heard a high-pitched cry. Jiro's light disappeared.

Dave pulled his Beretta, ran to the end of his aisle, swung down the next one, and pointed his flashlight at a chilling scene. A giant of a man dressed in black, gripping a long knife, crouched over a fallen Jiro. He raised the knife and started a downward thrust. Dave squeezed off four rapid-fire shots. The giant's knife hung in mid-arc, glittering in the flashlight beam, then the man turned and disappeared into the shadows.

Dave ran to Jiro. He checked quickly around him and knelt down. Jiro was on his back, left hand holding his right shoulder, eyes fogged with pain. Blood seeped through his fingers.

"Jesus, man!"

"Fucker must've been seven feet tall. Had a curved knife about two feet long. Surprised me. I threw my flashlight. Guess it messed up his aim. Otherwise, that knife would've gone right through my heart. He was about to finish me off when you fired."

Dave took off his shirt and wrapped it around Jiro's shoulder to staunch the bleeding, and helped him sit up. "Don't think I hit him. I was juggling the flashlight."

"No complaints from me. You saved my ass and all my other body parts."

"Gotta find out who's after you."

Jiro's smile was feeble. "Yeah, you don't want to break in a new agent."

Dave checked the bandage. "Nah, too much work. Looks like they fed us a bogus tip."

Jiro winced with pain. "Maybe."

Dave helped him to his feet. "Come on, let's get you to a doctor."

"I can't believe how big that guy was. Huge. Not just tall, huge. Asian face. Maybe Chinese. Dressed in black. All black."

four

The seismology department secretary stuck her head in the door. "Besides the hundred or so reporters out there, there's a hunk in a Navy uniform. Commander Steel. Says he's a friend."

"Coast Guard, not Navy," said Lani, and nodded an okay.

"Came by to see if I can help," said Dave. He took the chair next to Lani's desk.

She held back tears of frustration. "Dave, I didn't release that story to the *Times*, but nobody believes me."

He nodded. "Admiral Carson told me you called and said you weren't responsible."

"It was based on a memo I wrote to Sylvester Purvis, right after a meeting I had with him and Margaret Bradshaw."

"Not a memo to the *Times*?"

Lani tapped her desktop emphatically with the eraser end of a yellow pencil. "Purvis asked me not to release anything without his okay, and I gave him my promise. Then Margaret said Purvis wanted a memo outlining my case in detail. She said she'd walk it over to him. I worked on it all morning and put it on her desk about one. A few hours later the roof caved in."

"So he probably thinks it was you who sent out the story."

The pencil stilled. "That's what everybody thinks, and I'm

really in the doghouse. But I honestly don't know how my memo got from Margaret's desk to the *Times*. She claims she never got it. I suppose someone could have seen it there, read it, and for whatever reason gave it to Sinclair."

"Would Margaret have any reason to sabotage you?"

"I went over her head, and we haven't exactly been friends lately, but she could get me fired without pulling something like this."

"Anybody else out there who'd have a reason?"

"No." Her color heightened. "Whoever it is, I'd like to punch their damn lights out. I can't even leave the building." Her thumbnail dug into the soft pencil wood. "The reporters and TV cameras are out there waiting like circling sharks. They have my apartment staked out, too. I slept on the office couch last night. My lab assistant went over and brought me some fresh clothes."

"Is there a back door to this place?"

"Main entrance from the street, a parking lot entrance, and a building maintenance entrance in the back, next to the loading dock. All staked out."

"When does the building maintenance crew get here?"

"Late afternoon. Around five. Two men and two women."

"Do they wear uniforms, and how big are the women?"

Lani set down the pencil. "Yes to the uniforms. The women are from El Salvador. On the small side."

"Good."

A little before 5:00 p.m. the maintenance crew arrived. Manuel, the maintenance supervisor, handed Lani a plastic bag. "Hope it fits."

Lani pulled on a pair of dark blue coveralls with the company emblem, a green conifer and the words *Redwood Building Maintenance* stitched on the breast pocket. She piled her hair on top of her head and tucked it inside a dark blue baseball cap. With the dark eyes and golden brown skin inherited from her Hawaiian ancestors, she should look enough like a Salvadoran maintenance worker to pass casual inspection.

But would it get her by the eagle-eyed reporters milling around the entrances with their notebooks, microphones, and minicams? Her picture had been published by the *Times* in a follow-up story. It was a formal-looking photo from a SciPac faculty publication, and she didn't think it looked much like her.

Dave looked at her approvingly. "In five minutes, you and Manuel walk out the maintenance door together. Go straight to the van like it was just part of the job. Stay close together. I'll be waiting for you at Santa Anita and Colorado. Anything I can take?"

"My notebook." She handed him the briefcase-size computer.

Lani watched the five minutes tick off on her desktop computer screen. She said to Manuel, "Time to go." She snugged in close behind him and followed him out the door.

There were only a half dozen media people outside the entrance. The rest were around front and in the parking lot. One yelled, "Did you see her?"

Manuel shook his head. "I didn't see nobody."

A man holding a minicam blocked their path. "Hey, I'll give you a hundred bucks if you get me inside." When Manuel didn't respond, he said, "Make it two hundred."

Manuel said, "Listen, mister, I'm late for another job, so just get out of my way, okay?"

The cameraman looked closely at Manuel, then at Lani, and finally stepped aside.

Dave had been parked at Santa Anita and Colorado for only ten minutes, but it seemed like hours. Finally, a white van appeared in his side-view mirror, slowed, and pulled in behind him. A small figure in blue coveralls got out and walked toward his car.

Dave steered the Corvette onto the Foothill Freeway. "I'm driving you down to my apartment in Naples, near Long Beach. Use it as long as you want. I'll move in with a friend."

Lani said, "I hate to put you to so much trouble. I won't stay any longer than I have to. Maybe a couple of days."

"No trouble. Wait till it's safe before you go back."

The apartment was located on a little arm of a small-boat marina. As they walked across the lawn to Dave's ground floor unit, Lani asked if one of the boats tied up in front belonged to him.

Dave smiled. "No, I get enough sea duty. But a friend of mine owns a Viking twenty-eight. If you like to sail, we can take it out one of these days."

He gave her a tour of the apartment, then started throwing clothes into a duffel bag.

She said, "I appreciate everything you're doing, but just in case you think this might lead to something, I want you to know up front I'm not on the market. I'm engaged."

He stuffed a final pair of socks into the duffel and zipped it up. "Who's the lucky guy?"

"An island boy I've known since I was little."

Dave tucked the duffel under his arm. "I'm doing this because I like helping people. I'm not expecting anything."

"You mean you do this all the time? Put yourself out like this?"

"Sure, for friends. And I was hoping to get to know you better."

Lani removed the baseball cap, pulled her hair back into a loose twist, and refastened it with the dolphin clip. "Why?"

"You're smart, and you fight for stuff you believe in. I admire that."

She looked at him. "Not much more to know."

"I hope we can at least be friends. You know, you tell me a couple things about you, and I'll tell you some lies about me."

"Well, I am curious about how a saint got into the Coast Guard."

Dave laughed. "I play poker with the Pope. Listen, can a friend come by tomorrow evening and take a friend out to dinner? There's a great seafood place near here."

Dark eyes watched him. "Just as friends?"

"Just as friends."

"I'll be busy in the morning. Have to get the laptop online and catch up on work that's been stacking up. But call me tomorrow afternoon and let me know what time."

~ ~

Dave stood facing Admiral Carson's desk with a blue folder in his hand.

Carson cupped a hand over the phone and whispered, "Talking to the commandant. Be another minute." He wagged a finger toward his picture wall. "Check out my new addition."

Two dozen framed prints of historic Coast Guard ships covered the wall next to the floor-to-ceiling window. Dave studied the newest.

Carson finished talking and reseated the phone. "Civil War revenue cutter *Henrietta*—steel engraving. Pretty, isn't she?"

Dave flashed a thumbs up. "Beautiful."

The admiral closed a thick marine safety manual. "Regulation changes pile in from Washington so fast it's hard to keep up." He nodded toward Dave's folder. "Evacuation plan?"

Dave slid the blue file across the desk. "It's pretty thin. More of an outline of what has to be done. Couldn't fill in much detail because I'm getting zero cooperation from the local authorities."

Carson looked up in surprise.

Dave said, "It's pretty obvious somebody's passed the word to these coastal cities not to give us the time of day."

"Maybe they think it'll hurt business."

"But who put them up to it? It was a solid wall. Has to be orchestrated."

"Let me make a call," Carson said. "The city manager of Redondo Beach is in the Coast Guard Reserve. He was out on exercises with us last summer. Sit for a minute. I'll see what I can find out."

The admiral got right through to Ray Pinkton, City Manager of Redondo Beach, and laid out the problem in a straightforward way. After that, conversation consisted of, "mm-hmm, of course," and "I see."

Carson finally hung up and tilted back in his chair. "He was cagey at first. Thought he might be saying something out of school. Then he told me there was a meeting down at the Balboa Bay Club a few days ago. Mayors of most of the beach cities, plus the governor and his staff. Meeting was hosted by a guy named Harley Wamp, president of Southern Coast Land. They're the outfit that's developing this new city where Camp Pendleton used to be."

"And the outcome?"

"Apparently Wamp sold everyone on the idea that Dr. Leilani Sanches is a fraud, just in it for the publicity, there's nothing to worry about, and they should all stick together to block any emergency evacuation planning."

"They're risking millions of lives. Could be as bad as the Indian Ocean in '04."

"That was a while back, and people forget fast. Harley Wamp's on a mission to get Lani fired and squash even the slightest hint of evacuation planning."

Dave's face reddened. "He's afraid it'll ruin sales. What an asshole! The sooner Lani makes her case to the panel of scientists, the better. If she convinces them this threat is real, then the beach cities will have to go along with the program."

"It can take forever to get a group like that together," said Carson. "I'll put in a call to Purvis and tell him the Coast Guard is interested in a quick resolution."

"I'm seeing Lani this evening. Shall I tell her who's gunning for her?"

Admiral Carson nodded. "She should know who her enemies are, as well as her friends."

~ ~

The Ocean Grill looked to be only one step above a coffee shop, but it had a glorious view of Long Beach Harbor and the cook had a way with grilled fish. Their window table looked across the harbor's expanse to the stately *Queen Mary* silhouetted against the orange-red afterglow in the western sky. The waiter brought an ice bucket for their bottle of Stag's Leap Chardonnay, and a busboy lighted the candle in the net-covered, red glass hurricane lamp. Dave slid the bottle out of the frosty bucket and poured generously.

"Any idea when you'll be meeting with Sylvester Purvis's scientific panel?"

"None," said Lani. "I hope it's not too late when he finally gets around to it." The hurricane lamp spread a soft glow over the table as the outside light faded.

The waiter reappeared, a bulky man with dark eyes and dark hair graying at the temples. He spoke with a Balkan accent. "Fresh today we got Alaska halibut and Pacific salmon. Salad comes with and you can have mashed or fries."

"Halibut, please." Lani said. "And French fries."

Dave ordered salmon and fries, and the waiter nodded and left.

Dave had picked up a copy of *Points North*, an upscale magazine devoted to the business and social life of north San Diego County. He opened it to one of the center pages and showed it to Lani. "You know this guy?"

She studied the retouched photo of Harley Wamp in a hard hat and standing in front of a bulldozer. She shook her head. "Should I?"

He told her about the meeting at the Balboa Bay Club.

Lani looked out the window. The lights of the *Queen Mary* across the harbor were growing brighter as dusk deepened into night. When she turned to face Dave, her color was high, her expression grim, and her eyes full of indignation. "What gives this man the right to attack me like that? Who does he think he is?" She sent a fork spinning.

Dave was startled. "Hey, don't shoot the messenger."

She pounded the table. "This is crazy! I won't stand for it!"

"Don't let it get to you, Lani. It's all about money. He's afraid tsunami talk will hurt business."

Her dark eyes bored into him. "To destroy another person— to destroy *me*—and put five million people at risk for a few bucks. It's absolutely insane!"

The depth of her fury made Dave uneasy. "It's a bad rap, for sure. What do you think you'll do?"

"Fight it!" Her lips twisted into a grimace. "I have to convince Purvis that I didn't leak that story to the *Times*. Then persuade him to back me up… announce publicly there's nothing wrong with my science. It won't be easy."

Her face was flushed, jaw set. Lani's high emotion tweaked something inside him. It made her more alive and attractive, but at the same time thorny and disconcerting. He'd tried to connect with her anger, but found himself pushing it away instead of letting it in. This was one side of Lani he wasn't sure he wanted to handle. Just as well she was unavailable. He finally said, "Could be an uphill fight."

"Millions of lives are at stake. Plus my job and my reputation. I don't care how hard the fight or how long it takes. I'm not backing down."

The busboy set fish knives wrapped in maroon napkins next to the paper placemats. They sipped Chardonnay during the pause.

A younger version of the waiter came to their table. He wore a dark pencil mustache and a red-flowered aloha shirt with "Slava" on the name badge. "Hi, folks. We're having a little problem in the kitchen. Your order's going to be held up a few minutes."

"How long?" Dave asked.

Slava shrugged. "They started the charcoal late. We'll be ready to grill in five or ten minutes. If you like cold seafood I'll send an appetizer while you're waiting, no charge."

Dave said, "Okay, thanks, Slava," then asked Lani, "Where were we?"

The interruption had not cooled her anger. "No way am I backing down."

"If the experts agree with you, that'll help your case. Admiral Carson said he'd call Purvis and try to get him to move on that panel. We've got to clear you as fast as possible, and I need to get the beach cities working with me on the evacuation plan."

Lani's anger had subsided, smoldering. "Purvis didn't seem to be in much of a hurry. Lots of luck to the admiral."

"Hey, Lani, I'm in your corner. I'm not the enemy." Dave set his wineglass on the wet napkin.

She met his eyes. "Sorry. I'm glad not everyone's against me. Thanks. Mo' happy you my side, bruddah."

Dave smiled in relief. "How about that! Dr. Leilani Sanches, geophysicist, seismologist, writer of high-order mathematical formulae, and speaker of real island pidgin."

"Comes with the territory when you grow up on da islan'." She lifted her glass. "I could do a pretty fair hula when I was ten."

He was still trying to adjust to her sudden change—as if nothing had happened. "I'll bet you still can."

The small hand tilted back and forth. "Maybe. I'd have to practice."

"You sure were graceful moving around on the *Carlsbad* and in that little sub."

"Squeezing into a submarine and doing a hula are two different things. I might have to take off a pound or two."

He sipped his wine. "C'mon, be serious. You're what? Five-two and ninety pounds, tops, right?"

Lani tilted her hand again, neither confirming nor denying.

The waiter returned with a small platter of peeled prawns and scallops nested in ice. He set it on the table with crocks of tartar sauce and red cocktail sauce.

Dave sensed her pulling back. "Are you still mad?"

She spooned cocktail sauce onto her small plate. "Simmering down. Trying to focus on the best way to handle Purvis."

"Just tell me to back off if I'm poking my nose where it doesn't…"

She nodded. "Let's talk about other stuff."

Dave thought for a moment, casting around for a subject of mutual interest. "About the volcano. Why is it doing what it's doing?"

"You want the full lecture, or the short version?"

"How long is each?"

"The full shot is six hours, the short version only three."

Her joke surprised him and he broke into laughter. "Condense the short version, and very, very simple."

She thought for a moment. "Okay. My theory is there's a deeply buried hot spot. Hundreds of miles down in the mantle, and big. Perhaps thousands of cubic meters in size."

Dave closed his eyes. "I'm trying to visualize that. Like a huge lake, maybe."

"Except no flat surface. More like an enormous balloon-shaped cavity. Two-thousand-degree temperatures melt rock farther down in the mantle. That material rises and flows into the hot spot."

"What happens when the balloon fills up?"

"Heat and high pressure force the hot magma to rise out of the hot spot, upward toward the surface. The molten river finds seams and channels leading to the volcano."

Dave dunked a prawn in cocktail sauce and took a bite. "Obviously, no one has ever seen a hot spot."

"Too deep," said Lani. "They can't be observed or measured directly by any instruments we have now. We have to infer their existence and behavior by what we can see and measure on the surface and subsurface." She speared a scallop with her seafood fork, dipped, and nibbled. "End of lecture." A moment later, she added, "When I blew my stack, it wasn't aimed at you."

"I understand. But the next time I'm bringing my asbestos gloves." He dipped a fat prawn in red sauce.

Her eyes crinkled at the corners when she laughed. "That's me. What you see is what you get."

He wanted to say, "I like what I see," but he wasn't sure, so he said nothing.

"I don't know if what I see in you is what I get," she said. "You make little jokes, but that doesn't tell me much."

Color tinged Dave's face. "You're not the first to tell me that. Sorry."

Lani watched Dave for a moment. "We couldn't be more different. I'm impulsive… wear my heart on my sleeve. You're cautious and held in."

"I try to be more open, but I always find myself sizing up the situation first."

"I'm curious," said Lani. "Do you mind telling me about your family and stuff like that?" A man at a nearby table briefly monopolized the room with a loud, one-sided cell phone conversation. Dave waited till the man finished. "Sure, as long as we can get back to Lani after a while."

She nodded.

"Well…" he paused. Should he tell her about the ripper smuggling, shooting at a seven-foot giant flashing a knife, Jiro nearly dying? He shrugged. "My life has been pretty routine. Dull, really."

"You said you went to Colorado State before the Coast Guard Academy. Is that where you're from?"

"No, Cincinnati. My dad was a salesman for Procter and Gamble. Sold everything from soap to fruit drinks and ended up as national sales manager for one of their divisions."

"Is he still there?"

"He took early retirement to go into the sales training and seminar business. That's what he does now."

The waiter brought a basket of hot rolls and said their dinners would be up right away.

Lani said, "What did you learn from your father?"

Dave thought for a moment. "To be positive. Don't let the negatives get you down. Set reachable goals. Work hard to attain them."

"What else?"

"Listen to people. Tune in. Find out where they're coming from. And be cheerful. He always used to say people love a smile, hate a frown."

Lani looked at the hurricane lamp shadows playing on Dave's face. "You sound like Willy Loman, getting by on a shoeshine and a smile."

Dave smiled. "Willy Loman was out of touch with reality. I try to keep my feet on the ground. But I guess I sound pretty boring. That's what my ex-wife said when she filed for divorce."

She forked a scallop and bit into it.

Dave said, "Married right after I graduated from the academy. Only lasted a few months. Long time ago. No kids. No regrets."

"Besides boring, did she ever say she couldn't tell what you're thinking?"

"I guess that's how I still come off."

"Not boring. You obviously care about people, but I'm not sure how you feel."

Dave broke a breadstick and put the two pieces down on his cocktail napkin. "I try to be up front. But when I'm not sure about a situation, I hold back a little, see how things go."

"You sound like you're afraid of getting hurt again."

His brow wrinkled. "Well, one day she just picked up and left. Said she needed more excitement. I thought we loved each other, so it *was* a surprise. But I don't think that has anything to do with needing to size things up."

"Positive-thinking sales types are supposed to be spontaneous."

"That's my dad to a T, but my mother's more controlled, more intellectual. I got some of both. His gung-ho and her caution."

"Two tendencies bound to clash."

"Yeah, like a couple of billy goats colliding head-on. But only with people. Not with command decisions, problems to be solved."

"So are you sizing me up, then?"

Dave forked another prawn onto his plate. "No, that's settled. We're just good friends who like each other's company."

"Still feels like you're holding back. I can see why your ex-wife had problems. But I know you're a caring person, ready to help. That counts for a lot."

Dave twirled the stem of his glass. "Our job in the Coast Guard is saving lives. I thought about med school at one time, but spending all my days indoors in an office or hospital didn't do it for me. Geology sounded better because I figured I'd be outdoors. Then the Coast Guard thing opened up and that seemed ideal. I could be outdoors a lot and still help people."

She studied his face. "If you have to be cheerful and positive all the time, how do you handle loneliness and fear and sickness and people dying? Don't you ever want to cry?"

Dave stopped twirling the glass and folded a corner of his napkin. "No matter how big a load of garbage I'm carrying around, I cope with it. I have to lead by example. Inspire others to do their jobs well."

"Do you have more family?" The waiter arrived with two plates heaped with grilled fish, shoestrings, and green salad. Lani sniffed her halibut. "Smells wonderful."

Dave said, "I'm the oldest. Sister working for IBM and a little brother in law school. My mother's gone back to teaching. We get together at holidays, and all get along fine."

"Your background and mine couldn't be more different." There was pain in Lani's eyes. He waited.

"My folks had four boys. All big guys. Guess they got the Hawaiian genes. I was tiny at birth—only four pounds—probably got the Chinese genes. I came sixteen years after my youngest brother."

"Change-of-life baby?"

Lani sipped her wine. "My mother was at that age. I probably wasn't planned."

"You mean they weren't happy to have a little girl finally, to keep them company in their later years?"

Lani's mouth pulled up in a half smile. "My brothers had all left home. I can't think Rudy and Rose were jumping for joy with the two o'clock feedings and changing diapers when they thought they were through with that stuff a long time ago."

Dave topped the wine glasses. "What does Rudy do?"

"He was a sanitation worker, drove a garbage truck. He spoiled me with treats and called me his sweet Leilani, so I suppose he loved me. Love from Rose was a different story."

Dave tasted his salmon.

"She was busy doing volunteer work from the time I remember. I didn't see much of her. My Auntie Hazel picked me up at school, and I'd stay with her till my folks got home."

"Did you have friends to hang out with?"

"Friends? A lot at school, but there weren't many kids my age in our neighborhood. It was kind of lonely."

"How about when your folks came home?"

"Rudy was always worn out from working on the garbage truck all day. He'd fuss over me for a few minutes, then sit in his chair and watch TV till he went to bed. Rose would come rushing home complaining about too much to do, fix supper, then spend the rest of the evening making phone calls. She'd kiss me goodnight before bed, but I was never sure how much she loved me."

"How did you handle it?"

She speared a French fry, followed by a taste of halibut. "Stayed busy. I had to be the best at everything in school. Brought home tons of homework every night. Studied hard. I got into Kamehameha because I'm part Hawaiian. Joined every club on campus and ended up running most of them. I was even captain of the softball team."

"What position?"

"Shortstop. Batted three-eighty."

"Wow! Lani the home-run slugger."

"I just had the knack of seeing the ball and hitting singles." She swung an imaginary bat, and the bull-voiced cell phone user looked over. "I could go to either field, but my favorite was over the pitcher's head up the middle."

"You and Admiral Carson ought to start a team. He's always talking about his days in the minor leagues. Did you play in college?"

"UCLA and Michigan both recruited me for softball, but Princeton was where I really wanted to go. I decided to drop all outside stuff and concentrate on academics."

"Your folks still living?"

Lani nodded. "Rudy retired. They sold the house in Honolulu and moved to the country, out to the North Shore. Up on a hillside. If the tsunami hits they'll be okay."

Dave waited while the busboy refilled their water glasses. "You said you're part Hawaiian."

"Plus Chinese and Portuguese."

The busboy glanced at her, then left, ice cubes rattling in his pitcher.

"I'd say that particular blend produced one of the nicest women I've ever met."

Lani cocked her head. "Nicest? After I singed your eyebrows? I like compliments, but I'm not sure that fits."

He saw a spark of teasing humor in her eyes. "Okay then, how about beautiful and mysterious? Plus intriguing and irresistible."

"You're getting close," she said, and they both laughed.

Dave said, "Tell me about this island boy you're engaged to. Is he a three-hundred-pound Samoan who eats Coast Guard people for breakfast?"

She looked down. "I'm sorry, there's no island boy. I said that because I don't want any involvements."

"Why not?" Dave rested his fork on his plate.

"I'm still hurting from the last one."

"Oh?"

Candlelight reflected in her dark eyes. "Got married right out of high school to a guy just out of the Navy. Frank Fortney. Didn't last long. I thought I knew him, but I didn't."

"Did he run around?"

She grimaced. "He not only cheated on me, he drank too much, and the bastard got physical when I complained."

"You mean... like he hit you?"

"Beat up is more like it—but only once. He came home late from a party. I yelled at him. He slugged me and tried to tear my clothes off, but he was so drunk he fell asleep first. My face was all bruised. I went outside and trashed his pickup. Broke the windows, slashed the tires, and poured sugar in the gas tank. Packed my stuff and left."

Dave's eyes widened.

"I'd never been hit before. I still have bad dreams about it. This guy was so nice before we married. Such a loathsome piece of filth after. So I'm sorry, but I just don't trust men. No way to be sure what you're getting."

Dave said, "I tend to shy away from long-term commitments, too. How come you married so young?"

"It was an impulse thing. I fell hard for Frank and just went for it. Disaster."

"What happened after that?"

"I got a divorce and an injunction to keep him away. I went back to live with my folks, but I wanted to make my own way, so I waited tables for a living and took courses at UH Manoa."

"Fortney stayed away?"

"I haven't told you the worst part. He sold drugs to dealers."

Dave saw a flicker of fear in her eyes. "A distributor?"

Her breathing got shorter. "Big operator in the drug trade. I was afraid to turn him in, but I finally had to. He was stalking me despite the injunction. He'd follow me to work and school. Send me notes with death's-head drawings. I finally got so scared I blew the whistle on him."

"Where is he now?"

"They found a cocaine lab in his apartment. He got fifteen years in Halawa State Prison. My scholarship at Princeton came through, and I left the Islands. He's the main reason I haven't been back. I don't want to be there when he gets out. I hope he's out of my life for good, but I worry." She poked absently at her neglected salad.

"Any other reasons for not going back to Hawaii?"

She shook her head. "I didn't want to for a long time. Nothing there for me. But lately I've been wanting to go back and get reacquainted with my folks."

Dave flagged the waiter. "Two coffees, please." A busboy carted their dishes away. The waiter returned, placed two clanking cups and saucers on the table, and poured from a steaming carafe.

Dave said, "This has been an interesting evening."

She laughed. "Come on, Dave, you've got to do better. Interesting like good, or like a pain in the neck?"

"Stimulating," he said. "I'd like to do it again."

Her smile disappeared. "One dinner together, okay. Just friends. Two dinners together, something else. I don't think so."

"Fine."

~~

It was pre-dawn dark when Dave picked up Lani to drive her to work. Her subtle floral fragrance filled the car. The clock on the dashboard said 5:40 as they pulled up in front of the seismology lab.

"Thank heavens," said Lani. "All those reporters are gone."

"They probably left when they found out you'd flown the coop, but there'll be snoopers around, so don't get too complacent."

"If the coast stays clear, I'll go back to my own apartment tonight." She started to slide out, then turned and leaned back into the car. "You've been a big help. Thanks." She reached across and squeezed his hand.

Dave let her hand rest on his for a moment. "Call if you need a friend."

~ ~

Lani sat at her computer, studying the readings coming in from Seamount Gilman. After less than an hour of tracking the morning's numbers, it was clear to her that activity was diminishing all along the line: number of quakes, quake intensity, gas pressure, water temperature, magma flow.

She picked up the phone and alerted Margaret that Seamount Gilman showed signs of subsiding.

A few minutes later Margaret stood over her shoulder, studying the changing numbers. "It was only a temporary flare-up after all. Everything's headed down."

"The only thing that isn't is the crustal stress level along the fault line."

"But that's not a volcano reading. I think we can announce that your so-called tsunami threat is finished."

"I'd watch it for another week or so to make sure," said Lani. "This could be a momentary lull before it turns around and gets nasty again."

"Not with the numbers plunging like this. It's over. I'll tell Sylvester… uh… Dr. Purvis, that we should release a statement to the press saying the whole thing was a false alarm."

"Whatever you do won't make any difference to the volcano. If it decides to rest a day or two and then blow its stack, that's what it'll do. I think we should wait and see before we release anything."

"I'm on my way over to his office right now," said Margaret. "I'll let him decide."

Gus Belmondo saw Margaret leave. He stepped into Lani's office, green eyes worried. "What'd she say?"

"She's going to Purvis's office to recommend that he sound the all-clear. I'd planned to meet with him today to see if he'd back me up. Some developer is stirring up trouble."

"What kind of trouble?"

"Trashing my reputation." She watched columns of numbers flicker across her screen. "Releasing stuff claiming I made this up to get attention. Saying my science is phony. Now, with the volcano fading, I don't know how receptive Purvis will be."

Gus said, "That sucks. Everybody on the project knows you're doing good science."

"I hope Purvis agrees. Otherwise, I don't know."

The phone call from Purvis came less than an hour later. "Lani, in view of this latest information, I think we're just going to have to eat a little crow with the press and admit the thing has settled down and there's no longer anything to worry about."

"I think you'd be jumping the gun. We just don't know enough about this yet."

"I hear what you're saying, Lani, but everyone else is sure the mountain's going dormant. I've made the decision to announce that to the media."

"Dr. Purvis, I think you're setting yourself up for a potential calamity. If the volcano comes back and blows and triggers the tsunami, millions of people along the coast could be caught unprepared."

"I'll admit it's a risk," said Purvis. "But a small one, and one I'm willing to take."

"Does this mean you've decided not to convene the panel to hear my presentation?"

"I don't see any need for it now. If the volcano had continued to heat up, it would have been the thing to do, but now it isn't." He paused. "Lani, I've decided to put you on administrative leave for a while."

She didn't reply for a moment. Finally, "Why?"

"Three reasons. You violated the rules by going around your department head, you sent the tsunami story to the *Times* after you promised you wouldn't do so without my permission, and questions have been raised about the quality of your science. Whether you took shortcuts and didn't adhere to scientific method."

Lani swung away from the computer screen, her voice full of shock and anger. "Yes, I went over Margaret's head because I thought I had to. But none of the other stuff is true. You have to believe me. The *Times* story was based on a memo I left on Margaret's desk. She told me you asked for it."

Purvis cleared his throat. "Yes, but apparently it went elsewhere."

"I don't know who sent it out, but it wasn't me. And I'm sure of my science. So far, nobody's been able to show me where I'm wrong."

"You'll have an opportunity to defend yourself. I'm appointing a special academic committee to review your case and make a recommendation as to whether you should be reinstated, or discharged for conduct detrimental to the institute. In the meantime, your regular salary will continue but you are asked not to come to work. Someone else will fill your position."

"Even if the volcano comes back?"

"I don't think it will."

five

At the Blue Star offices in Hong Kong, Hacker poured hot water into a teapot to warm it. He leaned forward and inhaled the scent from one of the many canisters lined up on the table. "The English think they know tea," he said to Dixon Mallory. "They don't know shit about tea. They drink some dickhead blend like Earl Grey and think it's so damn great."

"What marvelous brew are you whipping up for us today?" asked Mallory, drily.

"That sounded a little bit snotty to me, Dixon. Just don't fucking patronize me, okay?"

"I know you're serious about your tea, and I respect that. And I know better than to try to patronize you, George. I think you're overly sensitive about some things."

"Anyhow, to answer your question, we're starting with a base of China Black. A Keemun from North China. Nice bouquet. Adding a little late summer Formosa Oolong. Very pungent. Then, a pinch of high-grown Dimbula from Sri Lanka. Plus three Indian teas. A second flush Darjeeling picked in June. A heavy Dum Duma from Assam. And an autumn Duar. Nice for blending."

Hacker poured out the hot water, then added tea leaves to the warmed pot. "Now, tea is a product after my own heart. You can make it with coolie labor and sell it at a good profit. But lately they've been paying the plantation workers too much."

"Squeezing profits," said Mallory.

"Yeah, drives up prices and spoils the workers. If I ran the tea business, I'd take care of that in short order. If the workers don't produce, they don't eat. If they make their quotas then they eat, but damn little. If they eat too much they get lazy and you can't get a decent day's work out of them. You got to keep them hungry."

Hacker had taken the pot to the freshly boiling kettle, and the blend was now steeping. "Wait'll you taste this. It's gonna blow you away. Get the aroma." He took the lid off the pot and put it a few inches from Mallory's nose.

"Very, very nice, George."

"Have to let it steep for a few minutes. Did I tell you we're sponsoring an orphanage?"

"I didn't know we were in that business."

"Not a business, Dixon. Just insurance. Some general told me this was a favorite project of the chairman himself. I figured it wouldn't hurt. I coughed up enough to get our name on the door. They're gonna call it the Blue Star Children's Home."

"You're a surprising man, George. Just a second ago you were talking about starving the tea pickers. Now you tell me you're underwriting an orphanage. I don't think you had to do it. Knowing the amount we put into the Peoples Liberation Army recreation fund, I'd venture to say our situation here is quite solid."

"Well, it never hurts to stay on the right side of the big shots. Besides, I was an orphan myself, you know. Got put in a dozen different foster homes before I said fuck it and ran away when I was fourteen."

Mallory waited a moment, watching Hacker with the teapot. "I just received an e-mail from our man in L.A. The FBI has put twenty-four-hour surveillance on our container ships unloading in San Pedro and Long Beach."

Hacker poured two cups from the pot. "They won't find anything. Hey! Get that bouquet."

"They've zeroed in on the provisioning trucks. They're videotaping the whole thing. Loading, then the empty crates coming back. They've had some agents sniffing around the Marine Providers warehouse, too. I don't like it."

"Is Yamaguchi still the agent in charge?"

"Yes," said Mallory. "He's working with a Coast Guard officer. A Commander Steel."

"Too bad Ho Kai Fat didn't kill that asshole in the customs yard. We'll just have to tell him to finish the job. I don't like people sticking their noses where they don't belong."

Mallory said, "We have to make sure nothing can be traced back to us. But you're right. If we don't take action soon, they might accidentally stumble onto something."

"We gotta get rid of those two. And the sooner the better. So what about the tea— pretty fucking good, huh?"

~~

"Yeoman Gates said you wanted to see me, sir." Dave had just walked into the admiral's office.

Carson stood near the tall window with his hand on a waist-high, round wooden stand. "Come see."

Dave examined the old mahogany and brass navigation instrument. "Binnacle, gimbal ring, and compass! The whole works. Beautiful!"

"Came off a 1920s British frigate. Top condition."

"Great addition. Goes with your model ship collection and the picture wall of classic cutters. Nice feeling."

"Frankly, I can't stand being in a dull office all day without some connection to the sea." He sat down at his desk and motioned Dave to a chair. "Is it true they put Lani Sanches on administrative leave?"

"She got a call from Sylvester Purvis yesterday. He's bringing her up before an academic committee for unprofessional conduct.

Until then, she's persona non grata."

"I used to have some respect for Sylvester," said Carson. "I knew he was there mainly to raise money and get support for the school, but I thought he had a modicum of guts and brains. Now it appears I was wrong. He has neither."

"Lani called me from La Jolla," Dave said. "When Richard Costello at Ocean Research heard what'd happened, he asked her to come down and work with him on the Seamount Gilman project. Costello also thinks this could be a lull and the worst is yet to come."

"That puts us in a bind." Carson stretched, as if to break the shackles. "The scientists still think the tsunami could happen, which makes evacuation planning a top priority. But Purvis is making it impossible to get the coastal cities or disaster agencies to cooperate."

"It won't be easy, working with zero help, but I'm trying to draft a plan that's simple enough to be carried out by local agencies on a moment's notice. There'll be multiple escape corridors, and procedures for notifying residents, controlling panic, and moving them along the escape corridors by foot."

"On foot, positively," said Carson. "If people try to drive out, it'll be nothing but gridlock. Millions would die stuck in their cars."

Dave's face was earnest. "The average person can walk three miles in an hour, so two hours should be enough time to get everybody out of harm's way before the wave hits, assuming we get a full two-hour warning and assuming the local authorities act immediately."

"Better start with our own people," said the admiral. "We need to be in a safe place with all communications functioning. Our air operation at LAX may get washed out, so let's move the heelos and fixed-wing units further inland now. Set up a temporary headquarters operation where we can stay dry. Once you get the phones and radio gear working, we'll move most of the staff. Just keep a skeleton crew here. Also, I want all boats and cutters ready to put to sea within thirty minutes."

"I'll get that started, then I want to take a heelo ride along the coast to locate the best escape corridors in each community."

The admiral nodded his approval. "Tell the air station to get one ready."

~ ~

The helicopter rose into a clear and breezy spring sky on a westerly heading. The midmorning sun slanted in through the plexiglass bubble, warming Dave's back and filling the cabin with light.

He seated his helmet and checked the intercom level. "Swing south to Del Mar, Baldy. Fly as fast as you want getting there."

The pilot set the turbojet power on full and steered the helicopter seaward while climbing to cruising altitude, then banked southeast and adjusted his rotor pitch for top speed in level flight. He turned up the intercom volume against the scream of the engine and *pop-pop* of the rotors. "We have a ten-knot tailwind, so won't take long."

"At Del Mar, do a 180 and fly north low and slow about fifty meters off the beach. Maintain about a hundred meters altitude."

"How come we're going so far south?" At age twenty-five, Baldy Spangler had only a little reddish-blond fuzz left on top, and a thick fringe that he liked to grow long, pushing Coast Guard limits. He'd come by the nickname "Baldy" honestly.

"The scientists tell us the area of maximum impact will be from Oceanside to Santa Barbara. If the tsunami happens, the whole coast'll be affected, but the part we're flying today will be in the greatest danger."

They flew at a thousand feet just off the breaker line, Dave dictating his preliminary observations about each beachside community into a handheld recorder.

Baldy said, "There's the Del Mar Race Track. Starting my descent and 180." He guided the main control stick down left, banked onto a reverse course, and steadied the craft at three hundred feet, just off the beach. "Will a hundred knots air speed be okay?"

"Give me the equivalent of seventy to eighty knots ground speed. I'll need time to dictate my notes. And be ready to go in for a closer look when I say so."

They worked their way up the coast, Dave dictating into his recorder about escape routes and assembly areas such as parks and stadiums where people could wait until given permission to return to whatever might be left. His notes would form the basis for the evacuation plan.

They'd covered Oceanside, the new city of Serenidad, San Clemente, Dana Point, Newport Beach, Huntington Beach, and the smaller towns in between. Now they approached Long Beach and Los Angeles harbors.

"Reduce ground speed to about thirty knots till we get past San Pedro," said Dave. "I want to give special attention to clearing the port area and getting as many ships out to sea as possible."

Baldy throttled back and changed the rotor pitch. "Adjusting for the headwind, this oughta give us about thirty knots ground speed."

As Dave talked into his recorder, he noticed a Blue Star on the funnel of a container ship anchored in the outer harbor. He wondered if Jiro was making any progress on the Marine Providers investigation. He dictated as his gaze swept the area below him. "I count twenty-one ships anchored in the outer harbor waiting for pier space. If given a two-hour warning, all ships in the outer harbor should be able to get to sea before the wave hits. They'd have to be on a common radio frequency and ready to comply instantly with orders. Coast Guard cutters might be needed as escort vessels. There are nine tankers pumping crude to the tank farms, and forty-three cargo ships tied up at piers in the two harbors loading or offloading. I don't think two hours is enough time to get any of those ready for sea and out of the harbor. To save lives, it would be better to leave them in place and evacuate the people."

They hovered over the harbor for another ten minutes while Dave scanned the ships once again with his binoculars. He finally nodded and pointed up the coast, indicating to Baldy to continue on to Santa Barbara.

~ ~

At first glance, Dr. Richard Costello's lab at Ocean Research Laboratories looked like a jumbled mess. Computer printouts, marking pens, and coffee mugs fought for bench space. Faded horror-movie posters lined the walls, Post-its clung to sides of computers, and *New Yorker* cartoons and a snapshot of a St. Bernard decorated a bulletin board.

In truth, the lab was fairly well organized. Four computer stations lined one wall. A workbench ran along the wall opposite, with two state-of-the-art electronic microscopes, Bunsen burners, racks of test tubes, petri dishes, glass slides, and other assorted equipment. Above the bench, shelves of glass jars held samples of ocean water, ocean creatures, bottom corings, and vegetation. Wet suits hung on coat racks at either end of the room.

At 3:00 in the afternoon, the lab was empty except for Leilani Sanches, who sat at one of the computers.

"They said I'd find you here." Dave walked toward her from the doorway, dodging around a bicycle parked inside the door. He wore jeans, tennis shoes, a white La Coste knit shirt, and a well-worn camel hair blazer.

She blinked in surprise. "What are you doing here? Where's your uniform?"

"It seemed like a nice day for a drive down to La Jolla. So I put on civvies, took the top off the Corvette, and here I am."

"Then who's running the Coast Guard?"

"I left Admiral Carson in charge. Told him to call me if he had any problems." He surveyed the cluttered room. "I thought scientists had neat and orderly minds."

"Orderly minds, but not always orderly habits." Lani smiled. "It's nice to see you."

Dave reached out and took her hand. "I was hoping you'd relent and let a friend take you out to an early dinner. I have to get back before midnight."

"I'm sorry, Dave. We better not. Besides, I promised Richard I'd meet with him at six to go over the latest volcano numbers."

So she was calling him Richard now. On the *Carlsbad*, it was Dr. Costello. But they'd been working together, so no big deal. "I understand," he said. "You have to earn your keep down here. What about the latest volcano numbers? Is Gilman starting to heat up again?"

Lani rechecked a block of numbers on her screen, and pushed aside the computer mouse. "I keep expecting it to, but this is day four and absolutely nothing is happening."

"That's hard to believe, after seeing it on the verge..."

"I know. I thought it would start a comeback by now. But the numbers say just the opposite—activity still receding. Despite that, I still believe my computer model will eventually prove to be right."

"What's happened with other volcanoes? If the activity subsides, does that usually mean the whole thing's over?"

"Not always." Lani capped a yellow highlighter. "There can be a hiatus of a few days or a few weeks before it comes back and builds up to a blowout."

"Any way to tell?"

"Usually, the longer the delay, the less likely it is the activity will come back. Every day that goes by without seeing these numbers spike normally means the chances of a comeback are vanishing. If it dies altogether, that's good news for the people along the coast, but it'll make me look pretty dumb."

"You have to have faith in your work. If you did everything right and your model tells you this will probably happen, then I would think the chances of its happening are fairly high."

"That's what I keep telling myself, but I can't help but worry that I missed something and I'll end up with egg on my face."

Dave frowned. "My worry is that this is lulling people into a false sense of security. They won't be prepared if the tsunami happens."

"All we can do is wait and see." She glanced at a framed photo beside her keyboard of a young couple and two small kids. She looked up and met Dave's eyes, felt her feelings rising, squashed them down.

Richard Costello came into the lab and smiled when he saw Dave. "How are you, Dave? Nice to see you again."

"Nice to see you too, Dick."

Costello slammed his briefcase down on the workbench and walked out.

Dave looked confused.

Lani said, "He hates to be called Dick."

"Yeah, I remember now. Damn, why did I go and forget that?"

"Only you and Dr. Freud can answer that one," said Lani, unable to conceal her smile.

Flushing, Dave said, "I better take off, but how about coming outside for a second. I'd like to take your picture before I head back."

They took the steep stairs to the top of the bluff above the lab. A cool, ten-knot sundowner breeze blew in off the Pacific. Lani removed the jeweled dolphin clip and started rearranging her hair.

Dave held up an open palm. "Wait. Let your hair blow. Now a big smile." He clicked and checked the shot in the view window.

She came over and looked. "Ugh."

Dave said, "No, perfect. Okay if I print it?"

"Only if you want to scare little children."

"C'mon—there's a free feeling about it."

They looked together at her picture in the camera window,

aware of the rumble of the surf and the salty tang in the wind off the sea.

Finally Lani smiled and said, "Okay."

At the bottom of the stairs, Dave took her hand. "I'll keep asking about dinner."

She squeezed and released his hand. "Thanks for coming down." She turned and walked back to the lab.

~ ~

At full tide, the container ship *Shanghai Star* rode high in the water, and the lines securing it to Pier 63 stretched tight. It had finished offloading its cargo of women's clothing, running shoes, snow blowers, power mowers, surfboards, and cellular telephones, all with American brand names stitched in or pasted on. The loading of the outbound cargo of navel oranges, computer chips, scientific instruments, and bales of Bakersfield cotton wouldn't start for another few hours.

The dock was empty in the fading light. A high bank of dark clouds had moved in, accompanied by a cold northwest breeze, the leading edge of an arctic storm on its way.

"Once again, what exactly are we doing here?" asked Dave.

Jiro's shoulder was heavily bandaged, his arm in a black sling. "We're going aboard with one of the crew. He's supposed to meet us here. He says he knows where the contraband is stowed."

"You mean this guy just calls and says he'll show you where the guns are?"

"We told the police to call us in if they picked up any Blue Star crew for drunk and disorderly. We grilled this guy for forty-eight hours straight before he finally broke. Admitted they're running guns and said he knows where they're hidden."

"What did you do—put him on the rack? He's taking an awful chance ratting on his bosses."

"He wants to immigrate. We told him he could stay and go into our witness protection program if he shows us where the stuff is."

"What happens if somebody spots us?"

"He says most of the crew's ashore and we can get in and out without being seen. Once we know exactly where the guns are, we'll get a search warrant and impound the vessel."

"If this guy's on the level, it could break the case open," Dave said. "We'd have cause for seizing and searching all Blue Star ships. If he doesn't show, is there another direction to go? Any other leads?"

Jiro nodded. "A tip just came in today. The informer's pretty reliable, so we think there might be something to it."

"How important?"

"He said a guy named Milo Wagstad is the main man here. We checked his rap sheet."

"Yard and a half long?"

Jiro spread his good arm. "Longer. Petty thief and pusher with two prior convictions, and a dozen arrests without being convicted. He's street-smart—might be hard to nail. But we've put a couple of our best people on him. If we can catch him in the act, it would be a big step forward."

Night had fallen. Dave pulled up the collar of his jacket as the wind picked up. "We'll need foul weather gear before too long. I can smell the rain."

"He should be here by now," said Jiro.

A tall, thin man appeared out of the darkness and spoke to Jiro in Chinese. Jiro answered, then said to Dave, "His name is Wu Lin. He says there's no one on deck now, so we can go up the gangway to the main deck, then he'll take us below to the guns."

"We have any backup?" asked Dave. "Just in case?"

"Four agents just out of sight. They'll come on the double if I give the signal." Jiro pointed to a radio in its small leather pouch on his belt. "I press the red button on top. They're here in two minutes."

They followed Wu Lin up the gangway. As he reached the

main deck, he motioned for Jiro and Dave to squat down, then held up his hand to wait. He took another two steps onto the deck, crouched, and looked fore and aft carefully. Finally he gave them another signal and they followed, creeping across the ship and aft to a companionway that led to the lower decks. He stopped at the companionway hatch and motioned them closer. When they approached, he bent and whispered something to Jiro.

As Jiro turned to translate for Dave, Wu Lin flicked out a knife, slit Jiro's belt, grabbed his radio and holstered pistol, and disappeared. Jiro barely had time to yell, "Hey!" before Wu Lin was gone.

A very large man appeared at the bottom of the stairs. He climbed toward them, a long, curved knife in his hand.

Jiro's eyes widened. "Jesus, it's him! Let's get out of here!"

They turned to go forward to the gangway, but three men stepped toward them. They looked aft, and that way was blocked by another three.

"We're in deep shit, man," said Dave.

"Jesus! No gun, no radio."

The crew closed in. Dave and Jiro heard the footsteps of the big man on the stairway, now only a few feet away.

Dave said, "Over the side!"

"Hope I can swim with one arm."

"That water's hard as concrete and ice cold," said Dave. "And it's a hundred feet down. Go in feet first with a hand on your balls, and pray like crazy."

The giant had reached the head of the companionway, long knife raised above his head. The crew rushed them.

Jiro put his good arm on the rail and vaulted over the side into the darkness. Dave followed, but not quite fast enough to avoid the first slash of the big guy's knife. He glimpsed the flash of the blade and felt a sharp pain on the bottom of his foot. The knife had cut through the shoe leather as if it were Cheddar cheese. But now it was free fall that seemed to never end, then the shock of slamming into cold ocean that numbed his senses and paralyzed his breathing, then down, down, down, deep into the black water.

At last he floated up until he broke the surface. He gulped for air, kicked off his shoes, slid out of his jacket, and wriggled out of his pants. Jiro thrashed in the water about twenty feet away. As Dave swam toward him, a light rain started to fall.

"I can't float," Jiro gasped, pedaling with his feet and splashing with his good arm.

"Arch your back. Belly up. Head back." Dave, treading water, put a hand in the small of Jiro's back and lifted him into a floating position.

Jiro gasped through chattering teeth, "C-c-cold, Dave."

"Keep floating till I get your shoes off. Then we're out of here."

Dave heard the *zing-snap* of a bullet. It missed his head by inches. Someone on the ship had a high-power rifle with a silencer. Probably a night scope, too, he realized. It would be only a matter of seconds before they zeroed in. The next two shots kicked up little geysers between Jiro's legs as he floated on his back.

"Take a deep breath," Dave said. "We're going down for a minute. Frog kick and paddle with your good arm." Dave grabbed Jiro by the collar and towed him under. He scissors kicked and sidestroked for nearly two minutes, then surfaced.

The rain washed over them in sheets, making it hard to get a breath, but helping screen them from the shooter on the *Shanghai Star*. With Jiro in tow, Dave had no choice… he had to swim with the outgoing tide. If they couldn't attract attention or grab onto a line someplace, they'd end up in the Catalina Channel on a dark, wet night with twenty-foot seas and absolutely no chance of being rescued.

"Keep frog kicking and paddling," said Dave. "We'll stay on the surface. Try to get in rhythm with my strokes."

He got a firmer grip on Jiro's collar and swam with the tide.

They came to the next ship tied up alongside the dock. There were lights on deck, but no one visible. His voice wouldn't carry far enough in the storm to attract attention, so he looked for a hanging line or a ladder. Anything to hold onto, but there was nothing but the massive dark hull of the ship.

Their swimming and the tide carried them past an unoccupied section of dock. Nothing but fifty feet of smooth, concrete wall. Then they drifted by another ship. No one on deck. Nothing dangling to get a grip on. Dave felt his arms tiring. The burst of energy expended during their escape, the cold water, and the effort of towing Jiro were taking their toll. He wasn't sure how much longer he could last.

Aboard the Greek freighter *Argolykos*, cook's helper Nick Pappas had been in the galley for six straight hours. Now he was on a well-earned break, leaning on the rail, looking at the lights of the other ships through the rain. He didn't mind the rain. It felt good after the long shift in the hot galley. He looked down at the dark water and could make out the moving rows of small, creamy wind waves. The light from a porthole illuminated a small patch up near the bow. He could see raindrops slanting down. And something was out there. Pappas leaned over as far as he could. He stared into the darkness and cupped his hand to his ear.

Dave stroked and drifted up to what might be his last ship. His strength was draining. He wouldn't last more than another few minutes. He studied the low-slung freighter with the deck closer to the water than the big container ships. Lights on deck, but not a sign of life. His spirits sank. Then a head appeared at the rail, aft of amidships, a white hat pounded by rain. The face peered out across the harbor. It was now or never. Dave yelled as loud as he could. "Help! Down here! Help!"

The man looked down. Dave yelled again. The face with the white hat disappeared. A spotlight went on, flooding Dave and Jiro with bright light, and a voice came through a bullhorn. "Keep swimming! We throw to you the line down. You hold on. We put ladder and come get you."

When Dave and Jiro finally struggled to the top of the ladder with the help of the four crew members who'd fished them out of the water, they were greeted by Captain Chris Karkalas. He was five foot six, carried a sturdy two hundred pounds, and had a large, round head with an oversized nose and days of black stubble on his face. His captain's cap was crusted with salt. The bullhorn still dangled from his hand. "Come. We got Greek coffee and ouzo. Best damn thing for crazy assholes swimming around L.A. Harbor in storm at night. Then we get for you dry clothes and feed to you fresh mousaka. Okay?"

With great effort, Dave lifted his hand and put it on the captain's shoulder. "You, sir, are beautiful. Just plain fucking beautiful."

~ ~

Dave and Jiro, blankets draped over their shoulders, wobbled down the gangway of the *Argolykos* to the waiting Coast Guard car. The driver, a young red-haired woman in Coast Guard uniform, held the rear door open. "I'm Seaman Hopkins, sir. My orders are to take you both to the emergency room, and then drive you to headquarters."

"Why headquarters?"

"Debriefing, sir. Captain Mazzini of Port Security and people from the police and FBI are waiting."

In the back seat, Jiro's voice sounded shaky. "Wasn't sure we'd make it. Jesus, what an ordeal!"

Dave said, "If the Greek ship hadn't seen us… God, I don't know."

"How's the foot?"

A quiet groan. "Hurts like hell. Knife went in deep."

"The docs will give you a shot and stitch it up." Jiro tugged the blanket tighter across his shoulders. "Maybe they'll give me something to stop my shakes."

Dave said, "I'm tired down to my toenails. Hope the damn debriefing is quick."

~~

A little after three in the morning, the Coast Guard car delivered Dave back to his apartment. All he wanted was to drop into bed and pull up a comforter. He opened the door, and there was Lani sitting in his big chair reading a book.

"I kept that key you gave me," she said. "I know it's late and I know it's crazy, but I needed to talk to someone… oh, you look awful!"

Dave limped across the room. The anesthetic they'd given him when they stitched up his foot had worn off. "I just damn near drowned in the middle of L.A. Harbor and I gotta get some sleep. Stay over. Talk in the morning."

She jumped from the chair. His gray-tinged features and obvious exhaustion scared her and sparked her own painful memories. "My God, Dave, I'm so sorry. What do you need?"

He shook his head. "Sleep, just sleep."

She put her hand on his arm and guided him into the bedroom. He sat on the edge of the bed while she tugged his shoes off, then got him to lift his hips so she could pull back the covers. She gently pushed on his shoulder and he tumbled into bed, still wearing the turtleneck and warmup pants he'd been given on the Greek freighter. She adjusted the pillow under his head, pulled up the covers, and turned out the light.

She rummaged around in the hallway linen closet and spotted a white thermal blanket. She spread it on the sofa, folded it back, and sat holding the blanket's fleecy corner. What pure hell Dave must have gone through to come out looking that bad. Her deep feelings for him stirred her own pain again. The shock, the betrayal she'd felt when her ex-husband had turned on her. She winced at the memory of his first vicious blow. Tears came now, and she hoped Dave would heal fast. She hoped she would someday too.

She kicked off her shoes and turned out the lamp. She stretched out under the thermal blanket and drifted off, thinking how close she felt to Dave.

She was awakened just before eight by a shaft of morning sun across the living room sofa. She showered, brushed her teeth, wrapped her long, black hair in a towel, and put on a blue terry robe she found hanging in the bathroom. She made instant coffee and toasted a slice of raisin bread.

About nine-thirty she opened the door to the bedroom and peered into the semidarkness. She crossed the room and sat on the edge of the bed, looking down at Dave's face on the pillow.

He opened his eyes and studied her for a long time.

She couldn't take her eyes from his.

He said, "Is it morning?"

"Nine-thirty, and you've only had six hours of sleep. I should leave and let you get some more."

He took her hand. "Please stay. Let's talk."

"Only for a minute—you need your rest. Shall I let some light in?"

"Not too much."

She went to the window and adjusted the Venetian blinds.

He said, "Looks foggy."

"It was sunny earlier. The fog rolled in a half hour ago."

She settled back on the edge of the bed and let him take her hand again. They were quiet, searching each other's eyes. The nasal hoot of the fog horn on the far jetty invaded the silence.

She said, "I worried about you last night. You looked so terrible." Her fingertip traced a line from his cheekbone to the corner of his mouth. "This was a deep crease and your skin was gray."

"It's nice to be worried about, but I'll be okay."

"Tell me what happened."

His eyes shifted away and the strain of the night showed on his face.

She said, "I know what physical assault feels like. Please tell me."

His eyes returned to hers. "I'd never doubted myself before. Never thought I'd be in a spot I couldn't handle. We were lucky."

She gripped his hand tightly while he told his story, beginning with the episode in the holding yard when the giant in black wounded Jiro, their walking into the trap on the *Shanghai Star*, the long knife slicing open his foot, the plunge into the harbor, the sniper shots that missed them by inches, the grueling ordeal of towing Jiro through bone-chilling water in a lashing rainstorm, and their rescue when his strength was fading and the ebbing tide was sweeping them toward open ocean. "The thing that scares me now…" His stare was somber, intense.

"That you almost died?"

"No, that I almost failed Jiro."

Tears welled in Lani's eyes. "So much pain. You went through so much pain."

Her heightened feelings wedged open his own sensory world. He was aware of her freshly-bathed, warm body scent, his own salty odor from a night in the ocean, her breathing and his breathing and the lingering hoot of the foghorn, and the faint cries of circling gulls, the diffused light of a foggy morning highlighting the soft look in her brown eyes, the shape of her nose and ears, her eyebrows and eyelashes.

She said, "Your eyes tell me you're feeling something deeply. Tell me."

He retreated from the moment. "You said you came over to talk about something."

"That can wait." His sudden change jarred her. She wanted the moment back. "You were feeling something."

"It all flooded in at once. I could smell, see, hear… everything."

"Like what?"

"Your smell— bath mixed with warm body. The foghorn and the gulls. Hear them?"

Lani's gaze shifted from his intense blue eyes to the blond stubble on his chin and the tousled sandy head on the pillow. The distant cries of the seabirds and the lonely sound of the horn seeped inside her and triggered a yearning she'd kept bottled up for ten years. She tried to hold it back, but it kept building. She whispered, "I better go," and moved to rise.

He gripped her hand. "Stay."

"You need your sleep."

"Not now."

"What then?"

"Tell me about growing up in Hawaii. The good things you remember."

Lani frowned in thought, then the frown turned to a smile. "Shave ice. There was a lady who had a little stand. She made the best."

"What was your favorite flavor?"

"The combo. She'd heap a big scoop of crushed ice into a paper cone and pour on mango, passion, papaya, and strawberry. On a sunny day with the trades blowing, walking barefoot, licking shave ice. Heaven."

Dave said, "We had a summer cottage on a lake in Wisconsin. That's where I learned how to sail and swim. Barefoot all the time, too."

Her laugh was easy, relaxed. "Going barefoot is such a free feeling."

Their eyes shared the pleasure of sensual memory.

He turned back the corner of the blanket.

She shook her head. "Better not."

He didn't release her hand.

"Oh, Dave, I'm deathly afraid of starting something that'll end with my heart in the trash can."

"I won't let it."

They held hands, looking into each other's eyes. He gently pulled the blue robe back to reveal a golden tan shoulder and the top of a breast that was a lighter, creamier tan. She didn't resist. He peeled the robe down to her waist. "Your body is beautiful."

Her eyes didn't leave his. "My breasts aren't too small?"

"No, they're perfect. And I like that dark patch around your nipples." He reached up and touched the towel she'd wrapped around her head. "Let your hair down."

She looked at him a long time before slowly unwrapping the towel turban and dropping it on the floor. She stood, letting the blue robe fall to the floor too, then fluffed out her cloud of black hair with both hands, pushed it behind her ears, and let it tumble down her back to the cleavage of her buttocks.

Amazed, Dave shook his head. "My God, Leilani, you are drop-dead gorgeous."

She bent and touched his lips with a fingertip, then slipped into bed beside him. He pulled her against his warm body and held her for a while. He could feel her shivering. "Don't be afraid. It's going to be okay." He sat up a moment to take off his pants and turtleneck, then stretched out beside her and put his arms around her.

She ran a hand over the stubble on his jaw.

"Shall I shave?"

She snugged closer. "No." She pressed her fingertips into his back. "You have a nice, strong body."

He kissed her eyes gently, then kissed her on the mouth and she responded. His kisses moved to her neck and down to her breast.

She cupped her breast and shifted his mouth to the taut nipple. He sucked gently and massaged her nipple with his tongue. When he drew away, her nipple was hard and bright pink and swollen.

"I'd better take care of the other one before it gets too jealous."

She propped herself up on the pillow, wrapped her hand around the back of his head, and pulled his mouth over to her other breast.

Smiling, she stroked his hair as he took her nipple in his mouth.

~ ~

It was past noon before they'd showered, dressed, and finished breakfast. Dave carried their cereal bowls to the sink, unplugged the coffeemaker, and poured the last splash. The smell of coffee lingered in the air. He parked his cup on the breakfast bar, where Lani sat perched on a high stool. He put a hand on hers. "Lani…"

"I was very impulsive this morning."

He tried to engage her eyes, but she looked away. He said, "I was going to say I've never experienced that kind of love before. But we both have to be sure."

She finally looked at him with worried eyes. "I forgot myself. But the red flag is back, bigger than ever—danger written all over it."

"You're afraid I'd mistreat you."

She nodded.

"And I'm afraid you'd dump me—I'd come home some night and you'd be gone."

"We're not ready, Dave."

"I don't know, I had the strong feeling that we belong together. I know I would never hurt you."

"Whatever our feelings in bed, this is the cold light of day."

"Maybe you're right. We need more time."

"Let's talk about the reason I came here in the first place. I need to talk something out."

Dave nodded.

"They won't let me stay at Ocean Research. The director had a phone call from Sylvester Purvis. SciPac doesn't want me involved in the Seamount Gilman project in any way. Since I'm still on Purvis's payroll, there was nothing ORL could do."

"That SOB really has it in for you. What are you going to

do?"

"That's what I came to talk to you about. They've set a tentative date for my academic hearing… late next week."

"Just as well they're not delaying. That way, you'll know one way or the other."

She frowned. "They're stacking the deck. Gus Belmondo wangled a list of the committee members. They're all cronies of Margaret and Purvis."

He wrapped a hand around his steaming cup, a leftover reaction to the cold of the harbor waters. "Will there be any scientists on the committee?"

Lani shrugged. "A couple, but not first-rank. I requested the best scientific minds on the faculty. Instead, I'm getting a hanging-tree posse."

Dave set his cup on the tile counter. "That's bad news. Chances of convincing them your work is scientifically sound suddenly go way down."

She rotated the stool seat away from Dave, disengaging his hand from her shoulder. "Somewhere between zilch and zero."

"What about the other charges?"

She spoke with growing heat. "I did *not* send that out to the *Times* and they know it. I admit I went over Margaret's head to go to Dr. Cohen, and if they want to gig me for that, so be it. But no way will I let them get away with saying I took shortcuts on my science. I'll fight them to the death on that one."

The blare of a boat's horn from the nearby marina channel floated into the apartment. Dave said, "Have you figured out how?"

"I'll sue them cross-eyed."

He picked up the storm warnings. "Lani, can't you talk about this stuff without blowing your stack?"

She looked at him for a moment, her color rising. "What, this isn't important?"

"Of course it's important. But the more upset you get, the harder it is to reason things out."

"What's to reason?" Her anger was suddenly in full sway. "They're dumping all over me. I'm hitting back. Hard! End of story!"

"Have you thought about all the ramifications of taking this to court?"

"I don't care about that. I just want to burn and bury those slimy creeps!"

"You'll need a high-powered lawyer to go against SciPac. They have the money to hire the best legal brains in the country."

Lani dumped her coffee down the drain, went to the window, and stood looking out with her arms folded. "I'll find one."

She was still upset, but quieter now. Dave said, "Hope you have a rich uncle. Finding someone to take your case on contingency won't be easy."

She walked back and stood looking up at him. "Sorry I overreacted."

"It's okay."

Her concerned eyes scanned his face. "Oh, Dave, I've been so wrapped up in my problems I forgot your foot and everything you and Jiro went through. You still look exhausted."

The note in her voice surprised him. He held her eyes. "You're worried about me—you care then."

"Of course I care. I care how you feel. That's all that means."

A puff of wind rattled a shutter in the quiet room. Dave hid the letdown feeling. "I'll be okay in a couple of days. Now, about a lawyer."

"There's a good law firm out there someplace that'll take me on. I'll keep digging till I find one. I've got to force SciPac to admit my science is right, and issue a statement clearing me."

Dave put both cups in the dishwasher. "A law firm on contingency won't settle for that. The only way they make money is getting a cut of a big damages award. SciPac will drag the thing out for months, maybe years."

"Then what should I do?"

Dave took his turn looking out the window for a few moments.

"How about going one-on-one with key people on the faculty? Persuade them. Get them on your side. Maybe they can pressure Purvis to appoint a legitimate committee."

"Won't work. I'm taboo. The word is out. No one on campus will talk to me. I have to do this my way. No other choice, despite all the obstacles."

"I just want to make sure you explore all your options."

"Believe me, nothing to explore."

He shook his head, grinning. "Once you get your mind set…"

Lani said, "I've been called stubborn and mule-headed. Are those the words you're looking for?"

"Plus relentless. I don't know what it would take to budge you. How about an 8.5 earthqua—"

Her words flew out before he could finish. "How about a hundred-foot tsunami?"

They stood searching each other's eyes.

Finally Dave said, "All I can say is, what can I do to help?"

"You can help me find a lawyer."

"I'll talk to Admiral Carson. He may have contacts. What happens if things don't work out? Do you have a plan B?"

"I can't even think about failure."

"But worst case scenario… you lose. What then? It must have crossed your mind."

She turned away from Dave and stepped to the door. "Can we take a walk? I feel cooped up."

They left the apartment and strolled along the promenade bordering the boat basin, Dave limping on his sore foot. The day was clear, the sun warmer than usual. High pressure had moved in and temporarily blocked off the usually dependable sea breeze. He waited for an answer to his question.

They stopped to watch seagulls swarming around a school of fish. "Hawaii State University has been after me for a long time," she said. "They e-mailed yesterday, and they still want me, regardless of the outcome here."

"Then you do have a fallback."

"I prefer to have it as an option after I win. I don't want to be forced into anything."

"What kind of position would it be? As good as SciPac?"

They resumed their stroll, looking down on an endless variety of small boats bobbing in their slips. "Much better. They're talking about a full research fellowship."

Dave's feelings jumbled. He was relieved when she said, "But I have to fight this fight first, so I'm here for a while."

"I'm glad. I hate to see you pass up an opportunity, but staying here means we'll have a chance to see each other."

Lani watched a small power boat chug up to a slip, cut its engine, and glide in. She looked at Dave and waited till their eyes met. "The only reason I'm tempted to take the Hawaii job right now is it would put us an ocean apart."

He took in a sharp breath. "I thought we clicked this morning. It wasn't that way for you?"

She rested her hand on his arm. "Everything was wonderful. That's the problem."

"Why is that a problem?"

"It was better when we were just friends."

"Why can't we be both? Friends *and* lovers."

She shook her head. "I can't manage it… trusting a man, loving a man, after the hell I went through. I will never let myself be that vulnerable again."

A mix of sadness and anger welled up in him, but he walled it off. "I couldn't go back to being just friends. It'd be too hard to be around you and not…"

"So I guess we'll have to call it a day." She gazed at the far breakwater, where the main harbor channel met the sea.

He had never known anyone like her. Bright. Impulsive. Passionate about everything. Roller coaster highs and lows. And obstinate as a mule. "I said it before and I mean it. I could never do anything to hurt you."

She turned and looked into his eyes, almost accusingly. "That's what Frank said."

Dave's voice sounded harsh in his own ears. "I'm not Frank." He watched her eyes cloud. His irritation slowly cooled. "We've both been wounded. Your abuse was a lot worse, but my ex-wife's desertion still hurts, too. Maybe if we take it slow… date for a while and gradually try to work things through…"

"Can't you see, Dave? I'm not ready. I don't know if I'll ever be."

He saw tears in her eyes, and some of his own sadness forced its way in. "Can we stay in touch?"

She didn't answer, and they walked back to the apartment in silence. Dave twisted the knob and nudged the door open with his shoe. Lani stood outside. She said, "I came over last night on a wild impulse. Stuck my toe in the water, but it's still too scary. Sorry. My sweater and overnight case are inside the door."

He retrieved her things and handed them to her.

She stood with the sweater draped over one arm, overnight case dangling from the other. The marina suddenly seemed empty. No boats coming in or going out. The birds had vanished. The surface of the water lay oily flat. The silent air smelled faintly of kelp and anchovy.

She said, "About staying in touch… my answer has to be… goodbye, Dave."

His eyes followed her until she disappeared around the corner of the building.

~ ~

"Mr. Hacker wants to see you," said Dixon Mallory's secretary when he returned from lunch at the Hong Kong Racquet Club. He walked down the hall to Hacker's office and found his boss once again brewing tea.

"Russian style, this time," said Hacker. "Mixed up some Keemum, Assam, and China Green." He turned the samovar spigot and watched the hot amber liquid stream out until the glass with the silver wire handle was half full. He handed it to Dixon on a silver tray. "Put in a spoon of that strawberry jam. It'll knock your socks off."

Mallory took the tray and set it down. "You wanted to see me, George?"

"What's the latest on *Shanghai Star*?"

"The ship was completely sanitized before she was boarded by the police. Ho Kai Fat and his men were gone and the ship was clean."

"Anybody say anything?"

"The captain and most of the crew had spent the night ashore. They took statements from the skeleton crew still on board."

"And?"

"Everyone stuck to the story—the Coast Guard officer and the FBI man did a quick inspection and left. Port security will hold the ship for seventy-two hours. Since there's no physical evidence of a crime, I think our Washington contact can be persuaded to override the local authorities and get her released."

"Yeah, we pay the sonofabitch enough. But what about Mr. Fat? He missed again. Didn't take care of those two assholes like we told him."

Mallory said, "I wouldn't replace the big fellow. He did everything right. It was a miracle those two survived. They should have been what the police call a couple of floaters."

"Shoulda been, but they weren't." Hacker spooned jam into his tea. "I'll give the big guy one more shot at it, but this time I want to talk to him personally to make sure it comes out right. I'm taking a trip to L.A."

"Why L.A.? Money's rolling in. All we have to do is stay with the plan."

Hacker watched his glass turning strawberry red. "Yeah, fucking jackpot if we stick with the plan. Just wanna make damn sure the plan doesn't get screwed up."

"You worried about the distributor?"

"Wanna make fucking sure nobody gets too bigheaded. Might have to get rid of some people."

"Your seat-of-the-pants feelings are usually spot on, George."

"And I wanna make sure our other investments there keep producing. I noticed a slowdown in one particular area, and I'm gonna give that associate a little surprise party. Walk in unexpected. He won't have time to think up excuses. I usually get to the bottom of things pretty fast that way."

"Do you want a car?"

Hacker stirred his tea and slurped loudly. "Yeah. Call the limo service and tell them to have a car at the airport. We don't need a driver. Ho Kai Fat can do that."

"Reserve it under your name?"

"No. Make it for Mr. Hotchkiss. And tell Ho Kai Fat to dress up and make sure he keeps his trap shut. Okay?"

Mallory nodded. "I have the latest Ripper report from the distributor. He called this morning and said he's opened up Denver. Chicago's next, as soon as he has the inventory."

"We never offered him Denver or Chicago. Any other problems?"

"The *L.A. Times* is on a crusade. They publish a Ripper scorecard every day. You know, eleven cops killed. Fourteen kids killed."

"Fuck the *Times*."

"They claim the Ripper's replacing the old-fashioned fistfight when kids have a score to settle."

"I could care less."

"But it's good publicity. And no one's been able to trace anything back to the source. This product will be one of our biggest producers when it's a hundred percent rolled out."

Hacker slurped more tea. "Maybe it's time to think about Midwest and East Coast distributors. More production's coming online, and we don't want the L.A. guy to get too greedy. Sometimes it goes to their head and they try to fuck you over."

"I see what you mean," said Mallory. "Are you sure you don't want to postpone your L.A. trip until after this tsunami thing passes?"

"Shit. Fucking tsunami. That's over. The volcano's gone back to sleep. Our guy on the scene says the whole tsunami thing was just a pile of crap in the first place."

"Oh, really?" Mallory's split-second eyebrow arch vanished before Hacker picked it up. "I hope he's right. Have a good trip, George."

SIX

At a little past noon, all the tables were taken in the oak-paneled dining room of the Merchants Club in downtown Los Angeles. The pace seemed unhurried, and men and a sprinkling of women in business attire talked in subdued tones.

Wamp's dry Manhattan sat in front of him as he checked off whitefish and house salad on the little menu card. "Made up your mind?" he asked Sylvester Purvis.

"Soup and a club sandwich will do just fine."

Wamp finished checking the cards and handed them to the waiter. "What's happening with little Miss Leilani? When does she get the ax?"

"That's all in the hands of the academic council. They set their own time for the hearing, and they have certain procedures to follow. I can't intervene."

"Don't play games with me, Sylvester. I know you can get her ass fired any time you want."

Purvis leaned earnestly toward him. "Harley, I know you're an important benefactor to the school and…"

Wamp snorted. "You don't have to kiss my ass and you don't have to use big words like benefactor. Let's just get it all out on the table."

Purvis studied Wamp. "Okay, Harley, here's the thing… we have the right people on the committee, and they're ready to get this thing done next week sometime."

"Then how come you're stalling me?"

"She has an employment contract. She can sue our ass off if we try to fire her without cause."

"You have cause, big-time. She made up this whole tsunami mess and gave it to the media without your permission."

"She claims she didn't send it out. She says somebody took an internal memo she'd written to me about the volcano and sent it out without her knowledge."

"Well, however it happened, it got smeared all over the front page of the *Times*, and the TV people got ahold of it and had a field day. The damn thing won't settle down till you get rid of her."

"I will, but I can't do it right now. I have to let the lawyers clear it before the committee can do its thing."

The color began rising in Wamp's face. He spoke in a quiet growl. "You're not listening, Sylvester. I'll lay it on the line. Southern Coast Land is one of your biggest backers…"

"I appreciate that, but…"

"But bullshit! I can fix it so you don't get another dime from us, and we have clout with a lot of your other backers. If you don't get off your ass and take care of this, I'll damn well see that your funding goes right down the tube. You'll have to close classrooms and fire half your goddamn professors."

"Come on, Harley. Back off. You want her ass canned and so do I. Give me a little time."

"Goddamnit, Sylvester, there's no time left. Even with all the spin we been putting out, like experts saying her predictions are based on unproven theory blah blah blah, and she doesn't know what she's talking about blah blah blah, the tidal wave scare won't go away. It's hurting business all along the coast."

"Yours in particular?"

Wamp gulped half his Manhattan. "Deposits out at Serenidad are going down the toilet. Our cash flow is hurting. Banks want their interest payments on time. Suppliers need to get paid. And we have investors who get very mean if we don't produce."

"I think I see the picture."

Wamp put a heavy finger on Purvis's wrist. "Here's a carrot-and-stick deal."

"I already know the stick," Purvis said.

Wamp took a set of house keys out of his pocket and put them in front of Purvis. "Here's the carrot. My beach house in Ensenada and all the high-class pussy you can fuck and all the booze you can drink."

Purvis's eyes brightened. "For how long?"

"As long as your pecker and liver hold out."

"Let me work on it. I'll have the lawyers speed it up, and I'll tell the head of the academic council we want Lani gone by next week. She'll cooperate. There are things she wants that I can make possible."

~~

The doorbell chimed in Lani's small ground-floor apartment in Altadena. It was midafternoon, and she had returned from Dave's only a few minutes before. Most of her neighbors were still at work. She opened the small peephole. A man's face came into focus. She gasped.

"Guess who got paroled," growled Frank Fortney, her ex-husband.

After a timeless moment of paralyzed fear, Lani turned and fled to her bedroom. No way out except the window. She heard splintering sounds of her door being smashed, and she yanked off the bedroom screen, cranked open the window, and had one leg outside when Fortney's big ham hands clamped around her arms, pulled her back inside, and threw her to the floor.

He stood over her. "You're not going anyplace. You're coming with me and you're going to pay for what you did." He reached down to grab her by the hair, but she jerked her head away, grabbed his wrist, and sunk her teeth into his forearm. He swatted her on the side of the head and staggered back, looking at the wound.

Lani sprang to her feet and snatched the phone off her nightstand. She punched in 9, but his heavy fist caught her flush on the temple. The blow launched starbursts in her head and sent her staggering into the wall. Her vision cleared enough for her to see the rage in the eyes of the charging Fortney. She threw the phone at him. It bounced off his forehead.

He roared, "That's enough out of you, you little slut!" He pinned her against the wall with one hand on her chest. He balled the other hand into a big-knuckled fist, drew it back, and delivered a vicious blow to her right eye.

For Lani, the whole world went black.

~ ~

Dave, Jiro, and FBI Assistant Director Lewis seated themselves around Admiral Carson's desk. The admiral said, "I ordered Port Security to hold *Shanghai Star* for further investigation, but Blue Star must have political connections. The word came down from somewhere on high to let her sail."

Dave said, "Damn! The bastards got away with it!"

Carson's mouth twisted in disapproval. "It stinks! The commandant is trying to run down the source, but it's too late to change anything. How are you two feeling?"

Jiro gripped the arm of his chair with his good hand and pushed himself slowly to his feet. "Must have sprained something when I hit the water. Hurts when I sit."

Dave looked down at the moon boot on his foot. "Sore foot, but otherwise okay."

Carson said, "Good. Now let's update the gun smuggling problem."

Jiro propped a hand on the back of his chair. "It looks for sure like Blue Star is deeply involved in smuggling the Rippers."

Dave said, "The whole thing was a setup. They planted somebody who'd break down and confess and then lead us into the trap. We were getting too close." Dave shifted his foot to a new position. "And I don't think they'd set out to murder FBI and Coast Guard people without orders from above."

"How far above?" asked Carson.

Dave said, "The crew can only take orders from the captain, and the captain receives his instructions directly from the owner. That means the owners of Blue Star Lines in Hong Kong must be in this up to their eyeballs."

"Where do we go from here?" asked Director Lewis.

"Research," said Jiro. "I'd like to get your okay to ask Washington to do a thorough background investigation of Blue Star Lines. Turn them inside out. Backgrounds of the owners, financial records and dealings, relationships with customers and banks, information on their subsidiaries."

"Write up the request and I'll okay it. We'll fax it in today."

Jiro rubbed his back. "There's a company in San Pedro called Marine Providers. They provision all Blue Star ships. Full boxes of supplies go into the ships, and empties come out."

"Could be the way the guns come ashore," Lewis said.

"That's our suspicion. I'd like them checked out, and I want to check out Blue Star's connections with the city of Hong Kong and the government of China."

"Be careful on that one," Dave said. "They've probably paid off a lot of people in high places. We don't want Blue Star to know they're being investigated."

"I'll mention that in the request."

Admiral Carson asked about the status of the Ripper supply.

"Frightening," Lewis said. "The cities on the Coast are saturated with those lethal little killers, and they're starting to show up in the mountain states and Midwest. If we don't break this case pretty soon, the whole country'll be swimming in the damn things. The cost in human life will be appalling. Especially kids and cops."

"Until I get the report on Blue Star," said Jiro, "about all we can do is continue surveillance of Blue Star ships and hope to catch them in the act."

As the meeting broke up, Dave signaled Jiro to follow him to his office. "I need a favor."

"Sure," said Jiro. "Anything."

"Lani's missing. I'm worried."

"That's a local matter. Normally I'd tell you to call the police, but let me see what we can do at the bureau. How long has she been gone?"

"Only three days. But I have a bad feeling. She's not answering her home phone, and none of her friends from SciPac have heard from her. I even called her folks. There are a lot of Sancheses in the Oahu phone book, but I kept calling till I got the right one. They haven't heard from her either."

"What's her mental state?"

"Pissed off at SciPac for messing her around. Ready to find a lawyer and sue."

"Not depressed?"

Dave shook his head. "The last time I saw her she was mad as hell, and gung-ho about carrying the fight and winning. Full of life. Forging ahead. Planning for the future."

Jiro studied his friend for a moment. "Do those future plans include you?"

Dave's pained grin was accompanied by a half shrug. "Afraid not."

"You love her?"

Dave walked to the window with his hands in his pockets. "I don't know. I miss her when she's not around. But she's quite a handful. Not sure."

"Not sure? I'd say you're in pretty deep."

Dave sounded annoyed. "She told me to take a hike, so it

doesn't make any difference. Let's just say I'm worried. Okay?"

Jiro put his hand on Dave's shoulder. "I'll try to find her for you. The bureau will help out unofficially. We can work with the local police. You have a picture of her?"

"I took this in La Jolla." Dave opened a desk drawer and handed Jiro the photo of a smiling Lani, her cloud of black hair flowing free in a ten-knot sundowner breeze.

"She's a knockout. Do I see Asia in her face?"

"Chinese and Polynesian on her mother's side."

"Anything else you can tell me?"

Dave was lost in thought for a moment. "Check out a guy named Frank Fortney. Lani's ex. Doing time in Hawaii."

Jiro punched in the name on his Palm Pilot. "I'll have the FBI office in Honolulu contact the state corrections people. If she's alive, we'll find her for you. Afterwards, I hope things work out okay. For both of you."

"Just find her, Jiro. Please."

~ ~

Harley Wamp's colon was in full spasm. Gas pains shot through every part of his gut and chest. "These are the shittiest figures I've ever seen," he yelled at Brett Giardino, his sales manager.

Wamp had walked in unannounced at the Ocean Aire Estates sales office, which was set up in a mobile trailer at the entrance to Serenidad Phase One. Giardino shrugged. "It's the tidal wave. People are looking but they're not buying."

"How many times do I have to tell you, the tidal wave shit is over with. You have to let your prospects know."

"Yeah, you can lead a horse to water, but…"

"You have to put your sales force in the right frame of mind. Make sure they understand the whole tidal wave scare was phony to start with. Cooked up by some featherbrain trying to get publicity."

"I've told 'em…"

"And if there ever was anything to begin with, it's all over with now. The volcano's gone dead and it'll stay dead. A tidal wave never has hit this part of the coast and never will. This property is a hundred percent safe. Now, what's the problem?"

Giardino pointed at Wamp, then himself. "You believe what you're saying, and I believe what you're saying, but the public doesn't believe what you're saying. That's the problem."

"I hired you to sell houses, not sit around and give me excuses. I don't care what you have to do, but I want to see some goddamn sales. Change the advertising. Offer incentives. Throw in a refrigerator if they sign up by the end of the month. Get a sales contest going. Two weeks on the Riviera to the top producer."

"I hear you, Harley. I'll build a fire under the sales crew, put the screws to the ad agency, and do everything else I can to sell these houses, but you gotta realize there's still gonna be a lotta resistance out there. Something big's gotta happen to change their minds. Like an official pronouncement by some high muckymuck that everything is officially okay. Otherwise, the buyers are still gonna hang back."

"I'm taking care of that. The top guy at SciPac is set to make a big all-clear announcement. It'll be plastered all over the papers and the TV news. But it'll be a few days before that happens, and we can't wait. You gotta kick some ass and get me some sales. Right now. We need those fucking down payments."

It was midmorning before Wamp pulled into his parking space in the Southern Coast Land building near John Wayne Airport. On the drive back to his office he'd admitted to himself that Giardino was right. Nothing would really goose sales till Purvis made his announcement. Even then, it would take a few weeks for people to accept the idea that everything was okay and think it was safe enough to buy near the beach. But the ass-kicking he'd given Giardino had probably done some good. It'd get the sales force off their butts and sharpen up the advertising. Maybe they'd even get a few more down payments.

Wamp's secretary, Holly Wiggins, cupped her hand over the phone and signaled to him as he came through the door. "It's Dr. Purvis."

Wamp nodded and picked up the phone in his office. "Is today the day?"

"We've run into a snag," said Purvis. "Lani's hearing before the academic committee was scheduled for today. I was to get the committee's report tomorrow morning and then hold a press conference tomorrow afternoon."

"So?"

"Lani didn't show up for the meeting. We've been trying to contact her to make sure she had the date and time right. But she's disappeared. Not at home. Nobody's seen or heard from her for several days."

The gas pressure in Wamp's gut started building again. "Damn it, Sylvester, it's not your fault she didn't make the meeting. It just proves she's so far off base, she's afraid to show her face. So fire her ass anyway and go ahead with the press conference."

"That's what I'm going to do," said Purvis, "but everything has to be run through legal to make sure we're doing it right. She could be out there in the bushes getting ready to slap us with a lawsuit. It'll take a few extra days."

Wamp's face went sunburn red. "Every fucking day you put this off is costing me millions of dollars. Put the heat on the lawyers. Get this thing done."

"Believe me, Harley, I'm pushing it along as hard and fast as I can. I want her out of here as bad as you, but I have to give the lawyers a couple of days to make sure there aren't any land mines. Better safe than sorry."

Wamp's voice went quiet. "If you don't wrap this up in a goddamn hurry, you won't be very damn safe and you're sure as hell gonna be sorry." He clicked off, but the intercom buzzed before he had a chance to slam the phone down.

Holly blurted in a strained voice, "There are two gentlemen here to see you, Mr. Wamp."

"I don't see anything on my appointment book. Who are they?"

Wamp's door suddenly swung open. George Hacker stepped into the office, followed by the seven-foot hulk of Ho Kai Fat. An anxious Holly Wiggins trailed behind them.

The heightened color drained from Wamp's face. He waved Holly out the door. He'd only seen Hacker one other time, the day the papers were signed making the Blue Star owner the controlling partner in Southern Coast Land. Seeing him now was a nightmare come true.

"I didn't put a billion dollars into this deal just to own land in California," said Hacker. "What the fuck happened to sales?"

Wamp swallowed hard. "Tsunami scare's killed the market. But I'm getting it fixed."

"Shake hands with Ho Kai Fat." Hacker nodded toward his seven-foot companion. "Mr. Fat's job is to make sure things get done right."

Wamp reached out and took Fat's hand. At first, he responded to the giant's firm handclasp by tightening his own strong grip. But as Fat squeezed tighter and tighter, Wamp's grip weakened and finally gave way altogether. He felt intense pain, then almost unbearable pain, shooting from the hand up into his arm and neck.

"That's enough," said Hacker. "We don't want to break any bones. Not yet."

Ho Kai Fat released his grip. Wamp, sweating and breathing heavily, let his injured hand dangle.

Hacker said, "The problem with Mr. Fat is he doesn't know his own strength. If I'm not around to tell him when to stop, things get out of hand. I'll be back in three days. So will Mr. Fat. That's how long you have to get sales back up where they belong.

Next time, I might just go down the hall to take a leak and forget to come back."

The morning sun trying to burn through the overcast spread diffused light into Admiral Carson's office. He patted the stack of blue-bound folders on his desk. "Good piece of work, Dave. Separate plans for every beach community. Escape corridors, assembly points, how to notify people and get them moving, crowd control, coordination of public agencies."

"Yeah, but I don't know if anybody's interested now that the volcano's died down." Dave frowned.

"I've been wondering about the urgency myself. Moving our operations away from the coast will eat up a lot of my budget. The funds may be better used in other ways."

"You can call it off, but you'll have to decide now. The first units are scheduled to move inland tomorrow."

The admiral leaned back in his chair. "What do *you* think, Dave?"

"All the experts are saying the volcano's gone back to sleep and there's no chance of anything happening. But the last time I talked to Lani, she thought this might be the calm before the storm."

"How long ago was that?"

Dave's brow creased. "It's been four or five days. Right after she came back from La Jolla."

"You haven't talked to her?" Carson rose and Dave stood at the same time.

"No, but I still think she's right. I'd go ahead with key parts of the move. Get the inland headquarters set up with all communications operating, and man it with a skeleton crew. Then we can move the rest on short notice."

"Sorry, Dave, but I disagree. I've been checking with the people at SciPac every day. The volcano readings are still down, and I can't justify the expense of even a partial move. I'm inclined to cancel. It's okay to go ahead and distribute your evacuation plans to the coastal cities, but that'll have to be the end of it."

"I hope we're not giving up too soon. I'll never forget my sub ride. The power inside that mountain is beyond belief. If it ever heats up again and blows, we could be facing the major disaster Lani predicted."

"My decision's final," the admiral said.

"I understand, sir, but if we don't take the threat seriously, then no one else will either. For now, I'll get these plans out to the mayors and city managers and hope they're never needed."

When Dave got back to his office he found a message to call Jiro Yamaguchi. He punched in the number.

"We've located her," Jiro said. "And your hunch was right."

Dave's inner alarm streaked into the red zone. "Frank Fortney? Shit, he found her!"

"We tracked them to an old house in a bad part of El Monte."

"Are the police on it?"

"El Monte PD's investigating as a favor to the Bureau. But not very fast because no complaint's been filed. They think it might be a domestic dispute, and they hate to get caught in the middle."

Dave's voice rose. "Damnit, Jiro, this is no domestic dispute. Her life is in danger!"

"I know. I saw Fortney's rap sheet. Real bad ass. Spousal abuse on three different women. Assault with intent. Battery. Drug dealing. I'll drive over to El Monte and build a fire under the chief."

"What's the address?"

"Better wait for the cops."

"I don't have time to wait, Jiro."

"Okay. 4312 Edgar Drive in El Monte. He's a big guy with a bad temper. Be careful."

~ ~

Dave parked in front of 4312 Edgar Drive. The 1950s tract house looked run-down. Peeling paint. Holes in the screens. An old Chevy sat on blocks on the dried-up devil grass lawn of the front yard. A tanned, muscular man with a blond crew cut bent over a low-slung Harley-Davidson, polishing the machine with a chunk of terry towel. He wore black spandex shorts and a tight black T-shirt that emphasized his biceps.

Dave went up to him. "Frank Fortney?"

The man flicked a glance at Dave. He might have been handsome once, but now his face was seamed with heavy lines from years of ugly self-indulgence. He continued wiping down the motorcycle.

"I'm here to pick up Lani."

The man draped the polishing rag on the handlebars and straightened to face Dave. "Get the hell off my property."

"Mind if I go in and talk to her?"

Fortney picked up a crowbar. "If you don't get your ass out of here right now, I'll split your skull wide open."

"Look, Fortney, I'm taking Lani back with me. That's the way it is."

Fortney laughed. "If you want trouble, mister, you've come to the right place. That little girl belongs to me."

"Move!"

Fortney tapped the crowbar in his palm. "I'm teaching her nobody messes with Frank Fortney. And that applies to you too, motherfucker!"

He raised the crowbar, lunged forward, and came down with a vicious blow aimed at Dave's head. Dave did a smooth pivot and sidestep, like a toreador avoiding the horns of the bull. He grabbed Fortney's wrist as the steel bar went by, jerked him forward with his own momentum, and slammed him to the ground. Fortney lay on his back, partially stunned. Dave picked up the crowbar and smashed the biker's right kneecap. Fortney let out a bellow of pain, tried to sit up, and fell back to the ground, moaning and holding his knee.

"Move an inch, I'll smash the other one."

The house was dark and smelled of beer and bacon grease. Lani was not in the living room, kitchen, or bathroom. He tried pushing open the bedroom door, but it was locked. He pounded on it with his fist. "Lani! It's Dave."

He put his ear to the door, straining to hear. He studied the old, warped door, wedged the crowbar into a gap near the lock, and popped it open.

Plywood covered the window, blocking out most of the light. Lani lay on her stomach in the darkness, arms outstretched toward the door, fingernails digging into the bare wood floor. He knelt and rolled her onto her back as gently as he could. She whimpered in pain. He slipped the crowbar under his belt, scooped his arms under Lani's small frame, and carried her out of the room.

Seeing her in the light, he groaned, "Oh, dear God." Beneath a ragged white T-shirt, she was naked from the waist down. She'd been brutally beaten. Her legs and arms were swollen, with welts and bruises in shades of purple, black, and yellow. "It's Dave, Lani. I'm taking you home."

Lani's eyes were blackened, one swollen shut and the other a mere slit. She tried to open the slit and reach a hand toward Dave's face. The effort was too much and the hand dropped back. The voice was faint, but it was clear to Dave the fire still burned. "I fought the bastard every inch." Tears began streaming down her tattered face.

She'd been beaten with fists and something that could break bones. A club or piece of pipe. From the angle of the foot, it appeared as though her ankle had been fractured. He lifted the T-shirt and saw cigarette burns on her breasts. The need to hold her and heal her flooded through him. Then he felt his anger rising almost beyond control. "I'm going out and finish that miserable bastard!"

He started to lower her to a sagging couch, but the motion shot more pain through her body. "No. Don't put me down. Don't leave me."

He lifted her back into his arms, dragging in a calming breath, then another. "Gotta get you out of here."

When he reached the open front door, he saw that Fortney had somehow pulled himself over to the motorcycle and was reaching inside a saddlebag. Dave settled Lani on the sagging sofa, bolted through the door, and dashed straight for him. Fortney jerked a pistol out of the saddlebag, aimed, and fired. Something hot tore at Dave's trousers, just as he swiveled and kicked sidewinder style as hard as he could. His foot drove into Fortney's hand, slingshotting the pistol across the yard. It bounced off the garage door and landed in the dirt.

Someone yelled. Jiro Yamaguchi and two police officers scrambled out of a black-and-white and ran toward him. He stood breathing raggedly, then carried Lani out of the house while the officers handcuffed Fortney.

Jiro said, "Thought you'd need help, so I convinced El Monte PD we had an emergency." He grimaced when he saw Lani. "Oh Jesus, Dave. Get her to a hospital!"

One officer said to his partner, "Read the suspect his rights, and call for backup and an ambulance." He slid behind the patrol car wheel.

Lani tucked her head against Dave's chest and clutched his sleeve. He looked at Jiro. "Use your FBI clout to get her a private room in a good hospital without going through a lot of red tape."

Jiro held out his hand for Dave's keys. "I'll follow in your car." He opened a rear door of the black-and-white and helped Dave get settled in the back seat with Lani. He said to the officer, "Huntington Memorial ER. Code three."

Dave limped though the swinging doors into the pandemonium of the ER lobby. He dodged a woman in green scrubs trot-pushing a gurney, the man strapped down and groaning with pain. Chairs lining the walls were full, people waited three deep at the check-in desk, and the amplified babble bouncing off the hard walls produced a chaotic din.

Dave's right pant leg had been cut away, and a thick bandage covered his outer thigh. After Lani had been admitted, he'd checked himself in for treatment of his gunshot wound.

Jiro rose from his waiting room chair. "How is she? And besides needing a new pair of pants, how are you?"

Dave glanced down at his bare leg. "Just a graze. It'll heal in a few days. Lani's still in there. Last I saw, the ER people had her rigged up with an IV in each arm."

They headed for the exit, Dave resting a hand on Jiro's supporting shoulder.

Outside the door, Jiro said, "I had to pull a few strings to get her a private room."

Dave shifted his weight to his good leg. "Thanks. They said she'd be in ER for a while. A trauma specialist and orthopedic surgeon are on their way. ER says she'll go to intensive care later. Eventually to her room."

"Who's picking up the tab for all this?"

"I called SciPac. Luckily, she's still on their medical plan. They located her primary care doctor. He'll be overseeing her case."

"What's her condition?"

"You know medical people. I'm not a relative, so they hardly give you the time of day. It looked to me like she was still in shock. Don't know when I'll see her again. They told me to wait till I hear from her primary care guy, a Dr. Rosen."

"Did they say when?"

"After he examines her. If I don't hear, I'll keep checking with the hospital."

Dave waited outside the door while Jiro brought the car around. As he was getting in, Jiro said, "Can you concentrate on other business?"

Dave clicked his seat belt home. "What's happened?"

Jiro steered through the parking lot toward the street. "We just got the research report on Blue Star. I haven't had a chance to read it carefully, but it looks like Washington came through for us in a big way."

The trip to FBI headquarters in the Federal Building at Wilshire and Sepulveda included a stop at a shopping center, where Dave picked up a pair of jeans. In Jiro's office, Jiro handed Dave a copy of a thirty-four-page research document. They read in silence for more than a half hour. Dave scratched an occasional note on a pad.

Finally, Jiro said, "Pretty mind-boggling. Blue Star owns half the world. Including Marine Providers."

"Yeah. But the one that blows me away is their controlling interest in Southern Coast Land. That's run by Harley Wamp, the guy who's been gunning for Lani."

"Connection or coincidence?"

"That's what we'll have to find out." Dave sighed. Pain from the bullet wound made his whole leg throb.

Jiro said, "The fact that they own Marine Providers makes our theory a little more solid. If they're getting the guns off the ships into their trucks, the rest is easy to figure out."

Dave tapped the report. "Sure. The Rippers probably disappear among thousands of other boxes in the Marine Providers warehouse."

"We don't have enough evidence for a search warrant. I'll set up a surveillance detail. We'll find out how they're getting the guns out of the warehouse to the distributor."

Dave stared out the window. "Do you know how that crud got his hands on Lani?"

"I'll call El Monte and see if they've interrogated the guy yet."

Jiro spent a long time on the phone, mainly listening. He hung up and swiveled back to Dave. "They interviewed Fortney in the hospital prison ward at County General. Got him to talk before the public defender showed up."

"What'd he...?"

"Apparently kicked in her door, coldcocked her, and tossed her in his pickup. Altadena Sheriff's office joined El Monte PD in the investigation. One neighbor had reported hearing a fight, and seeing a man carry an unconscious woman out of Lani's apartment."

Dave's hands bunched into fists. "I should've worked him over with that crowbar. Hope to God they're throwing the book at him."

Jiro nodded. "Kidnapping, aggravated assault, battery, torture, rape, and attempted murder for trying to put a bullet in you. They'll need statements, and you and Lani will both have to testify at some point."

"I'll cooperate now. Lani will testify when she can."

"The DA wants to put that shithead away for good. He'll need your statements soon as possible."

Worry lines rippled Dave's forehead. "He can have mine tomorrow. That miserable bastard has got to do major time. Let's make sure some lawyer doesn't find a loophole and get him out on a technicality."

~ ~

Sylvester Purvis listened to the background hum of the conference line as he waited for an answer from SciPac's lawyers. Finally, Martin Snyder, the head of the firm, said, "With respect to sufficient grounds…"

"Right."

"Was Dr. Sanches's failure to appear before the committee voluntary, or for reasons beyond her control?"

"The notice of the meeting went by registered mail. The receipt with her signature is sitting on my desk."

"You didn't answer my question. Do you know if a valid

reason for not attending occurred after she signed the receipt?"

Purvis paused before answering. "Possibly."

"I don't understand."

"She may have been kidnapped."

"Either she was or she wasn't. Where is she now?"

"Her lab assistant called a few minutes ago and said she was taken to Huntington Memorial Hospital. After a police rescue."

"If the police report corroborates her story, you have no choice but to reschedule the hearing. If you don't, you're wide open to a lawsuit."

Purvis drummed fingers on his mahogany desk. "What about announcing there's no chance of a tsunami? Declare the volcano's dead."

The lawyer cleared his throat, a professional distancing. "I don't understand the question."

"Remember, we talked about announcing the two together. Her firing and the all-clear on the tsunami."

"No, now you have to separate the two. If you have a valid scientific basis for your volcano announcement, then I see no problem. But you can't do anything about Dr. Sanches until after the hearing."

Purvis said, "Okay, Marty, I understand," and disconnected. He stepped to the water cooler outside his office, then returned to his desk. He drummed his fingers again and shifted around in his leather swivel chair. He'd been getting erections thinking about the goodies waiting for him at the Ensenada beach house. Somehow he had to satisfy Harley Wamp.

He would schedule a press conference announcing the all-clear. He'd try to convince Wamp the all-clear was the really big thing, and Lani was an unimportant side issue, to be handled in due course. Maybe that would be enough.

He wanted to track the volcano numbers for another day or two, to be sure it was staying dormant. He'd schedule the press conference three days from now. He called Margaret Bradshaw's office and got her voice mail. He hung up and called the seismology lab. Gus Belmondo answered.

Purvis said, "Anything new on Lani?"

Gus's normally chipper voice was subdued. "Nothing since I called you. Her Coast Guard friend, Commander Steel, said he'd keep me posted. I'll let you know when I know."

"Are the volcano's readings still down?"

"Yes, sir. The numbers are still dropping. All except the crustal stress readings."

Purvis said, "I know that crustal stress sensors were embedded in the seafloor along the Murray fault line several years ago, but that has nothing to do with the volcano."

"No, sir. Not directly. But a fault line collapse could destabilize the area."

"Are the stress numbers that high?"

"Not at the present time, but they are going up."

"Getting back to the volcano itself, are the readings now low enough to assume it's dead, for all practical purposes?"

"No active volcano is ever dead, Dr. Purvis. But it appears to be headed for a state of dormancy. Number and size of earthquakes keep getting smaller. And gas pressure inside the mountain has subsided to the point where it's hardly detectable."

"How long since the last spike?"

"There was a minor spike in gas buildup three days ago, about the same time as the last earthquake swarm. Didn't last long and nothing over 2.5. Quiet since then. All readings are still sliding or have bottomed out. It appears the volcano's going dormant, but without Lani here to interpret, I can only give you my best guess."

"Is that the consensus of the rest of the people on the project?"

"I haven't tried to get a consensus. But if you'd like some outside opinion, I'll call Richard Costello down at Ocean Research Labs and ask him to call you. He's one of the best in seafloor seismology."

"If he can call me today or tomorrow, I'd appreciate it." Purvis sat for a minute after seating the handset. He'd better wait till he heard what Costello had to say.

He buzzed his assistant. "If Harley Wamp calls, tell him I'm out. You don't know when I'll be back, and you don't know how to reach me."

seven

Dave, a red knit sweater over his open-throated white shirt, thumbed through an old issue of *National Geographic* in Dr. Jeffrey Rosen's waiting room. A half dozen patients waited to be called. The inner office door opened. A tall woman in flowered scrubs announced, "David Steel."

He followed her down a hall lined on both sides with consulting cubicles. She opened the door at the end of the hall. A small, wiry man with thinning blond hair rose and offered his hand across a cluttered desk. The handshake was warm, the hazel eyes were honest, and Dave liked the man right away. On the wall he noticed four diplomas and a framed photograph of a younger Jeff Rosen leaning against a net post, holding a tennis racquet and a large trophy.

Dave settled in a chair. "When I called, you said you'd examined Lani. Can you tell me anything about her condition?"

"The only reason I agreed to meet with you is that you brought her to the hospital and seem interested in her welfare. But she hasn't authorized me to divulge anything about her case to anyone, so I really can't comment on her condition."

Dave pushed ahead. "Right now, I'm all she has here. Her folks are in Hawaii. I want to help however I can."

Rosen softened a little. "Maybe the best way you can help is to give her some space for a few weeks. She needs a chance to recover. Physically and emotionally."

"Does that mean I shouldn't go see her?"

"What exactly is your relationship? Are you engaged?"

Dave shook his head. "No, nothing like that. Really close friends, I guess you could say."

Rosen studied Dave with a clinical expression. "She told me no visitors. No calls. No exceptions. That's the order I left with the hospital."

Dave fought off a wave of deep disappointment. But the sinking feeling was too strong—he finally had to let it in. "That's not what I expected. Of course, I'll do whatever it takes to help her."

"Keep checking with the hospital. They'll let you know if she's changed her mind." Rosen glanced at his small, marble desk clock. "Sorry I couldn't be more helpful."

Dave took the cue and got up to leave. He wanted to say *Thanks for nothing*, but said instead, "Thanks for your time, Dr. Rosen."

~ ~

Dave sat in his parked car feeling frustrated. He wanted desperately to help Lani, but he couldn't even get in to see her. Maybe it would help if he knew something about the healing process after episodes of abuse. He remembered Amy Fenstrom, a psychiatrist he'd played mixed doubles with at the club. They'd talked while waiting for a court. She'd been interested in how stress was diagnosed and treated in the Coast Guard. They'd also touched on how the Coast Guard dealt with abuse of rank. He picked up his cell phone, got her office number from information, and waited for the connection.

"Hi, Dave. My next patient is due anytime, so I can't talk more than a minute or two."

"How about lunch?"

"Sorry. I'm booked solid all day, including the lunch hour. But I can meet you for a drink after my last patient."

"What's near your office, and what time is good?"

"The Plaza has a nice bar and lounge. Six-thirty?"

Dave arrived early and took a table in a quiet corner. The Plaza's Whaler's Cove was a low-ceilinged room with a whaleboat bar and a rope-framed mirror on the back wall. Two dozen round maple tables with spindly Windsor chairs were evenly spaced through the room. Most of the happy hour crowd had left, but a few hung on and the early diners were beginning to drift in. Most of the bar stools and about half the tables were occupied.

He spotted Amy at the door and waved her to the table. He was surprised to see her in a drab, shapeless, dark blue dress. He knew she had a killer body and good taste in clothes.

She saw his look. "My patients seem to feel more comfortable if I dress conservatively."

Dave said, "Better not let them see you on the court."

A waitress in a pleated mini and blue-striped T-shirt took their drink orders. Lounge babble and canned music floated in the background.

Amy said, "You haven't been around the club. Are you still seeing Andrea?"

He shook his head. "I have something, or I should say *someone* else on my mind."

"For a minute there I was hoping the someone might be me," said Amy. "I was jealous as hell when you got cozy with Andrea. But your body language tells me it still isn't me."

He smiled. "I'm really flattered, but this is about a girl I met on a Coast Guard project."

"You're obviously in pain, so why don't you spill the whole thing. Normally I'd charge one-fifty an hour, but since I've always had the hots for you, this'll be free."

Dave said, "Her problem is trusting men."

Amy raised an eyebrow. "Her problem, or your problem?"

Dave waited while the waitress set Amy's white wine spritzer, his Beck's draft, and a bowl of snack mix on cocktail napkins. "I was hoping to gradually win her trust. Then this bastard of an ex-husband kidnapped her and beat her to a pulp."

"How long ago?" Amy plucked a peanut out of the snack mix.

"She was rescued day before yesterday. He had her for five days and nearly killed her. She's in intensive care at Huntington Memorial."

She finished chewing the peanut. "Obviously, this will make trusting men harder than ever for her. How do you feel about that?" She looked at him intently.

"Before the kidnapping, I was hoping I could change her mind. Now, she won't even see me." Dave lifted his sweat-beaded beer and sipped through the foamy head.

"So you feel…"

"A little resentful, I guess. I'm the guy who went in there and laid out that shithead, and got her out of there."

"Was she conscious?"

"Barely. But she recognized me."

Amy sipped her spritzer. The ice clinked in her glass. "So you think she should be grateful and magically change? Suddenly trust you implicitly?"

He shrugged. "I hoped that's the way it would work."

"I interned at the busiest trauma unit in Chicago. Did my residency in psychiatry at the same hospital."

"Guess you saw some bad cases."

"Every kind of abuse you can imagine."

"And…"

"Reality time, Dave. No matter how hard you try, there's absolutely nothing you can do. If change is to come, it has to take place within *her*."

Dave waited, trying to absorb the message. "That's hard to

swallow. I thought maybe I had proved to her…"

Amy leaned closer to him. "Rescuing her is great, and so is being considerate, since that's the kind of man you are anyway. But you can't force change from the outside. It has to come from something inside her, not from something you do for her, no matter how trustworthy you make yourself look."

She stirred her drink. "What kind of girl is she? That might be a clue as to whether change is likely."

"Bright and ballsy. Doesn't seem to be afraid of anything."

"Except trusting a man, right?"

Dave sipped his beer. The squint lines around his eyes deepened. "She took a terrible beating. Will she ever get over it?"

"If she's as strong-willed as you say, she may have a chance of eventually overcoming her fear of entrapment. What do you know about her background?"

Dave told her as much as he remembered from their talks.

Amy was silent at first, sipping her drink. She finally said, "It's impossible to do a meaningful diagnosis without meeting the person and having some one-on-one therapy sessions. So whatever I tell you might be totally off the mark."

"I'd still like your take on it."

"She came sixteen years after the last of the siblings?"

"That's what she said." Dave ran a finger over the condensation on his beer glass.

"Let me get this straight. All her brothers were gone. Her father left for work at five every morning. And her mother was busy all day doing volunteer work?"

"Lani stayed with an aunt after school."

Amy waited till the bartender's loud blender cut off. "No wonder she's tough. Had to fend for herself right from the start. Does she feel that her folks loved her?"

"She thinks her dad loved her. Even though he was dog tired when he came home, he'd bring her treats and make a fuss over her. But he went to bed early, played golf with his buddies on weekends, and didn't spend much time with her."

"And her mother?"

"Preoccupied with her work. Too busy to give Lani any attention—or love, I think."

"So Lani came from a sterile environment, and then married an abuser. Never had a chance to learn about loving and trusting."

"I know she has it in her. She can be very tender."

Amy nodded. "Mmm-hmm. But will she let those feelings come out? Will she trust them when they do?"

Dave drained an inch off his beer glass. He slowly set it back on the damp cocktail napkin. "Sixty-four thousand dollar question."

Amy said, "There's no way to tell if or when she'll make the breakthrough. Maybe never. You have a big decision."

His voice was low, reflective. "To wait or not to wait."

Amy nodded. She looked away for a moment, then refocused on Dave. "So how did you pick this one?"

His grin was forced, masking the pain of rejection. "Lord only knows. We're not much alike. I like to stay in control, sail a steady course. She's open, out front, holds nothing back. Totally different experience for me. I think about her a lot."

Amy laughed and stirred her wine spritzer. "A case of opposites attract. She has Mr. Predictable here squirming and reexamining his priorities."

Dave echoed her laugh. "Guilty, Your Honor."

Amy's expression changed from amusement to concern, but she didn't speak. Loud laughter came from a table of four men with loosened neckties. Finally, "If she does change enough to say yes and you marry her, it's more than likely the least little thing could send her fleeing. You'd probably be working overtime to keep things on an even keel."

"You mean if I slipped up and did something to shake her trust…"

"Be ready to go through six kinds of hell to patch things up.

Could be a lifetime struggle."

Dave stared at his beer. "Right now, we're just good friends. I'm only trying to help her out."

"Of course."

He pointed to her glass. "Time for one more?"

Amy shook her head. "I'll take a raincheck. Maybe you'll be back on the market next time. I'll wear a different dress."

∼ ∼

When his assistant announced that Dr. Costello was calling, Purvis dropped the paper clip he'd been unwinding and punched the lighted button. "I've been wanting to talk to you about Seamount Gilman."

Costello said he'd been away, but he'd been checking the volcano's readings several times a day.

"In your opinion, is the possibility of a major eruption and tsunami definitely behind us?"

"It appears that's the case, but I'd be reluctant to make such a flat prediction."

Purvis was disappointed. And worried. He picked up the bent clip. "Why not?"

"It has all the earmarks of a volcano going dead. Magma's no longer flowing in, but there's still a trace of low-level activity. Until we get total subsidence and it stays completely dead for a year, I just wouldn't want to go out on a limb. Mount Saint Helens showed signs of subsidence for a few days just before it blew."

"What do you think the chances are of the volcano heating up again and actually exploding? Five percent? Ten percent?"

"It's not like forecasting the weather, Dr. Purvis. I wish it were as simple as picking up a storm front on radar. Every volcano does its own thing."

Purvis thought for a moment, twisting the clip into a triangle. "I understand that your opinion of what would happen in case of a full-scale eruption is not as drastic as Lani's."

"Lani and I had an honest difference of opinion after looking at the same data. My estimate of the chances of a big-time tsunami hitting the California coast after an eruption are quite a bit lower than hers."

"But both your estimate and Lani's are based on a major blow-out the size of a Saint Helens, right?"

"That's one of our points of difference," Costello said. "I'm not sure the eruption would be comparable to Saint Helens. I'm not sure it would fracture the crust or collapse the mountain. If it did spawn a tsunami, I'm not sure it would be big enough to threaten the California coast. But if activity ever starts up again, and the pressure builds as high as it was and keeps on building, then it's not inconceivable that we could have a Saint Helens. I wouldn't discount Lani's theory altogether. At the moment, there's no sign of a buildup. In fact, the activity is so low it's hardly measurable."

"What's your own unofficial opinion? I won't hold you to anything."

"Dead, for all practical purposes. What do your SciPac seismologists say?"

"The consensus seems to be there is no present tsunami threat and chances of one hitting Southern California in the foreseeable future are zero. I'm inclined to make that announcement to the press."

There was a pause before Costello replied. "I'd agree there's no present threat. But someone would have to define foreseeable future for me. I don't think it'll happen, but if the mountain decides to heat up again, a destructive blast at some point is not out of the question."

"So you don't think I should sound the all-clear?"

"That's your call, Dr. Purvis."

Purvis hung up and sat at his desk for a few minutes, holding an internal debate on the pros and cons. A light blinked on his phone and his assistant said the school's finance director was on the line. "What can I do for you, Jerry?"

"Southern Coast Land stopped payment on their last contribution check."

"The five million?"

"That's right."

"Damn!" Purvis kicked his wastebasket and sent it flying across the room. He needed that five million to pay bills and meet payroll. Harley Wamp. What a miserable asshole. He took a deep breath and got his rage under control. *Well, shit, I was about to make the decision anyhow.* "I'll take care of it, Jerry. It'll clear the bank by tomorrow."

He buzzed his assistant. "Call a meeting. Four o'clock this afternoon, my office. Head of earth sciences, head of seismology, head of press relations." Purvis sighed. "And get Harley Wamp on the phone."

~~

George Hacker had paid a Hollywood producer $10,000 to move to another suite at the Beverly Hills Hotel so he could occupy the presidential cottage. He sat over breakfast wearing red silk pajamas over his squat 185 pounds, and a black silk robe with a green dragon stitched on the back. He shoved his breakfast tray aside and looked at the banner headline on the front page of the *L.A. Times*. *TSUNAMI WARNING A MISTAKE, SAYS SCIPAC PRES*. Hacker sounded like a hen cackling as he laughed. "Your handshake did the job, Mr. Fat."

Ho Kai Fat sat silently in a chair next to the door.

"That little squeeze let our friend Harley know we were serious, and he let his friend Sylvester know *he* was serious. That's the way things get done. Harley oughta sell a buncha houses now. If he doesn't, we know how to get his attention, don't we, Mr. Fat?" He cackled again.

Ho Kai Fat's voice sounded deep and hollow. "Two men come."

"That'll be Milo Wagstad and his number one helper. Let 'em in."

Milo was short, skinny, and thirty-fivish, with thin brown hair, a receding chin, protruding teeth, and the small black eyes of a rodent. "I got a call from Hong Kong. Said to come here for a meeting and bring Deshaun Spence with me."

"You must be Wagstad. Spence is your number one assistant?"

Milo nodded. Deshaun Spence, a six-footer with a beachball rump, opened a hand in a half wave.

"You can call me Nick," said Hacker. "Meet my associate, Mr. Fong. We wanna talk to you about your distributorship."

Milo spoke heatedly. "And I wanna talk to *you*. First you cut my commission..."

"You're selling more merchandise, so you get the money back."

"Yeah, some. But now you're taking away territory. Deshaun and me, we worked our ass off to get the Ripper business going here on the West Coast."

Hacker picked up the teapot from the breakfast tray and topped off his cup. "Sure, just stick with the Coast and you'll be a rich man."

Milo's rat-like eyes flicked around the room. "You don't get it. We're starting to move stuff real good over there in Denver. Just getting ready to go into Chicago. Fucking gold mine, Chicago. Then some asshole calls from Hong Kong and says Chicago goes to another distributor. That sucks. I should get Chicago. I should get the whole fucking country. I earned it."

"Why not think it over, Milo? Still plenty of business to dig up here on the Coast. And you can keep Denver. We'll throw in the mountain states. Lotsa money still to be made. But you gotta let the resta the country go. Decision's been made upstairs."

"If there's one thing I know how to do, it's sell Rippers. I know how to get salesmen. I know how to let the kids know where to find 'em. Got my network set up."

Hacker hauled his squat frame out of the chair and retied the silk belt on his robe. "Right, and it makes sense to keep building up the territory you know."

"Makes more sense to let me set up the whole country. I can make more money for everybody that way. No need to bring in other distributors. How about telling that to the people upstairs in Hong Kong?"

"The people upstairs think three or four distributors who know their own territories can sell more Rippers than one guy from outta state."

"Shit. Wouldn't take me but five minutes to learn everything there is to know about Chicago or New York or anyplace else."

"Why don't you think about it?"

"Nothin' to think about. And tell the people in Hong Kong some guy down in Mexicali is knocking off the Ripper and wants to use my network to sell his guns. Coast to coast."

"You're threatening to switch?"

"Not if I get the rest of the country."

Hacker studied Milo for a long time. "Okay. I'll tell Hong Kong you're not happy with the West Coast. We'll see what they wanna do."

Milo nodded at Deshaun and headed for the door. Ho Kai Fat rose to open the door. When Milo passed, the big man held up a restraining hand that froze Deshaun Spence in place. With the other hand, he delivered a crushing karate chop to the back of Milo's neck. Everyone heard the sound of his spine snapping. He crumpled and fell back into the room.

"Mr. Spence," said Hacker, "would you like to be our new western distributor? And you won't get greedy like Milo, will you? You'll be happy with the Pacific Coast and mountain states?"

"Yes, sir," said Deshaun. "Real happy. I'm not a greedy person."

"Where's Milo's car?"

"We came over in my Beemer," said Deshaun. "Valet parked it."

Hacker thought for a moment. "Mr. Fong, is my packing case big enough for this shithead?"

Ho Kai Fat went to the closet, pulled out Hacker's large suitcase, and dropped it down beside Milo's body. He nodded.

"Stuff him in the suitcase, put him in the Beemer, and you two go get rid of the garbage."

"I know a guy in South Central," said Deshaun. "Runs a place that hardens steel and other shit like that. The furnace runs two thousand degrees. I've used him before."

"He's reliable?"

Deshaun nodded. "He won't say nothin'. He knows better."

"Okay. You two get going. As soon as Mr. Fong tells me it's been taken care of, Deshaun is officially our new Western U.S. distributor. And Mr. Fong, stop at a luggage store on the way back and buy me a new suitcase. Alligator. Top of the line."

Ho Kai Fat put Milo's body in the suitcase, picked it up, and went out the door.

Deshaun Spence followed close behind.

~~

Pushing paper was not Dave's favorite duty, but he accepted it as part of life in the Coast Guard. He'd just finished writing a modification to the evacuation plan. He buzzed his assistant, Yeoman 1st Class Luke Martinelli. "More evac plan changes to keyboard."

Martinelli moved quickly, with short, springy steps. He scooped the pages out of Dave's outbasket. "Anything else, sir?"

"Yes. Set up a radio link to the skippers on interdiction patrol. Conference call. I'll be expecting progress reports on container ship violations. Thanks, Luke."

Another light blinked on Dave's telephone as he reached into his inbox for the next piece of paper. The intercom buzzed. Martinelli said, "Personal call for you on three."

"Commander Steel."

"This is Lani, Dave."

It was the first time he'd heard her voice since he'd left her in the emergency room ten days before. He was surprised at how strong she sounded. He said, "I tried to call…"

She broke in. "I was such a mess, I didn't want anyone to see me. And they wired my jaw, so I couldn't talk for the first week, anyhow."

"He broke your jaw?"

"Jawbone was cracked, but now on the mend. Still have soft casts on ankle and forearm. They were fractured."

Dave was engulfed with the same rage he'd felt when he'd found her at the house in El Monte. "Damn it, that guy's got to be thrown in the slammer for good!"

Lani's voice, which had started to flag, suddenly crackled with energy. "It's my anger that keeps me going. The sooner I recover, the sooner I can nail that bastard. The police left word they need my statement. I'll do whatever it takes."

"How are the bruises?"

"Not pretty, but the swelling's almost gone."

"When can I come see you?"

"They're discharging me day after tomorrow. Why don't we wait."

"Sure. I'll call you at your apartment in a couple of days."

Her voice softened. "I appreciate what you did."

"I wasn't sure you'd remember."

"Just little snips. Like a dream. But I remember being in your arms. I didn't know anything else till a few days ago. Dr. Rosen told me what happened—he'd seen the police report."

"When I heard the name Fortney, it rang a bell. I knew you were in trouble."

She sounded drowsy. "Nap time. Call me in a few days, okay?"

~ ~

Dave parked under a tree in front of Lani's apartment complex. He pulled his red knit sweater over a tan sport shirt, then threaded his way along a hedge-lined walkway and skirted a small swimming pool. He spotted her apartment number scrawled in grease pencil on a makeshift plywood door, and rang the bell.

She opened the door and it was clear to Dave that she had not yet recovered. She'd lost so much weight, her small body had an emaciated look. Her face had regained its shape, but deep bruises still showed in purple and yellow. Fatigue lines furrowed her cheeks. She wore long sleeves and pants on a warm day, probably to cover the bruises on her arms and legs. One sleeve was pushed up to accommodate a forearm brace. One pant leg rested atop an ankle cast that looked like a foam boot.

He wanted to give her a reassuring hug but saw her hesitation. Instead, he reached out and took her hand. "Wonderful to see you up and around… you look great."

She drew him inside and closed the door. "Cut the bull, Dave. I'm not much to look at, but I'm still ticking."

He grinned. "Same fighting spirit—otherwise I'd worry." He nodded toward the plywood door. "Temporary?"

"They're putting in a new one."

"Ready for some lunch?"

She nodded. "Not very hungry, but I know I should eat."

"Can you walk on that ankle?"

She smiled. "Hobble is more like it. If I hang on to your arm."

He presented an elbow and waited till she had a firm grip. "Altadena's foreign territory to me. Know a quiet place with good food?"

"Bella Napoli's pretty reliable. Small but nice. Ten-minute drive."

~ ~

The patio was shaded with large umbrellas advertising Campari. The hostess showed them to a table off by itself, away from the burbling fountain. She dealt out menus. "Something to drink?" Her eyes took in Lani's bruises.

Lani said, "Ice tea. Anything stronger would knock me flat on my you-know-what."

Dave thought for a moment. It was a warm day and he was off duty. "An Italian beer—Peroni if you have it."

After the hostess left, he turned to Lani. "Did the doctor give you a prognosis? Any idea how long before everything heals?"

She shook her head. "It'll be slow. Months."

"You were going to file suit against SciPac for a fair hearing. Where does that stand?"

A young man wearing a red cobbler's apron over black walking shorts appeared with their drinks. "Would you like to hear our specials?"

Dave said, "How's your Caesar salad?"

The waiter signaled a thumbs-up, and pronounced the word "excellent" with an Italian flourish. "Etch-a-lent-tay. Very fresh."

Dave nodded. "Don't spare the shredded cheese."

"Make it two," said Lani. She waited till the server was out of earshot. "I've been trying to sort out my priorities."

Dave poured his beer into a chilled glass. "Getting well should be number one."

She stirred her ice tea and tipped the lemon wedge into the glass. "Right after I give the police my statement." Her rising color emphasized the bruise marks on her face. "The most important thing in the world is making sure that slime gets what's coming to him."

Dave gave her a look. "Not at the expense of your health."

"Giving that statement will make me feel better than all the pills in the drugstore. I just wish I could remember more of what happened."

Dave said, "Just tell what you remember. I gave my statement last week. It'll fill in a lot of the blanks."

"Dr. Rosen recommended a lawyer. She agreed to take my

SciPac case and go with me for the police interview. Anyhow, priorities are the police statement and getting well." She sipped ice tea through her straw. "Once I have my strength back, I'll be ready to take on SciPac."

"I hope you're all the way back before you take on a court battle."

Her eyes softened. "That brings up a point. I'm going to Hawaii to finish my recuperation. It'll take the pressure off for a few weeks. I want to see my folks, anyhow. While I'm there, I'll talk to Hawaii State about that research fellowship."

It was a punch in the gut. "You think you'll stay in Hawaii?"

She shrugged. "Depends."

"On what?"

"The HSU offer, and how I feel after I think about things. Whatever happens, I have to come back to testify against Fortney, and work with the lawyers on the SciPac lawsuit."

"But coming back to stay… is that option still open?"

She met his eyes and moved her hand slightly, as though she meant to reach out to touch him, but pulled it back. "I know you put your life in danger when you came to help me. I'll always be grateful."

"Now you can cut the bull. You don't owe me anything. I only did what anyone would do."

She wanted to hear he'd done it because he cared. But she wasn't ready anyhow. Just as well.

They sat in silence until the salads arrived. The waiter unfolded a stand and rested his tray on it. The Caesars, mountains of shiny chunks of romaine lettuce in wooden bowls, were served first. Then an extra bowl of shaved Parmesan cheese, followed by a basket of bread wrapped in a red napkin. "Bread's right out of the oven." He topped off Lani's ice tea glass from a large pitcher, giving her bruises a fleeting glance. "Another beer?" he asked Dave.

"No thanks."

The waiter palmed his tray, folded the stand, and headed back to the kitchen.

They worked on their salads for a few minutes. Finally Lani said, "I know what I said hit you wrong."

He set his fork down. "If we ever do get around to a relationship, I don't want it to be based on gratitude."

"I see where you're coming from." She had stopped eating too. "We'd need a more solid base. Mutual respect. Sharing. Commitment."

"And liking each other."

She met his eyes. "I like you already, very much. It's that I don't want a man in my life right now. Any man. I can't go even partway down that road, because I might not be able to stop until I find myself in a spot I can't handle."

"Maybe it's not in the cards right now." His voice was matter-of-fact.

She reached across the table and put her hand on his. "If I hurt you, I'm sorry."

Dave put his other hand over hers and smiled. "No biggie. And this doesn't mean I'm giving up. Come on, let's finish our lunch."

She gently withdrew her hand. "I'm not very hungry. I'll just finish my tea."

He set his napkin on the table beside his salad. "When are you leaving for Hawaii?"

"Next week. I have two more physical therapy sessions, plus a final appointment with Dr. Rosen. He's referred me to a doctor in Honolulu. He wants me to continue my physical therapy." Her eyes moistened, and she turned her head away.

He felt Lani's pain, and unexpectedly, his own. He wanted to put his arms around her and try to bring some comfort to them both. But the time was not right. "Maybe we should get you home."

"My first time out. Pretty tired."

He left a fifty-dollar bill on the table.

At her door, he said, "Let's stay in touch."

"I'm not sure that's best."

He tried to smile.

Lani's eyes brimmed with tears again. "I guess this is Aloha."

Dave squeezed her hand. "Take care of yourself." He turned and headed for his car.

The Mexican border agents hardly glanced at the black limo as it crossed over into Mexicali from Calexico at nine-thirty on a weekday morning. The limo drove slowly through town and continued south past irrigated farmland and into the Baja desert.

"We're almost there," Deshaun Spence said to Hacker. "We can get a good look at it from that hill."

Ho Kai Fat turned off at the next dirt road and drove to the top. They emerged into an ocean of hot, dry air and walked to the rim of the hill. Hacker raised a pair of binoculars.

"So that's where they're making the knockoffs." He scanned the one-story concrete block structure, which stood in the middle of five acres of cleared desert. Thirty or forty cars angled nose-in, in neat parking spaces around the building.

"Yeah, that's where me and Milo went to talk to the guy about selling his guns and ammo."

"Wonder where they got a machine that makes that small a caliber cartridge?"

"Don't know where they got it, but they got it. He showed us the machine. Looked real new. Loads powder in the casings and seats the bullets. About fifty people sit at long tables and put the guns together."

"Guns any good?"

"Don't have the nice feel the Ripper does, but it gets the job done."

"Do you know what the boss's car looks like?" Hacker handed the binoculars to Deshaun.

Deshaun swept the parking lot and stopped when he spotted a silver Rolls near the front entrance. "There it is. He's in."

"You sure the charges are set?"

Deshaun said, "They better be, or there's one Mexican general gonna have more than one hole in his ass. Tol' me he'd put his best demolition team on the job. They was supposed to start around midnight and have it all wired and ready to go by five this morning. I give him the first ten thousand. He gets the other ten after."

"Local police taken care of?"

"Yeah. I give him another five for the police chief. The official report'll say it was a accident. Electricity set it off."

Hacker said, "He's supposed to say static electricity caused a spark and the powder storage went up."

"Right. That's what I told the general. He said he'd tell 'em to say that."

"Then I guess everything's set. Can we do it from here? It's over a mile."

Deshaun pulled a black plastic wand out of his pocket. "General says the remote's good for two miles as long as it's line of sight."

Hacker checked his watch. Five minutes after ten. "Let's do it, Deshaun."

"There's fifty people in there. You sure?"

Hacker's face reddened. "I'm sending a fucking message. I wanna make damn sure it's loud and clear. We don't let other people horn in on our business. So do it! Now!"

Deshaun still hesitated. Hacker grabbed the wand out of his hand and pressed the red button.

The whole building lifted off the ground on a cushion of smoke and dust. It hung in space for a moment before flying apart. By the time the shock wave of the blast swept over the three on the hill, the building and every thing and every person in it had disintegrated into dust, and become part of the black-and-white cloud billowing upward thousands of feet into the hot desert air.

"I never seen nothin' like it," said Deshaun. Awe etched his features.

Ho Kai Fat said, "All gone. All dead."

"Let's get the hell out of here," said Hacker.

~ ~

Lani had been away from the Islands for nearly eight years. When she'd left for college, a whole new world had opened up for her. First at Princeton and later at SciPac, she'd found an exciting new life where knowledge, talent, and hard work counted and gave her power over her life. She kept finding reasons for not going home. Now, as she stepped out of the small B&B in the hills behind Honolulu, the soft feel of the air, the warmth of the morning sun, and the smell of the trade winds brought back pleasure as well as echoes of pain. *Makes me want to go barefoot and suck on shave ice.* She laughed.

At Hawaii State University, she was shown into the office of Dennis Chung, Dean of the School of Earth & Marine Sciences. A neatly trimmed black beard ran along his jawline, framing a smiling young Hawaiian face with inquisitive brown eyes.

"We've had our eye on you for a long time," said Chung. "Top of your class at Kamehameha, cum laude at Princeton, rising star at SciPac."

"I guess you know the rising star fizzled."

"From what I hear, you got caught in a political crossfire. I've talked to our own seismologists and volcano people, and also called John Morehead at the Tsunami Warning Center at Ewa Beach. Plus Richard Costello at ORL."

Lani nodded, waiting.

"They all say your theory is based on valid science and think such an event is within the realm of possibility. We're still watching Seamount Gilman very closely. A wave big enough to hit California would hit us first and hit us like a ton of bricks."

"I haven't been in a lab for weeks. Anything new with Gilman?"

"Still dormant," said Chung. "Even the signs of low-level activity have disappeared. But that doesn't mean your science was bad. It just means you can't outguess a volcano. Anyway, how about coming to work for us?"

"I'd like to, but it depends on the offer."

"Before I tell you about the position, I want to say there are a couple of reasons we'd like to have you. One is that you're smart and have a bright future. The other is you're Hawaiian. We like to keep our best brains at home. The offer is a full research fellowship."

"In seismology or volcanology?"

"The School of Earth & Marine Sciences is multidisciplinary. We were impressed by the way you used a number of scientific disciplines to arrive at your Seamount Gilman conclusions."

She grinned. "I used a little bit of everything. Volcano science, mathematics, seafloor seismology, oceanography, computer modeling, you name it."

"That's the kind of research we'd like you to do here. Find out how to best use all lines of inquiry to understand the dynamics of natural events."

"So my work here wouldn't be restricted to volcanoes or tsunamis?"

"No. We'd like you to get a feel for what we do and who we are, and then write a research proposal. Your project should utilize a variety of disciplines to help us further our knowledge of how the planet works."

"Would you expect me to teach?"

Chung's phone rang and his answerer clicked on. He muted the volume before the message started. "Probably a weekly seminar for grad students. Think about a subject."

"How will I learn the ropes?"

"To begin, we'd rotate you around to several of our labs,

starting at our oceanography lab. After a while, you'd work with our people at the volcanology center, and then you'd go over to the volcano observatory on the Big Island for a spell to work with U.S. Geological Survey."

"Any others?"

He smiled. "I was just getting started. After the volcano observatory you'd do a stint with our sea floor mapping research group. Finally, some time with the Marine Seismic Observatory. They install ocean floor seismic sensors and process the incoming data."

"I know. Sounds like fun."

He handed her a sheet of paper. "This is the formal offer… salary, benefits, and all that stuff."

Lani studied the numbers. "This is very good. Can I take a few days to think about it?"

Dennis nodded. "No problem. We want to wrap up our staffing for the fall semester in two weeks. Can you give us an answer no later?"

"I won't take that long. I'd like to check out the lab facilities."

"Which one would you like to see first?"

"How about the lab that runs the Marine Seismic Observatory?"

"Sure—MSO. We operate it in partnership with Woods Hole."

"I'm very interested in the sensor data coming from the Murray Fracture Zone near the volcano. I'm keeping an eye on crustal stress."

Chung lifted his phone and punched in three numbers. "I'll see if the director has time to work with you for a few days." He spoke into the phone. "Is Jonathan there? This is Dean Chung."

He listened for a few moments, then looked at Lani. "He's away—with one of our research vessels putting down a new sensor on the Murray."

Lani leaned forward. Her voice rose. "Near the volcano?"

He spoke to the phone. "Gilda, do you know where on the

Murray?" He nodded and glanced back at Lani. "They're putting down a high sensitivity, state-of-the-art seismometer on the north side of the Murray fault line five kilometers west of Seamount Gilman."

Lani said excitedly, "I've been after the International Research Institute for Seismology for months—trying to get them to install a new station on the Gilman site. I've been out of the loop—I didn't know they…"

"National Science Foundation came through with the funding about a month ago. Woods Hole had already developed the seismometer and we had the instrumentation package ready, so we launched the project."

"I've got to be at that lab when the data start coming in from the new sensor."

Chung turned back to the phone. "I'm sending someone over there to work with you for a few days. Leilani Sanches." A pause. "Right, the one from SciPac. Can you find her a desk and a computer—get her familiar with the setup?" Another pause. "Great. Thanks, Gilda."

He replaced the phone and smiled. "Gilda Epstein is assistant director. She says she's dying to meet you. She'll set you up early tomorrow and give you as much time as you need."

"Fantastic!" said Lani. "I'll check in with her first thing in the morning."

Dennis stood up, smiling, rubbing his beard. "Good. Let me know if you need anything else. And get back to me on the offer as soon as you can."

"I will. By the way, while I'm here, I'd like to meet John Morehead at the Tsunami Warning Center."

Dennis laughed. "Tsunami John. Great guy. He can smell a tsunami before it happens. I'll set up a meeting for you."

~ ~

That night, Lani called her mother at the retirement village near Kawela Bay. "Hi, Rose. I'm in Honolulu."

Rose delayed answering for a moment. "Why didn't you let us know?"

"Last minute thing. I'm talking to Hawaii State about a fellowship."

"You're moving back?"

"Don't know yet. Depends on things at HSU. I'd like to come by and see you and Rudy."

"Oh, my! Hawaiian Relief has been keeping me in a lather. I'm running night and day. But I'll try to make time somehow."

Lani said, "It must be the annual benefit dinner."

"I'm chairing the whole thing this year. The governor's coming, plus all the high-power movers and shakers from downtown. We expect about five hundred. Top people from all the islands."

"Wow! I can see why you're busy."

Rose sounded out of breath. "Only three weeks to go and I'm having menu problems, seating problems, publicity mix-up. Everything's in a mess!"

"You'll get it straightened out. You always panic and everything always comes out really well in the end. I'm sure it will again."

"I've never been responsible for the whole thing before."

"I can put off my visit…"

"No. When can you come?"

"Tomorrow? Midafternoon?"

"Oh, dear!" Rose's voice was panicky. "That's the only time I can get the decorating committee and the florist together."

"Rose, check your calendar. Tell me a good time."

"Day after tomorrow. Before ten in the morning. That's the only time…"

"I'll be there at eight. Tell Rudy I love him. See you both then."

~ ~

Lani went back to see Dennis Chung the next day. He said, "Still want to spend a few days checking us out?"

Lani said, "For sure. Ready to start."

"Good!" He rose from his chair and walked to a wall map of the campus. He pointed to a blue dot, then a block of buildings. "You're here. The IRIS data center and the oceanography lab are both at HGC—Hawaii Geophysics Center. Gilda Epstein has a desk and computer waiting for you over there."

Lani made her way across campus to the HGC Building and up the stairs to the data center. Gilda Epstein took both of Lani's hands in hers. Her smiling face had a freckled, eager, blue-eyed, freshly scrubbed look. She wore short blonde hair, was about Lani's height, a little over five feet, but with wide shoulders and a round, stocky build. Her white lab coat nearly touched the floor, giving her the appearance of a large marshmallow.

Gilda said, "I've been wanting to meet you for ages. Your work on the Seamount Gilman model is absolutely brilliant."

A bit overwhelmed, Lani said, "That's very nice to hear. I'll be around for a few days getting acquainted. While I'm here, I'd like to get up to speed on the new seismic observatory you're putting down on the Murray Fracture Zone."

Gilda led Lani to a cubicle with a desk and state-of-the-art computer. "Your new home while you're here. After you boot, click on the IRIS icon."

"Any data coming in from the new seismometer?"

Gilda shook her head, eyes on Lani's faded bruises under her makeup. "You're limping. Everything okay?" There was concern in her voice.

Lani waved a dismissive hand. "Getting over an accident. I'm fine."

Gilda said, "Right now we're only getting signals from the original seismic observatory located about two hundred kilometers south of Seamount Gilman."

"Still close enough to give us usable data," Lani said. "But the new one will be right in the neighborhood, and much more sensitive."

"State of the art," said Gilda, eyes bright with enthusiasm. "The original observatory was put in some years ago on the old Hawaii-2 undersea telephone cable. Since then, seismometer development has advanced by light years. The new ones penetrate much deeper into the crust."

"My hope is the deeper signal will give us something new on the volcano."

"I guess that's possible, but all the other numbers say it's dormant. I just checked a few minutes ago."

Lani sighed. "I know I might be in for another letdown, but I think there's a chance of activity deeper down in the crust. Something the old sensor isn't picking up."

Gilda opened a door to an adjoining room with a large, flat video screen mounted on the wall above a computer desk. She said, "This is our satellite link with the ship that's installing the new seismometer—cameras are on deck and on the remotely operated vehicle."

"Is the ship on station?"

Gilda nodded. "As scheduled, it's working on the north side of the Murray, three miles from the base of the volcano."

Lani's voice carried high excitement. "In the heart of the action—when the action comes back."

"You don't give up easily, I can see that." Gilda's round fingers caressed the mouse as she clicked an icon on her desktop. A real-time display of the working deck of the 220-foot research vessel appeared on the screen. She said, "They almost completed the installation yesterday, but had to suspend operations due to weather. Let's see what's happening this morning."

Lani said, "Weather's clear and it looks like they're busy on deck."

Gilda studied the activity. "They've launched the ROV. It must be back at work on the bottom. I'll get the remote vehicle's external camera so we can see what it's doing." She tapped her keyboard.

Lani studied the murky picture on the big screen. "The arm is lowering something into that hole—is that the new sensor?"

"It's going down into the caisson—wired to that instrument package in the frame next to the hole."

Lani said, "Is that a fiberoptic line going to a broadcast buoy on the surface?"

"There's a communications module in the buoy—it'll send the data via satellite directly to our data center and simultaneously to the IRIS network."

"When do you think we'll have the new data?"

"They have to make sure the sensor unit is securely in the hole, then they go through a testing checklist to confirm that all the contacts are solid and everything's working. Maybe they'll start transmitting sometime tomorrow."

Lani's look of disappointment passed quickly. "I'll spend the rest of the day getting familiar with the lab. Tomorrow I'm spending some time with my parents. Haven't seen them for a long time. And I want to shop and relax a bit. I'll come in day after tomorrow."

"The data from the new seismometer should be flowing in by then. Feel free to roam at will for the rest of the day." Gilda swept her lab-coated arm in an expansive gesture. "If I don't see you before you go, I'll see you in a couple of days."

Lani went to her cubicle and flicked on the computer to check the current status of Seamount Gilman as measured by the present seismometer setup. It took only a few seconds to see that the mountain was dormant—maybe dead altogether. In another 48 hours the new data would start coming in. It was not likely it would reveal anything new, but Lani still couldn't hold down her anticipation. The one person in the world with whom she longed to share her excitement was Dave Steel. The idea gripped her. But that was crazy. She'd told him staying in touch was a bad idea. She wondered how he was.

As if on cue, her cell phone chimed. She plucked it out of her sling bag and checked the window. Dave! Should she answer? If she did, where might it lead? Was she ready to see him again? Ready to consider committing to a relationship? She felt short of breath. If she just had more time. If she could only be sure. The phone chimed again. She edged her thumb toward the talk button. *What should I tell him? How will I feel when I hear his voice? Maybe it would be better to talk later, after I've had more time to think.* She eased her thumb away from the button. She stared at the phone in the palm of her hand until it stopped chiming.

eight

The multicolored balloons and pennants attached to the Ocean Aire Estates sales office in Serenidad mamboed in the afternoon breeze. Hacker's black Lincoln limo glided to a stop outside. Harley Wamp walked up to meet him.

Hacker lowered his tinted window. Ho Kai Fat slid his giant-size body out of the driver's seat and stood close by. Hacker sat motionless behind his dark sunglasses for nearly five minutes. Wamp started to lean down and say welcome three different times, but he couldn't tell if they were making eye contact, so he waited. Finally, Hacker said, "What the fuck's this all about, Harley?"

"I thought you'd want to come help us celebrate a hundred million in deposits. We're pouring a little champagne for the sales people."

"I don't like parties. Get in front with Mr. Fat, and we'll take a ride. I want to see the property."

Wamp did as he was told. Ho Kai Fat settled behind the wheel and waited for orders. Wamp pointed to the main road that would take them through the entire development. Hacker nodded.

As the limo pulled out, Wamp said, "A hundred million in deposits means over a billion in sales. The mortgage paper's being processed. The whole billion-plus'll be going in escrow in a month to six weeks. Then into our bank account as soon as the move-ins start. Thought it was worth a few bottles of champagne."

Hacker looked out the window as they drove slowly through mile after mile of houses in different stages of construction. Painters and landscape workers added the finishing touches to the houses in phase one, known as Ocean Aire Estates. In phase two, Sea View Mansions, roofers, plumbers, electricians, and drywall people worked on houses newly framed. Framing was still in progress in phase three. Carpenters filled the air with noise and sawdust from power saws, and shot nails into fresh pine lumber. In phase four, a fleet of ready-mix concrete trucks, cylinders slowly turning, poured foundations, retaining walls, and driveways for a dozen houses at a time. Bulldozers and scrapers kicked up dust clouds as they graded lots in phases five and six.

It took a little over an hour to drive the twenty miles from the north end of the project near San Clemente to the south end near Oceanside.

Hacker peered out the window as he spoke to Wamp. "A billion in sales and you think it's time to celebrate?"

"It's only the beginning," said an uneasy Wamp. "The sales crew is hot. They're selling every minute."

"They better be. It'll take a hell of lot more than a billion to pay off all the goddamn bills. Lot of fucking money going out to these contractors. And the banks are really sticking it to us with the interest. When do you hit two billion?"

"Not till we're selling in phase two."

"When is that?"

"As soon as the models are finished. Another two, three weeks."

"Kick some ass, Harley. I'm giving you a week to get those fucking phase two models open. And I expect to see deals closing twenty-four hours later. We need that next billion and we need it fast. I'll be back to see you in eight days. Mr. Fat'll be with me. All

I can say is, phase two sales better be in high gear by then. You're gonna be one sorry sonofabitch if they're not. Now get your ass outta my car and get this place moving."

Wamp opened the door and put a foot out. "But..."

"Shit, Harley, get a ride back with the grading sub, or call sales and tell 'em to pick you up. This isn't a fucking taxi service. I've got more important things to do." Hacker motioned to Ho Kai Fat and the car pulled away. Wamp did a quick two-step to close the door and back away without getting knocked to the ground.

Hacker put in a call to Dixon Mallory in Hong Kong on a secure channel. "I think I got the problems at Serenidad solved. It'll be another cash cow for us very damn soon. How's our new distributor doing?"

"Deshaun Spence is turning out to be first-rate," said Mallory. "Ripper sales are up. He's easy to work with. Definitely a good choice."

"I have one last little problem needs to be taken care of before I come back. Make it two. The FBI asshole and the Coast Guard guy."

"We have to be careful, George. FBI can get nasty if one of their own gets hurt. And the U.S. Coast Guard can shut us down."

"They can't do anything if it's an accident. Things can happen out of our control. Put on your thinking cap, Dixon."

Mallory delayed a moment. "I'll come up with something and get back to you."

"Goddamnit, Dixon, get your thumb out of your ass and do it today, not tomorrow. I don't care how messy, just make sure it finishes the job. Permanently. I don't like people messing around with my business. We got rid of the Mexican. Now we gotta swat these other two flies."

The Coral Reef Village retirement community perched on a hillside above Oahu's north shore. Rudy and Rose Sanches lived in a one-bedroom, wood-frame bungalow that opened onto a sweeping view of Kawela Bay and the ocean beyond. Red bougainvillea covered one side of the house, and plumeria trees had dropped a carpet of yellow-white petals on the volcanic rock covering the small front yard. Lani paused at the gate, then went to the door and knocked.

The door opened and Lani stood face to face with her mother, her father a few feet behind. Rose Sanches was an inch or two taller than Lani and fifty pounds heavier, with striking brown eyes under plump lids and thick black lashes that gave her a dreamy look, which was quite misleading. She opened her arms and Lani stepped in and embraced her. Then Lani took her father's hands and kissed him on the cheek.

Rose gushed, "Oh, Lani. I'm so thrilled!" Her busy brown eyes flitted over the bruise shadows along Lani's jaw, and widened. She quickly covered with a smile. "You look… so wonderful. And I love your hair." As if a switch had been flicked, her voice lowered and her eyelids drooped. "I know I said I'd have time if you came at eight, but something came up. Super urgent."

Lani was not surprised that her mother had let her down again, but she still felt hurt and irritated at the thoughtlessness. "You can't even stay long enough for coffee?"

Rose shook her head. "I'm late as it is. I'll catch something later."

Lani couldn't disguise the pique in her voice. "I just drove two hours through heavy traffic to get here."

"I know I put you out." Rose's voice reflected a mix of panic and plaintiveness. "But the printing company misspelled some big donor names—five hundred programs ruined. If I don't get right on it this minute, we'll be too late to reprint and end up with no dinner programs and a major disaster. I hope you understand."

Lani was struck by how much her mother's flowing movements reminded her of her Hawaiian grandmother, and how much the facial expressions and nonstop energy reminded her of her Chinese grandfather. "Can't you get someone else to handle it?"

Rose raised her hands and fanned the air, as if chasing away a bad smell. "That's the problem. I let someone else do it the first time. Now I've got to fix it."

Same old Rose. Rushing off to fix problems and save the day. "Okay, so go. We'll get together later."

"Stay and talk to your father. He'll fill me in." She gave Lani a peck on the cheek. "Goodbye, dear."

Lani waited till she heard Rose's car start and tires crunching on the coral drive as she drove away. She turned to her father. "Isn't this your golf time?"

Rudy shrugged his big shoulders. He had a round, weathered face topped by springy iron-gray hair. His brown eyes were steady and understanding. "My daughter's more important. I play golf alla time."

"Let's talk out on the lanai. We can watch the waves breaking on the beach."

They sat in the weathered bamboo chairs. Rudy said, "Yeah. Nice view."

"You still play golf with Kenny Lau?"

"Kenny and Chester Akahue and Quentin Farmer. We tee off at seven every day. I told them I couldn't today. They're playing without me."

"You guys all worked together at Sanitation. When I was little, they used to come over for beer." She was standing at the railing now, turning to talk to him.

He nodded. His laugh was a low rumble. "Yeah. We all rode the garbage truck. Known them most of my life."

Lani tried not to let bitterness show. "Rose is still busy saving the world."

Rudy shifted in his chair. "I feel bad she left like that. But Hawaiian Relief is a big deal to your mother. They use the money for clinics for the poor people."

"Sure it's important. But so was the Red Cross drive and the Christmas toy drive and all the other drives that kept her so busy."

Rudy rose from his chair and went to stand beside Lani at the railing of the lanai, gazing at the sea beyond the breakers. "She never did that when she was raising the boys. She started after they left."

"I guess all that energy she was using to raise my brothers had to go someplace."

"She couldn't sit still. And she always worried about poor people and sick people."

Lani added, "And saving the dolphins and birds and reef fish."

"Don't make fun of her, Lani. She really cares about that stuff. Always trying to make things better for others—and a better world. She has a good heart."

Lani had complained enough. That's the way Rose was, and she just had to accept it and move on. She watched large white-capped waves roll into the bay and break on the sand in a foamy explosion. The surf was so heavy, she could hear its muffled boom high on the mountainside. A big tsunami would wipe out everything. The white sand beaches, the cars in the parking lots, the homes, the surf shops, the surfers, the sunbathers, the cars on the highway. Everything and everybody.

Rudy pointed downhill. "Man, look at those breakers. Must be a big storm out there someplace."

"Are the tsunami warning sirens still working?"

"Yeah, once a month. A few people always forget it's a test and start running."

She patted her father's shoulder. "How are you doing, Rudy? Everything okay?"

"Oh, sure. Feel good. Play golf every day. What could be better?"

"I worry about you guys sometimes."

"Why? We're both fine."

"Who would take care of you if you got sick?"

"We take care of each other."

"I mean later."

"When we're real old, you mean?"

"You and Rose must have talked about it."

"She brings it up once in a while, but why think about that stuff now? Cross that bridge when we come to it. Hey, I'll fix us a pot of coffee. Gilbert Apia came by with a real good blend from the Big Island."

Lani walked with her father to the kitchen. She watched him plug in the pot and spoon out the ground coffee. "That's going to be pretty strong."

He flexed a bicep. "I like it strong in the morning. Gets me going."

She spotted a pink bakery box sitting next to the sink. "Something from the Portuguese bakery?"

Rudy's low chuckle bubbled out. "Malassada. Real fresh. I went down there early this morning."

Lani arranged four of the sugary fried doughnuts on a plate. "They smell so good. Been a long time since I had malassada." She licked sticky sugar from her fingers. "Don't you ever think about getting older?"

"I guess so. Once in a while." They sat at the table while the coffee perked.

Lani said, "You're both healthy now, but one of these days you guys will need some help. When you need a caregiver, who do you want that to be?"

He shrugged. "We thought it would be your big brother Hector. But his work keeps him overseas alla time."

Lani nodded. "He dropped me a note from an oil platform in Saudi Arabia. I know Paul is at some airbase in Spain."

"Your other two brothers are busy raising families. Eleven kids between them."

"So I would have to be the one. Right, Rudy?"

He nodded. "That's what your mother said, last time we talked about it."

"In that case, you have to get stuff together for me. All your records, your health information, your finances, where everything is. Your bank accounts, safe deposit box keys, deed to the house, your will, insurance, all your records. And who your lawyer is, your doctors, your tax man."

Rudy stretched his mouth down in a grimace. "How soon you want it?"

"Not right this second. But I'd like you and Rose to start getting a package together. Make up a list of everything I should know, including phone numbers. I'll come back later to go over all your stuff with you."

Rudy said, "I'll tell Rose you want it. Now we talk about Lani, okay?"

She said, "Coffee's ready." She lifted the stem out of the coffeemaker and poured billowing black streams into two mugs. "Everything's fine with me."

"You got marks on your face. Yellow—like old bruises. You been in an accident?"

Lani blew steam off her coffee and set the mug on the table. "You remember Frank Fortney?"

The question jerked Rudy stiffly upright in his chair. His voice became loud, gruff. "That sailor? The one who beat you up?"

She gripped the handle of her coffee mug. "He was in L.A.—found out where I lived."

Rudy pushed his chair back and stood, hands on hips, broad shoulders pulled back, his sun-darkened face now even darker. "He beat you up again?"

She nodded. "Pretty bad. Put me in the hospital."

He raised a fist. "I should have killed that guy the first time. I bought a gun but the cops already had him in jail."

"I'm glad you didn't shoot him. Then I wouldn't have a father to talk to. You'd be in prison."

"Some people shouldn't even be on the face of this earth."

"He's back in jail. This time they'll put him away for good."

Rudy sat down. "Not good enough. Somebody should beat that man to a pulp. Break every bone in his rotten body. Then shoot him down like a dog."

"The prosecutor's asking for life with no parole. He thinks he'll get it."

Rudy placed a big, rough hand gently over his daughter's. "I'm real sorry that happened to you, Lani. You healing up okay?"

"Physically I'm not in pain. A little tender still, but getting better. It's the mental part I'm having trouble with. I can't get over it." Her eyes moistened.

"It'll take time."

She smiled. "Sure. Come on. Let's eat up some of this good stuff." She pushed the pastry plate toward her father.

He scooped up a malassada, took a big bite, and chased it with a gulp of coffee. "Real good."

She ate a bite of doughnut and held it thoughtfully in her hand. "I was gun-shy of men before. Now I'm even more so."

Rudy was still for a moment. "All men are not like that."

"Rationally, I know that's true. But I'm afraid to take a chance with another man."

He studied his daughter. "Any man in particular?"

She smiled. "His name is Dave. He's in the Coast Guard."

"Another sailor?"

"Yes, but this one's straight-arrow. Very caring man."

"He loves you?"

She sipped her coffee. "He says he misses me when I'm not there. And once in a while I have this sudden pang—I miss him so much it hurts. It goes away but it keeps coming back."

"So you want to be with him, but you're afraid of what might happen."

"That's about it. I'm like a kid who's been burned by a hot

stove."

"All stoves act the same. But not all people. Only a few burn you. Big difference."

"I don't know, Rudy. Can I trust him? I guess it boils down to that."

"You think he's the kind of man who'd hit you?"

She shook her head. "He acts nice now, but how can I be sure about later? He could turn into a monster."

"After that punk Fortney beat you up the first time, you told us you'd never trust a man—never get married again. Now he did it again. I can see why you feel so strong about it."

"But I've never missed anyone before. Never had this feeling of needing to be with someone."

Rudy finished off his malassada and swigged more coffee. "Some men hit their wives. Most don't. I never laid a finger on your mother, but that doesn't mean everything was always perfect between us."

Lani said, "I guess most married people have their problems. You guys hid yours pretty well. I never felt any tension between you and Rose."

"Maybe that's because we'd both say what we had to say, and then it was over. We never carried around unfinished business."

"Do you mind telling me what the main issues were?"

"I know you feel like Rose never gave you enough love. Never gave you enough time."

Lani nodded.

"We argued about that. It wasn't she didn't love you. She loved you a lot. But the problem was—you came a lot later."

"I know. Sixteen years after Nigel."

Rudy chuckled his low, rumbling chuckle. "You were our little surprise package."

"I suspected as much."

"Hey, don't worry about it. You got lots of company. Most kids on this earth aren't planned for. It was wonderful to have a little girl after all those boys."

"Then what was the disagreement between you and Rose?"

"We talked about should she stay home again and be a full-time mom, or could she keep on doing her volunteer stuff and ask her sister Hazel to help out with you."

"Auntie Hazel was really nice," said Lani. "She'd pick me up at school and take me to her place till Rose got home. But I always wanted more from my mother. More attention. More love."

"Heck, we all want more of that."

Lani laughed. "I guess no one ever gets enough."

"But she tried real hard to be family on weekends. Remember how we all used to snorkel at Hanauma Bay and watch the surfing at Sunset Beach? Take a picnic?"

She nodded. "You're right. There was love in the house, even if I didn't think I was getting my share."

"Love in the house was the thing. I ask your mother why she won't stay home and take care of you full-time. She said she loved you, but she worked real hard to be the best fund raiser on the island. All the charities wanted her, and it would be real tough for her to give it up."

Lani's gaze traveled out through the lanai to a piece of pale blue sky and lingered there for a few moments. "So Rose was hitting her stride in something she loved to do."

Rudy waited till he had his daughter's attention again. "And what if you marry this friend and you have kids?"

Lani nodded. "You must be a mind reader. I'd be facing the same decision."

"Exact problem Rose had. Give up work, or try to do both."

"I could never give up my work. I put in too many long, hard hours getting where I am. And I love what I do. Like any working mom, I'd have to do both."

"Rose put in twenty years raising the boys. She started doing part-time volunteer work after Nigel was in school, and pretty soon she was doing it full time. She had ten years in her new career when you came. She said if she had to give up her work and go back to full-time housewife, she'd fall apart."

Lani nodded but didn't speak.

Rudy said, "It took me a while, but I finally understood it was best for her health if she kept working and gave you as much time and love as she could. We got Auntie Hazel to help. And I tried to do what I could when I got home."

Lani smiled. "I'm seeing Rose in a rosier light." They both laughed.

"So what about this friend of yours—Dave?"

"I think I'd like to have someone I love and trust to talk to about stuff like this—but I don't want to give up my independence."

"You know, when you were eighteen it was a lot easier to make a mistake, and you made a big one. Lots of girls do the first time out. They fall for the wrong man."

Her burst of laughter had an ironic ring. "School of hard knocks in more ways than one."

Rudy smiled sympathetically, but he didn't laugh. "Sure. Now you can trust your own judgment better. You probably know when something is wrong. Or something is right."

"So you're saying trust my instincts." She stirred her coffee and sniffed the aroma. "Maybe. Not sure."

Rudy picked up another malassada. "A minute ago you told me how hard you worked to get where you are—be a scientist."

She sipped her coffee and waited for Rudy to finish his thought.

"You never call and I'm no good at writing letters, so this is first chance I have to tell you how proud you make me. Your letter about being the first one to figure out about that volcano—I read that to my golf buddies twice, and called everyone I know."

Lani patted her father's arm. "Thanks, Rudy, that means a lot. But now the volcano's gone dormant. I think it will come back, but hardly anyone agrees with me."

"Not true." He waved a protesting hand. "Scientists from HSU or the warning center come on TV almost every night. They yammer back and forth, but end up saying pretty much the same thing—the volcano died down but could wake up some day—like *boom*!—and make a big tsunami. They say the Islands should start getting ready."

Lani applauded. A smile spread across her face. "That cheers me up! Hawaii's doing it the right way." Her smile faded. "But it's not working that way on the mainland." She told him how she'd been removed from her job by SciPac for political reasons. "They're gambling with millions of innocent lives."

Rudy held his nose. "They smell like bad, greedy people."

"So now my big dilemma is, should I go back and clear my name? Or forget it and take the job at HSU?"

"Rose told me you're talking to HSU. They make you an offer?"

She nodded. "Good one. Fellowship. Seems like a perfect fit for me."

"It'd be real great to have you close by. But to get your name cleared back on the mainland—how big a fight we talking about?"

Lani almost gritted her teeth. "Enormous. I'm not afraid of a fight, but this one is tougher than most, uphill all the way. Lawyers, the whole shot."

"After you win, will you have to take your old job back?"

Lani nodded. "If I go back and take them on, I'll be demanding a public apology—*and* reinstatement. That's the only way I can really prove I was right."

"Will HSU hold the job for you?"

She shook her head. "They need an answer in a few days. I'll have to give it up if I go back to the mainland."

"You really want your father's advice, or you want to sort things out on your own?"

"I'm awful close to this thing. I'd like to hear your opinion. I'll make my own decision."

"Seems to me you should go back to the mainland."

"Really? I thought you'd rather see me stay here."

"Maybe you'll come back later. I know you, Lani. You're a fighter. You don't want to leave L.A. till you set things right. And you should talk to your friend Dave. Have a heart-to-heart. Find out for sure if he's the one you want."

"You're complicating my life, Rudy." She took the last doughnut and pulled it in two, half for her father, half for herself.

~~

Ho Kai Fat steered the limo through congested six-lane traffic on the I-5, heading back to the Beverly Hills Hotel. They had passed Anaheim and the industrial area of Santa Fe Springs and were approaching downtown Los Angeles, its cluster of highrises barely visible through the thick haze.

The phone rang and Hacker glanced at the message window. "What do you have, Dixon?"

"I've spoken with some of our captains, and I have a suggestion as to how we might go about this."

Hacker put Mallory on the limo speaker and lit a cigar. "Let's hear it."

"We have a ship enroute to Long Beach from Taiwan. The *Nanjing Star*, with a cargo of agricultural chemicals. She's due in there next week."

"*Nanjing Star*'s not a container, right? Regular old cargo tub."

"Right, a cargo ship with four holds. One of those holds is full of drums of a chemical called parathion Z, which is used for crop dusting. It's in liquid form, and very deadly to insects and parasites, but not harmful to human beings in the open. The insecticide is too diluted in that kind of setting. But in an enclosed situation, a few leaking drums can create a lethal concentration of gas."

Hacker emitted his barking laugh. "I like your thinking."

"The hold would have to be tightly sealed."

"Yeah, seal the hatch with duct tape and then get rid of it after the job's done. Dog the doors down tight from the outside after they go in."

"That would produce the right conditions."

"Would they smell it when they first went in?"

The connection with Hong Kong faded for a moment, then Mallory's voice came back strong and clear. "... has a slight odor, but nothing overpowering. Nothing that would make them suspicious."

"How long would it take?"

"Not long. If the hold's properly sealed, they'd be dead in five to ten minutes."

"Who's the captain?"

"Jim Reedy. He's been with Blue Star for twenty-three years."

"Yeah, I know Reedy," said Hacker. "He'll do what he's told."

Mallory said, "Put some specialists aboard as soon as they dock. Pinhole leaks in about two dozen drums should do the trick."

"Yeah. Just so Reedy doesn't remember a fucking thing when the cops start asking questions."

"I'll make certain all he says is he gave permission for the inspectors to board and gave them run of the ship."

"Yeah, but that's all! He was busy doing other stuff."

"Don't worry, his story will be that the two inspectors went below to check out the cargo and were apparently overcome by the fumes. The drums must have been damaged during loading and the whole thing was a terrible accident. That's all he'll know or say."

Hacker said, "Okay, I'll take it from here. Ho Kai Fat will be ready with his top men. Tell Reedy to stand by for orders."

Dave opened his fridge door and pulled out a cold Corona. He wore a T-shirt and chinos and planned to spend the evening fine-tuning the evacuation plan. His chiming cell phone said "FBI."

"What's up, Jiro?"

"I know this is last-minute, but how about doing a stakeout with me tonight?"

"What time and where?"

"Have to be in downtown L.A. by ten. Pick you up at nine. And wear a dark sweater."

"What or who are we staking out?"

"Looking to nail one of the top Ripper pushers."

∼ ∼

The illuminated clock on the dashboard said 3:19. They sat in a dirty brown, ten-year-old Chevy Cavalier parked near Fourth and Soto. A thin, cold ground fog had moved in, but they could still see the corner under the faint glow of the street light.

"Not a soul on the street," Dave said.

Jiro grunted. "Stakeouts are always dull. Usually nothing happens, period. Sometimes nothing happens for a long time and then suddenly you have more than you bargained for. The LAPD has picked up some of the kids involved in these shootings."

"And got them to talk?"

"These aren't hardened criminals, mainly scared kids. Thirteen, fourteen years old. Quite a few from good homes. It wasn't hard to get them to tell where they got their guns. LAPD made up a list of the ten hottest locations and asked the FBI to give them a hand. This is one of the hot corners."

"Right now, it's a very dull corner. What happens if we catch the seller in the act?"

"Try to get him to finger his supplier. If he talks, we might be able to work our way back up the line till we find the real source."

"If he doesn't talk?"

"Plan B. We're still trying to get someone into Marine Providers. They've called one of our guys back for a second interview, so we might have a chance there."

"This is pretty damn dull work."

Jiro blew an exasperated puff of air out his nose. "You said that before. Let's talk about something else. What's happening with your love life these days?"

Dave slid further down in the seat and laced his fingers behind his head. "At first, I didn't think I was in love with Lani, but it turned out I was."

"Then you were the last to know."

"That obvious, huh?"

"Anybody could see you were in pretty deep."

"Problem is, I don't think she loves me."

The incoming call light blinked on Jiro's receiver. He pushed the headset against his ear, listened, shook his head. "Not for us. How do you know?"

"Before she left, I told her I wanted to stay in touch. Twice. She said no both times. Doesn't want a man in her life. She says she likes me—but obviously not enough. It's pretty clear. Time to move on."

Jiro shook his head. "'After what Fortney did to her, I can understand. Maybe she just needs more time."

"If I thought there was a chance, I'd keep trying. But it feels like a one-way street."

"Women do change their minds. Feeling the way you do about her, it might be worth another shot."

"She really had her heels dug in. I might have to wait forever."

"Is that the only reason?"

Dave was quiet for a moment. "I was dumped once. I don't want to raise my hopes and then get rejected again. So, time to get back in the swim."

"Paddling toward anyone in particular?"

"There's a girl over at the tennis club I was going with before I met Lani. My mixed doubles partner."

Jiro's receiver light flickered again and he pressed a headphone against his ear for a moment, then hung it back on its hook.

Dave kept talking. "She's just the opposite of Lani. Tall. Five eight or nine. Blonde. Very athletic. And very affectionate."

"Oh, yeah? Then why don't you sound more enthusiastic?"

"Just give me a little time, that's all."

At 5:25 a.m. a figure came out of the shadows, stood under the streetlight for a few moments, head swiveling in all directions, then came directly toward the brown Cavalier.

"He's checking us out," said Jiro. "Slide down as far as you can. The glass is tinted but he can still pick up a shape if it's back-lighted."

Dave heard footsteps and felt the car sway as the man pressed the edges of his hands against the glass to try to see in. After a minute or two, he heard footsteps receding. Jiro nudged him, indicating it was okay to look out. He slowly pushed himself back up in the seat. When he looked at the corner, he saw two people under the streetlight. An exchange was going on. The first man passed something to a smaller person. The small person appeared to be handing money over to the first man.

"I'm making the bust," said Jiro. He drew the Glock from his belt holster, shouldered his door open, and sprinted toward the two people under the light.

"FBI! You're under arrest," he yelled.

The two men ran. The smaller man headed in the opposite direction, the bigger one past Jiro, in the direction of the car. Dave got his door open just in time to dive out and leap for the man as he streaked by. He wrapped his arms around churning legs, felt them slipping free, finally latched on to a pair of ankles, cinched up tight, and brought the man down. Then Dave was on him, pushing him face down on the sidewalk and pressing a knee into the small of his back. He pulled one of the man's arms across his back in a hammerlock. Jiro pulled the other arm around and cuffed the man.

They pulled him to his feet and found two Rippers in his pockets, plus a dozen clips of ammo and four fifty-dollar bills.

"Where's your license to carry?" said Jiro.

The man had a shaved head, a scraggly black mustache, and a defiant glare. "Fuck off."

"Even if you had a license, Rippers are illegal and selling one is a felony. Ten to twenty in Pelican Bay. What's your name?"

"Fuck off. You can't prove nuthin'."

"The little guy was a cop," said Jiro. "You're nailed."

"Still ain't sayin' nuthin'."

"That's okay. LAPD will be here in a minute. They'll scan your mug and prints and have your sheet on their screen in five minutes. My guess is you have at least one prior, maybe more. If you have two, this could mean life. But maybe I can give you a break."

"Whaddya mean?"

"We want your supplier."

"Sheeit. I give you my supplier, man, and I'm same as dead. Jail ain't no fun, but at least I'm alive."

Jiro let it rest for a minute, then said, "Think about it."

There was another pause. The man finally asked, "What kinda deal?"

"Thirty days suspended on a misdemeanor instead of life on three strikes. Plus we'll get you out of town if you want. I think I can sell it to the prosecutors. But you have to do something for us."

The man stayed quiet.

Jiro said, "Tell your supplier you're out of stock and have some buyers. You need a dozen guns and a hundred clips today. Set up a meeting."

An LAPD patrol car pulled up. A blue-clad female officer got out and bent down to Jiro's window. "We'll take charge of the prisoner," she said.

"Maybe I can do somethin'," said the man in handcuffs.

Jiro looked at the officer. "Can you give us about five minutes, Sergeant?"

"I'll have to mug and print him first, then you can have your five minutes."

She put the man's thumb in a wire holder attached to the small digital camera and took a flash shot, then close-ups of his full face and profile. "Okay, he's yours for five minutes. Signal when you're ready."

The sergeant got back in the patrol car, and the man gave Jiro his cell phone number and a pager number. "Put in my number. He'll call me back. He changes pagers every day, so won't do no good to keep the number." Jiro called the pager and punched in the number. Five minutes later the cell phone rang and Jiro put it to the man's ear.

"I'm all out and need a dozen plus a hundred clips. Got me three new buyers hot to trot."

He listened and nodded. "Okay. I got it." He nodded and Dave switched the phone off.

"Where?" asked Jiro.

"Down in Pedro. Avenal Park. Fourteenth and Dodson. Ten tonight."

Jiro got out and talked to the sergeant. She made a call, then said they'd have to take the suspect in and book him before Jiro could make his pitch to the division commander to get him released for the operation.

As Jiro and the sergeant talked, a rap sheet appeared on the monitor in the patrol car. The man's name was Ruben Castro. He'd done time for two prior felony convictions. Jiro nodded and said they'd follow the sergeant to Lincoln Heights Division headquarters.

nine

The fog bank still hung offshore, leaving the night clear and a crescent moon rising in the eastern sky. Dave, alone in Jiro's old FBI Chevy, parked at the top of a rise on the west side of San Pedro where it butted up against Rolling Hills. Below, he could see Ruben, the gun pusher, standing next to a fire hydrant at the edge of the small, deserted park. Jiro hid somewhere in the park. Two LAPD plainclothes detectives waited in an electrician's van close by. If all went according to plan, Ruben's supplier would show up in the next two or three minutes. As the exchange took place, Jiro and the LAPD would move in from two sides and arrest the supplier. Dave hoped the operation would be that simple.

Another ten minutes dragged by before a black Mercedes slowed and parked a few feet from the fireplug. A man wearing warm-ups and a baseball cap got out and motioned for Ruben to come to the car. The two of them stood talking next to the open car door. The man in the baseball cap reached into the car and brought out a small package. Ruben took it, peeled four bills off the top of the roll that had been provided by the FBI, and handed them over.

Jiro came running out of the park with gun drawn, and the two detectives launched themselves out of the van. Ruben and the man in the cap dived into the Mercedes and slammed the door. Jiro pulled at the handle of the locked door and started yelling at them, "Come out or I'll shoot!"

The other cars seemed to materialize out of the night. A moment before, the street was empty. Now seven cars lined the curb. Doors flew open and young men piled out and surrounded Jiro and the Mercedes and the two cops. There were at least thirty of them, some with guns, some with knives. They began closing in.

Dave started his car, grabbed the radio mike, and called for help. He gunned the car over the curb onto a grassy strip that ran between the street and the sidewalk, stomped down on the accelerator, and headed for the fireplug at the bottom of the rise. Shouts and scattered shots sounded as the gangbangers jumped out of the way.

Dave had the old brown Cavalier up over seventy when he sheared off the fire hydrant and smashed into the Mercedes. A high-pressure geyser shot fifty feet skyward and crashed back down like Niagara Falls.

The impact caved in the side of the Mercedes and shoved it to the other side of the street. The frantic squawking of its car alarm joined the blaring of the Cavalier's stuck horn. The front of Dave's car resembled a compressed accordion. The air bag kept him from being hurled through the windshield, but the high-speed impact rammed the dashboard and steering wheel back into the car, pinning a stunned Dave against his seat. Despite the gushing water, a strong smell of gasoline filled the air. Tongues of flame started licking out from under what was left of the car's hood.

Fast-closing sirens from backup patrol cars rose above the roar of the geyser, the car alarm, and the stuck horn. The would-be killers and their seven cars disappeared as quickly as they'd arrived. Dave recovered enough to disengage the seat belt. He struggled to free himself from the steering wheel wedged against his chest, finally wriggled out, and jammed his shoulder against the door. He stumbled away from the blazing car and collapsed face down in the wet street, seconds before the fire reached the gas tank and the car exploded in a searing ball of red, yellow, and orange flame.

Jiro ran over and knelt beside Dave. He turned him over, checked for damage, and helped him sit up. "You okay, man?"

They stayed that way for several minutes: Jiro kneeling, a hand on Dave's shoulder to keep him from tipping over, torrents of water cascading down onto their heads.

Jiro said, "What is it with you? You let me get into these terrible jams, then you bail me out at the last second. But we always end up getting wet. Can we do the next one in the middle of the desert?"

Dave said, "How about Needles? Colorado River runs right through it."

Jiro nodded toward the bashed-in Mercedes, now surrounded by twelve LAPD officers in shooting stance, weapons drawn and pointed. "Let's see what we've got in our trap."

While the fire department and a water and power crew shut down the cascading hydrant, Jiro knocked on the still-intact driver's door with the butt of his pistol. "Ruben, you and your friend better come on out now. All your buddies took off. We have a dozen cops here and a SWAT team on the way."

There was no reply. Jiro turned and yelled at the nearest police officer. "Who's commanding?"

The officer, clad in safety vest and gripping a riot gun, nodded toward a lieutenant.

Jiro bellowed for the benefit of those in the Mercedes. "Lieutenant! We need tear gas canisters and launcher! Over here!"

The lieutenant yelled back, "Ferguson! Tear gas! Now! Ready to shoot!"

Jiro spoke again through the window glass. "If you don't come out now, the situation's going to get out of my hands and turn ugly. You know, some trigger-happy rooky'll start shooting and everybody else'll blast away and you guys'll end up like hamburger." He paused briefly. "Or a tear gas grenade'll set the car on fire and you guys will burn to death. Play it smart. Come on out with your hands up."

After another few moments of silence, Jiro pointed to the car window and stood back. An officer stepped in and smashed the glass with the butt of his riot gun, and the lieutenant yelled, "Shoot the canister through the hole! On three! One…"

Ruben came out first, followed by the man in the baseball cap.

~ ~

Jiro, wearing his blue FBI windbreaker, waited with Dave in the cool dawn air in front of the LAPD Harbor Division in San Pedro. Dave had pulled a blue sweatshirt over his T-shirt.

Jiro flapped his arms to keep warm. "I wish that damn messenger would get here."

"How many pictures are coming over?"

"Blowups of the ten top executives at Blue Star came in from Washington yesterday."

A dark gray Crown Victoria slowed to a stop. The passenger window lowered and a young man in shirt and tie leaned over and stuck a large manila envelope into Jiro's waiting hand. Jiro yelled, "Thanks, Mike," as he disappeared through the swinging doors with Dave close behind.

Inside LAPD's Harbor Division, Ruben Castro was sent to a holding cell. The man with the cap was escorted to an interview room. Jiro and a detective from Lincoln Heights sat across a table from him. Jiro had the large manila envelope in front of him. Dave sat against the back wall and observed. A second detective came in, plopping a file down on the table as he sat. He opened the file and took out a mug shot, then looked at the man in the baseball cap. "Your picture says Deshaun Spence, your prints say

Deshaun Spence, and your rap sheet says Deshaun Spence. Stop playing deaf and dumb, asshole."

Deshaun looked at the ceiling. "Not sayin' nuthin' till my lawyer gets here."

They sat in silence until the lawyer arrived about twenty minutes later, a fiftyish, sad-faced man in a brown tweed suit. The detective picked up where he left off. "You were observed selling illegal firearms by four witnesses. We have the guns and ammo in question, and you were found with the marked currency in your pocket. You're looking at twenty to life at Pelican Bay. Folsom if you're lucky."

The lawyer laughed. "This is so obvious. You want something from this guy so you planted all the evidence. You put the money in his pocket when you searched him. The guns could have come from anywhere. No way you'll get a conviction on this one."

Lincoln Heights detective Ray Ruiz, whose knowing dark eyes had seen just about everything during his twenty years on the streets, said, "Besides the three law enforcement officers, we have an independent witness. Commander Steel here is with the United States Coast Guard. He also observed the transaction."

The lawyer said, "Where's his uniform?"

Dave held up his Coast Guard ID.

"It could still be a setup."

Detective Ruiz said, "Deshaun's friend Ruben Castro has signed a statement and says he'll testify that Deshaun sold him the Rippers. I think you should advise your client to cooperate."

The lawyer leaned toward Deshaun. The two men whispered back and forth for a few minutes. The lawyer said, "What exactly do you guys want?"

"Deshaun's ass," said the detective.

"C'mon, be serious."

The detective said, "We're asking the judge to hold him without bail."

The lawyer scoffed. "No grounds. No case. But let's talk.

Maybe we can work something out."

Jiro said, "We want to know if Deshaun has ever seen any of these people." He tapped the manila envelope.

"What people?" asked Deshaun.

"People from Hong Kong," said Jiro. "We know that's where the guns come from."

"Shit, I don't know nobody from Hong Kong."

The detective said, "Your choice. Look at the pictures, or spend the rest of your life in prison."

The lawyer asked, "You mean all he has to do is look at pictures and say yes or no?"

Jiro nodded. "We want Deshaun to study each photograph carefully and then tell us if he knows the person or he doesn't."

"Then you'll reduce the charge?"

"That's up to the prosecutors."

"Depends on how much he cooperates," said the Harbor Division detective.

"No felony, no third strike?" asked the lawyer. "Reduced down far enough to get him out on reasonable bail?"

The detective shrugged. "If he gives us what we want, we might talk to the prosecutors and recommend something like that to the court."

"What happens if you don't like his answers?"

"We expect Deshaun to cooperate and identify anyone he knows or has met," said Jiro.

The lawyer hesitated, then nodded to Deshaun.

Jiro took out the first eight-by-ten photo, mounted on a stiff backing. He handed it to Deshaun. "I want you to take the picture and study it for twenty or thirty seconds. Then tell me whether you know the person. Okay?"

Deshaun reached out and took the first photo. He held it at eye level for a moment. "No. Never seen that dude."

Jiro said, "Wait. I want you to *really* look at it."

Deshaun looked again, as if studying the picture. "No, man.

Told you I didn't."

They went through the same ritual nine more times, Deshaun saying that he did not know the person.

"Okay, that's all for today," the Harbor Division detective said to the lawyer. "Deshaun goes back to his cell, but we'll talk to the prosecutor about reducing this to a bailable offense. If he does, you can get him out tomorrow or the day after."

The photographs had been mounted on a thin microchip material that recorded and transmitted Deshaun's physiological changes to a polygraph in an adjoining room. Each time he handled a photograph, changes in respiration, blood pressure, heart rate, perspiration and other galvanic measurements were recorded on the machine.

Jiro, Dave, and the two detectives went into the polygraph room. The operator said, "Everything was flat except for number four. On that one we got a real spike. The machine went crazy." He pointed to a section of the graph where the lines shot up to a peak, almost going off the paper.

Jiro laid out the ten photos, left to right in numerical order. He looked at a sheet that listed the names. He shook his head and pointed at the face in photo number four. "My list says that's George Hacker, owner of Blue Star Shipping. But that doesn't make sense. He's one of the wealthiest and most powerful men in the world. Why would he be associating with a lowlife like Deshaun Spence?"

~~

Lani woke early, anticipating her first look at the data coming in from the new seismometer. Her ankle swelling had gone down overnight, but it still hurt when she put her weight on it. After her shower, she pulled an elastic brace over the ankle and examined the bruise marks on her face. They had mostly faded to yellow with faint traces of blue, but still required plenty of makeup.

She arrived at the data center on the HSU campus just after

6:30 a.m. The place was empty. She went to her desk and booted the computer. She clicked on the IRIS icon, then on the link to the new seismometer on the Murray Fracture Zone. Instead of seeing new data streaming in, she read a message saying the Murray link was out of service. To ease her letdown, she took a ten-minute stroll to the food court and had a cup of coffee and a breakfast roll. She didn't know where the school got its pastries, but they didn't compare to the stuff from her father's favorite Portuguese bakery.

She walked back to the HGC Building, lingered on the ground floor reading notices on the bulletin boards, finally climbed the stairs to the second floor, and checked back into the data center at 7:20. Gilda Epstein's marshmallow form stirred around in the little kitchen alcove, making coffee.

Lani said, "I was in earlier but the link to the Murray sensor was down."

Gilda's blue eyes were warm and her freckled face creased in a toothy smile. "I'm not surprised you were in by dawn's early light."

"It's just that I'd like to know if the deeper signal shows anything."

"When they ran their tests yesterday, they found some glitches in the new setup. Hopefully, they'll have it all fixed sometime this morning. We'll get an e-mail when they start data transmission."

Lani emitted a deep sigh. "I'll be down the hall checking out your satellite oceanography lab. Let me know when the new sensor's online."

"The very second we're notified." Gilda left the kitchen alcove and turned toward her office.

Lani was fifty feet down the hall, heading for the satellite lab, when she heard, "Lani!" and the rapid *squeak squeak* of rubber soles on vinyl flooring. Gilda was rushing to catch up, white sleeves waving.

"E-mail just came in," she panted. "New seismometer's online.

Let's go see."

They hurried into her office to look at the data on the larger screen, and Gilda clicked on IRIS, then the Murray link. The screen began streaming data.

"These numbers don't look much different," said Lani, disappointment in her voice.

Gilda shook her head. "They've calibrated the equipment to send out data signals on two levels. Now we're looking at the transmission taking in the first ten kilometers of the earth's crust. That's about the limit of the old equipment."

"How do we go to the deeper signal?"

Gilda slid the mouse arrow to a blue L2 in a small box in the corner and clicked. "Level two takes in the bottom ten kilometers of the crust and the first kilometer or two of the upper mantle." The numbers on the screen scrambled for a few moments, then a new stream of information rolled across the screen.

They studied the new numbers in silence. Lani saw that the signals were layered in ten bands, each representing a thousand meters of thickness in the lower half of the crust. She watched intently for a half hour, her shoulders gradually sagging. "All flat. Nothing. Not a sign of activity, even at these deeper levels."

"Certainly appears the fault line is quiet—as is the volcano." Gilda's ample white-clad body tilted to the computer screen, her hands lingering over the keyboard.

"Let's check crustal stress in that lower tier."

Gilda typed in a command and touched Enter. "Pretty high." Her voice contained a note of surprise. She studied the moving graph line representing the degree of crustal stress creeping forward and upward through the grid. "Whew! That fault line is under a lot of strain."

"But still no seismic activity," said Lani. "I don't understand it."

Gilda switched back to the lower level seismic signals. "Nothing going on. But all this data is being recorded and stored, so we can do other stuff for a while and check this later. The historical grid charts display all continuous activity as far back as you want to go."

Lani nodded. "Let's give it a few more hours, then take another look."

"I told Marvin Louder at Oceanography you'd be coming in this morning. He's got a pile of stuff for you to read, and he's set aside time to give you the two-dollar tour."

"Good," said Lani. "I'll try to get up to speed on satellite oceanography. If I'm not back by nine, would you peek and let me know if you see anything?"

~ ~

Marvin Louder was a vigorous-looking man in his early forties. He was slim with a dark crew cut and energetic brown eyes. He stood about five ten and wore running shoes, khaki shorts, and a white knit tennis shirt. He looked like he probably ran 10K before breakfast every morning.

He explained how their array of dishes on the roof of the building picked up data from five different satellites, processed it through their banks of receiving equipment, and converted the information to visual displays in real time. He stopped in front of three large video monitors. "At the moment, these three screens show grid overlays of the ocean between Hawaii and the mainland."

Lani nodded. "We have a similar system at SciPac. One is weather, two's surface conditions, and three shows information on ocean currents—direction, size, speed. What about seismic data—contour of the bottom, subsurface activity?"

"Next room," said Marvin. He opened the door to the connecting office. Lani scanned the three monitors a final time and stepped toward the open door. Someone shouted her name and she turned.

"Lani!" Gilda's round, lab-coated figure appeared in the door to the main hall behind her. "Come! Look at the chart!"

"I'll take a raincheck, Marvin. Thanks for your time." She trotted to catch up. As they entered Gilda's office, Lani saw a large grid on the screen with short, undulating lines on four levels, stretching left to right.

Gilda pointed to a spot on the wavy line at the bottom of the screen. "You were right. Seismic activity."

Lani tracked the horizontal line representing the deepest point, where the earth's crust met the hot plasticity of the mantle. About forty minutes after the new seismometer went online, there it was… "A spike!"

They studied the small peak in the otherwise flat, wavy line. Gilda said, "Not very big and it lasted less than a minute, but it was a definite spike."

Lani spoke rapidly, a new brightness in her voice. "Look at the location—right under Seamount Gilman."

"Time of spike—Alaska standard—zero eight forty-three."

Lani glanced at the clock in the corner of the computer screen. "Forty-five minutes ago."

"We better wait and see if we get another spike. If so, how big and where."

Lani nodded. "That's the only way to find out if this is an anomaly or part of a pattern."

"By the end of the day we should know whether your volcano is dead or alive."

"I'm pulled two ways." Lani's smile was rueful. "It's safer dead. But it validates my theory if it's still alive."

"How you feel doesn't matter a whit to the volcano," said Gilda. "It'll do what it's going to do."

"I know. I preach that same sermon all the time. Let's take another look around four. Right now, I'm going back to the satellite oceanography lab and see if Marvin has time to finish the tour."

Gilda said, "Good, I have ton of work on my desk. See you

late p.m."

Lani finished her tour of the satellite lab with Marvin a few minutes after 11:00. She was settling down to read the stack of background material when her cell phone chirped. She was surprised to hear her mother's voice, and even more surprised to hear, "Can you meet me for lunch today?"

"Aren't you too busy?"

"I had a long talk with your father last night—you two had a nice gab session. I'd like to make up for having to run off yesterday morning."

Was her mother's change of heart guilt driven, or did Rose really love her and really care? That was the hope she chose to nurse. "Sure. What time and where?"

"How about the Moana at one? Banyan Court?"

"Can we do twelve-thirty? I have to get back to the lab."

"See you then. I'll make a rez."

Lani was fifteen the last time she'd been to the Banyan Court with Auntie Hazel. They would go to the beach at Waikiki, and Auntie would give her money to rent a surfboard, then read while Lani surfed. Once in a while, Auntie would say, "Let's see how the other half lives," and they'd walk through the sand to the Moana and sit at a little round table under the old banyan tree. Lani would have a Coke with a cherry in it, and Auntie Hazel's pina colada came foamy white with a tiny parasol and a slice of pineapple. Now the Banyan Court's furniture was new and the place had been spruced up, but the big tree was still there and so was the gorgeous view of Diamond Head.

Rose sat at a table set with terra cotta linen and sterling flatware. Lani bent and kissed her on the cheek and Rose smiled up at her. A server appeared. Rose said, "Mango ice tea today, Bernice."

Lani said, "Make it two."

Rose opened a palm toward Lani. "Bernice, this is my

daughter, Lani."

The server, a thirtyish woman wearing a white top, red vest, and white bell-bottoms, looked at Lani. "A pleasure to meet you." She turned back to Rose. "I'll be right back for your order, Miz Sanches."

"You must eat here a lot," said Lani. "Everyone seems to know you. The hostess fawned all over me when I told her who I was meeting."

Rose laughed. "I'm a big customer. I book a lot of fund-raising events here."

"So Rudy told you about our long session."

Rose nodded. "It seems we have some issues to discuss."

Lani waited.

Rose said, "I can see how my being busy all the time made you feel like I didn't love you."

"Wow! You get right to it, Rose."

"You know me."

Lani studied her mother's face. Her brown eyes were still lively as ever, and the skin still smooth and pretty for someone in late middle age, though her chin had started to sag and creases around the mouth and chin were etching deeper. "Rose, even when you were home it seemed like you were too busy for me—always preoccupied." She felt out of breath suddenly. "I was never sure you loved me."

"I was forever doing a juggling act, with a million things to think about." Rose wrinkled her brow. "It's one of my big regrets. I want you to know for sure I was crazy about you when you were little, and I love you now. I've always cared about you very much."

"The problem is, I could never feel it. I can't explain why."

Rose's mouth pulled down, giving her a forlorn look. "I know I wasn't there for you enough and I worried about it—felt bad I couldn't give you more."

Lani smiled. "Hey, it's okay. Water under the bridge."

Rose said, "The other question is, do *you* love *me*? I've never been sure, either."

Lani's eyes widened. "I wasn't prepared for that one."

"The boys always go out of their way to tell me they love me when they call or e-mail. You've never done that."

"Now it's my turn to say I'm sorry. I do love you, Rose. But I've always wanted more, and I always hoped you'd want more from me. You know, real mother-daughter love."

Rose's shake of the head, pursed lips, and half smile signaled regret. "I guess we're two of a kind."

Lani slid a hand across the table. "I've said I love you. You say you love me. Now we can both move on."

Rose smiled and put her hand on Lani's. "Amen. Point two. Rudy said Frank Fortney found you on the mainland."

Lani touched the fading bruise mark along her jawline. "Close call, Rose. If Dave hadn't saved me, I don't think I'd be here. The doctors said another day of those beatings might have finished me."

Rose gasped. "I had no idea. I'm so sorry." After a moment, "Dave is the new man in your life? Your father said something…"

Lani blinked. "This day's full of surprises. Most children resent parents prying into their private lives, but you never did that. I really wanted you to."

"Okay, I'm prying."

"If there is to be another man in my life, he's the one. But I'm not sure I want any man right now."

"Rudy says he's another sailor."

"Coast Guard, Rose. A full commander. Wonderful guy. Just not sure I'm ready to trust him."

Rose looked into her daughter's eyes. "I can see you want to."

Bernice arrived with their mango ice teas. "Special today is papaya stuffed with bay shrimp."

Rose nodded. "One of my favorites. I'll have that."

"Make mine a BLT," said Lani. She waited till Bernice was out of earshot. "I'm not sure exactly what love is. I sure do miss him.

Sometimes it gets very intense. But it wouldn't be a good marriage if I kept waiting for the time bomb to go off."

"Does he know about your doubts?"

"I'm afraid I overdid it. I told him everything was off—I didn't want to see him anymore."

"Now you've had second thoughts."

Lani nodded. "The longer I'm away from him the more I think about him. Rudy says if my feelings are this strong, I should rethink it. He told me your marriage has had its stresses and strains, but you guys always air it out when you disagree."

Rose's smile reflected both pleasure and pain. "We've had our share of shouting matches. Rudy squirms if things are left hanging, so we always try to clear the air."

"He told me it keeps you guys from carrying around a load of regret or resentment."

Rose sipped at her tea, leaving lipstick on the straw. She looked seaward when a conch shell's hollow moan announced the return to shore of a catamaran. They watched a brown-skinned young man steer the double-hulled craft through the surf while a boatload of tourists paddled in rhythm to his chanted cadence. Finally, she said, "He's right about no resentment—we never indulge ourselves that way."

Lani blinked again. More surprises. "What about the regrets?"

"Your father's a dear man, Lani. True blue. I love him very much."

"He thinks you're pretty special too."

"I know he does. That's why I never told him I sometimes have this feeling that I could have done much more with my life."

"You wish things had turned out differently?"

Rose sipped more ice tea, this time a long pull. "We married young. Had Hector when I was nineteen. Then three more boys two years apart. I was thirty-five by the time the last one—your brother Nigel—started middle school."

"You were what when I came—forty?"

"Forty-one. I had ten years of part-time and full-time volunteer work under my belt. I found out I was a talented manager. I had what it takes to organize big drives, motivate people, get results."

"I know that feeling of accomplishment. I don't blame you for not wanting to give it up."

"That's when the doubts crept in. I knew deep down I was capable of managing anything out there—even the biggest corporation. But I'd given that up to have a family. If I'd finished college, gone on to get my MBA…"

"You'd have taken a career over the family?"

Rose frowned. "I didn't say that. I wouldn't trade my family for anything. But those were hard times, raising the boys. We couldn't afford help. Rudy was dog tired when he came home. But we got through it together."

"That has to be a reward in itself."

"I suppose so. I know it's too late and there's nothing I can do to change things, anyhow. I try not to play the what-if game, but sometimes late at night I can't help wondering how things might have been."

"We're on opposite ends of the experience. I'm happy being a scientist. Fulfilling in lots of ways. But I often wonder how it would feel to be married and have kids."

"Which brings us back to your Dave."

"I've been trying to visualize a life with him."

Rose sighed. "I know Rudy would like to see you get back together with this man. I'm not so sure that's the right thing to do."

Lani felt let down. She'd expected encouragement. "Why not?"

"You worked hard getting where you are. I've checked around. You're one of the best in your field. Ninety percent of the women in the world would love to be in your shoes."

Lani shrugged. "I suppose so."

"Would you be willing to give up your work to raise a

family?"

She shook her head. "I'd have to juggle, like other working moms."

"That can be exhausting, and you'd always be worried about shortchanging your kids. I know about that."

"It sounds like you're against the idea of Dave and me getting back together."

"Not so much against it, as wanting to make sure you think about it carefully. I'd hate to see you lose what you've worked so hard to achieve."

"Did Rudy mention my problems on the volcano project?"

Rose reached a hand across the table. "I'm so proud of you, Lani. All the media here say your work on that was brilliant. So what happened? You stepped on some toes?"

"It's a long story—but yeah—that's about it." Lani's color heightened. "Special interests in L.A. were dead set against any open tsunami debate—bad for business. They decided to shut me up—trashed my name and ridiculed my work—trying to make me the goat."

Rose looked at Lani with a worried expression. "You inherited your father's macho genes. Never afraid of a fight. Meet trouble head-on. But if you can work at HSU and be closer, wouldn't it make more sense to…"

"I'd always have that other thing hanging over my head."

"I'm sure you'll be proven right and vindicated over time. You could avoid all that unpleasantness on the mainland. Be respected and happy in your work here. And it would be nice to have you close by in case we need you."

"I'll think about what you've said, Rose. And about what Rudy said. And my own feelings. At some point, I'll make a decision."

~~

After lunch Lani walked down Kalakaua, Waikiki's main

boulevard. She needed time to think about her talk with her mother. She window-shopped for an hour, looking at the latest island fashions, wondering if people really wore some of the strange stuff in the store displays. Finally she bought a pair of earrings at an open-air stall, retrieved her car from the Moana, and returned to the campus at 3:30.

As she entered her office, a yellow Post-it note clinging to her monitor screen caught her attention. Gilda wanted to see her ASAP. She dropped her sling bag on a chair and quick-stepped next door to Gilda's office.

"Come look at this." Gilda flashed her a smile and tapped her computer mouse to clear the screen, then brought up a chart displaying the new observatory's seismometer readings over the past seven hours.

Lani said, "Can you isolate the bottom graph line and enlarge it?"

Gilda clicked and tapped. A full screen image of the deepest line appeared. "Here's the bottom line, so to speak. Twenty kilometers below the ocean floor—where the crust meets the mantle."

Lani took in the situation at a glance, and a jolt of excitement coursed through her. Her eyes brightened, her speech quickened. "Gilda! A pattern of spikes! First at eight forty-three. Second at ten fifty-one. Then twelve forty-nine. Every two hours, plus or minus a few minutes. Something's going on down there!"

Gilda nodded. "Not big—all in the 3.0 range. But your mountain's alive and kicking. The announcement of its demise was somewhat premature."

Lani sank into a chair. "But alive and kicking which way? Still dying? Or is this the first sign of new magma starting to push back into the mountain? Or something else entirely?"

"Could be any of the above."

"We should give Dean Chung a heads-up."

"Better let me e-mail the official report, since you're not yet on the payroll." Gilda tapped furiously for a few moments and clicked Send. "I told him we've detected new activity and will keep watching."

"That's all we can do. We'll have to wait to see what it does." Lani gazed out the lab window, her eyes traveling up Makiki Valley toward the top of the Pali, and lingering on the rain clouds gathering along the spine of the Koolau Range.

"What's that faraway look in your eyes?" asked Gilda.

Lani jerked her eyes away from the cloud bank and her mouth twisted into a half smile. "Oh, nothing. I had this sudden urge to call someone. Tell them about the volcano."

"I've flagged Dennis Chung, so it's not a state secret. Why don't you call?"

"My heart wants to, but my head tells me to wait a little longer."

"Based on past experience?"

Lani's eyelids drooped into a squint. "Only one, but it was a five-star disaster."

"So you're being super careful this time—before getting in too deep." There was real concern in Gilda's voice.

"I've tried to apply clear, rational thinking—but I'm very confused right now. I'd rather talk about it later."

"I don't know if I've been in your exact spot, but I did go through a couple of bummer relationships before I found my husband." She jotted a number on a slip of paper and handed it to Lani. "Home phone. Eldon's on a lecture tour in China for a couple of weeks. I stay up late reading. Call whenever the spirit moves you."

Lani reached over and touched Gilda's soft hand. "Thanks for caring. I'd rather work through this myself. If I get stuck, I'll remember your offer."

~~

Dave sat at a table in the tennis club coffee shop with his doubles partners Andrea, Kim, and Wilton. He'd played Wilton two sets of singles before joining the women for three sets of mixed doubles. It felt good to be out on the court again, working up a sweat, focusing solely on the flight of the yellow ball, letting the breakup with Lani and all his other problems fade into the background for a while.

He tasted his ice tea and glanced at Andrea. Her blonde ponytail stuck out the back of her tennis cap, and her face was flushed from sun and exertion. On the court, she chased down every ball, constantly bounced on her toes, and never stopped moving. She was divorced, worked as a part-time ticket agent for American at LAX, and had a three-year-old son at home.

"Great to see you back here, man," said Wilton. "Where you been?"

Dave sipped more ice tea. "Just had too much stuff to do. Finally decided to take a week off and told the admiral he'd have to run the Coast Guard for me while I'm gone."

Wilton and Kim laughed, said they had things to do, picked up their tennis bags, and left.

Andrea set her water bottle on the table and studied Dave with dark sloe eyes. "You really have a week's leave?"

Dave nodded. "Yeah. I need to sort some stuff out."

"You haven't called in a while. Have you been going out with someone new?"

Dave hesitated. "Sort of, but not exactly. Anyway, just too many problems. Didn't work out. How about you?"

"Oh, I go out once in a while, but there's nothing serious going on."

They were both silent for a few moments. Dave finally asked, "How's Alex?"

"He's a sweet little guy, but getting into a very demanding phase. Wants everything his way. I left him with my mom for the morning."

"Do you have time for lunch?"

She looked at her watch. "I told my mother I'd pick Alex up

before twelve."

Dave nodded. "Sure. I understand."

Andrea started packing her tennis bag. She stopped and looked at Dave, then reached into the bag and brought out a cell phone. "Let me see if she can keep him till later."

Dave went to the men's room while she made her call. When he got back, she said, "Mom says everything's okay. He's down for a nap now. She can keep him till four."

Dave smiled. "Wonderful. I don't like the showers here, so I'll go home and change. I can pick you up at your place in about an hour."

"No need to go all the way over to Naples and then back to Seal Beach. You can change into your warmups at my place. I junked the water-saver showerhead and put in the old-fashioned kind. You'll like it."

~~

Andrea's second floor condo on Seal Way was decorated in cream and beige, which gave the place a light, airy feeling. The view through the sliding glass doors and past the balcony was of waves breaking on the beach and blue ocean to the horizon.

"If you don't mind, I'll shower first," said Andrea. "There's wine in the fridge."

Dave took his glass of sauvignon blanc out to the balcony and sat in the sun. The air was so clear he could see Catalina Island. He'd left the sliding glass door open and could hear the shower going in the bathroom. He thought he heard Andrea calling and went in.

"Would you get me a washcloth? They're in the linen cabinet."

Dave took the blue one off the top of the stack, slid the shower door open a few inches and handed in the washcloth. "You need any help? I scrub a mean back."

"That's impertinent of you, sir, and you are being much too

forward. But if you take your clothes off first, we can discuss the matter."

Dave stripped off his tennis clothes and got into the shower. Andrea handed him a bar of soap and the washcloth and turned her back to him. He liked her shape. Her butt was rounded and her hips wide enough to create a taper at the waist. Her legs were long, but nicely proportioned. He lathered soap on her back, then scrubbed gently with the washcloth in a circular motion, starting at the neck and working down. The water verged on too hot and she'd set the shower head on pulse.

He worked down to the base of her spine and started slowly massaging the cheeks of her buttocks with the soapy washcloth. He put his chin on her shoulder and whispered, "Better do the other side." He reached around and soaped her breasts, massaging each with the washcloth until he felt the nipples swelling. He massaged downward to her stomach and finally her pubic bush.

Dave put his hands on her hips and slowly turned her toward him. They kissed under the pulsing shower.

~ ~

They lounged on the patio in terry robes, soaking up the afternoon sun, her feet propped in his lap. Two wine glasses and the bottle of sauvignon blanc sat on the table.

Dave said, "Haven't had a chance to relax like this in a long time."

"Been through a rough patch?"

He splashed wine into both glasses. "Yeah, lots of problems."

"Work or personal?"

"Little of both."

Andrea slipped the sunglasses on her head down over her eyes. "Who was she? Anybody I know?"

Dave shook his head. "Someone I met. But it's over."

"You sure? Your voice doesn't sound like it."

"Maybe I need a little more tennis to snap me out of it."

"That can be arranged."

He massaged her foot. "And a little more of this R&R."

"Maybe we can arrange that too, as long as Mom's willing to watch Alex."

They were quiet for a few moments, listening to the muffled boom of the surf. Dave said, "I have a few more days of leave. Hope your mom's available."

She wiggled her toes in his hand. "I think she'll do it between bridge afternoons. She plays twice a week. I'll ask."

"Fantastic."

"Does that mean you'd like to be around more?"

Dave sipped his wine, still holding her foot with the other hand. "Sure. But I don't think you want me hanging around with lewd thoughts on my mind when Alex is here."

"I would if you plan to stay. It'd be nice having a man around the house. Do you like Alex?"

"Yeah, I think we'd get along."

"Why don't we both think about it," she said.

"Yeah, make sure it's what we want."

Andrea took off her sunglasses and peered into the living room to look at the driftwood clock on the wall. "It's after three. I better get dressed." She pulled her legs back and stood up. Her robe hung open. She bent down and kissed him, and held his face close to hers with a finger on his cheek. "We make a good team."

"I know."

She kissed him again. "Think about it."

Dave smiled. "Let's see how it goes."

"Mom sits Alex again day after tomorrow. I think I can get her to keep him till four."

"Great. Meet you at the club at ten?"

She nodded. "I'll reserve a court. Oh, and before you go, your wet towel goes in the hamper and be sure to pick up all your tennis stuff."

~ ~

The message from Yeoman Gates on Dave's machine said to call Admiral Carson at the earliest. He punched the autodialer and waited to be put through.

"Your XO's in sick bay," said the admiral.

"What's wrong with him?"

"They hit a sudden squall about a hundred miles off the coast, on their way to check out that Russian trawler fleet. Riley was on deck. The storm knocked him down and almost washed him overboard. Two broken ribs and a broken collarbone."

"How's he doing? Any complications?"

"The doctors say they'll have him back on duty in a few weeks, but you'll have to take command of the group. Urgent. Sorry to cut your leave short."

"No problem. I can be there in forty-five minutes."

"The *Farallon* brought Riley in. You can go directly aboard and proceed back to join the other two cutters."

"Aye aye, sir. Anything new on the volcano?"

"No. Purvis at SciPac called me yesterday and said it's still dead."

"Right. I'll report when we've contacted the Russians."

~ ~

Dave stood on the bridge with Lieutenant Elaine DuBois as the *Farallon* cleared Angels Gate, heading into a four-foot westerly chop on a course of 220 degrees. He thought about his day with Andrea and wondered if he really wanted a relationship with her for the long haul. She was good looking and good in bed. They got along well. He could probably come to love little Alex, and maybe they'd have more kids. She was probably a good hostess, which wouldn't hurt his Coast Guard career. But what else did they have in common besides tennis and sex? She could be a nag and that would get old. And would he come to love her? That was the real question.

His thoughts strayed to Lani. He couldn't help wondering how she was and what she was doing at that moment.

~ ~

At a few minutes before 5:00 p.m., Gilda's ampleness filled the width of Lani's open door. She'd shed her lab coat and wore a short-sleeved blue linen top with a tan silk skirt. "I need to do a little shopping before the stores close, so I'm off and running. See you in the morning?"

"Hey, you look smashing—that top matches your gorgeous blue eyes. I have a call in to Dennis Chung. If he can see me in the morning, I'll stop there first."

Lani's phone burbled as Gilda waved goodbye. Dennis Chung's secretary said, "The dean asked me to tell you eight-thirty is open. He'll expect you then."

Lani spun her chair around to her view of Makiki Valley and the clouds hugging the spine of the mountain range. Decision time. Stay or go. She loved it here at HSU. Good people to work with, topnotch facilities, unlimited opportunity to do advanced research in her field. But there was that black cloud she'd left behind. Could she live with herself without first fighting that battle as hard as she could fight it? And what about Dave? Could she keep putting that off, or must she also resolve that one way or the other?

Next morning, Lani parked in the structure and walked quickly across campus to Dennis Chung's office. His door was open, revealing the familiar clutter. He motioned her to a chair and studied her for a few moments before speaking. "Judging from the expression on your face, I think the news you bring is not necessarily good for Dennis Chung or Hawaii State University."

"I'm sorry, Dennis. The offer you made is fantastic. I see lots of opportunity here for me, and I really like HSU. But I've got to go back. SciPac smeared my name, and I have to take care of that."

"You're putting that first?"

She nodded. "Top priority. I'll fight them with everything I've got."

"I know the new observatory is picking up a trace of low-level activity, but for all practical purposes the volcano's still dormant. They'll throw that at you. Are you sure it's worth it?"

"Dormant but not dead. We may be seeing the first inklings of a resurgence."

He nodded. "But that's not the point, is it?"

She smiled. "You caught me with one foot on my soapbox. You're right. The point is they railroaded me and smeared my name for their own selfish reasons. Even if the volcano remains dormant, my opinions were based on good science. And I did not release that information to the press. I'm going to find out who did and why. And I'm going to convince that academic committee I'm right and get myself reinstated."

Dennis said, "You better find a good lawyer."

"I have to represent myself before the committee, but I already have a lawyer who'll help me with my legal rights. She's hired a private investigator to find out who leaked my memo."

"That'll take money."

"I'll find it somehow."

"Do you have anyone back on the mainland who can help out?"

Lani nodded. "There's a friend. He told me he wants to help."

Dennis smiled. "You might have some Chinese in you, but you're not very inscrutable. Your face tells me this friend is more than a friend."

Lani blushed. "I didn't know I was that transparent. Yes, he's much more than a friend."

~ ~

She arrived at her office in the HGC Building at 9:15 and said good morning to Gilda. "Are the spikes still showing up on schedule?"

Gilda nodded, bright sunlight from a nearby window glinting on her hair. "Clockwork. Every two hours, give or take."

Lani said, "Check with you later." She left answering machine messages for Rudy at home and Rose at her office telling them her decision. Then she called Dave at Coast Guard headquarters in San Pedro. He was away, so she asked for Admiral Carson.

She told the admiral, "I've decided to return and spend full time going after SciPac. I need to talk to Dave about it. Is there any way I can reach him?"

"Afraid not, Lani. He's out on patrol duty for another two weeks, and the crews aren't allowed to receive or make personal calls unless it's an emergency. Anything I can do?"

"When will you know his actual return date?"

"Probably a week and a half. When they're two days out, I can give you their arrival time within a couple of hours."

Lani gave the admiral her cell phone number. "Please have him call the minute he steps ashore."

Admiral Carson said, "I'll give this to Yeoman Gates. She'll make sure he gets the message."

Lani called her apartment house manager to see if the new door had been put in. The manager said there was other damage, so they'd decided to redecorate the unit. The painters hadn't finished and the carpet and new door were still to be installed. She couldn't move back in for a week.

～～

The flight from Honolulu touched down at LAX just after ten at night. Lani still had the key to Dave's apartment, so she could stay there for the few days till her place was ready. Walking in the door brought back good memories and painful ones. How much she'd missed him! How badly she wanted to be in his arms again! When he came back in two weeks, she'd tell him she'd looked into her heart, that she loved him and wanted to be with him.

In the meantime, she'd be busy. She found a lined pad in the top drawer of Dave's desk and began writing down things to do the next day, starting with a call to her lawyer.

The phone rang as she was halfway through the list. After the third ring, the outgoing message started and a few seconds later a woman's voice came through on the speaker. "Hi, lover." The voice was throaty, suggestive. "I'm sooo glad we're back together. Things were sooo wonderful after tennis. Got your message about sea duty. When you get back I'm ready for more doubles. Hope you are too. And let's keep talking long term. Call me. Love ya."

Damn him all to hell! Men are all the same. Cheat on you when your back is turned.

~ ~

Lani sat at the desk a long time. She briefly blamed herself for waiting too long, but the momentum quickly swung over to Dave's fickleness and infidelity, and stuck there. She wadded up her page of notes and threw it in the wastebasket. She called a taxi, picked up her things, and went out the door. Her anger kept building as she stood in the damp night air waiting for the cab.

She saw the taxi turn the corner, moving slowly. She waved, and the cab speeded up, then coasted to a stop in front of her. She slid into the back seat.

"Where to?" asked the driver, a small, lean man wearing a Dodgers baseball cap.

"Where do I go when I'm mad enough to wring someone's neck?"

The cabbie laughed. "Whoa. I don't know, lady. Maybe to the drugstore to pick up some Prozac."

"I don't think anything will calm me down right now. Just take me to a decent motel."

"Closest Holiday Inn is on Pacific Coast Highway in Long Beach. That okay?"

"Sure." She sat in bitter silence during the twenty-minute drive, anger and disappointment boiling inside her. She tried deep breathing to calm herself, but it didn't make her feel any better.

They pulled up in front of the Holiday Inn. "Here we are, lady."

She towed her luggage up to her room, set it aside, and sat on the bed. Her anger refused to subside. She felt betrayed and discarded. She hated Dave.

Inconsiderate, self-centered bastard! He set me up and yanked the rug. If he didn't love me enough to wait, he could have told me. If he loved me, he would have tried harder. Sent flowers or something. Didn't even have the guts to tell me he'd found someone else. If that's the way he is, I'm better off without him.

She slid off the bed, searched for the TV remote, and finally found it in the nightstand drawer. She turned on the TV, then clicked it off before the picture took shape. She tossed the remote on the bed and started pacing the small room.

Fortney just breaks bones. But emotional abuse hurts as much—maybe more. Dave played mind games—stabbed me in the heart. How could he?

This was one of those times in her life when she really had to talk to someone. So many feelings were churning in her, she couldn't think straight. Maybe talking would relieve the pressure, let her sort out the problem and look at it rationally. But who to call? Not her mother. Lani still wasn't close enough to her to spill something like this. She remembered Gilda. She hadn't known her long, but she liked and trusted her. And Gilda had said to call anytime—she stayed up late reading.

Lani checked the time. Midnight in L.A.—ten in Honolulu. She pawed around in her sling bag till she found her cell phone and the slip of paper with Gilda's number. She sat on the bed and tapped in the ten digits.

Gilda picked up on the third ring, her voice alert. Lani said, "Hope I'm not interrupting anything important."

"Hi, Lani. No. I'm reading a dull research paper and looking for an excuse to put it down. How was your trip? How are things in L.A.?"

"Trip fine. Things in L.A. horrible."

"What's the problem?"

"He dumped me."

A pause. Gilda's voice was filled with empathy. "Ohhhh, Lani. That's terrible. So you went to see him, and he what? Just showed you the door—boom, like that? What happened?" Lani imagined the concern on her friend's fresh, freckled face.

"I didn't even have a chance to see him." Now that she was putting it into words, all of Lani's anger, humiliation, and heartbreak gushed up to her throat and strained to spill out, but she fought hard to control her feelings. "I was in his apartment when a message from his sweetheart came in. What a shock!"

"Sweetheart? Oh, God! What a shock! Total heartbreak!"

Lani broke into tears. Through her sobs, she said, "I usually don't cry, but this was the last straw."

"Men can be no-good, cheating turds—most worthless bastards on the face of the earth."

Lani brought her crying under control. "It hurts like hell, but I'm not going to let it get me down."

"That's the spirit. Tell me what she said. What did she sound like?"

"Sexy voice. I don't remember the exact words, but something about long-term plans and sleeping together again. Disgusting."

There was a pause. "Well, it sure sounds awful, but let me play devil's advocate. Are you certain he feels the same way about her?"

"You should have heard her—so lovey-dovey it was sickening. Couldn't be any clearer about what's going on. When she said mixed doubles she sounded like Mae West."

"Don't you think you ought to find out for sure? Give him a chance to explain?"

"Not much left for him to explain. Besides, I have my pride. The dumping will have to be on *my* terms. When he calls, I'll just tell him 'Sayonara, Buster' before he has a chance to say anything."

"I sure know how you feel." Gilda sighed. "Men can be such dismal bastards. But I'd hate to see you lose out on something you want so much without finding out for sure." There was no response from Lani, and she continued. "Have you done anything on your end to confuse the issue? Make him believe things were over?"

Several things flicked across her mind. The call she didn't take at HSU, and the farewell scenes at his apartment in Naples and hers in Altadena, when she'd told him things were over. But her anger quickly smothered her flash of guilt. "Bottom line is he didn't love me enough to keep trying. I'm not interested in a guy who quits the first time a girl says no."

"Depends on how firmly you said it, and how sensitive he is to rejection—like if he's been hurt before. I think you should let your emotions simmer down before you chisel this thing in stone."

"Darn you, Gilda. I wanted a shoulder to cry on, and you're making me think."

Gilda laughed and Lani joined in. Gilda said, "You still have a sense of humor—all is not lost. My shoulder's available all night if you want, but I'd like to see you use those smart brains of yours to decide what's best for your future."

"So you think I ought to call him? Tell him I heard the message—ask him to come clean?"

"It's your decision, but I think you should at least consider it."

"I don't want to sound like a jealous wife—or beg or put myself in any kind of down position."

"Just be straightforward, like you always are. Say something like I heard the message, and it really upset me because I came back to see if you still want a relationship."

"If he says no, it's a double dump. That would be the ultimate humiliation."

"What if he says yes?"

"Then we'd have to sort out this other woman thing."

"You have to decide how important he is to you."

"It would be hard to risk having my feelings trashed again."

Gilda said, "By the way, I should have been arguing the other way—I'd love to have you back here at HSU. So would Dennis. He told me to twist your arm and get you back. But your happiness comes first."

Lani had a hard time holding back fresh tears. "Thanks, Gilda. I'll let you know what happens."

ten

Hacker had been trying to eat less. His new Hong Kong wardrobe was already too tight and he hated the idea of getting measured again. But the thought of dieting had made him so hungry he'd ordered a breakfast of a six-egg omelet, two thick slices of honey-baked ham, a round of Camembert, and a basket of croissants, buttered toast, and assorted Danish.

Ho Kai Fat sat by the door of the Beverly Hills Hotel bungalow as the room service waiter laid the food on the table. Hacker had taken the first few bites of his omelet and was spreading a thick layer of Camembert on a croissant when the phone rang. It was Dixon Mallory in Hong Kong. He put him on the speaker and continued eating.

"Our FBI source just reported in," said Mallory.

"About time. We pay the sonofabitch enough. What's he have to say?"

Mallory, over the chomping and smacking sounds of Hacker's eating, said, "One of their agents has been hired by Marine Providers. He's working in the warehouse operating a forklift."

"Any chance of him running across anything?"

"None. They'll keep him away from certain areas. I think we can use him for our own purposes. Feed him misleading information and get the FBI checking out leads that go nowhere. That'll divert their attention and get them so frustrated they might give up."

There was a pause while Hacker finished chewing. "No way, José. He's gotta die in an accident. Send a message to those cocksuckers."

"That will just stir up a hornet's nest at the FBI. They'll know it wasn't an accident. They'll be out for revenge and put extra people on the case, and could well put our inside source at risk. They'd want to know how we knew."

"Screw the FBI. Those assholes gotta be taught a lesson. Anybody screws with George Hacker, they pay the price."

"That's just not a very good idea, George. In fact, it's dangerous. Think about it. We can talk later."

Hacker slapped the table, rattling the plates and silver. "Give the order, Dixon! Don't argue with me. Just give the goddamn order. I want that fucker dead. The messier the better. Maybe his forklift hits a corner, brings down a wall of shelves, and he gets crushed under a couple tons of cans and bottles. Something like that. You understand me?"

Mallory replied in a resigned voice. "Okay, George. I'll give the order. One other item. The captain of the *Nanjing Star* wants to know if everything's on schedule."

Hacker said, "Ho Kai Fat's boys are ready to fix the chemical drums as soon as she docks, but the Coast Guard guy is doing sea duty and won't be back for a week and a half."

"The *Nanjing Star* is due in there next week. I'll tell the captain to delay his arrival."

"Yeah, slow him down by three days. That'll work out about right."

"Okay, George. I'll get on a secure channel to Reedy and give him his orders."

~ ~

Lani called her apartment house manager from the motel in Long Beach. The manager said she could sleep in the apartment if she could stand the paint smell and be out by eight each morning for another few days. She caught the Blue Line trolley to Union Station, then the Gold Line to Pasadena. She transferred to a bus that took her within a block of her apartment in Altadena, and she walked the rest of the way. The door stood open. Paint buckets and a radio blaring hard rock sat on a drop cloth in the entry. She crunched across rolls of butcher paper covering her floor, dodging around one painter on a ladder and another kneeling in the hall trimming the baseboards. She shoved her suitcase under her bed and turned on her answering machine. Her attorney, Gloria Haskins, wanted her to call.

Lani's Corolla stood in the carport coated with two weeks of dust. She ran the windshield washers long enough to give her a clear view of the road and headed for Maggie's Diner. Her stomach told her lunch was overdue.

She called Gloria Haskins from the restaurant. Haskins said, "I've been trying to locate you. SciPac came through with a date for the hearing. They agreed to put three from our list of scientists on the committee. But it's still weighted the other way."

"Has the PI been working on this?"

"She's been digging. I think we're on the trail of the smoking gun. Do you have your scientific case ready to go?"

"I finished writing it in Hawaii. It's still in draft form, but I can do the final edit tonight."

"We'll put it into presentation folders for you and make up copies for the committee. When can you come to my office for a couple hours of rehearsal?"

"Tomorrow?"

"Booked all day. How about ten-thirty day after tomorrow? We can go till twelve, then wrap it up over lunch."

"I'll be there."

"Good. We'll have one more session with the PI the day before your meeting. That should get you primed and ready to go."

~ ~

Lani timed her arrival at SciPac so she would not be even a minute early to her meeting with Purvis's hand-picked academic committee. She wheeled a backpack to the end of the long conference table, pulled out thirteen inch-thick presentation binders in blue covers, and stacked them next to her place. From her briefcase she drew a file folder and set it in front of her. She sat looking at twelve unfriendly faces.

The closed hearing was chaired by her former boss, Margaret Bradshaw, at the opposite end of the table. She wore a gold monogrammed M in the lapel of her gray business suit.

Margaret said, "The volcano's been stone dead for nearly a month. I can't understand why you've chosen to come back and try to convince us that your work and your behavior have been anything but irresponsible. You failed to appear before this committee earlier. The only reason we're giving you this second chance is because our legal department has advised us to do so."

Lani's eyes darkened, but she held her anger in check. "This volcano is not stone dead. The seismometer recently installed on the Murray shows seismic activity continuing at a low but persistent level."

Margaret's knuckles whitened as she gripped the arms of her chair. Her sapphire ring caught the light. "What's this nonsense about seismic activity?"

"It isn't nonsense," said a white-haired man in his fifties, one of the well-tenured professors in the seismology department. "Our deep tracking gear started picking it up a few days ago. I notified you by e-mail."

Margaret stared. "My secretary dropped the ball again—she's supposed to flag me."

Lani said, "Even though eruptions have vanished and seismic activity has dwindled to a trace, I stand by my work. I believe it accurately represents the geophysical situation at Seamount Gilman, whether the mountain eventually goes dormant or reactivates."

The white-haired professor looked at Lani. "Dr. Sanches, in our opinion these new seismic readings represent the volcano's last flicker of life and don't materially change the situation. Most of us here simply do not agree with your findings."

Lani held up one of the blue-bound reports. "My findings are here. All the readings from every instrument, minute-by-minute, plus all my computations, all my conclusions. I'm ready to present, discuss, debate. However you want to handle this, I'm ready."

The same man, Dr. Jeremy Dunston, said, "Even if you convince us there was some logic to what you were trying to do, that still doesn't excuse you for sending your theories to the press without permission."

"I didn't."

There was silence. "What do you mean, you didn't?"

"Just that. I did not release the information to the *Times* or anyone else. I promised Dr. Purvis I wouldn't, and I didn't."

The woman seated next to Dunston, a research fellow in geology, rested a forefinger on a stapled memo in front of her. "This is a copy of an e-mail from you to Porter Sinclair at the *Times*."

"It's a copy of a memo I wrote to Dr. Sylvester Purvis, not to Porter Sinclair."

"Then how did Sinclair's name get on it?" asked Dunston.

"Ask Dr. Bradshaw," said Lani. "She's the one who told me Dr. Purvis wanted a full written report. She told me to leave it on her desk. I did."

Everyone looked at Margaret. She laughed. "Oldest trick in the book. If you're guilty and there's no other way to wiggle out, try to pin it on someone else."

Dunston focused his gaze on Lani. "If it comes to your word against Dr. Bradshaw's, I'm afraid you'll lose."

"It's more than my word against hers. I have a file assembled by Universal Investigation Service."

Dunston leaned forward. "You hired a private detective?"

Lani nodded. "My law firm tells me Universal's one of the best in the field. Considered extremely reliable, and used by the biggest corporations."

The geologist tapped his pencil. "We're trying to keep this a dignified hearing. When you bring in lawyers and a detective agency, this could turn into a circus. Drag the school through the mud."

"SciPac has dragged my name through the mud. I have every reason to turn the tables and do a little dragging of my own, but that's not what I'm here for. I'm here to set the record straight. My work has been based on scientific method. I'm ready for a full discussion on that. And I did not release the memo." She tapped the file folder in front of her. "I have documented proof."

There was a buzz of conversation around the table. Margaret Bradshaw rapped the side of her water glass with a pen to get attention. "Speaking as committee chair, it's not a good idea to allow a questionable, outside report into our deliberations. This is an academic disciplinary hearing, and I don't think things like that should be considered."

"Disagree," came one comment.

"Why not?" came another.

"I think we should be able to see what she has," said still another.

Margaret's face flushed, but her voice was steady. "Let's be sensible. If we let that report in, this hearing will turn into a farce, and we just can't let that happen. The chair rules any such information is not admissible in this hearing."

There was a clamor around the table, and Jeremy Dunston said, "Margaret, I don't think you have the right to make such a ruling. It's pretty obvious the committee wants to hear whatever Lani has to say and see whatever she brings in here in her own defense. I move that she be permitted to do so."

Several people could be heard yelling, "Second the motion," and there were ayes and yesses.

The color in Margaret Bradshaw's face deepened. She started

to speak, but clamped her mouth shut.

The research geologist said, "Okay, Lani. Let's see whatever it is you have."

"Before I pass around copies of the investigator's report, let me tell you what they found. On top, there's a copy of the memo as it was originally written, addressed to Dr. Purvis. The date and time, eleven forty-three a.m., as shown on the file on my hard drive, is noted. Next is the same memo, with Dr. Purvis's name removed and Porter Sinclair's name substituted. I assume whoever made the change scanned my memo, changed the addressee, underlined my name as the sender, and e-mailed it to the *Times*."

"How do you know that for sure?" asked Dunston.

"The e-mail log at the *Times* shows it was received at fourteen forty-eight the same day, a little over three hours after I finished writing it and two and a half hours after I dropped it on Margaret's desk."

Dunston's pencil pointed at her. "You could have done that yourself to make it look like someone else did it."

"The university's main server keeps a record of all e-mail transmissions. This one was sent from Margaret Bradshaw's computer to the *L.A. Times* at fourteen forty-six."

"You could have sneaked into Margaret's office when she wasn't there."

"She was there at the time it was sent."

"How do you know that?" asked Dunston.

"There was a witness. The witness was interviewed by the investigator. The witness's statement is included in the file."

Margaret Bradshaw rose from her chair. "This has gone far enough. Everyone knows this woman is lying to save her own skin. I don't see any point in listening to any more of her fairy tales. I'm closing this meeting." She slapped her briefcase down on the table. "This meeting is adjourned."

No one moved. Finally Dunston said quietly, "I don't think you can do that, Margaret. I believe Roberts Rules say adjournment takes a motion, a second, and a vote."

Margaret remained standing. "Okay then, the chair moves to adjourn. Do I hear a second?"

Silence. Margaret picked up her briefcase. "I, for one, refuse to sit around here and listen to these lies. I know if Dr. Purvis were here, he'd feel exactly the same. I'm leaving, and any of you who value your relationship with the president of the university would do well to leave with me." She walked to the door. A few others got up and started gathering their things.

Lani was momentarily thrown off balance by the sudden turn of events. She rose, drew a deep breath, and with all her strength, belted out, "Hold it right there, Margaret!" If she'd been onstage, her words would have carried to the last row in the balcony.

Margaret stopped before she reached the door. She turned to face Lani. Everyone else froze in place.

Lani said, "Whatever your relationship with Sylvester Purvis might be, he will do nothing to protect you when the truth comes out. He won't jeopardize his own reputation and that of the university."

Lani looked at the others. "I don't want to have to take this to court to get justice, but if I have to, I will. I'll not only sue the university and Sylvester Purvis and Margaret Bradshaw for damages, but I will file suit against each and every one of you in this room today as accessories, and for conspiracy to deprive me of my rights under the academic charter. I've retained a damn good law firm and I have a very complete private investigator's report which proves I was purposely defamed and slandered by this institution. Make no mistake. I *will* clear my name and I *will* get my job back. It's up to you. Either you give me a fair hearing right here and now, or be prepared for one very loud and messy lawsuit spread all over every paper and every TV station in town."

There was silence again as the two women glared at each other from opposite ends of the room. Jeremy Dunston finally cleared his throat and looked at Margaret. "It seems to me that threats from both sides should be ignored, and we should continue to hear Lani's side of the story. Our duty as an academic committee is to conduct an unbiased hearing."

Margaret remained by the door, watching the others gradually take their seats. She said, "You're all being taken in by a very clever manipulator. Her claims are so transparent, they're laughable. I'd say those who can see through them have futures at SciPac. But those who can't…" She waited, shrugged, and left the room.

There were calls for Dunston to take the chair in Margaret's place. He looked at Lani. "Okay, Lani. You may continue."

"The witness is Margaret's secretary. She told the investigator she remembers my coming in around twelve-twenty on that day after Margaret had left. She remembers that I tried to hand her a report, but she was getting ready to go to lunch and told me to just leave it on Margaret's desk. She saw me go in and put the report there. She got back at one-fifteen, and Margaret a half hour later, around a quarter to two."

Dunston asked, "And then?"

"She says Margaret called her into her office to pick up a batch of papers for distribution. While she was there, she saw Margaret take the item I'd left on her desk and put it in her scanner. It stuck in her memory because my report had been printed out on a buff paper stock, which was quite distinctive."

"Does she remember what time that was?"

"Around two-fifteen. The e-mail was sent to the *Times* at two forty-six, about a half hour later."

Dunston wagged his head back and forth. "Hmmm. I don't blame you for trying your best to build a case, but so far it's all circumstantial. No one actually saw her send that e-mail. She could have been scanning something else on buff stock. I can see how you're trying to tie it all together, but I'm not sure it's proof enough."

"There's one other item," said Lani. "Private investigators aren't bound by the same rules as the police. They occasionally have to do things people aren't supposed to do in order to find what they want."

The geologist said, "If your private eye got something through illegal means, I'm not sure we should consider it. But what did he get?"

"It's a she and she's an expert computer hacker. She hacked into Margaret's computer and printed out the complete list of files on her hard drive. I've highlighted one file on that list. It's the same date and time she was seen scanning the buff pages, and carries the same file name as my original. She didn't bother to change it. SMGREP4SP, which is my shorthand for *Seamount Gilman report for Sylvester Purvis*."

There was another buzz around the table. Lani drew a sheaf of stapled three-page copies of the private investigator's file out of the file folder and passed them around. She waited while everyone read it.

After a few minutes, Dunston said, "Margaret's not here to explain her side of it, so the committee will have to reconvene when she's available. But while we have you here, let's get to the other part of our hearing, which is whether you used accepted scientific method in reaching your conclusions on the condition of Seamount Gilman."

Lani distributed the thick blue folders and began taking the committee through the report page by page. Lani's presentation and the questions it stimulated lasted for more than two hours. At the two hour and eleven minute mark, she finished giving a long answer to a complex question and waited. There was some side conversation and rustling of papers but no more questions.

Dunston made a brief note and put down his pencil. "I'd like to thank Lani for her presentation. I think she surprised us by wandering off the well-worn path a few times." He waited for the laughter to die down and continued. "But that's the way progress is made in science. To look at data in a new way. To challenge the old theories and make us traditionalists defend ourselves. I personally don't think there is anything irresponsible or shoot-from-the-hip in Lani's work. I see it as well documented and well thought through. But each member of this committee must make his or her own decision on this, as well as on the matter of who released the memo to the press."

Lani said, "Thank you all for hearing me out. I am asking for two things. I want my job back. And I want the university to hold a press conference announcing my reinstatement, clearing me of any wrongdoing, and saying that my work meets scientific standards."

"Duly noted, and we'll take all of that under advisement," said Dunston. "The committee will ask Margaret Bradshaw to return later today so we can hear her side of things. Then we'll go into executive session to make our decision and deliver our recommendations to Dr. Purvis."

"When will I hear?"

"Dr. Purvis will contact you after he's made his decision."

~~

Hacker's laugh was ugly. "Nothing to be afraid of, Harley."

Ho Kai Fat stood in front of Wamp's desk, hand outstretched. Wamp rolled his chair away from the desk. "No."

Hacker laughed again. "Go ahead. We're just saying you did a good job getting phase two open on time. It's like a pat on the back. I told him easy and friendly. He won't hurt you this time."

Wamp had a sick smile on his face. He stuck out a tentative hand. Mr. Fat grabbed it and clamped down hard and fast, like a crocodile's jaws snapping shut. He kept squeezing. Wamp bared his teeth, gulping air and snorting. He tried to twist his body away from the pain, and tears came to his eyes. Hacker tapped Ho Kai Fat's arm, signaling for him to stop.

Wamp sat in his chair, head bowed, rubbing his hand. "What was that for? I thought you said I was doing a good job."

"You do okay when I'm on your back. Getting phase two

open just shows what can be done when you kick enough ass. But you needed a little reminder about what happens if you start slacking off, so just make damn sure you keep selling houses. We got a lot of fucking bills to pay, so you gotta keep goosing the cash flow."

Wamp planted his feet on the carpet and rolled his chair back to the desk. "You're not going to like what I have to say, but it won't do any good to mangle my hand again. That won't help the situation."

"What situation?"

"Just before you came in, I got a call from Sylvester Purvis at SciPac. Little Miss Leilani's back. Ready for a fight. She's got herself a lawyer and a private eye. She's threatening to sue their ass off if they don't reinstate her and hold a press conference saying her science was legitimate. I yelled at him and said we'd cut off support and wreck the goddamn school if he did that. Didn't faze him. He says he has no choice because she has him by the balls."

"He's going to do it?"

Wamp nodded. "He'll say her theory holds water. That'll hurt sales, even if the volcano's dead. Eventually people'll forget about it and sales'll come back, but it'll put a chill on cash flow for a month or two."

Hacker grinned. "You're not thinking, Harley. There doesn't even have to be a goddamn press conference."

"What do you mean?"

"If she disappears before they call it, then they don't have to have one, do they?"

"Listen, George, if disappears means murder, then count me out. That's a line I don't cross."

"Yeah, well, that's why you're the flunky and I'm the boss. You haven't learned that you gotta do what you gotta do, or you end up at the bottom of the shit hole."

"I can't go along."

Hacker watched him, his small gray eyes bemused. "You don't

get a vote, my friend. You're in it up to your ass, whether you like it or not. You'll fucking well do what you're told. And the first thing I'm telling you to do is get a picture of Leilani for Mr. Fat."

Wamp buzzed his secretary and told her to bring in the press clipping file. He pulled out the *L.A. Times* follow-up story and laid it out on the desk. "This is the only picture I have."

"How tall and how much does she weigh?"

"Never met her. I've heard she's a small woman."

Hacker looked at Ho Kai Fat and handed over the clipping. "Give her the same treatment we gave the distributor."

"What was that?" asked Wamp.

Hacker brought his hand down in a vicious chop. "Mr. Fat broke this guy's neck nice and clean, and threw the fucker in a blast furnace."

"Jesus!" Wamp's voice quavered.

"Mr. Fat'll be waiting for her sometime and that'll be that. No Leilani. No press conference. No problem. You can just keep right on selling houses and putting money in the bank."

"I still don't like it."

"You don't have to. But if you don't keep your mouth shut now and forever, you'll end up the same way. Is the picture clear?"

"Very clear."

~ ~

Dave, sunburned and windburned from two weeks of sea duty, still didn't have his land legs as he walked off the pier and over to Coast Guard headquarters. He asked Cynthia, Admiral Carson's secretary, if the boss was in. She nodded and tilted her head toward the admiral's door. He knocked and stuck his head in. "Thought I'd report in before going home for the day."

Carson pointed to a chair. "I saw *Farallon* dock awhile back. Thought you'd probably drop by. How did you leave things with the Russians?"

"They were a good fifty miles inside the EEZ line. With GPS, there's not much to argue about. We escorted them outside the zone and left the *Point Buchon* there on station for a few days—make sure they don't come back in."

"Anything else to report?"

"We followed a Blue Star freighter into port. Looked like they were piling junk on the fantail. The *Nanjing Star*. I'll call the harbormaster and find out where she's docked."

"Did it look like a violation?"

Dave nodded. "Might be a fire hazard. I'll pick up Jiro Yamaguchi tomorrow and we'll go take a look. Might be an excuse to board and inspect."

Admiral Carson said, "Okay, but watch your step. The last time you two boarded a Blue Star you both ended up in the drink."

Dave smiled. "I hope they're not dumb enough to try the same trick twice. Don't worry. We'll be careful."

The admiral glanced at a row of brass-clad dials on his wall, showing temperature, atmospheric pressure, wind velocity, humidity, and naval observatory time. "Four thirty-six. Day's almost gone. Take what's left of it off and get some rest."

"Thank you, sir. I'll report tomorrow morning after we inspect *Nanjing Star*."

Admiral Carson smiled. "Lani Sanches is back in town. Wants to talk to you."

Dave was surprised by his rush of relief and elation. He'd realized during the long hours on patrol that he still loved Lani deeply, but doubted he would ever see her again. He'd resolved to concentrate on his work and try to put her behind him. "Where can I reach her?"

"She called and told me she was coming back to get her name cleared. Asked for you. I passed the message to Yeoman Gates. When you leave, ask Cynthia for the number."

Dave tried not to show how anxious he was to make the call. "So she's fighting to get her job back?"

"Doing a damn good job of it. I wasn't in when she called

after the meeting. She told Yeoman Gates things went well, and chances are good she'll be reinstated and get an apology from the school. She's waiting to hear officially. Now get out of here and make that call."

Dave snapped a quick salute and went to Cynthia Gates's desk. "Your boss says Lani Sanches left a phone number for me."

Cynthia looked stricken. "She did. But I can't give it to you."

Dave said, "I don't understand. Why not?"

"When she called the second time…"

"I know—about her meeting—the admiral told me."

"That wasn't the main reason she called—it was to ask me to tell you specifically *not* to call. She said she doesn't want to see or hear from you under any circumstances. Period. Her words."

Dave's heart plunged. "Did she say why?"

Cynthia's eyes were sympathetic. "She sounded angry—upset. That's all I know."

Why had she jerked him around like that? He felt cheated, annoyed, and determined. "I'll call her anyhow. Have to find out what's going on."

"Sorry, Commander."

"Don't worry about it, Cynthia. When the news is bad, it's no fun being the messenger." Before he turned to leave, Cynthia whispered, "Good luck, sir."

~ ~

Dave opened the blinds and let the late afternoon light flood his apartment. He got a beer out of the refrigerator and flicked on his answering machine. Andrea's message was the fourth of seven. He felt acute discomfort as he listened to her voice.

His gut reaction was the truth teller: Andrea was not for him. He hadn't missed her when he was on patrol. He hadn't even thought about her much. The few times he did, the thoughts stirred no emotions, positive or negative. He didn't look forward with any great pleasure or anticipation to being with her. It all added up to one conclusion. He didn't love her.

He'd have to level with her. It would be a painful call, but he had to make it. *I'll call tonight around nine, after she gets Alex to bed.*

The big thing right now was to find out what was happening with Lani. He didn't have her new home number. When he'd tried to reach her cell phone in Hawaii there'd been no answer. She always had the cell with her, so either she'd chosen not to answer or had changed over to a Hawaii area code. Nothing to lose. He called the old cell phone number. To his surprise, she picked up on the second ring.

Dave said, "I just got back. I hear you're giving them hell over at SciPac."

"So far so good," she said. "I have to go over tomorrow morning for a meeting with Sylvester Purvis. He's to tell me the decision of the committee."

"Admiral Carson said you wanted me to call, then Yeoman Gates said not to call. Confusion reigns. What's going on?"

Lani sounded emphatic. "Yeoman Gates had it right. I did not want you to call."

"Can we talk about it? I'd really like to see you. I can be there in an hour."

"Not a good idea, Dave. I'm in the middle of this fight for my life. You have your own plans and your own life to live. I think we should leave it at that."

"I've had hopes we'd somehow be able to see each other again. Can't we at least have lunch or a cup of coffee?"

She drew in a shaken breath. "No, I just think it's better if we don't."

"Lani, you sound so, well, cold and formal. I don't under—"

Her words were controlled, but the underlying anger was unmistakable. "Oh, I think you understand very well."

Dave felt adrift. "I do?"

Her anger flared. "Don't play dumb with me! I heard that woman's message."

"Jesus. How did you…"

"You damn dummy! I came back to see if you're still interested. I had the key to your apartment. I was going to wait for you."

"But Lani, I don't love her. I love you. Let me expl—"

"Explain what? How you lead women on and then throw them in the dumpster? You know what you are? An oversexed, despicable, rotten bastard who'll do anything, promise anything to get a woman in bed, and never give a damn how much it hurts. I'm glad I found out the truth when I did. Now you and that adolescent gland of yours can go straight to hell!"

Dave listened to the dial tone for a few moments and finally jammed down on the Off button. He had to straighten this out. Let her know he loved her. Make her understand Andrea was a rebound impulse—a mistake. He hit Redial. Busy signal. *Damn it to hell!* She'd probably taken her phone off the hook.

He juggled the handset in the flat of his hand and had a sudden impulse to throw it through the window, but took a deep breath and slowly reseated it on the base unit.

Had he been that much of a jerk? Had Lani given him any signal that she'd changed her mind? No. She was totally unreasonable, and somehow he'd have to get past her hurt feelings and pride and get her to listen. But how? Drive to Altadena and hope she'd let him in? Write a letter? Send flowers? Whatever he did, he'd have to do it right.

Okay. But first he had to check out the *Nanjing Star* violation. He called Jiro and told him about the pile of junk on the *Nanjing Star*'s fantail. "It's our chance to inspect every inch of a Blue Star ship. We have to do it early tomorrow morning before they clean up the mess, and before they start unloading cargo."

"How early?"

"I'm going over to headquarters now to pick up a Coast Guard vehicle and some other equipment. I'll sack out for a few hours on the cot in my office. Meet me there at 2:00 A.M. I'll leave your name with the guard."

He soaked in a long, hot shower and then put on his winter blues. He grabbed his keys and went out the door.

~~

Lani wiped her eyes and blew her nose. Her anger had finally given way to an enormous sense of loss—she'd just cut the person she loved out of her life. For now, she would focus on getting her job back and clearing her name. She'd concentrate on that, and nothing else. She began reading over the list her attorney had given her of the subjects most likely to come up at tomorrow's meeting with Purvis. The outcome would not be negotiable. She would settle for nothing less than full reinstatement and a public apology.

An hour later, she realized the words on the page were not making sense. She couldn't concentrate. Her thoughts kept drifting to Dave. Anger and hurt peaked and ebbed. During her calmer moments, she wondered, had she been too harsh? Too quick to condemn? He'd said he loved her. Should she have listened? Her friend Gilda told her to hear him out, but when the crucial moment came she'd given him a tongue lashing instead. He deserved it, but was it the right thing?

How much of this was her own fault? In Hawaii she'd finally realized how much she loved the guy, but had been afraid to tell him. Now he was involved with another woman. She'd lost him, and there was nothing she could do about it. *I just have to move on.* She let out a long breath and started again at the top of the page. Halfway through item number one she stopped.

She closed her eyes and tried to clear the static from her thinking and place herself in an open frame of mind. She'd blamed Dave for everything, but was it totally his fault? She'd never told him she loved him, in so many words. It had been such a struggle to reach the point where she could say it. When he'd wanted to stay in touch, she'd said no, it was over. When he tried, she wouldn't take his call. But to suddenly find out he'd chosen someone else so quickly was too cruel a blow. As Gilda said, it broke her heart. She was still furious at him for not waiting longer. For being so fickle. She'd made the right decision. Let him go.

She wandered around the living room of her small apartment. Hurt feelings and wounded pride kept clouding the issue. She continued pacing, then suddenly stopped. Wait a minute. Why was she giving up so easily?

What did she really want? To pretend that Dave didn't matter and swear off men again? Retreat to living alone? Or should she admit that being with Dave was the thing she craved beyond measure? She'd accused him of giving up too easily, and now she was doing the same thing. Quitting at the first sign of a problem.

If he really was in love with her, shouldn't she give him a chance to prove it? And shouldn't she really be going all out to get him back? She was fighting to get her job back and clear her name because that's what she wanted and deserved. *I should be fighting for Dave as hard as I'm fighting for my job.*

She was startled by the ring of her phone. The little window on the handset said Admiral Carson. She thumbed the Talk button. "Admiral?"

"No, this is Yeoman Gates calling for the admiral. The inundation maps you requested came in from U.S. Geological Survey. I can fax them to you in black and white, or e-mail in color."

"E-mail, please. Color is better for my purposes."

"One map shows computer-simulated flood areas for a hundred-and-fifty-foot wave, the second for a two-hundred-foot wave. Is that correct?"

"Yes, that's what I asked for. How do they look?"

"Scary."

"Perfect. They'll help me illustrate a point in my meeting with Dr. Purvis at SciPac tomorrow."

"Good luck on that, Dr. Sanches."

"Please call me Lani."

"Okay, Lani. I'm Cynthia. I gave your message to Commander Steel."

"I'm sorry I saddled you with that. Was it unpleasant?"

"For him, yes—judging from the look on his face."

"What do you mean?"

"He was devastated when I told him you didn't want to see him anymore. His face, his shoulders—fell like a punctured sponge cake. Only for a second. Then he straightened up and you couldn't tell. But I saw how hard it hit him."

Another pause while Lani let things sink in. "Then he really does…"

"Care for you? Couldn't be more obvious."

Lani clicked off, but Cynthia's call had tipped the scale—and then some. She keyed in Dave's number, and felt deflated and a little desperate when his answering machine came on. Was he with that other woman? A stab of jealousy slowed her, but it didn't stop her. She left her message: "Dave, I love you. Please call right away. We have a lot to talk about."

~ ~

Riviera Beach was one of those small Southern California beach towns that had its heyday in the 1920s, slumped during the Depression and World War II, then gradually built back up and became fashionable again. The streets were narrow, the low-rise architecture stucco and red tile roofs. The Riviera Beach Emergency Response Office was a volunteer operation. Gladys Miller, sales manager for the local radio station, had been made director of the ERO after years of going to meetings and spending her evenings teaching CPR and earthquake safety.

A few days after the volcano had been declared officially dead and the tsunami scare over, Mayor Max Hausman handed Gladys a tsunami evacuation plan from the U.S. Coast Guard. She threw it on her desk when she got home and carried a drink out to her beachfront balcony. She sat in the fading light, sipping and watching the waves crash on the sand. The surf was high. Her eyes drifted out a few hundred yards where the big breakers were forming and fastened on one wave line starting to build. She watched it grow as it rolled toward shore, swell to a six-foot crest, curl, and smash down on the beach with a heavy *thud*, followed by a booming echo.

She had always lived near the ocean and knew its power. She'd been caught in a riptide once and remembered how helpless she'd been. And lucky. A lifeguard had rescued her. She wondered if a volcano in some faraway place could really start a tidal wave big enough to hit her beach. An earthquake had started the Indian Ocean tsunami in back in '04. She remembered watching the destruction on TV. She closed her eyes and tried to imagine a hundred-foot wave rolling across the sand. The imaginary onrushing wall of water towered high over her three-story building, on the verge of smashing into it and sweeping her away. She gasped and opened her eyes.

Gladys went back to her desk and started reading the plan. She made notes. The next morning, she called the Coast Guard office in San Pedro with a list of questions. She spoke to Commander Dave Steel, who told her the warning system would give her only two hours to evacuate the entire population, and urged her to get her community ready to activate the plan at a moment's notice.

She took her proposal to the mayor. He wasn't enthusiastic, but he said she could put on her rehearsal when he was attending the mayors' conference. She persuaded Police Chief Oliver Rendell and Fire Chief Milford Van Dam to cooperate. They staged a dry run, using police and firefighters to supervise volunteers from other city departments and local civic groups. Every street and every block near the beach was patrolled by a person wearing a blue armband, ready to execute traffic and crowd control.

Ho Kai Fat waited in the shadows a few feet from Lani's door. In black pants and shirt, black shoes, and black watch cap, he blended perfectly into the shadow cast by the juniper hedge from the pale light of the corner street lamp.

It was 5:25 a.m. Fat's men had reported that she left her apartment at 5:30 every morning for a forty-five-minute run. When she came out, she always paused to check the handle to make sure she'd locked the door. Except for the streetlight, it was pitch dark and the streets were deserted.

When she stopped to check the door, it would take Fat less than two seconds to step from the shadows and deliver the lightning-fast downward chop that would break her neck. He had a throw rug to wrap the body in. He would put it in the car trunk and she would be on the way to the annealing furnace less than three minutes after she stepped out the door. No trace of her would ever be found. Her disappearance would always remain a mystery.

Lights came on inside. A few more minutes and the job would be done. He checked his watch. One minute to go. He waited. He heard a click and saw the doorknob turn. The door started to swing open. He rose onto the balls of his feet, raised his arm, stiffened the huge, hard-edged hand.

The telephone rang inside the apartment. The door closed. He relaxed his stance. His window of opportunity—the total darkness and quiet streets—would hold for another fifteen minutes. Maybe a wrong number and she would be right back out.

The fifteen minutes passed. He gave it another five. She still didn't come out. The first faint glow edged up the eastern horizon. It was necessary to leave. A seven-foot foreigner dressed in black would be sure to cause comment. He would come again the next day.

Lani hoped it was Dave when the phone rang. But the caller

was Sylvester Purvis.

"I apologize for calling so early, but something's happening with the volcano."

She caught her breath. "Gilman's come back?"

"I don't know how serious it is, but I wanted to find out if you'd be interested in going over to the lab and taking a look."

Lani took off her headband. "But I'm on administrative leave."

"I've been going over the committee's report. You and I were scheduled to meet about that later today."

"Yes, to hear your decision?" She tightened her grip on the phone.

"Lani, the committee accepts your science, and thinks you may not have sent the memo, but you did violate university rules by going over…"

She wanted to throw the phone right in his face. "Then why are you calling me at five-thirty in the morning? Do you want me to go to the lab, or don't you?"

"If we can work something out on a conditional basis."

She tried to keep the irritation out of her voice. "Not interested, Dr. Purvis. Maybe you should send someone else to the lab."

"What if we work out a short conditional period?"

Time to go fo' broke. "You know my bottom line. Full reinstatement or get ready for a lawsuit. And I expect to be in full charge without anyone looking over my shoulder, and that includes Margaret. So, do you want me back, yes or no?"

There was no reply. Had she stepped over the line?

Finally Purvis said, "Yes, we want you back."

Relieved but still cautious, she said, "Does that mean I'm reinstated?"

Another long pause. "Yes."

She pumped a fist. "No interference or second-guessing?"

"I'll reassign Margaret. That puts you in complete charge."

"So things look that bad."

Purvis said, "Get over there and give me a report as soon as you can."

She skipped her shower and scrambled to get her makeup and clothes on. When she jogged out her front door, the sun was coming up behind the Sierra Madres.

She trotted into the SciPac lab about twenty minutes later. A half dozen people clustered around her old work station, watching the monitor.

Gus Belmondo saw her first. "Hey! Look who's back!"

There were smiles and pats on the back as Lani sat down, but she was all business now. "Somebody bring me up to date on the numbers."

She made notes as people threw figures at her, then settled into her chair and studied the readings coming up on the monitor. She clicked from SciPac's own seismograph readings to satellite infrared readings to ocean bottom seismometer readings and magma flow transport readings.

A half hour of studying the numbers made the picture clear. The quakes running in a fifty-mile band along the fault parallel to the seamount chain were increasing in number and size. The focal depths of the shocks were fairly shallow, between five and ten kilometers down. The Richter Scale readings ran between 6.0 and 7.0. If the magnitudes increased and a swarm of quakes above 7.5 swept along the fault line, a number of things would happen.

The shocks could open up massive fissures under the volcano, allowing a flood of magma to surge into the mountain, at the same time opening cracks in the side of the mountain that would let more water seep in, creating a lethal mix. The magma would boil the water and the mountain would become a giant pressure cooker. All it would take would be one big shock directly under the mountain to rupture the bulge, drain the magma, and fill the mountain with high-pressure steam. The pressure would keep building, but it wouldn't have anyplace to go. The mountain would explode.

The phone rang. Purvis asked, "How do things look?"

"Not good."

"Do you think the mountain will blow? If it does, do you still think it'll cause a tsunami?"

"If the quake activity keeps escalating, I'd say there's a high probability of a catastrophic event."

"How catastrophic?"

"I'd get ready for a two-hundred-foot wave."

~~

Low clouds rolling in from Baja mixed with the thick coastal fog and dampened the waterfront in a soupy drizzle. At a little after midnight, Ho Kai Fat and six men came aboard the *Nanjing Star*. They disappeared below, came up thirty minutes later, and sealed the number four hatch with foot-wide duct tape to make it airtight. As the deck crew rigged a tarpaulin over the hatch, Ho Kai Fat signaled to the captain, then led his men off the ship.

Three hours later, Dave, a sleepy-eyed Jiro beside him, drove a Coast Guard Cherokee onto the pier alongside the ship.

"Don't know if we can see anything in this muck, but here goes." Dave aimed a spotlight into the fog and could make out the jumble of flammable junk on the ship's stern. "There it is—our reason to board and search."

"Yeah, but at three in the morning? I'm seriously sleep deprived."

"Have to do it before they unload," said Dave. He stepped out of the Cherokee with his bullhorn, wearing a blue pullover sweater with three-stripe shoulder boards and a blue garrison cap with the Coast Guard badge and commander's silver leaf on the front. He aimed the bullhorn at a seaman standing watch at the head of the gangway. "Ahoy, *Nanjing Star*. Inform the captain the U.S. Coast Guard is coming aboard."

He stowed the bullhorn and adjusted his gun belt. They made their way up the gangway to the main deck. The man on watch said, "Captain's coming. He was asleep."

After a few minutes, a tall man with a long face and a brown hairpiece that didn't match his sideburns came to meet them. "I'm Captain Reedy. What can I do for you gentlemen?" His accent was probably Australian.

"The debris on the stern is a fire hazard," said Dave. "That makes this vessel unsafe. We'll have to conduct a full ship inspection."

"I'm sorry, Commander. The garbage hauler was late. That stuff'll be gone later today—no need to inspect. Besides, can't it wait till daylight?"

Dave shook his head. "You're scheduled to unload at seven, and we have to inspect while your cargo's intact. Please turn on all ship's lights above and below decks. The pier loading lights will be coming on in less than a minute."

"Isn't there some other way we can do this?"

"Those are the rules, Captain." Powerful lights from poles on the pier suddenly bathed the ship. "Agent Yamaguchi will take pictures of the violation, then we'll inspect the rest of the main deck. After that, superstructure and bridge, living quarters, and storage areas. Then we'll check out the engine room and the holds. Be sure that junk on the fantail is cleaned up by the time we get back here to the main deck."

"Sure, I'll take care of it, Commander. You have the run of the ship."

Dave had expected more excuses, more attempts to dissuade. "Why don't you stay with us, Captain, in case we have to get into a locked area or something?"

Captain Reedy nodded. They walked to the stern. Jiro pulled a digital Pentax out of his windbreaker pocket and snapped pictures from different angles.

Dave studied the pile of junk. It was a curious assortment. Cardboard boxes, provision crates, bags of waste paper, old clothes, all getting soggy in the drizzle. He said to Captain Reedy, "This is not typical Blue Star. You guys are usually shipshape."

"Had some roaches below, so we decided to clean out the ship. We expected the rubbish haulers to meet us when we docked. Turns out they can't be here till later, but we'll move the stuff onto the dock till they get here."

"Better get that approved by the harbormaster," said Dave.

Jiro finished taking his shots, and the three of them began walking slowly toward the bow. Dave had the captain open storage lockers and take the covers off the lifeboats. He shone his flashlight into every hidden corner on deck and probed with a walking stick the spaces he couldn't see.

When they reached the bow, Dave scanned the main deck back to the stern. Something was out of balance. After another moment of studying the deck, he said, "The hatch cover on hold four is the only one with a tarp over it. How come?"

"That'll come off before we unload," said Reedy.

Dave headed for the stern. "Let's take a look."

The captain ordered the tarp removed. Four crewmen untied the ropes and pulled back the heavy canvas.

Dave knelt down and poked at the duct tape. "Why is this hatch cover taped down?"

"It's warped, so we tape it when we're underway to keep the cargo dry. The crew will peel it off when we get the ship ready for unloading in a couple of hours."

Dave considered his explanation and nodded. They moved on, touring the bridge, the galley, the dining areas, and the living quarters. The captain asked if they'd like to take a break for a cup of coffee.

Dave said, "Don't mind a break, but we'll skip the coffee." They sat on a dining table bench near the galley.

"Are we getting a passing grade?" asked the captain.

Dave studied Reedy. "That's what puzzles me. Everything so far has been shipshape. Piling all that flammable junk on the stern doesn't make sense, Captain."

Reedy laughed. "Yes, very embarrassing. We were just trying

to get rid of the stuff, but our timing…" His beeper sounded, and he checked the window. "First mate wants to see me. Be right back."

Dave said, "Bring the ship's papers. I want to see the manifest."

When Reedy was out of sight, Jiro said, "I don't get it. It's like they were inviting an inspection. He said they have cockroaches, but I didn't even see a trace."

"Yeah, he's trying to convince us they're just trying to keep the ship clean. Maybe, maybe not."

"I vote for maybe not."

"I don't think the condition of the upper decks means anything, anyway. What we're looking for is probably in one of the holds. That's where we'll take our time and really check things out."

Jiro's fingers tapped out a rhythm on the mess table. "The holds'll probably look okay too. The whole thing could be for show. Like Blue Star's trying to convince us they're not really running guns."

"You might be right, but let's give it a try. Maybe we'll get lucky."

When the captain came back with the ship's papers, Dave looked at the manifest. "I see you've got bagged agricultural fertilizer in holds one, two, and three, and liquid pesticide in drums in number four. Is that right?"

"Correct," said Reedy. "Where do you want to start?"

Dave said, "We'll work from number one back to the stern. We'll do number four last." They spent more than two hours inspecting the first three holds. By 6:00 a.m., they stood in front of the lower deck bulkhead door leading to hold number four.

The captain's beeper sounded. He checked the window. "First mate again. Go ahead and start your inspection. I'll be back in a few minutes." He started to leave.

Dave stuck a hand out. "Hold it. Let me take one more look

at the manifest. I want to see exactly what kind of pesticide you have in this hold."

Reedy handed over the manifest. "Parathion Z for crop-dusting."

Dave nodded. "Says here the stuff comes in twenty-deciliter drums. How many to a pallet?"

"Eighteen. Three by three, stacked two high." Reedy began spinning the dogging wheel to open the bulkhead door. "Go on in. I'll be back in ten minutes."

Dave took a step toward the door and slipped. He steadied himself. "How come the deck's wet down here?"

Reedy took his hand off the dogging wheel. "Drizzle," said Reedy, pointing upward. "Crew tracks it in from the main deck."

Dave's forehead wrinkled. "The entrances to the other holds are dry. This one's got damp footprints all over. How come?"

"Someone probably came down to oil the dogging wheel."

Jiro nudged Dave and pointed at the deck. Both men saw a clear imprint of a wet, twenty-inch shoe.

Dave ran his fingers along his gun belt, over to the butt of his 9 mm Beretta. "You'd better stay with us, Captain."

Alarm showed on Reedy's face for a millisecond, then disappeared. "If you want to start without me, I'll come back and join you in less than five minutes. Just let me get this door open." He started spinning the wheel counterclockwise again.

Dave grabbed Reedy's wrist and slowly disengaged his hand from the wheel. "We'll do this hold exactly like the others. The three of us together, in case we have questions." He stared at the captain.

A suddenly flustered Reedy said, "Now really, gentlemen, there's no need to delay…"

Dave spun the dogging wheel till the door to the hold cracked open. He extended his hand toward the opening. "After you, Captain."

Reedy glared at Dave in silence, eyes wide.

Dave grabbed Reedy's lapels and backed him against the gray

steel bulkhead. "Your choice, Captain. We can throw you in this hold and lock the door…"

The color drained from Reedy's face. "No! You can't…"

Jiro pulled his Glock and leveled it. "Yes we can!"

Dave shoved Reedy toward the door. "And we damn well will."

The captain held out a hand. "Please, gentlemen."

"Or you can tell us what the hell's going on here, and personally escort us off this ship."

Jiro jammed his gun into Reedy's belly. "Now!"

Reedy didn't hesitate. "I give my word. Let's go topside, and I'll explain." He started up the companionway.

Jiro held the gun on the captain till they got to the top of the companionway, then palmed it. When they stepped onto the main deck, they found their escape route blocked by a dozen and a half thick-necked men with big arms and greasy skin. Behind them stood a mountainous form in black, his long knife at the ready.

The captain said nothing to disperse them, so Jiro poked the Glock into Reedy's back. The captain still didn't speak. The giant in black thrust his long knife straight above his head, then brought it down slowly, inch by inch, until the tip pointed directly at Dave and Jiro. He grunted, "Ha!" The gang moved in.

Jiro swept the pistol from Reedy's back, held it high for all to see, then pressed the barrel against the Captain's temple. "Stop, or I blow the captain's head off!"

Dave held his Beretta in the Weaver stance and aimed at Ho Kai Fat. "Back off or I shoot!"

They hesitated, then came to an uneasy halt, like dogs straining at their leashes. After a long minute, one of the men lurched forward a step, but froze in place when Dave swung his pistol on him.

Jiro shouted, "I pull the trigger on three!" He took a deep breath. "One…"

Dave said, "We mean it, Captain. Call off your goons."

The muscles bulged in Jiro's neck. "Two!"

Reedy swept a hand up. "Make way! Captain's orders! Let us through!"

The men waited till the giant in black lowered his knife, then slowly stepped back to open a path. Jiro kept his Glock against Reedy's head. Dave gripped the back of Jiro's jacket, fanning his pistol in small arcs, and they moved as a tight threesome to the head of the gangway. Dave spun Captain Reedy around and shoved him hard into the wedge closing in behind them. The confusion gave Dave and Jiro time to run halfway down the ramp. They edged backward the rest of the way. Dave fired two quick rounds across the top of the gangway. Heads stayed down.

They scrambled into the Cherokee. Tires smoked as they sped away. Dave made a U-turn at the head of the pier and parked about a quarter mile from the freighter. He shut off the motor. "I want to watch them, and I want them to see us watching."

Jiro finally holstered his pistol. "As long as we're far enough away to get a head start if they come after us. Too many to hold off by ourselves."

Dave tapped numbers on his cell phone. "I'll get an armed party on board to check out that hold, and detain the captain and the big guy for questioning."

"Tell them to move fast, or the hold will be clean and the big guy'll be long gone."

It took Dave five minutes of heated conversation and pulling rank to convince a lieutenant commander that the situation was urgent enough to immediately dispatch a heavily-armed boarding party.

"How long will it take them to get here?" Jiro asked.

"Twenty if we're lucky."

"Hope they're not too late."

"I can't believe we damn near walked into it again."

Jiro nodded. "Real bad shit was waiting for us in that hold."

Dave glanced at his wrist chronometer. "Oh-six-twenty-three.

Hope we can keep them on the ship till backup gets here."

Jiro put his window down. Foggy dampness flooded the car. He ran his window back up. He said, "That agent we planted in Marine Providers warehouse was badly hurt on the job."

"What happened?"

"A couple hundred cases of cooking oil fell over and almost crushed him. He's in intensive care, but the docs think he'll make it. The story is he cut a corner with his forklift and knocked over the stack. I don't believe the story."

"You think they were on to him?"

Jiro nodded. "Looks like there's a leak in our office. We're investigating."

Dave shook his head. "All part of a pattern. The trap they set on the freighter, then this. Courtesy of those wonderful folks in Hong Kong."

After a few moments of silence, Jiro said, "While we're waiting, give me another update on your love life."

Dave grimaced. "Complicated. I talked to Lani last night just before I left. She'd found out about Andrea and read me the riot act. I told her I loved her and Andrea was a mistake, but she hung up on me."

"Wow! You sure know how to keep things from getting dull."

"I already took care of one thing—phoned Andrea from the office and broke it off. Painful, but the right thing to do, whether I get back with Lani or not."

"How'd Andrea take it?"

"Really pissed off. I'm not popular with women these days. She and her son Alex were just leaving to spend a few days with her mother in Anaheim Hills."

"What next?"

Dave studied the *Nanjing Star*. "Get Lani back. I've been trying to decide whether to go to Altadena and park on her doorstep, or send flowers, or make my case by e-mail."

"So which will it be?"

"All of the above. I've composed an e-mail in my head. I'll send it as soon as I get to a computer. Then on my way to Altadena, I'll stop at the florist and pick up a dozen long-stem red roses with a card saying, 'I love you. No one else. Only you.'"

Jiro flashed a thumbs-up. "Good plan, Dave. I approve."

The radio squawked. "Boarding party should be there in three minutes or less." Dave started the engine and shifted into Drive.

Jiro moved his hand to the butt of his Glock. "Ready to rumble."

Dave's cell phone rang. He listened and shoved the gear lever back into Park. He said, "Yes, sir," several times during the call. Finally, "I'll get right on it." He radioed the boarding party to scrub the mission, clicked back into Drive and floored the pedal as he cranked into a U-turn. He screeched out onto the street and goosed the Cherokee up to 70 in a 35-mile zone without saying a word.

Jiro said, "What is it?"

"Admiral Carson's orders. Forget the *Nanjing Star*, cancel the boarding party, and get my ass back to base."

Jiro's eyes widened. "What the hell's going on?"

"Tsunami. Got to activate the emergency evac plan. Now. Then get ready to escort a bunch of ships out to sea."

"You mean…"

The Cherokee swung around an eighteen-wheeler. "That volcano everybody thought was dead just came back to life. It could blow any time. Every second counts."

"An honest-to-God, for-real tsunami," Jiro said, awe in his voice.

"How about a two-hundred-footer."

eleven

Lani stayed at her work station all night, fascinated by the heavy seismic action along the fault line that had started more than twenty-seven hours before. The time display in the corner of her monitor said 06:49. The earthquake swarms had not slacked off. The pressure inside the volcano had continued to climb and was now at its most dangerous point, but for the moment the mountain was still intact. She could feel the fatigue of her all-night vigil. She needed to stretch out on the cot in the women's lounge and sleep for an hour or two.

She got up, legs aching. Gus yelled, "Whoa!" She looked back at her monitor, and her heart started racing. The seismometer reading had spiked up to 8.0. She checked her other readings. The shock was shallow, and close to the mountain.

Gus said, "Is this it?"

She slid back into her chair. "Let's check... epicenter right under the Murray fault, four hundred meters from the volcano. Look... crustal stress highest I've ever... oh, oh... stress numbers sinking... fast. Oooh! They're gone!"

"My God! The Murray's collapsed!"

"Massive," Lani said, hanging on to her composure. "One whole side of the fault dropped a hundred meters along a fifty-kilometer line. That could trigger more quakes—start a domino effect."

Gus started whistling something tuneless. "Waiting is the hard part."

"Tell me about it."

Gus said, "Hey! Another big jolt. Nine point one! Right under the mountain!"

Lani checked the time. 06:54. "If it ruptures the bulge…."

Four minutes later—at 06:58:20—all the readings on the screen scrambled. Lani began isolating the gyrating numbers and analyzing their meaning. She looked at Gus. "The mountain just exploded!"

He rolled his chair closer to the screen. "Look at that energy release!"

"Thirteen thousand kilotons—equal to a thousand Hiroshima-size A-bombs." She switched to a satellite view. "Concussion should kick off a big tsunami!"

Gus's feet danced. "Yeehah!" He watched a column of smoke, ash, and chunks of mountain shoot skyward from a boiling sea. "The blast punched that column through a thousand feet of water and straight up to the sky. Debris cloud's rising fast—a mile—mile and a half—topping at three."

Lani couldn't hold her feelings in check. Elation and dread rolled into an overwhelming charge of emotion. "Dear God, there's over a million tons of debris hanging up there. When it slams back down into the ocean, it'll start the second wave."

"The eruption had some downward force, too," said Gus.

She switched back to an ocean floor profile. "Better believe it. Pulverized the earth's crust directly under the volcano, broke through to an empty magma chamber. The sides of the mountain that weren't blown upward are collapsing inward into the hole."

Gus shook his head in disbelief. "Looks like that crater belongs on the moon."

"The mountain collapsing into the hole starts the third wave. And the biggest. Those three waves will surge outward one after the other in all directions at nearly six hundred miles an hour."

Gus gritted his teeth. "Ouch. Look out, Hawaii."

Lani nodded. "The initial wave will hit Hilo and the windward side in two hours, the mainland, from San Diego to Portland, in three. The three waves are probably spaced a hundred miles and twenty minutes apart."

"Wave size?"

Lani studied her numbers. A refrigerator motor kicked on in the nearby coffee room, breaking the early morning quiet. "The first two waves will be killers. A hundred to a hundred fifty feet high. The third will be your superkiller—two hundred."

"Lord have mercy," said Gus. "Nothing on the ocean floor between here and the volcano to slow the speed."

"Nothing. The waves will follow the contour of the bottom till they reach shallow water, then build to their full height as they climb up the land slope."

"That'll be one terrifying sight," said Gus. "Three massive walls of water the size of high cliffs sweeping over our local beaches."

"Let's confirm what we think is happening." Lani clicked the Earthworm icon on her screen and studied the stream of numbers coming out of the tsunami warning network's computer processing center in Palmer, Alaska, where data funneled in from seismic networks, arrays of sensors, and tsunami warning stations all over the Pacific. The Earthworm program transformed raw data into an instant picture of events as they happened: location and magnitude of the shock, wave size and speed, and expected arrival time.

"My God. Catastrophic."

She put on her headset and called Tsunami John at the Pacific Tsunami Warning Center in Honolulu. He said, "Can't talk now, Lani. We're evacuating windward side, all islands. All I can say is it's multiwave and it's one big mother."

She called Arlene Pinsky at the Palmer Center and confirmed

that the Earthworm readings showed the formation of a three-wave train that could exceed fifty meters, or a hundred fifty feet when it hit land. The ETA for the Southern California shoreline was approximately 09:42 Pacific Standard Time. An emergency alert had been issued to all authorities.

Lani checked the time: 07:06. Two hours and thirty-six minutes to get five million people moved back from the beach. She put in a call to Sylvester Purvis and gave him the news. She listened for a moment, said, "Of course," and clicked off.

Gus waited for Lani to say something. Finally he asked, "What'd he say?"

She laughed. "He said if the media calls, be sure to give the university credit for predicting the tsunami."

"What a hypocrite. Guess we should start preparing an official log."

"That can wait. In a day or two we'll set up a timeline simulation, using all the data from all the sources over the last day and a half. Satellites, surface sensors, ocean floor sensors, everything. It'll tell us exactly what happened and when. We'll log from that."

Tears shone in Gus's eyes, and his voice was hoarse. "First I was excited. Now it's starting to hit me—what this means for millions of people."

"They can't get everyone off the beach in two hours. It'll be one of our worst disasters." She put her hand on his shoulder. "But nothing more we can do now. You might as well go home. I'll stick around awhile in case anyone calls."

~~

When the mayor of Riviera Beach, Max Hausman, heard the news, he didn't know what to do. He finally called his old friend, Police Chief Oliver Rendell. It was 7:14. "Ollie, you heard about the…?"

The alarm in the mayor's voice alarmed Rendell. "About what?"

"Tsunami!"

"You mean the volcano's…"

"Big time. All over TV."

"When's it…"

"Nine-forty."

"Shit! You mean we got two hours to…"

"…move forty thousand people off this beach. That's it exactly!"

"Shit, Max, you gotta be kiddin'. How in hell am I suppose to move forty thou—"

"Don't you have that Coast Guard plan?"

"Coast Guard? No, you gave that to Gladys—the emergency—"

"Oh, yeah, I forgot. But she's only a volunteer."

"You made her head of the whole deal."

"We better stick with our sworn personnel."

"That mean you want me to do it?"

"Why the fuck you think I'm calling?"

"Then tell Gladys. She did a lot of work on this and she'll be madder than hell. And tell the fire chief." Rendell walked to the window with his phone. Cars backing out of driveways jammed the narrow streets. People streaming out of apartments and condos on foot bumped and shoved, trying to get around the cars. "Shit! Cars! Blocking the street! That's gotta stop! And I mean right now!"

The mayor said, "Yeah, the county emergency people told me no cars. That's what they're saying on TV, too. But people aren't—"

"I'll damn well put a stop to that even if I have to pull my gun."

The touch of fear in Rendell's voice raised the mayor's anxiety even higher. "Stay calm, Ollie. Let's just move ahead and get this done."

Chief Rendell's voice got squeakier. "But we got a goddamn panic starting out here. Fucking riot."

"Don't wimp out on me, Ollie, for Crissake," the mayor shouted.

"We got a job to do. Settle down."

That seemed to quiet Rendell. "Where do we start, Max?"

"Meeting in ten minutes. My office. You and me and the fire chief. "

"Gladys?"

"Well, yeah, I'll try to reach her."

Rendell watched the crowd push a car over on its side, people still in it. "Jesus, this is awful!"

~ ~

Gladys Miller was buttering an English muffin and letting her first cup of hot coffee cool when her station's drive-time DJ interrupted the latest hit song with the first tsunami warning. It was 7:17. She called the mayor at home to have him declare an emergency so she could take over. His line was busy.

She called the deputy mayor, who was also the head of the city council, but her line was busy too, as was the police chief's. She finally got through to the fire chief, who'd just seen the tsunami report on TV.

He said, "I'll get my department ready and try to get hold of the mayor, but don't wait around for somebody to declare an emergency. We got one, that's for damn sure. So just take over, Gladys. It's your ball game."

"I can be at city hall in five minutes," she said. "I'll set up the emergency command center in the mayor's office." She hung up, put on a sweatshirt, warm-up pants, and tennis shoes, grabbed her purse, and turned to leave, but the phone rang before she could get out the door.

It was Fire Chief Van Dam calling back. "Mayor says Ollie Rendell's in charge."

"The police chief? But we all agreed…"

"I know, but His Honor's changed his mind."

Gladys pounded the air with her free hand. "I'm the only one who knows how to get everybody moved in time. That jackass is going to get people killed."

"We gotta convince him, Gladys. Meeting's in his office in eight minutes. Be there."

She set off on a ten-block run to the mayor's office. On the way she saw signs of blossoming confusion and panic. A sport utility backed recklessly out of a garage and mowed down three people who'd just come running out of a neighboring apartment house. A mob gathered around the sport utility and started smashing out its windows with anything at hand. Thousands streamed into the old beach town's narrow streets. Only one major boulevard could get them across Pacific Coast Highway to safety, but many were turning into dead-end streets and then trying to fight their way out when others followed. Things were off to a dreadful start.

The mayor and fire chief were there when Gladys got to the mayor's conference room. The police chief arrived three minutes later.

Mayor Hausman said, "I have the highest regard for you, Gladys, but Ollie and I've been working together for a long—"

Gladys slammed her purse down on the table. "Max, what in God's name do you think you're doing? Things are out of hand down on the street. I have my organization ready to go!"

The mayor looked at Chief Rendell. "Ollie, can you get your people down there and restore order?"

Rendell shook his head. "Not enough of us, Max. Only got fourteen in my whole damn department."

The mayor pointed at the fire chief but spoke to Rendell. "Use Milford's people."

Gladys said, "Stop it! Stop it! If you try to wing it, people will die. Go with the plan and we'll get them out."

The mayor hesitated. "What do you think, Ollie?"

Rendell shrugged. "It's your call, Max."

The fire chief said, "Gladys has this thing organized, Max."

"Say yes, for God's sake," she yelled. "People are getting

trampled to death down there!"

Mayor Max Hausman was unable to make a decision. He sat paralyzed. The sounds of confusion and panic down on the street grew louder.

~~

The tsunami streaked toward the California coast. With nothing further to do at the lab, Lani punched in Admiral Carson's number.

Carson said, "Warning just came in. The communications officer's on his way over now with details."

"Where's Dave?"

"Aboard *Farallon*, but I'm sending a heelo for him. He'll be commanding a task force of cutters and air units."

"I want to come down there."

"Stay where you are."

"I've got to come down. Where are you?"

"Signal Hill Park on Cherry between PCH and Willow. But the freeways are gridlocked. Dave will call you when he can."

Lani called Sylvester Purvis. "You owe me big time. I need a ride on the SciPac helicopter. Set it up for me right away. I'll be at the landing pad in twenty minutes."

~~

The SciPac helicopter hovered over Signal Hill Park. The pilot leaned over to Lani. "No room to get in there. The park's small, two choppers down there already. Looks like Coast Guard." He pointed south, toward Long Beach Community College. "I can put you down on that football field. Looks like they're setting up a receiving area, but I can land over in the corner. You'll have to walk a few blocks to get back here."

Lani nodded. The pilot settled down on the field. She jumped out and started jogging up the street toward Signal Hill Park.

~ ~

TV and radio stations broke into their regular programs with tsunami alerts at 7:13 a.m. Most people in the beach cities heard the warnings and tried to get out. Whether they would make it to safety before the first wave hit came down to agility, fate, and how fast and how well their local police and disaster organizations responded. But a few people, either through bad luck, bad timing, or an inability to understand or accept, didn't get the message at all.

~ ~

At 6:10, an hour before the first TV warning, Pepe Cardenas unlocked the kitchen door of the Driftwood Grill in Manhattan Beach. It was his job to chop the lettuce, load the salad bar, make the hamburger patties, and get the place set up for lunch. He'd be the only one there until the cooks and waiters came in around 11:00.

Pepe knew only a few words of English, enough to get by when the waiters told him which table to clear. Today he'd brought in a new mariachi CD, borrowed from his brother-in-law. It was straight from Mexico City and he'd been waiting for weeks to get his hands on a copy. Now he had it all to himself with nobody around to tell him to turn it down. He slid the disk into the CD player, which he'd plugged into the restaurant music system, and jacked up the volume till every speaker in the place was jumping off the wall.

He didn't hear the phone when it rang at 7:40 that morning. He usually ignored the phone anyway, because of his limited English. When the police car with the bullhorn drove by at 8:00, warning all people in the area to leave immediately, the mariachi trumpets were hitting it hard and Pepe was washing lettuce and stomping to the beat of the music.

~~

Osteoporosis had put Martha Cannon in a wheelchair. She told her son Richard, who was in TV syndication and lived in Beverly Hills, that she wanted to spend her last remaining years near the ocean. He'd looked first in pricey Santa Monica, then checked out Venice, where he'd finally found an old house on a side street just off Speedway, only one short block from the beach.

He'd installed a wheelchair ramp from the porch to the sidewalk, and remodeled the interior so that Martha could take care of herself. Counters, stovetops, sinks, and shelves were lowered to wheelchair height. Mrs. Haskell, the housekeeper, came in at 11:00 every morning to fix Martha's lunch and tidy up the place. She left around 2:00. Otherwise Martha lived on her own, which was the way she wanted it.

Her routine didn't vary. After lunch she napped for a half hour, then steered her electrically operated chair over to the boardwalk. She cruised the boardwalk as far north as Navy, then headed back. Along the way she'd stop and visit with the T-shirt sellers, the food stand owners, the aroma therapist, the massage therapist, the jugglers, mimes, musicians, and street people. She'd get back around 5:00, mix herself a dry martini, and heat up something in the microwave for supper.

Going to sleep at night had always been a problem. Martha got around it by reading till midnight, then tuning in a late movie on cable. She'd drop off watching a second movie, wake up about 10:00, fix tea and toast, and wait for Mrs. Haskell to arrive, so that she could bathe and dress for the day.

Four hours before Seamount Gilman exploded, Martha had been watching Laurence Olivier and Merle Oberon in *Wuthering Heights*. Just after 3:00 a.m., she tilted the back of her chair to the reclining position, tucked a pillow under her neck, pulled a blanket over her knees, and closed her eyes.

Her cordless phone rang at 7:48, with a recorded warning

that a tsunami would soon inundate the area. All persons living within two miles of the shoreline were ordered to evacuate immediately. She'd heard something about a volcano a few weeks before, but she hadn't paid much attention. She turned on the TV. The solemn-looking announcer said the three waves comprising the tsunami would together be the largest in recorded history. The first would strike land in less than two hours. She wondered if the networks were doing this to get more viewers—they never failed to blow things out of proportion in order to up their ratings. She tried to phone her son, but the circuits were jammed. She decided to wait. She felt certain he'd call or come over to take care of things. He was very dependable that way.

It was midnight before Patsy Fryman finished reading the legal brief. Satisfied, she put it in her black leather case, took the elevator down thirty floors, signed out at the security desk, and made the trip from Century City to her new apartment in Hermosa Beach in forty-two minutes. She fed her parrot, an African Gray named Willie, brushed her teeth, and was in bed by 1:30.

Patsy was a thirty-year-old blonde with shoulder-length hair kept exquisitely smart by visits to the stylist every Friday. She'd waited months to get the apartment on the strand. The rent was too high, even on her lawyer's salary, but she loved the view, loved the area, and was willing to give up other things to have it.

She still hadn't unpacked everything, but she'd get that out of the way little by little, then tackle the much-needed redecorating. She didn't have to be in superior court in Torrance till 11:00, so she turned off her phone and beeper, set her alarm for 9:00, closed her eyes, and went to sleep to the boom of the surf.

Arjun Singh had been recruited as a computer programmer by Hughes when he graduated from India Institute of Technology in Delhi. He was from a small village on the coast north of Madras, and his people had been fishermen as long as anyone knew. To Art, as he was known at work, fishing was second nature. He spent most of his spare time doing it.

Art had scheduled a day off on the day the volcano erupted. He got up at 5:00 and headed for one of his favorite fishing spots, a small bay on the south side of Point Vicente. His tide table said low tide at 05:55. That meant he could get out to the farthest rock in the string of rocks that jutted out from the shore about a quarter mile. He'd fish all day, then return when the tide ebbed again late that afternoon.

He parked in the fishing access lot off Palos Verdes Drive, got his poles, tackle box, and lunch out of the trunk, and took the winding path down the hundred-fifty-foot cliff to the stony beach below. It was flat low tide, so he walked on the wet bottom out to the fifth rock, then climbed up and rock-hopped out to the last one.

The patrons of Shannon's Irish Pub in Sunset Beach called him Uncle Jack. It was hard to tell how old he was. His thick hair was turning from brown to white, and there were deep folds in his sunburned face and crows-feet around his bright blue eyes.

He tended bar at Shannon's from six in the evening till two in the morning. It was the first regular job he'd held down in many years. He was trying to save money for the first time in his life so that his daughter with the three kids and her husband could buy their first house.

Jack had been bitten by the wanderlust bug early. He'd dropped out of high school and lied about his age to join the Marine Corps, where he served a two-year hitch. Then he worked as a steward on a cruise ship. On his second voyage, he trained as a sous-chef in the ship's galley. After cruising for a few years, he'd taken a job as a roustabout in the oil fields on Alaska's North

Slope. When the cook quit one day, Jack told the boss he could run the dining hall and did that for a while. He picked up subsequent jobs as seaman, ship's cook, lumberjack, smoke jumper, and mechanic on a formula-one racing team.

His jobs always paid well, but he managed to spend everything he made. Now, facing retirement on a skimpy social security check, he was doing his best to hold down a steady job, save some for his daughter, and keep a little for himself.

The customers at Shannon's loved Uncle Jack. He listened well, spun a good yarn when called upon, made honest pours, and slipped in a free round from time to time. In the past few months he'd noticed that he was a lot more tired at the end of a shift than he used to be.

At a few minutes after 2:00 a.m. on the day the volcano exploded, Jack escorted the last few drinkers out of the bar, finished counting his cash, locked up, and went back to his apartment on Fifth Street, only a few yards from the sand. It was a small studio that fitted his needs perfectly. He'd made a deal to rent the place at a lower rate during the off-season. He would have to move out in a couple of months, at the end of May.

Exhausted, Jack put his false teeth in a jar, took off his hearing aid, crawled into bed, and turned off the light. The phone rang at 7:20. It took a few rings before he sensed it, but the vibration finally woke him up. He grabbed it without bothering to put in his hearing aid. Somebody was yelling something faint and frantic. He said, "Sure, sure, okay, okay," hung up, and went back to sleep.

~ ~

Dave sat over a mug of coffee in *Farallon*'s wardroom. At 07:05 an out-of-breath ensign stuck his head in the door. "Sir, Admiral Carson's on a secure channel. Urgent." Dave ran to the bridge and got the word that he had two hours and forty minutes before the first wave hit.

The admiral said, "Baldy Spangler's heelo is on its way over."

"Communications guy on board?"

"Affirmative. Plus a flight mechanic. As operations chief, you're in charge of all surface and air assets—cutters, boats, heelos, and fixed wing. From Santa Barbara south."

"Can we reconfirm priorities, Admiral?"

"Number one, get all craft in coastal waters out of harm's way—pleasure boats, fishermen, Catalina ferries, whatever. Into deep water as far offshore as possible."

"Number two?"

"Move ships at anchor in Long Beach, San Pedro, and other outer harbors into open ocean. Order the harbormasters to get crews off all ships tied up dockside and clear their harbor areas of all personnel.

"Number three, at 09:10, regardless of where your cutters are, order them to break off and head offshore at flank speed. They're to remain ten miles out until ordered back in."

"What about moving people back from the beach?"

"Local disaster teams are doing that. Not our job."

Dave radioed patrol assignments to his skippers and pilots, sending one fixed-wing observation plane to cover Point Mugu to Santa Barbara and another aircraft to patrol Oceanside to Point Loma. He ordered the San Pedro and Long Beach harbormasters to have all ships in their outer harbors make ready for sea and stand by for Coast Guard instructions.

When Baldy picked him up, they circled over the seventeen ships lying anchored in the two outer harbors. Dave radioed orders to start engines and weigh anchor, giving each ship its place in line. They hovered above each one to make sure the captain understood and was getting underway. It took thirty-five minutes to get the procession heading out to sea in an orderly fashion.

At 07:45 they circled over the harbor one more time before heading south. As they flew over the breakwater, Dave saw a large cruise ship inbound toward the Port of Long Beach entrance. He called the harbormaster, who confirmed that the *Grand Palace* had already been ordered to reverse course and sail to deep water.

Dave told Baldy, "Fly along the beach down to Dana Point. After that, let's circle out to sea and up to Point Mugu to warn any strays we can find. Then we'll come back along the beach and help the cutters finish clearing the area."

Dave sent units to warn off sailboats getting ready to start a race outside the Long Beach marina, to herd boats fishing the kelp beds off Huntington Beach toward open sea, to intercept a Catalina ferry coming into Newport Harbor, to head off a fleet of tall ships sailing into Marina del Rey, and to break up a powerboat race outside King Harbor.

~ ~

At 7:45, Max Hausman, the mayor of Riviera Beach, still sat in a paralytic stupor. Police Chief Oliver Rendell, Fire Chief Milford Van Dam, and emergency response coordinator Gladys Miller waited.

Gladys picked up the carafe of water from the middle of the conference table and tossed its contents into the mayor's face. "Wake up, Max!"

He shook off the water, but his breathing stayed heavy, his eyes still stared with panic, and he didn't utter a word.

Gladys looked at the others. "We've got to decide. He can't."

Van Dam said, "Gladys takes over. That's my vote."

Rendell nodded. "Gotta get our asses in gear. What do we do, Gladys?"

"Just like we rehearsed. The radio stations tell the volunteers to report to their posts. Police supervise volunteers south of Riviera Boulevard, and firefighters north. Stop all cars and take away their keys. Funnel pedestrian traffic into Riviera from north and south so we can get them across Pacific Coast Highway. Keep your walkie-talkies on channel three. Give me status reports every five minutes."

Baldy's helicopter circled back over San Pedro at 09:00. The coast was clearing out nicely. An armada of ships and boats of all sizes and descriptions made way to deep water. Time to order his own people to safety. At 09:10 he instructed all Coast Guard surface units to proceed due west at twenty knots and to give Catalina and the Channel Islands a wide berth. That would get them into deep water with time to spare.

Dave spoke loudly over the beat of the rotors. "Before we head back, let's take another look at that cruise ship."

Even though the *Grand Palace* had been instructed to reverse course, the ship still lingered south of Queen's Gate entrance to Long Beach Harbor, as if waiting for outgoing ships to clear so it could come into port.

Baldy said, "She hasn't moved."

Dave focused his binoculars. "Twelve decks. Probably two thousand people aboard. Something's wrong." He radioed the Long Beach harbormaster. "U.S. Coast Guard inquiring about the *Grand Palace*. Why aren't they proceeding to open water?"

"Harbormaster to Coast Guard. *Grand Palace* reports problem in the engine room. Loss of power. Suggest you contact them on ship-to-ship channel."

Dave switched channels. "*Grand Palace*, this is the Coast Guard. State your situation."

A voice replied through the crackle of static in Dave's headphones. "First officer here. We had a blockage in the fuel lines. Chief engineer just reported the problem fixed and full power restored. Starting our turn now. Expect to reach deep water in time."

Dave signed off and said to Baldy, "Thank God for that."

"Amen." Baldy tapped an earphone. "Admiral Carson calling."

Dave clicked to the air-to-ground channel. "Yes, sir."

"Dave, the FBI just called. Jiro Yamaguchi is stranded out at the end of pier four hundred in San Pedro. He's been doing solo surveillance since early this morning and nobody told him to leave."

"We're right over the area." Dave spotted a lone figure at the end of a large expanse of loading dock. "Let's go down and get him."

The flight mechanic lowered the basket, and Jiro hopped on while it was still moving. When they had him inside the helicopter, he said, "I'm glad I didn't have to swim home. I forgot my mask and fins."

Dave patted Jiro on the shoulder and said to Baldy, "We still have time to make a fast sweep of the local coastline."

At first glance everything looked clear. Then they saw a powerboat adrift just off Redondo City Beach. Dave pointed. "They must've come out of King Harbor and lost power."

Baldy brought the chopper directly over the drifting boat. Four people on deck waved frantically. Baldy said, "The crew plus Jiro makes five. We can only take three more. This bird will fly with eight aboard, but not nine. Not sure there's time to come back."

"Lower me down in the basket. I'll explain it to them," Dave said.

"I'll go along," said Jiro.

"Don't do anything crazy, you guys," said Baldy. Dave nodded as he and Jiro climbed into the basket. Baldy signaled the flight mechanic to send them down.

Dave and Jiro jumped out as the basket touched the deck. Dave told the boaters the hoist could lift only two at a time. He helped the two women into the basket and signaled the chopper to lift away.

When the basket came down for the last load, Dave looked at Jiro. Jiro nodded. Dave told the two men to get in and gave the lift signal.

They watched the two men disappear into the chopper. Dave waved Baldy off and the chopper pulled away. They were alone on a dead boat, drifting toward shallow water. The first tsunami wave, high as a seven-story building, was in sight and coming at them.

"Surf's up," Dave said.

"And me without my boogie board."

twelve

Ho Kai Fat pulled the limo up in front of the construction trailer a little before 6:00 a.m. He opened the door for George Hacker and Harley Wamp. The three men entered the trailer for a meeting with the construction superintendent. Hacker said he wanted to see how hard Wamp could kick ass to move the project along faster.

The meeting ended at 7:10. They drove through the development, heading for the I-5 Freeway. Wamp's cell phone buzzed. He put it to his ear and listened. His face turned white. "Are you sure?" He pressed the Off button. "Fucking volcano erupted. Tsunami's coming."

Ho Kai Fat turned on the radio. A somber announcer's voice warned people within two miles of the shoreline to clear the area. "NOAA's tsunami warning service advises that a series of giant waves arriving here at approximately nine-forty this morning will demolish everything within two miles of the coastline. If you live within two miles of the beach, you are advised to walk inland immediately. Do not try to drive your car or take household possessions. The streets are clogged. The safest procedure is to dress quickly but warmly, wear shoes, carry money and identification, and walk inland at a brisk pace. Police and emergency officials will direct you to a safe assembly point where you can wait until the danger has passed. There will be three separate waves, so do not try to go back after the first or second wave. Wait till the all-clear is given by the authorities. We repeat. A series of three large tsunami waves up to two hundred feet high will strike the Southern California coast at approximately nine-forty this morning…"

Hacker pointed a stubby index finger at Wamp. "You just cost me a fucking fortune. And now you gotta pay, you stupid asshole. You shoulda listened to that Hawaiian girl. Shoulda cut our losses when we had a chance. With phase two open, we're in awful fucking deep."

Wamp protested, "But you're the one who pushed me to open phase two."

"Yeah, and you're the one who said the tsunami stuff was bullshit."

The limo went down the hill and through an underpass to a frontage road on the beach side of I-5. Cars loaded with construction workers streamed uphill past them. The limo passed a bulldozer and earthmover storage compound on the beach a few hundred yards from the water. The area was surrounded by a ten-foot-high chain-link fence with angled razor wire across the top. The gate was secured with heavily padlocked chain.

Hacker told Ho Kai Fat to stop in front of the fence. He cocked his head toward Wamp. "Throw him in. Time to cut payroll."

Fat opened Wamp's door, grabbed the terrified man's ankle, and pulled him out. Wamp shook loose from Fat's grip for a moment, scrambled to his feet, and tried to run. But Fat grabbed him by the shoulders and lifted him high in the air. He juggled Wamp's thrashing body for a few moments, then adjusted his grip so that he held him face up, one hand on his seat, the other in the middle of his back.

"In he goes," ordered Hacker.

Ho Kai Fat ran toward the fence and launched Harley Wamp

through the air in a high arc that just cleared the top of the razor wire. Wamp glanced off the cab of a skiploader and came down hard on compacted earth. He lay on his side, gasping and kicking spasmodically.

"Oh, God. Something's broken," Wamp moaned. "I can't move. Help me."

"We're sending a little tsunami to float you out of there," said Hacker. "It'll be along any time now. Have a good swim." He motioned for Fat to head for the freeway.

The on-ramp was jammed, the freeway gridlocked. "Make a U and go back to the underpass," Hacker ordered. "Keep driving uphill till we get as high as we can go. Then we'll walk." It took a few minutes to get to the highest street in the complex, a hillside five hundred feet above sea level with a spectacular view of the coastline. Ho Kai Fat parked the limo. The two men hiked up a trail to the top of the ridge. The hills were green from the spring rains, the sky was clear, and a light breeze blew from the southwest.

From the top of the ridge, Hacker could see the entire twenty-mile length of the Serenidad development. He laughed a barking laugh. "You know, Mr. Fat, that fucking insurance company didn't want to give me disaster and acts of God on this place, so I told 'em I'd pull the whole account. Ships, subsidiaries, everything. They knew they'd lose millions in premiums, so they finally said okay. Now, I'm really gonna stick it to 'em. Tell 'em my losses are five times as much as they really are, settle for three times as much, and they'll think they really drove a hard bargain." He barked again. "You know who'll end up paying me off? Mister average working slob, when his insurance premiums go through the roof."

It was 9:48. Hot Kai Fat pointed. Hacker saw the surf ebb rapidly into the base of the first wave, leaving a half mile of kelp-strewn ocean floor. The wave was already as high as a construction crane, turning muddy, still growing, and coming fast. It carried the faint sound of thunder. They watched, hypnotized.

~~

At 8:27 Gladys Miller hadn't heard from Chief Rendell for almost twenty minutes, despite repeated calls on channel three. Two minutes later, he finally called in. "I'm shorthanded. Not even half the volunteers showed up."

"Are you getting people out?"

"As best we can. Cars are still crapping things up."

"Can you control the crowd okay?"

"Yeah, people are scared, but they're behaving okay right now."

"Can you get them out by nine?"

"Maybe nine-thirty if they stay cool."

Gladys said, "Keep telling them everything's okay."

Now that Chief Rendell was in the middle of the action, his voice sounded steady. "I'm worried they could start freaking out around nine or so, when they think the wave's getting close. Then I'm not sure what'll happen."

"I just talked to Chief Van Dam. Most of his volunteers showed up, so he's in pretty good shape. I'll see if he can spare some people. I'm coming down, too."

"Not even sure you can get through, Gladys, and it's dangerous as hell. Stranded cars everywhere, people backed up for blocks. Least little thing could set off a stampede."

"I'm not afraid, Ollie. Maybe one more pair of hands'll help get everyone out."

"I'm at Tenth and Seaview," said Chief Rendell. "Good luck."

~~

Dave and Jiro's crippled boat drifted to within a hundred yards of the beach. Fascinated, they watched the monster wave swelling offshore, then were suddenly swept toward it as the undertow sucked the little boat a thousand yards out in a few seconds, into the wave itself. They were lost in a roaring turbulence of churning mud and sand, gripping the handrails of the little boat with all their strength. The buoyant craft bounced and jolted, tilted and shipped water, and finally rode up the face of the hundred-foot wave, into the foaming curl at the top.

Dave caught sight of a rescue basket dangling just above them. Baldy had come back, but the wave would strike land and break at any moment. The basket powered steadily downward. It was within inches of their grasp, but the wind created by the mountainous wave blew it away from their outstretched hands.

Each time it swung back they lunged out to grab it. Finally, they gripped the bottom of the basket's tubular frame, using every bit of their strength. They felt themselves being reeled upward. There was a jerk as the chopper darted forward from the hovering position, momentarily snatching them from the wave.

The wave moved faster than the helicopter. The charging wall of water curled over them, engulfing them in an irresistible sucking force that tore at their hands as they struggled to hang on.

The chopper tried to gain speed, but the wave pulled the two men under with such force that all the helicopter could do was keep pace. The laboring hoist was no match for the downward drag. Dave and Jiro clung desperately to the metal basket as they bounced in the foamy crest of the hundred-foot wave.

The wave broke on the uphill slope, the crest curling and smashing down in a stew of mangled lumber, tile, carpet, tarpaper, shingles, furniture, streetlights, canned beans, Land Rovers, telephone poles, and chimney bricks. The helicopter strained to pull Dave and Jiro out of danger by accelerating vertically, but the immense power of the breaking wave finally tore them loose.

Dave felt the basket's frame ripped from his hands. The turbulence spun him around and around. He beat his arms, trying to swim to the surface, but was knocked under, tumbled head over heels, swirled, stretched, bent, corkscrewed, banged against the hard edges of debris.

The churning finally stopped. He found himself floating upward in calm water till he broke the surface. He dragged great swallows of air into his starved lungs, astonished to discover that he was in a swimming pool. Jiro popped up a few yards away, coughing and flailing. Dave sidestroked over, grabbed him by the collar, and towed him to the shallow end. The two accidental surfers struggled to their feet and looked at each other. Dave pointed. Wedged against a corner of chain-link fence still standing was a broken sign that said, *Starlight Motel Pool–No Lifeguard On Duty.*

The wave raced more than a mile inland on the uphill slope and gradually lost most of its punch. But it possessed enough power to shove Dave and Jiro down to the bottom of the pool again when it surged over them on its way back to the sea.

When they resurfaced and made their way back to the shallow end of the pool, Jiro shook his head. "Jesus Christ, I can't take much more of this!"

Dave pushed Jiro out of the pool. "The next one's due any minute. It'll make that first wave look like a ripple."

It took Gladys Miller almost an hour to fight her way through the mob. The closer she got to Tenth and Seaview, the more desperate things became, and she had to flatten herself against a concrete block wall to keep from being trampled. Chief Rendell was perched on top of the wall. He reached down and pulled her up. "Nothing more we can do," he told her. "Either they make it or…"

"How many left?"

Rendell eyeballed the street. "Seven or eight hundred. Maybe half'll get out."

Gladys wrinkled her nose. "That smell…"

"Some are so scared they're shitting their pants."

She struggled to absorb the chaotic scene before her. A river of terrified, desperate people, crushed together in a narrow street, pushing, milling, trampling over fallen humans, some dead, some about to die, some hurt and moaning and fighting to stand. Those down were kids, old people, sick people, and the unlucky. Gladys covered her ears, trying to block out the sounds of sobbing, screaming, pleas to God, frantic cursing, shrieks, and bellowed threats. Mothers cried out for lost children, wives for husbands. Panic ruled.

"Guess we're stuck, Ollie. Hope the end is quick."

Rendell shook his head. "I know a way out."

She just stared at him.

"There's a utility tunnel under the street. When the tail end clears that manhole in a couple minutes, we'll just have time to get down there and run like hell along the tunnel. It turns the corner at Riviera and goes right across PCH."

"Can we really get out?"

"Should beat the wave by five or six minutes."

Gladys thought for a moment. "You go ahead, Ollie."

"Are you nuts? There's no way to help now."

She shrugged. "Maybe I can get some of the kids into the tunnel."

The last of the stragglers stumbled by. Rendell turned to lower himself down the face of the wall. "I'll wait in the tunnel at the Riviera intersection. If you're not there in five minutes..."

"I'll do my best. Thanks." She watched him dodge the bodies littering the street on his way to the manhole. He lifted off the cover and disappeared. Gladys hung by her hands from the top of the wall for a moment, and then dropped to the street. She looked for kids down but still alive, but most were dead and mangled. Crushed heads, shattered arms and legs, intestines spilling from ripped abdomens. She finally spotted a little girl trying to sit up.

Gladys ran to her. "Can you stand?"

The girl, about six, nodded and got to one knee. Gladys pulled her to her feet, put an arm around her and guided her to the manhole. "Down the ladder and go that way!" She pointed to Riviera. "And run as fast as you can!"

She got two more into the tunnel and was going back for another when the first wave smashed into Riviera Beach. The three kids in the tunnel got safely across PCH with Ollie Rendell. Gladys died reaching out for a frightened four-year-old boy.

∼ ∼

Pepe Cardenas finished in the kitchen at 9:38 and went into the dining room to refill the paper napkin dispensers. He was listening to the mariachi music, taking the plastic wrap off a fresh pack of napkins, and thinking about his sick mother in Sinaloa when the first wave hit.

He couldn't understand what was happening. He heard a loud crash, and suddenly he was under water, helpless, strangling. The restaurant broke apart all around him. It was endless rolling, spinning, no up, no down, hitting things, bouncing off. The light went gray, then black, then he came back from the dark with air on his face and a bright sky above.

He grabbed something. The frond of an uprooted palm tree. Now he was being sucked back out to sea by the ebbing wave, pulled farther and farther away from shore, until the water disappeared underneath him, stranding him on the ocean floor a half mile from the beach. The bottom was wet, shiny, muddy, masses of kelp all around and a man's body tangled in it. *Madre de Dios!* Live fish flopped everywhere. He tried to stand, but he was too weak and fell. He got to one knee, then stood again and stayed upright. He moved toward land.

The going was hard. His feet sank into the wet sand and mud, got snagged by kelp. He threw every drop of energy he had into the task, and was almost back to dry beach when he heard a noise behind him, coming from the sea. The low rumbling roar got louder and louder, closer and closer. He looked over his shoulder. *Madre de Dios. So big, so gigantic. No creo. I don't believe.* Those were Pepe's last thoughts.

~ ~

At 8:30, Martha Cannon heard an amplified voice coming from Speedway which ordered everyone to stop what they were doing and walk inland: "Do not take possessions. Do not try to drive. The streets are closed to cars. Wear shoes and immediately walk inland, away from the beach."

She rolled her chair to the front window. The street in front reminded her of mob scenes in the movies, people fleeing the monsters from outer space. She couldn't go out into that. She didn't know what to do. She'd wait a little longer.

It was 8:45 and her son still hadn't called. The TV said the first wave would hit the coast at 9:40. The street was deserted. It was time to leave. She got a warm jacket from the closet, scooped her purse off the living room table, and steered her chair down the ramp. As she turned onto the sidewalk, she cut the corner too closely and her right wheel dropped into a slot between the sidewalk and a low brick retaining wall.

She kept pressing the power button, but the chair wouldn't budge. She tried and tried to free the wheel, but it was jammed tight and the battery was running down. It had been five years since she'd been able to stand by herself, even longer since she'd walked. She wondered if she had the strength to slide out of the chair, roll over to the wheel and pull it out, then get herself back in the seat.

Martha lay sprawled on the sidewalk, tugging at the wheel, when she saw the greasy pant legs and taped-up tennis shoes. She looked up into the leathery, sun-and-wine-browned face of Monty, one of the street people she knew.

"Where's everybody?" Monty asked.

She told him about the big wave. He picked her up and started walking north along Speedway. "This'll be faster than your chair," he said. "Brooks is the closest street."

It had been years since Martha had been in a man's arms.

Monty smelled of old sweat and cheap wine, but she liked his strength, his caring, his courage. She put her head against his shoulder. The first wave caught them as Monty turned the corner onto Brooks.

~ ~

At first Patsy Fryman thought there was construction going on outside. She rolled over in bed. But the pounding got louder. The numbers on her clock radio said 7:26. Someone was yelling. A man's voice. "Patsy! You in there? You gotta get out! Patsy! You in there?"

She put on a robe and opened the door. It was Owen, a neighbor who lived with his male partner. He'd helped her carry her stuff from the U-Haul into her new place. "Didn't you hear about the tidal wave?"

Dazed, she shook her head.

"That volcano exploded. Tsunami's coming!"

"Now?"

"I think in about an hour. They won't let you drive, so walk inland on Pier. Quick!"

She put on jeans, sweatshirt, and tennis shoes, grabbed her purse, and went out into the crowd that milled toward Pier Avenue. It was slow going for twenty minutes because some jerk was trying to drive away in his BMW. The mob stopped him, and his car now blocked part of the street. Once she got to Pier, the pace picked up. Hermosa police and firefighters were keeping the crowd moving.

Patsy had crossed Hermosa Avenue when she remembered Willie, her African Gray. She'd had the parrot for five years and loved it as if it were her child. *Oh my God, I can't leave Willie!* She turned and tried to fight her way back through the surging crowd. People yelled at her and fought her off. She dodged, wriggled, struggled, tried to make headway, but it was like swimming against a riptide. Someone kicked her in the ankle. She lost her footing and went down. Legs, knees, shoes ground into her, hitting her in the head, the stomach, all over her body.

A black hand sticking out of a dark blue firefighter's shirt pulled her to her feet and dragged her to the edge of the crowd, then into a bookstore that fronted onto the street. "What's the matter with you? You crazy or something, trying to go back against that crowd?"

"But I *have* to go back for Willie."

"You mean there's a baby back there?"

"No, my parrot. But he's just like my baby. I love him as much."

The firefighter, short and barrel-chested, shook his head. "I'm sorry. I can't let you go back for a bird."

Patsy started to cry.

He said, "I know how you feel. I got a dog I'm crazy about. But no way you're getting back through this mob."

"Are there any police or firemen back there who can go in and get him for me?"

"No, sorry. We got our hands full saving people. Now, get back out there and go the same direction as all the rest. Okay?"

Patsy hung her head for a few moments, finally nodded. "But look, if I give you my key do you think there's a chance anybody could get back to 17B Tenth Court and…"

He shook his head. "Sorry, Miss. The wave's too close, and I don't swim too good."

Patsy inserted herself back into the moving stream of people and trudged ahead with the others. At 9:42, when the first wave hit, she was in Andrews Park just off Aviation. There were radios in the crowd and word soon spread that everything within a mile of the beach had been wiped out. Nothing was left on the ocean side of Highway One.

She'd lost everything. Her apartment, furniture, clothes, car, and dear Willie. She didn't know where she'd sleep, how she'd get to work, where she'd get clothes or food. She was beginning to grasp the depth of the disaster. For the first time she felt fear, apprehension, and heart-sinking loss. As she wondered what to do next, she saw the firefighter who'd saved her and called out to him.

He made his way to her. "You're the parrot lady."

She nodded. "Willie."

"Real sorry I couldn't save him for you—there was just no way."

She visibly sagged, and he steadied her. She said, "I know. You were very brave to go in and pull *me* out. I could've been trampled. Thanks."

"Hey, just my job," he said quietly. "You take care now."

She watched his back disappear into the crowd, then burst into tears.

∼ ∼

It was almost 7:00 before Arjun Singh had everything the way he wanted. He'd cast one line, baited with live anchovy, directly off the point of the rock into deep water where calico bass and halibut bit. On the second pole he'd used live sand crabs and cast into the surf back toward shore for surf perch and bonito.

The sun came up behind the cliff; it was a clear day, the sea peaceful. The series of storms that had come down from Alaska the last few weeks were over, the foggy mornings still another month or two away, the weather absolutely perfect for a day of fishing. He took off his windbreaker and fished in a white T-shirt with UCLA on the back.

The first bites came within minutes. He pulled in two calicos from the front pole, and had no sooner gotten those off the hooks when his other pole jerked and he pulled in a fat surf perch. A few minutes later a ten-pound halibut took his newly baited hook. He had a bit of a fight landing that one. Then the surf perch hit again.

The fish stopped biting about ten minutes before 9:00. By

then he had thirteen fish on his string and was thinking about all the nice dinners ahead. He usually listened to the radio when he fished, but the activity had been so hectic he hadn't had time to turn it on. He finally got it out of the tackle box and tuned to 1070, which had national news on the hour.

He frowned as he listened to the broadcast. Something about a tsunami. At first he thought the tsunami was headed for Indonesia or Japan, then it sank in that a tsunami was on its way *here*! A series of three monster waves would hit all along the Southern California coast starting at approximately 9:40. Forty minutes from right then! He'd been so totally into fishing, nothing but the water, sun, sky, and fish existed.

He looked around. The place was deserted. Nobody on the rocks or beach. Only his Toyota pickup in the lot on top. Maybe someone had tried to warn him, but he couldn't have heard over the waves crashing against rocks. The tide had started coming back in almost three hours ago. Some of the smaller rocks were under water, so he couldn't scramble back. He'd have to swim, and the water would be over his head all the way to the beach.

He took off his shoes and jeans, waited for a wave to surge around the rock toward shore, and jumped in. A strong current carried him away from the rocks but parallel to the shore. He stroked steadily, trying to get to the beach, but he made little headway against the tide. Finally, he caught the crest of a large wave and body surfed almost all the way in. He stood up in waist-high water and struggled ashore.

His watch still worked. It said 9:46. Turning, he saw the first tsunami wave forming in the distance, pulling the surf out to meet it, exposing shiny ocean bottom past the rock where he'd fished. Ignoring the winding path to the top, he charged up the side of the cliff, grabbing onto clumps of grass, small bushes, rocks, clods, anything that would give him a handhold or foothold. He was within a few feet of the top when a clump of grass in his hand gave way. He slid twenty feet back down before stopping, then started his ascent again.

He'd made up half the lost distance when the wave struck. It slammed into the cliff, surged up the face, and Art was gone in an instant, like an ant hit by a garden hose. He was under water, being swept someplace by an incredibly powerful force.

The wave traveled another forty feet to the top of the cliff, over the fishermen's parking lot, and up the hill across Palos Verdes Drive to the steps of the Wayfarers Chapel. And that is where it deposited a dazed but breathing Arjun Singh in T-shirt and jockey shorts, before retreating back to the sea.

~ ~

Uncle Jack had no way of knowing he'd poured his last drink, told his last tall tale, made the final deposit into his savings account. He was asleep when the wave took him. His dream about reading bedtime stories to a five-year-old granddaughter went seamlessly into a nightmare about a flood of shockingly cold water ripping him from his bed, paralyzing his breathing, forcing salt water into his lungs. Darkness came within a few seconds. The next day, his body was picked up by a Coast Guard cutter two miles out to sea.

~ ~

The Coast Guard emergency operations center in Signal Hill Park pulsed with activity. Two helicopter landing areas had been staked out. A chopper settled in for a landing on one, while another heelo lifted skyward from the second. Admiral Carson ran the operation out of a forty-foot Winnebago. Three communications vans, a dozen cars, and several small trucks were parked in a semicircle around it. People seemed to be running in every direction. When Lani entered the admiral's RV, he stood with one hand on a makeshift desk yelling into a telephone headset, "Dammit, Baldy, why did you let him do that?" He saw Lani and clicked off.

"Any news on Dave?"

The admiral looked at her a moment. "He rescued four people off a drifting boat, but he and Yamaguchi had to stay on the boat. The helicopter went back for them, but they were washed off the rescue basket."

Lani gasped. "But…"

"We don't know what happened after that. All we can do now is pray a lot." He punched the air-to-ground radio channel. "Baldy, is that you coming in on pad two?"

"Right, Admiral. I have to refuel."

"Let me know when you're ready. I want to check first wave damage, and see where Dave was."

"Affirmative. We can launch again in five minutes. You won't like what you see—it's pretty bad out there."

Carson took off his headset and glanced at Lani. "I'll find out what I can."

"Take me along."

Carson shook his head. "Sorry. The Red Cross is setting up a receiving center over at City College—tents, feeding lines, field hospital. They'll need volunteers."

"I just came from there, but I'll go back and try to help. That's where I'll be if you find out anything about Dave." Lani picked up a pen and scribbled her cell phone number on a pad on the admiral's desk. "Will you let me know?"

Carson squeezed Lani's hand.

Baldy flew a little north of due west to the area behind Redondo City Beach. "Last I saw, the wave broke just before Pacific Coast Highway, and they disappeared."

"You didn't see what happened to them?"

"No. It was a mess—buildings flying apart and trees and cars churning around in the water. Their chances weren't very good. Probably got sucked back out to sea. Maybe not much point looking for them around here."

Carson shook his head. "Wouldn't know where to start.

Either they made it and we'll hear from them later, or they didn't."

Baldy continued hovering, but he didn't reply.

Carson pointed. "Fly north along the beach as far as Santa Monica. There are some low spots along that section of the coast I'm worried about."

They flew over a flattened Manhattan Beach. As they approached what remained of the Chevron Refinery and the Hyperion sewage treatment plant in El Segundo, Baldy glanced seaward. "Oh, my God! Here comes the second wave!"

They watched in awe as the wave formed and shaped itself, first as a wrinkle in the expanse of blue, running just behind the breaker line along the coast as far as the eye could see, then the undertow draining the surf toward it, baring a wide expanse of ocean bottom as the wave changed to a muddy brown and swelled to the size of a ten-story building. It surged up the beach and over the land, pulverizing everything in its path. Anything left standing after the first wave was smashed into kindling, swept ashore for more than a mile, then sucked back out to sea.

The wave wiped out the runways and maintenance hangars at LAX. It didn't quite reach the control tower or the passenger terminals. The chopper hovered over Marina del Rey, home port to thousands of pleasure boats, all of which had already been ripped from their moorings and either crushed and scattered like flotsam at the high tide line or sucked out to sea. The entire Marina and Venice Beach area, a natural, low-lying wetland, had been hit hard.

With no upward slope to impede it, the wave washed almost two miles inland before losing momentum and pulling back. Hundreds of buildings that had been just out of reach of the first wave—houses, apartments, condos, stores, offices, gas stations, warehouses, shopping centers, hospitals—were knocked off their foundations and ground into rubble by the enormous, fast-moving second wave.

The main boulevards were packed with people trying to move inland. Many made it to safety before the wave caught up.

Some didn't.

"They all could have been saved if everyone had been better prepared," said Carson. "Look! Some of those idiots at the tail end of the line are turning around and chasing the receding wave. They're crazy!"

"They're looking for loot," said Baldy. "Grabbing stuff washed loose. They get in a frenzy and forget another wave is coming."

A police helicopter swooped in low over the looters, ordering them over a bullhorn to move inland. Most ignored the warnings and kept on chasing the receding wave back toward the ocean. "It's lunacy," said Carson. "Hundreds, thousands of them. Like lemmings, running toward certain death."

Baldy took his chopper in low over Santa Monica. The palisade and natural upslope of the ground had kept the first two waves from going more than a half mile inland, but everything in that half mile, which included the heart of downtown Santa Monica, had been pulverized. Very little remained intact, and the third wave was still to come.

Admiral Carson received a call from Coast Guard control. "Commander Steel's alive, sir. He just called in. Wants to talk to you."

Baldy grinned and gave a thumbs-up sign. Carson said, "Patch him through."

"We're in a parking lot at Torrance and Prospect in Redondo. And don't ask how we got here. The FBI is picking up Jiro, and I'd like Baldy to fly me over the port area to see if any Blue Star ships were beached."

"We need all personnel ready for search and rescue when the third wave washes back out. There won't be a second to lose. There'll be hundreds of people trying to stay afloat out there. We have to get as many as we can as fast as we can."

"I hear you, sir. But I need to check something out before the third wave hits. If my hunch is right, it'll save thousands of lives in the future."

"Okay, as long as you do it before the third wave comes ashore. Once that hits, take a quick look at the shoreline to size up the situation, then firewall it straight back here. Understood?"

"Understood, Admiral."

"Now get out into the middle of the parking lot where Baldy can see you, and be ready to execute the rescue plan."

Baldy dropped Admiral Carson at the Signal Hill Park operations center and headed off to pick up Dave.

The admiral watched Baldy's chopper lift off and fly west for a few moments. Walking toward his Winnebago, he said, "Damn!" He hadn't told Dave that Lani was trying to find him. At least he could let her know Dave was alive.

He made a quick search of his desktop for her number, but a hundred message slips and other papers had piled up since he'd left. When Yeoman Gates buzzed and told him that the commandant was on the line from Washington, he took the call.

~~

Baldy spotted the lone figure standing in the middle of the empty parking lot. He touched down within a few yards of him and Dave climbed aboard. Baldy said, "Bloodshot eyes, torn shirt, that must've been one hell of a party."

"You have no idea. Fly over west basin. That's where the tankers were anchored."

They were over L.A. Harbor's west basin in just under four minutes. Baldy banked right and pointed. "See where the outer harbor narrows into the main channel?"

Dave nodded.

"When the first two waves came in, the main channel squeezed all that water down and shot it into west basin like a high-pressure fire hose." Baldy banked left and flew up to the end of the basin.

"Yeah," said Dave, "like a tidal bore. It washed those tankers pretty far inland. I count six."

The tankers were scattered in a semicircle on both sides of what was left of the Harbor Freeway. Two rested on their keels, one was upside down, and three lay on their sides.

Dave said, "That one over by the golf course, on its side. Blue Star on the funnel. Take me down."

Baldy hovered fifty feet over the tanker. "Too windy. Can't go lower on account of downdrafts. I can let you down in a harness, but the wind might bang you against the hull."

"I only have a few minutes. I'll take the chance."

Baldy handed Dave a cordless headset. "Call if it gets too rough. I'll pull you back up."

Dave pointed to a survival knife on Baldy's belt. "Can I borrow that, too?"

Baldy slipped the leather scabbard off his belt and handed it to Dave.

Dave strapped on the knife, cinched the harness, and hooked it to the cable. "Ready!"

Baldy lowered Dave to within a few feet of the hull, but the harness swayed in the twenty-knot westerly, blowing him around in a wide arc, like a carnival ride. When the wind dropped for a moment, Baldy put Dave down within three feet of one of the several hundred white boxes stuck to the bottom of the ship.

Dave stood on the wet, sloping hull, his bright orange harness attached to a cable that trailed after him. He worked his way over to a white box, knelt down and felt it with his free hand, then stood and kicked it. The box didn't move. He pulled out the hunting knife and sliced through three inches of Styrofoam to the inside box, which had been heat-sealed in heavy, waterproof plastic. He sawed through plastic wrap and cardboard with the serrated side of the knife and pulled out a Ripper sealed in a plastic bag.

He continued cutting the box apart. He found 48 Rippers inside. At the bottom was a small electronic motor made up of a computer chip, a fuel cell battery, and some coils of wire connected to a thin metal strip fastened to the outside of the box. The strip was stuck fast against the hull. He cut away the small motor and jammed it in his pocket when he heard Baldy's voice on the headset.

"Third wave's coming! I'm pulling you up!"

Baldy took them up to a thousand feet and headed toward the ocean. They were just over the outer harbor breakwater when the third wave began to rise like a mythological creature out of the sea.

"Water's draining out of the harbor!" Baldy said. "Good God in heaven!"

Dave was mesmerized by the massive mud-brown wall building higher and higher as it charged toward land. "Two-hundred footer for sure!" He thought of Lani and how hard she'd fought to get people to believe this was possible.

They watched as the mammoth wave swept over the breakwater and rolled through the loading docks and warehouses, over Terminal Island, and into Long Beach and Wilmington.

Baldy said, "I can't believe the power of that thing. All that damage. Bam-bam-bam. My God!"

"Let's get the hell back," said Dave. "We've got work to do."

~ ~

Yeoman Gates met Dave as he stepped off the chopper. "Admiral Carson just left for a disaster response meeting at Cal State Long Beach. He left you orders to start the offshore rescue operation immediately. You're to use his desk while he's away."

Dave sat down in Carson's chair. The baseball bat stood in the corner. "He brought his lucky charm."

"It goes where he goes."

Dave nodded and got down to work. He radioed orders to all Coast Guard ships and aircraft to commence the rescue phase, ordering cutters, helicopters, and fixed-wing aircraft to their preassigned patrol areas. Fixed-wing craft would act as spotters, directing boats, cutters, and helicopters to the rescue sites. He told Baldy to get a large heelo ready as an airborne command center.

"Full crew?"

"No swimmer," said Dave, "but your best flight mech and a communications specialist who can work fast relaying orders."

While Baldy set up the helicopter, Dave called the Torrance FBI office. Jiro was still there, and he told him what he'd found on the hull of the beached Blue Star tanker.

"How do the boxes stay on?"

Dave's radio squawked. "Just a second, it's one of our spotter planes." He gave the pilot the patrol altitude and returned to Jiro. "Magnetically. The hull is iron. The electronic motor has enough power to make a strong magnetic field. I guess they turn off the magnets by remote control from the bridge, and the boxes float to the surface."

"But how...? Wait a minute! Commercial fishing boats! They go out before daylight, but they can probably spot the white boxes in the dark."

Dave spoke quickly. "So if the ship releases the boxes at four or five in the morning, a fishing boat picks them up on the way out, puts them in the hold, and piles the catch on top."

"Bingo!" said Jiro. "I'll have Washington trace ownership of all boats in the San Pedro fleet. I'll bet some are owned by Blue Star. And Marine Providers owns a seafood distribution company. That must be the link."

"The whole San Pedro fishing fleet managed to put to sea before the first wave hit, so they're still around."

"What happened to Fish Harbor?"

"Nothing left but the bollards," said Dave. "The fishermen will be busy putting things back together for a few weeks."

"That'll give us time to run our investigation and nail the right guys. Now I've got some news for you."

Dave's radio squawked again. He put Jiro on hold, then came back. "Sorry. Too crazy here. Gotta go!"

"Give me one more minute!"

"Okay, but quick."

Jiro rushed his words. "Deshaun the gun pusher was hired by George Hacker himself, chairman of Blue Star."

"You sure?"

"We got Deshaun to talk. Convinced him he wouldn't last a day outside, and he'd be better off in the witness protection program. After he ID'd Hacker's photo, he said he met this same guy and his assistant in a fancy suite at the Beverly Hills Hotel."

"Assistant?"

"Yeah. Asian. Large. Killed Milo Wagstad on Hacker's orders. That's when Deshaun got the job."

"Sounds like you can get Hacker for murder."

"Multiple homicides. Deshaun said Hacker pushed the detonator button that blew up that plant near Mexicali. Fifty-five people killed."

"Hacker's a real sweetheart," said Dave. "The assistant—how large is large?"

"It's the guy with the knife. We ran background checks and ID'd him as Ho Kai Fat, a psychopathic bad ass from Hong Kong. In this country a couple of years. Good at torture and assassinations."

"Any idea where Hacker is?"

"Not sure, but we just put out an alert and circulated his picture."

Dave shouted in an anger-charged voice, "We've got to get that sonofabitch before he leaves the country."

"My exact sentiments. We'll keep on it till we find him."

Baldy appeared in the door.

"Duty calls, Jiro." Dave hung up and strode out to the waiting helicopter.

thirteen

After watching the first wave wipe out most of his Serenidad development, Hacker climbed back into the limo and told Ho Kai Fat to find a back road to take them east over the mountain. Fat tried two roads that led nowhere. He found success on his third attempt: a little-used road through a pass that took them to Temecula, close to the I-15 freeway.

"Find an airport, Mr. Fat. Time to get back to Hong Kong. Los Angeles doesn't interest me anymore."

Ho Kai Fat emitted a hollow grunt.

"LAX probably got wiped out, but there's gotta be other airports around where we can catch a plane to Chicago or New York. Stop at that gas station and we'll find out."

They pulled into the full-service lane and waited, but no one came out to the car. Hacker opened his door and walked into the station office. He found the owner and a mechanic watching television. "Live coverage," said the owner. "Third wave just hit. Can't believe the damage. Those folks down on the coast are really in big trouble."

Hacker agreed it was a terrible disaster. He asked about the nearest open airport, and was directed to Ontario, about fifty miles away.

As Hacker listened to directions to Ontario, a California Highway Patrol car pulled into the station. The trooper entered the little office and paused to watch the TV. Hacker headed back to the limo. On his way he glanced inside the open window of the patrol car. A telefaxed copy of his own picture lay on the passenger seat.

They drove north on I-15, and Hacker told Ho Kai Fat about the picture. "They may have all the airports staked out. But the one we're going to is in a little jerkwater place called Ontario. Maybe they don't have it covered yet. We'll check it out before we go in."

Ho Kai Fat cruised by the Ontario terminals three times. Hacker said, "Plainclothes watching the doors, plus some uniforms around too. Probably more inside. Better not take a chance."

From the back seat of the limo, Hacker kept punching airline numbers until he got through to San Diego, but Lindbergh Field had been hit hard and was out of commission. The only other airport in the area with departing flights was Burbank.

The closer they got to Los Angeles, the more chaotic traffic became. It took them nearly five hours to reach Burbank. They parked in an outer lot and Hacker took a shuttle to the terminal. Through the window of the shuttle, he saw plainclothes and uniforms covering all doors. He stayed on the shuttle and rode back to the limo.

"We'll have to get out some other way." He called Hong Kong, but Dixon Mallory wasn't in. No one knew how to locate him. Hacker ordered his staff to find Mallory immediately, or there would be hell to pay. "Sonofabitch is probably fucking one of his girlfriends," he muttered. "Let's get back to the hotel and see about getting my presidential suite back. We can wait for Dixon's call there. Besides, I'm horny as hell. I need a little action myself."

~ ~

Lani had worried about Dave all day, waiting to hear. She tried to put the dread of losing him out of her mind by plunging into the work at hand. By the time the third wave struck and receded at around 10:30 that morning, more than five thousand refugees had crowded onto the Long Beach Community College campus. More poured in throughout the day. She helped set up cots in the gym, pitch tents on the athletic field, dig latrines, and set up field kitchens and first aid stations. She unloaded trucks, handed out blankets, worked on the food serving line, and helped a nurse at the first aid station. Now, as night fell, she felt overwhelmed by exhaustion.

She hadn't taken a break all day. She got a cup of coffee from the kitchen and found a vacant spot in the corner of the field. She sat cross-legged on the grass and sipped her coffee. She'd been so busy dealing with immediate problems, she hadn't had time to think about the enormity of the disaster. Now she did. She studied the stunned looks on the faces of the survivors.

These people had lost everything. Homes, cars, belongings. Many had lost family and friends. The scene was being repeated in many hundreds of parks and football fields all along the coast. Probably five million people had been washed out of their homes. The system just wasn't ready to handle the aftermath of such a catastrophe. Not enough food, not enough blankets, not enough medicine or doctors or counselors. It would all get there eventually, but now people were hurting. They were physically miserable, in shock, despondent about their losses, and filled with anxiety about the future.

She had tried to get through to her parents earlier, but phone service to the Islands was out. She hadn't worried about them too much because their house was high on a hillside, well above the danger zone. She punched in their number again. This time she heard the ring on the other end. Rose answered and said they were both okay. Between sobs and hysterical laughter, she told Lani they'd watched the wave roll partway up their mountain. The windward side below them had been swept clean—little remained other than debris and flattened vegetation. Everyone had headed for the hills as soon as they heard the tsunami warning sirens. She and Rudy had taken in two other families until things could get straightened out.

Finally Lani allowed herself to think about her own situation. Anxiety about Dave hit her hard. She hadn't heard anything since Admiral Carson told her how Dave and Jiro were lost. The admiral had promised to call as soon as he knew anything, and that had been more than eight hours ago. The adrenaline that had kept her going through the day now drained away. She knew there was still so much to do. But her heart ached, and she had to know, one way or the other, if Dave had survived. She'd tried to call the Coast Guard emergency operations center several times but could never get through. Her cell phone still had battery life. She tried again.

Yeoman Gates answered. Lani asked for Admiral Carson.

"Sorry, he's not here. Can I take a message?"

"Tell him Lani Sanches called. Here's my number…"

"Oh, Lani, this is Cynthia. Commander Steel was asking about you."

"He's alive?" She tried to absorb the news.

"Yes, both the commander and Special Agent Yamaguchi came through okay. We don't know how, but they did."

"Really? I…" She couldn't finish. She started giggling, the giggles turning to laughter, then tears.

Cynthia waited out the spasm of relief. "I guess it was some kind of miracle—somebody up there must be watching out for him. Right now he's busy running the offshore rescue operation, so I don't know when he'll be back."

Lani gave Cynthia her number. "Please tell him to call me as soon as you hear from him."

Cynthia's voice was warm and understanding. "I will. I promise."

Lani shed tears of joy and relief before heading to the kitchen tent. It was dinnertime, and they'd be needing help.

~~

Ho Kai Fat drove the limo west, away from Burbank, through the San Fernando Valley to the 405 Freeway, which connected the Valley with the west side of Los Angeles. It was starting to get dark. Hacker looked at his watch and calculated the time difference. Ten in the morning in Hong Kong. Mallory ought to be in by now. His phone rang.

Mallory said, "Sorry I didn't get back to you sooner, but I'm on my way to Beijing and stopped by the office to pick up some papers. The transportation ministry is finally signing the contract on the Persian Gulf oil business. What happened to Serenidad? Anything left?"

"Fuck that, Dixon, I gotta get out of here. The cops must've connected me with the Rippers. Anyway, they're looking for me. All the regular air terminals are being watched. I need an airport to fly out of, a business jet with long-range tanks, and a pilot that knows how to get to Hong Kong. You have to take care of this before you go to Beijing."

"When do you want to fly?"

"Tonight. Has to be tonight."

"I'll go to work on it immediately. Let you know as soon as I can."

A block from the 405 Freeway, Hacker saw it was jammed and nothing was moving. "Is there a surface street that goes over the hill to Sunset?"

Ho Kai Fat turned south on Sepulveda. "This go same way."

"Okay, Mr. Fat, it's getting late and I have things to do. Let's see how fast you can make this thing go."

Traffic slowed to a crawl about halfway up the Sepulveda pass. After a few minutes of stop-and-go, Hacker said, "Come on, Mr. Fat, drive on the shoulder. Let's get past these stupid assholes."

The limo was almost too wide, but Ho Kai Fat maneuvered the big Lincoln along the shoulder, occasionally scraping against brush and rocks on the hillside. He squeezed back in line when the shoulder disappeared, and passed again when the lane widened on a curve. He gradually worked past the long line of stalled cars until they reached the intersection at Mulholland Drive. A California Highway Patrol officer directing traffic spotted the limo squeezing through on the shoulder.

After receiving a traffic ticket and a lecture about foreigners needing to learn the rules of the road in California, Ho Kai Fat stayed in the downhill line on Sepulveda and they eventually reached Sunset Boulevard. Mallory's phone call came in as they turned east toward Beverly Hills at 6:40 p.m.

"Be at Jet Aviation at Santa Monica airport before ten tonight your time. It's a Gulfstream Three with a seven-thousand-mile range. The pilot, copilot, and steward all have years of major airline experience. You'll be in good hands, and back in Hong Kong early tomorrow morning."

"I gotta make two calls," Hacker told Fat. "First the hotel, then the call girl service. It's been a hard day. I need to get laid before I fly for sixteen hours."

The hotel assured him that the presidential cottage was available and would be ready for him when he arrived.

Hacker punched in the number of the call girl service. "I gotta have two of your girls right away. Presidential cottage at the Beverly Hills Hotel. Gotta be young, tall, good looking. Classy. No dogs, no midgets. Nice round asses and big tits, no fashion model crap. If they're pretty and do what I want, there's a grand in it for each one. And they gotta be there in a half hour. I'm hot to trot and don't have much time."

Once inside the cottage, Hacker told Ho Kai Fat he'd be having company in a little while. "In the bedroom. Make sure I'm not disturbed. Understand?"

Ho Kai Fat nodded.

"Do you know how to get to the Santa Monica airport?" Fat nodded again. Hacker said, "We gotta be there before ten, so better plan to leave here no later than nine. Depends on how soon the girls get here. Maybe we can leave earlier."

At a little after 7:00, the doorbell rang and Ho Kai Fat let two girls into the cottage. They were both in their late teens. One was a tall brunette, the other a tall blonde. Both had nice round asses and big tits.

~ ~

The sun had long since dropped below the horizon in the western sky. Over the past nine hours, operating from the left seat of Baldy's helicopter, Dave had orchestrated the rescue of more than five hundred people. They'd been found clinging to capsized boats, tree limbs, chunks of shingled roof, telephone poles, front doors, and picnic coolers between Santa Barbara and Point Loma and as far offshore as fifteen miles.

"No light left," said Baldy. "Even the afterglow's gone."

"Yeah, twenty to eight. No survivor sightings by the spotter planes for the past three hours. I think we've found as many as we're going to find tonight." Dave punched in the task force radio frequency. "Let's wrap it up for today, and report back on station at daybreak tomorrow. Please confirm."

He stood by while the cutters, spotter planes, and helicopters acknowledged the order. He spoke again to the task force. "We'll start the day by doing one more sweep to make sure we got all the live ones. Then we start the bad business of collecting the floating corpses—there are hundreds, maybe thousands. I'll see if we can get the Navy to give us a hand. I'm not sure our cutters have enough deck space. Sunrise is oh-six-twenty. Let's be on station by oh-six-hundred."

"I'm heading for the barn," said Baldy.

~ ~

They walked into the Winnebago at ten after eight. Cynthia told Dave he had two urgent messages. One from Leilani Sanches. The other from Jiro Yamaguchi, who had also e-mailed two photographs.

When he heard Lani's name, Dave's fatigue vanished. "Lani? Really? Is she okay? Did she say how I can reach her?"

"One question at a time." Cynthia handed him the slip of paper with Lani's number on it. "She's working with the Red Cross over at the community college. She said I was to have you call a second and a half after you came back. No later. So call."

Dave hesitated. "But Jiro wouldn't have called if he didn't have something urgent on the gun smuggling deal. Maybe I better…"

"If you don't call Lani right now, I'll personally kick your ass right out of this Winnebago."

Dave cocked an eyebrow.

"With some help from Baldy," Cynthia added.

Baldy nodded agreement. "I've been waiting a long time to kick some sense into this guy."

Dave laughed and picked up the phone. "Appears I've been outvoted." He punched in Lani's number. She answered after two rings. "It's Dave, Lani. Wonderful to hear your voice."

"Oh, Dave, I'm standing here spooning out hot beans to a long line of people but they'll just have to wait because I want to ask you something. Did you get my message on your answering machine?"

"I left the apartment right after we talked—haven't had time since to check for calls."

"Oh, dear. My message says, 'I love you.' I should have told you a long time ago, but I think I loved you too much to tell you I loved you. Does that make any sense?"

He heard laughter in the background and a male voice telling Lani to give him the ladle and go ahead and take a break. Dave felt like he could float away. "Well, yeah, I guess so, but I'm not sure."

"I was afraid to say I love you, because I felt so vulnerable. It was hard to take that first step. But my feelings for you are so strong, I've been able to put those fears behind me."

Dave felt almost overwhelmed. After a pause, he said, "I'm kind of speechless…"

"About that woman on your answering machine—I'm serving notice right now she's in for a fight."

"Lani, you're the woman I love. You're the one I want to spend my life with. The other thing is over. Actually, never was."

"I have to see you, Dave. I can walk it in forty-five minutes. Will you wait?"

"I'll try to stay put if I can. It depends on what's happening and where they might need me."

"I'm coming over anyway. Wait for me if you can."

"If I have to leave, we'll see each other when I get back."

Dave looked at the pictures Jiro had e-mailed: George Hacker and Ho Kai Fat. He punched in Jiro's number.

"Hacker's been charged with murder and we think he's still in the area," Jiro said. "We want to get the bastard before he leaves the country."

"Any doubt he's the one behind the Ripper smuggling?"

"None. And we have witnesses who'll testify that both he and Fat were implicated in the murders of at least two people here and dozens more in Mexico."

"Any idea where he is?"

"We had a report from the CHP. One of their officers issued a ticket to a limo with occupants fitting the description of Hacker and Fat. Stopped them at Mulholland, going south on Sepulveda."

"South? Headed where?"

"Maybe LAX," Jiro said.

"But LAX took a bad hit. Airport's closed."

"He might not know that. It's possible he'd go there, find it's not operating, and keep on going south to John Wayne in Santa Ana, or turn around and drive east to Ontario or Palm Springs."

Dave said, "Freeways are jammed. Wherever he's headed, it'll take him a long time to get there. He's probably still in the area."

"I don't think he knows we're after him yet, but he's probably figured it's only a matter of time and he better leave while he can. We're covering all the regional airports, plus train and bus stations. We have a good description of the limo, so there's an APB out on that."

"What if he decided to lay low for a few days? Where would he hide out?"

"I don't know why he'd do that. It'd just give us more time to find him. If he did, maybe the Beverly Hills Hotel, where he stayed before. But that's a long shot, and I don't want to put any manpower on it. It's taking all our agents, plus a lot of local police, to cover the major airports and bus and train terminals."

Dave thought about all the people who'd died because of the Ripper scourge, mostly young kids and hard-working police officers with families. "I want to get this guy as much as you do. Maybe more. I don't go back on duty till daybreak—I'm going to spend tonight helping you find the SOB."

"Check out the Beverly Hills Hotel if you want, but don't be too surprised if he's not there. Makes more sense for him to leave the country on the first flight he can get. I'll alert Beverly Hills PD, but they're stretched thin too and might not show up."

"No problem. I'll have Baldy fly me over to the hotel."

"Watch out for the big guy. He's deadly."

Just as Dave hung up, Admiral Carson called on his way back from the emergency meeting. He said, "Don't leave till I get there."

Dave asked permission to use Baldy's heelo to assist the FBI. "We're on the verge of smashing the entire Ripper operation. I have a hunch about where he's holed up."

"Arresting the guy is their job," said the admiral. "Ours is keeping the contraband from coming in."

"Best way to keep the stuff out is to nail the guy who's bringing it in. I think it's a legitimate use of Coast Guard personnel and property."

"That's a stretch, Dave, but okay, as long as you don't put yourself in harm's way. If this man's armed or there's any trouble, just back away and let the police handle it. Is that understood?"

Dave said, "Aye, aye, sir," and signed off. Baldy announced he was refueled and ready to fly. Dave told Cynthia to tell Lani he'd be back as soon as he could.

They flew northwest over the endless carpet of light that was L.A. at night. "We just passed over the Baldwin Hills," Baldy said. "That clump of tall buildings ahead is Century City, then the black patch after that is the L.A. Country Club, ends at Sunset Boulevard. I'll turn right when we get to Sunset."

The chopper settled down on the lighted helipad on the roof of the Beverly Hills Hotel at 9:10 p.m. Dave unbuckled his gun belt and set it on the rear seat. "So they won't think I'm holding up the place."

He slipped out of the chopper and double-timed into the hotel. There was a mirror on the inside of the elevator door. He saw a tired man in a rumpled working-blue uniform with silver leaves on the collar and a two-day stubble on the chin. He decided to talk to the bell captain instead of the front desk. The bell captain was filling out a storage tag at a stand-up desk in the corner of the lobby. Dave showed him the two pictures. "I'm with the Coast Guard. We're looking for these two suspects in a smuggling case."

"Coast Guard? Shouldn't you guys be out rescuing people from the tsunami?"

"That's my day job." He stepped around the desk and came nose-to-nose with the bell captain. His voice contained barely controlled rage. "Look, I haven't slept for two days, I'm tired, pissed off, and for goddamn sure I do not need any shit from anybody. Now, are they here?"

The man backed away a step and shook his head. "No, but they *were* here. In the presidential cottage. Only stayed a couple hours. Left not more than twenty minutes ago. I helped the doorman put the bags in the limo."

"Where'd they go?"

"They didn't say."

Dave looked into the bell captain's eyes and knew he was telling the truth. He patted him on the shoulder and went back to the helicopter. "Just missed them," he told Baldy. "If they're going to John Wayne, Jiro's crew will pick them up. But if they're not, where else would they go? Burbank, Ontario, and Palm Springs are already staked out. So what's left?"

"Business jets fly out of Van Nuys and Santa Monica. He could have chartered one."

"What's the range of a business jet?"

Baldy thought for a moment. "Normally a couple thousand miles. But they can be fitted with long-range tanks."

"How would we find out if anyone's rented a business jet with long-range tanks?"

"They'd have to file a flight plan with Air Traffic Control." Baldy changed the frequency on one of his radios and called Los Angeles Center. He told the controller what he needed and was given a telephone number. Dave, listening on his earphones, punched the number into his cell phone and handed it to Baldy.

Baldy asked for the shift supervisor. "This is the U.S. Coast Guard," he said. "Can you tell us if any flight plans have been filed for international flights out of either Van Nuys or Santa Monica?"

Baldy answered the supervisor's questions about his identity and why he needed the information, and waited.

The supervisor came back on the line. "Two international flight plans have been filed, one out of each of those airports. Van Nuys has a Learjet leaving for Mexico City. Santa Monica has a Gulfstream Three filing to Hong Kong nonstop. Departure times for both are ten p.m. local time."

Dave looked at the time display on the instrument panel: 21:39. Twenty-one minutes to get to Santa Monica airport and stop Hacker from getting away. Baldy lifted off while Dave called Jiro's cell phone and Admiral Carson at the emergency operations center. Jiro said he'd try to get the Santa Monica police to send backup, but SMPD had their hands full and not to count on it. The admiral told Dave he'd helicopter to Santa Monica to back him up.

~~

Ho Kai Fat stopped the limo in front of the Jet Aviation hangar at nine minutes to ten. The night manager came out of the office, the words Jet Aviation circling a blue globe stitched on the front of his white windbreaker. "The plane and crew are ready to go, but you'll have to come in the office first to settle the bill and sign some papers."

Hacker handed the man his credit card. "Put us on board and bring the paperwork to the plane, and get a move on. We're in a hurry."

The night manager escorted them to a white Gulfstream sitting at the head of the taxiway, door open and stairs down. The cabin attendant, a man in his thirties with curly blond hair, greeted them. He wore a short-sleeved white shirt with black shoulder boards, and black trousers. He showed them to luxurious leather lounge seats and took their drink and dinner orders. The captain, he explained, would talk to them in a few minutes.

The Jet Aviation man came up the stairs and the captain came off the flight deck at about the same time. Hacker signed the documents. The captain said, "We've filed for a ten p.m. takeoff slot and are standing by for an okay from Los Angeles Center. Should be cleared for departure by the time we get to the runway."

Hacker watched the cabin attendant bring down the metal arm that secured the door and felt the vibrations of the jet engines starting up. The captain's voice came over the speaker. "Please fasten your seat belts. We're starting our taxi roll."

Hacker heard the high-pitched whine of the engines and felt the plane move. After taxiing for less than a minute, the plane stopped. He heard a faint rhythmic noise coming from somewhere. *Thud thud thud.* He looked outside, but didn't see anything. A strong light of some kind flooded his window.

Over the intercom, the captain said, "There'll be a slight delay. Please be patient."

"Find out what's going on!" Hacker yelled at the cabin attendant, who was already headed through the curtains to the flight deck.

He came back down the aisle with an alarmed look on his face. "Some damn fool has just landed a helicopter on the taxiway, right in front of us. We're blocked. Can't get to the runway. And he's shining his spotlight on us."

"Quick! Get us out of here," Hacker ordered the attendant.

"I'll have to check with the captain…"

"Just do it!" Hacker nodded to Ho Kai Fat, who rose from his seat, the long knife gleaming in the cabin light.

The cabin attendant opened the door, the stairs extending automatically. "Back to the limo," Hacker told Fat, and they took off running.

In the helicopter, Dave said, "They're running for it!" He leaped out of the chopper and sprinted after the fleeing men.

Baldy yelled, "Hey! Wait!" He unsnapped his safety belt and kicked his door open. He started to slide out, then checked the back seat. *Damn!* He grabbed Dave's gun belt, launched himself out the door, circled around the helicopter and chased after the disappearing figure of Dave.

"Your gun!" yelled Baldy. "You forgot your… ah, shit." He kept running in the direction of footsteps, but finally lost them and gave up.

Dave, adrenaline pounding, ran wide open with a floating spring in his step, feeling as though he had a gale force wind at his back. He was closing the gap rapidly. Hacker and Fat ran straight to their black limo, then suddenly changed course and disappeared through a side door in the main hangar.

Dave reached the closed door, opened it cautiously, and

slipped inside. It was massively dark, except for a line of light showing under the office door. He dropped his hand to his hip, feeling for his service pistol. No gun! *Damn! Out of the habit of wearing it.* His heart thudded for a moment, but he couldn't back out now. He felt along the wall, working his way toward the office door. He was within a few feet of it when the hangar lights flooded on.

Dave stood face to face with Ho Kai Fat. Fat placed the tip of his razor-sharp long knife against Dave's Adam's apple.

"It's the Coast Guard guy," came a voice from behind Dave. "Where's your pal?"

"FBI'll be here before you can get away, so you might as well surrender to me. That way, you won't get hurt."

"That's the funniest bullshit I ever heard," said Hacker. "You're gonna come with us and tell the pilot to move his chopper and stay out of our way. Then you're taking a nice ride to Hong Kong. With you aboard, they won't try to force us down. Move!"

Ho Kai Fat spun Dave around, moved the cutting edge of his long knife against Dave's jugular, and marched him into the glare of Baldy's floodlight. Hacker whirled his hand above his head and pointed upward, motioning to the chopper to lift off. He bellowed, "Get out of our way or this guy gets his throat cut."

~ ~

Lani arrived at the Winnebago at 9:31 p.m. Cynthia Gates said, "Dave took off a few minutes after he talked to you. He just called in on the radio link for Admiral Carson."

Lani looked down to the other end of the Winnebago and saw Carson talking into his headset mike. She got to his desk as he disconnected. "Was that Dave?"

Carson's thoughts were obviously elsewhere. It took him a minute to acknowledge her presence. Finally he said, "He's trying to keep a nasty character named George Hacker from leaving the country."

"Dangerous?"

Carson nodded. "Very." He strapped on a gun belt. "Haven't worn this old Navy Colt for a long time, but I remember how to use it." He walked toward the door.

She blocked his path. "Let me go with you. If Dave's in danger, I want to be there. He might need me."

"You could get hurt, Lani, or killed. These are bad guys."

She spotted the admiral's baseball bat and picked it up. "I'll take this along."

Carson frowned. "Okay, bring the damn thing and let's go! It's my lucky bat and we're going to need some luck."

At 21:44 the admiral's helicopter lifted off. "Can you make Santa Monica Airport in fifteen minutes?" he asked his pilot. "Lieutenant Spangler and Commander Steel have a head start. They'll need our help."

The pilot, Lieutenant Commander Alicia Rodriguez, said, "I'll fly low and firewall it." She lifted off, shoved the throttle all the way forward, and trimmed the rotors for level flight. The faint howl of the chopper's twin jets mixed with the rapid beat of the rotors as they rocketed ahead. "Should get us there in fourteen minutes, thirty-three seconds. So why not kick back and enjoy the music." She grinned at Lani. "I smuggle my own CD changer aboard. The admiral pretends not to notice."

"All she plays is country western," said Carson. "No classical, no jazz, no soul, no rock. Just country. Drives me nuts."

"How about Hawaiian? Got any IZ or Genoa Keawe?"

"The only Hawaiian I have is Hawaiian War Chant. Don't know who's singing. But there's a lot of them and it's loud."

"Okay, if that's all you've got."

"But first you have to listen to 'Wabash Cannonball' with Roy Acuff. Always inspires me when action's at hand. Then the war chant. By that time we'll be there."

When the twangy sounds of "Wabash Cannonball" invaded the intercom, Carson said, "Oh, for God's sake," and took off his helmet. Alicia's head bobbed to the rhythm, and Lani thumped the baseball bat in her lap. When "Cannonball" ended and the war chant began, Lani sang along.

Admiral Carson watched Lani for a moment and put his helmet back on. He laughed. "You're like a Hawaiian chief getting ready for battle."

Lani nodded and held up the bat. "My war club."

"We're here," said Alicia. "There's Jet Aviation down at the east end of the airport. Baldy's heelo is right in front of that white Gulfstream."

"My God!" said Carson. "What's going on down there—they've got Dave! Put down behind the Gulfstream."

Alicia brought the helicopter down behind the jet, out of the floodlit area. Lani started to follow Carson out of the chopper, but he shook his head. "You'll get hurt." He hopped out, landing in a low crouch, and moved under the belly of the jet to approach them from behind.

"They know we're here," Lani said to Alicia. "I'm going to circle around behind those small planes and come at them from another angle." She jumped out before Alicia could protest and disappeared in the forest of Pipers and Cessnas.

Carson stayed in the darkness under the Gulfstream, working his way toward the three men caught in the glare of the floodlight. He was within ten feet of Hacker's back when Hacker turned his head. "I know you're there. If you try anything, this asshole dies. Ho Kai Fat cuts his throat in half a second, and my Ripper goes off if I'm hit. So whoever the hell you are, throw down your gun and come on out!"

There was no choice. Dave would die. Carson threw his Colt out onto the tarmac and walked into the light.

Hacker and Fat were focused on the Colt and the figure emerging from the shadows. Lani stepped in from the other direction, cocked the lucky bat and swung through as if stroking a clean single into center field. She caught Ho Kai Fat squarely in the testicles with the meat end of the bat.

The big man's eyes lost focus. He sagged to one knee, the knife sliding out of his hand. Hacker turned just in time to meet Lani's second true swing of the bat. The blow landed solidly between his eyes, just above the bridge of his nose.

Carson scooped up his Colt and shoved the barrel into Ho Kai Fat's neck. Hacker was out cold, sprawled across the yellow line of the taxiway. Dave stood perfectly still, not quite believing his eyes.

The admiral stared at Lani. "God Almighty, that was as beautiful as it gets. Your warrior ancestors are smiling this day, I'm sure."

She dropped the bat and put her arms around Dave, pulling him to her, resting her head on his chest. "I couldn't let them take you away from me, not after all the trouble we've had getting together." She looked up and met Dave's eyes. "After all, you're going to be my husband and the father of my kids. Right?"

Dave's bewildered state passed. He smiled for the first time. "I'm not sure."

Lani pulled away and put her hands on her hips. "Not sure about what?"

"Not sure I'd be marrying the same girl. I'd just gotten used to the one who was stubborn as a mule and always spoke her mind. Now I find out, on top of that, she's fearless and hell on wheels in a fight. That's more than I bargained for."

"Sorry," Lani said. "That's what you're getting, so get used to it. And for heaven's sake, will you please take a bath, get a haircut, and put on clean clothes before the wedding. I don't want to embarrass my friends."

Admiral Carson was the first to start laughing. Dave broke up next. Lani joined in, but her laughter soon turned to tears.

Dave put his arms around her. "I love everything about you, Lani. The whole package."

She brushed tears away. "The whole package wants to know

if you're ready to take on the whole package."

He nodded, smiling. "I guess we better make it official. Will you marry me?"

"To da max, brah," she said. "Fo' real, garans ballbarans."

Dave started laughing again. "Care to translate?"

Lani let out a long sigh of frustration. "How can you get so high up in the Coast Guard and still be so dumb? Don't you know I just said yes two different ways in pidgin?"

"Just wanted to be sure."

epilogue

The three-wave tsunami took more than eight thousand lives. Most of the fatalities were people who didn't hear or understand the warnings in the first place, or went back into the area before the last wave hit, or were unlucky enough to be where local disaster agencies just weren't able to get all their people away in time.

The landscape within a mile of the beach had been flattened. The homes, apartments, offices, schools, cafes, markets, and shops that had been there the day before were swept away or reduced to a jumble of litter. Where five million people had lived and worked became a ghostly desert bordering the sea for two hundred miles. Property losses were so vast, calculations proved difficult, but most estimates exceeded five hundred billion dollars.

FEMA and other government organizations came in with aid money and loans to help people rebuild. State and local agencies concentrated on preventing disease and rebuilding infrastructure. A program to replace the major sewage treatment plants that had been located near the ocean received top priority.

The clearing and reconstruction process started slowly but gradually got going full tilt. Building materials and construction crews poured into the area. Streets were repaved, utilities gradually restored, trees and shrubs brought in for landscaping. It would take years to get everything repaired and rebuilt, and the beach area would never look the same, but people were putting their lives and their homes and businesses back together. Hope prevailed.

Lani Sanches stayed on at SciPac for several months, but found she didn't feel free to do her best work as long as Sylvester Purvis still ran the operation and Margaret Bradshaw lurked in the background. Lani received a new offer from Hawaii State University that gave her just about everything she wanted in rank, privilege, salary, and the freedom to do research on her own schedule.

She hesitated for a long time because she was engaged to Dave and wanted to be near him. She finally accepted the offer and left for Hawaii.

Harley Wamp's body was never found.

At the request of the Mexican government, George Hacker was extradited to stand trial for the bombing murder of fifty-five workers in the arms plant outside Mexicali. Despite attempts to bribe officials with massive amounts of dollars and euros, Hacker was found guilty and sentenced to life. In a dispute over control of the prison drug traffic, he was stabbed to death in the exercise yard of the Baja California territorial prison in Tijuana.

Ho Kai Fat was given a life sentence in Folsom for the murder of Milo Wagstad.

Sylvester Purvis remained as president of SciPac. Margaret Bradshaw was reinstated as head of the seismology department after Lani left for her new job in Hawaii. Margaret was not totally satisfied with that arrangement, and during an evening of sex and heavy drinking at her apartment, told Purvis she wanted more. She wanted him to divorce his wife so that they could marry.

Purvis told her it wasn't in the cards, and if she kept pressuring him he'd have to fire her. She said he couldn't do that because she had tenure. He said he'd turn the academic hearing file over to the board of trustees, showing that she'd framed Lani. Then she'd be history. She got a butcher knife out of the kitchen drawer and plunged it into his neck as he was mixing a vodka martini. He died from loss of blood. Margaret drew life in Tehachapi.

Admiral Carson got a third star and was assigned to headquarters in Washington as vice commandant of the U.S. Coast Guard. Before leaving San Pedro, he told Dave Steel he'd been worried about his performance since Lani had gone back to Hawaii. He said he was looking into ways and means of solving the problem.

Dave found out that Carson's way of solving the problem was to promote him to the rank of captain and transfer him to the Fourteenth Coast Guard district in Hawaii as commander of Coast Guard forces based at Sand Island in Honolulu.

The crater blasted out of the earth's crust by the explosion of Seamount Gilman became a mecca for volcanologists, seismologists, and oceanographers. Hawaii State University established a permanent, self-sustaining undersea laboratory at the site. Lani Sanches was appointed director of the undersea lab. She spent about half her time there, working with visiting specialists from dozens of countries around the world.

Lani and Dave married. Dave wore dress whites with a maile leaf lei draped around his shoulders, and Lani a traditional wedding gown with lei and crown made of white orchids. The wedding took place in a chapel near Waimea Falls, on a hillside overlooking Waimea Bay.

When Lani's father, Rudy, gave the bride away, he was cheered on by Lani's four brothers, their wives and nineteen kids, and half the sanitation workers on the island of Oahu. Lani's mother, Rose, sobbed through the entire ceremony. Jiro Yamaguchi was best man and Yeoman Cynthia Gates served as Lani's maid of honor. Dave's parents and brother and sister sat on the Coast Guard side of the aisle. Admiral Yarnell Carson, Richard Costello, Lieutenants Elaine DuBois and Baldy Spangler, Lieutenant Commanders Alicia Rodriguez and Justin Riley, Dennis Chung, and Gilda Epstein were among those lending moral support.

At the reception at Rose and Rudy's house, sticking out above the mountain of wedding gifts, was something in a long cardboard tube. It was marked *for the bride only*, and signed *Yarnell Carson*. The note said, "You've earned the right to own the lucky bat. Keep it out where Dave can see it as a reminder that he strays at his own peril."